PRAISE FOR NATE CROWLEY

"A nautical sci-fi space battle zombie horror comedy adventure tale, there's something in it for everyone, if just by the law of averages."
The Guardian

"This better be fucking good, then."
Dara Ó Briain

"Gory, gross, glorious."
Cassandra Khaw

"Surreal and occasionally horrifying."
The Daily Dot

"Increasingly weird and hilarious."
Buzzfeed

"An oddly wistful tale set in a thoughtfully constructed fantasy world."
Not Enough Scifi

An Abaddon Books™ Publication
www.abaddonbooks.com
abaddon@rebellion.co.uk

First published in 2017 by Abaddon Books™,
Rebellion Publishing Limited, Riverside House,
Osney Mead, Oxford, OX2 0ES, UK.

10 9 8 7 6 5 4 3 2 1

Editor: David Moore
Cover: Oz Osborne
Design: Sam Gretton & Oz Osborne
Marketing and PR: Rob Power
Editor-in-Chief: Jonathan Oliver
Head of Books and Comics Publishing: Ben Smith
Creative Director and CEO: Jason Kingsley
Chief Technical Officer: Chris Kingsley

ISBN: 978-1-78108-556-1

THE
DEATH
AND
LIFE
OF
SCHNEIDER
WRACK

NATE CROWLEY

Dedicated to my dad; I wish you could have stayed long enough to see this printed.

PART ONE
THE SEA HATES A COWARD

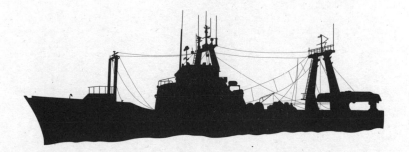

Alone, alone, all, all alone,
Alone on a wide wide sea!
And never a saint took pity on
My soul in agony.

The many men, so beautiful!
And they all dead did lie:
And a thousand thousand slimy things
Lived on; and so did I.

I looked upon the rotting sea,
And drew my eyes away;
I looked upon the rotting deck,
And there the dead men lay.

The Rime of the Ancient Mariner,
Samuel Taylor Coleridge

The boy stood on the burning deck
His lips were all a-quiver
He gave a cough, his leg fell off
And floated down the river.

Eric Morecambe

THE *TAVUTO*

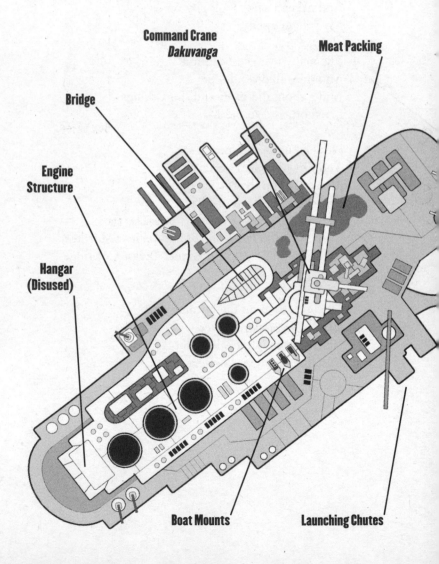

Command Crane
Dakuvanga

Meat Packing

Bridge

Engine
Structure

Hangar
(Disused)

Boat Mounts

Launching Chutes

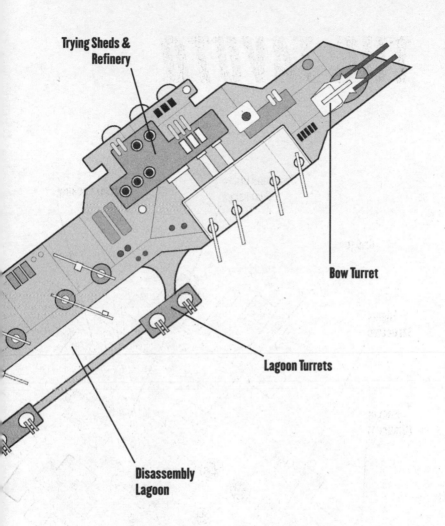

Trying Sheds &
Refinery

Bow Turret

Lagoon Turrets

Disassembly
Lagoon

CHAPTER ONE

WHERE WAS THAT bloody book? One of the high shelves, surely, where the old volumes were kept. The ones about history, or at least the really good legends. He was going to need the pole to get it.

The sun poured through the windows of the old library: even with his eyes shut, it blazed sepia through the lids. All around him was the sound of paper, dusty pages shuffling as the old fellows fumbled through them. It was louder than usual.

He searched for the hooked pole, the one for reaching the top shelves—and found it already in his hands. That was good. But he had forgotten the name of the book he was looking for.

Never mind. He knew it was on the top shelf, up there with the siegecraft and the politics and... the other one. The book with all the fish in it. He knew he didn't want to look inside that one very much. He would avoid that book.

His eyes were still shut, but that didn't matter—he knew the row by feel. He just had to lift the pole high enough, run it along the spines of the old volumes and... there. That was the right one. The leather was soft and the book was heavy, lent resistance by the pressure of old words around it, but it came loose with a solid tug.

He held the book in his hands. It was good and thick, and... maybe a little damp? That didn't matter—it was the right one. His eyes were closed, but somehow he could still read the title: *Schneider Wrack*. The words puzzled him briefly until they snapped into place—the book's title was his name. Which he'd somehow forgotten. Schneider was becoming increasingly suspicious that all of this was a dream.

The rustling of old thumbs on ancient pages grew louder all around him, almost aggressively. Some of the readers had started murmuring as well; it was distracting. The flicker of pages started to make his own thumbs itch to open the book, and his arms began itching too. He wasn't sure why, and it made him feel uneasy. It didn't matter though: he had to look in the book.

But once he had prised open the cover, sticky against the frontispiece, he found he couldn't read the words inside. They were there, rich and black and swarming, but they wouldn't come into focus.

Of course! His eyes were still shut. He had to open his eyes! But he'd been dreaming for so long. Schneider knew if he opened his eyes, he'd have to stop dreaming. And he wasn't certain that would be alright. Still, there wasn't much of a choice—he had to read what was inside that book, even if it meant waking up.

He struggled to ungum his lids, and the groaning of the old fellows grew louder around him. Like a dressing peeled from an old wound, he felt his eyelids begin to lift. But then he realised, far too late, that the book in his hands had changed.

It wasn't the book with his name. It was the book about the fish. The one he didn't want to see inside. There were horrible things in there, blank-eyed and wounded and long-toothed. A dictionary of demons. He tried to cover the pages with his hands before his eyes could open fully, but it was no good. His arms moved slowly, and they itched so badly. The groaning around him grew into a howl; he felt cold spray against his scalp.

His eyes opened.

Schneider Wrack stood among grey offal, before the hill-high carcass of a monster. In his hands, a twelve-foot length of gore-streaked wood; at its tip, a pitted blade hooked on a sagging strip of blubber.

Pebble-hard rain smacked against the back of his scalp, his shoulders. A hissing wind snatched the reek of blood from his nostrils, then whipped back, loaded with salt and liquid-thick decay.

Lightning smashed the image of bones against his retina; titanic bones shrouded in strands of white flesh. Schneider was standing inside a wound. Something grey and chitinous scuttled, convulsing, across his foot.

He wanted to scream, but he was already screaming—or trying to. His lungs pulled thick and wet against a closed throat, struggling against oneiric resistance, the paralysis of dreams. But this was a dream no longer. He was awake.

At last the liquid loosened: his chest heaved in half a gallon of air and let it out again in a weak roar, the ghost of a shout.

Shuddering like a new thing, Schneider looked down and stared at the soup of blood and grey fragments washing around his ankles. He screamed again.

This time, it came easier. A low moan, crude and primal. Salty liquid trickled from his lips, like the prelude to a drunken spew, yet no feeling came from inside, just a long, frightened wail from the base of his chest.

The noise trembled against the walls of the wound—and was answered. Schneider heard a pained howl from his left. And then from behind, all too close. Even as he jerked away in terror, a fresh wail came from the right, and his head snapped round to see its source.

Schneider looked straight into the withered, wrinkled, old-fruit features of a corpse.

It was stooped, ruined. Drenched in black fluid, its eyes watery above a ragged mouth, while its hair hung slick like the pelts of storm-drain vermin. In its hands, a billhook like Schneider's; on its back a shirt that was hard to distinguish from sloughing skin.

Gasping, Schneider recoiled from the apparition, straight into the sodden arms of another. He thrashed to disentangle himself. Grey teeth gnashed and clattered inches from his neck, and he rammed the butt of his billhook backwards hard.

Edging into the monster's wound with his blade shaking in front of him, Schneider quailed before a sea of twisted faces; a crowd of ghouls that seemed to look straight through him with their cloudy eyes.

A howl rose black and dreadful from their throats, and the ring of faces began to close in. Lightning splashed their outstretched arms with light, making them flicker as they reached out to pull him in.

Schneider stumbled, his foot slipping on a fat-shrouded vein. He fell on his arse and scrabbled back into the dark, away from the stretching claws. His billhook caught on something and fell from his grip, and he cowered from the monsters with his arms shielding his face.

But they weren't after him; they were after the meat. Stepping over him as if he were so much offal, they waded into the carcass and began tearing flesh from the wound with their billhooks, with rusted knives, with their own hands.

Their hands.

Crouched into a ball as the ghouls surged over him, Schneider blinked hard to chase the rain from his eyes, and looked for the first time at his own hands.

While he already knew what he was looking at—the swollen grey prunes of his fingertips, the bloodless white gashes that streaked his forearms—it was a long time of shivering and staring before he could face up to what it meant. He was a dead man.

Schneider screamed once more; a wail of despair that rejoined the rolling chorus his first cry had triggered, before drowning in thunder and crashing waves. No longer conscious of his own voice as a discrete part of the cacophony, he threw back his head and moaned to let the horror out. But more only flooded in.

Blackness rose. As his vision began to fade, he became aware of a deeper sound beneath it all; an abyssal groan swelling at the edge of hearing. It grew and grew until it shook the floor, then emerged, piercing, on the salt wind. The monstrous flesh around him shook with the noise, and Schneider's dimming sight was drawn to its source, at the jagged conclusion of the monster's great grey body.

There, above a mass of figures straining with hooked ropes, a sawtoothed jaw gaped in silhouette against a weak sun, and blasted out a death scream. Black blood geysered from the giant mouth; it thrashed once, then twisted and fell lifeless. The last thing Schneider saw before he blacked out was a rush of thin bodies, scrambling onto the head of the monster with knives drawn, to begin flensing it.

CHAPTER TWO

A LIGHT BLAZED against darkness, an angry stain orbited by sparks, swelling as sense came back to him. With the return of light came sound: the creaking of chains, the rasp of a great mass dragged across a rough surface.

Heat licked Schneider's face, and a cable cut into his shoulder. As the glow ahead grew more intense, it pooled around shadows; human figures stooped and trudging under burdens. He willed the dark from his eyes, strained like a drowning man to breach full consciousness again.

He broke surface, and awareness came all at once—he was deep in a crowd of the shuffling dead, yoked to ropes and moving forward across rain-puddled metal, with an enormous weight at their backs. He turned; behind them was a truck-sized slab of sinew and grey fat, moving on a slick of grease and gore, away from a pandemonium of butchery.

At the end of the lump's snail-trail was the carcass of the

monster. Night had fallen, and the thing had been stripped down to a raw red hill, stickled with spars of bone and swarmed over by the clambering, restless dead. Banks of floodlights turned the night outside their beams to ink, cast long shadows where other teams of wretches struggled forward with their hillocks of flesh.

The heat grew more intense. Turning back ahead, Schneider saw he was approaching a tall archway, its searing glow resolving into a glimpse of further industry. Inside the bright space, dark figures stirred and prodded at huge vats, their sides licked by flames. Crucibles ascended on clinking chainwork, poured bubbling torrents down chutes and into barrels, while yet more harnessed cadavers dragged bars to skim the slag from the molten grease.

Looking into that Hadal throng, Schneider felt his body grow heavy with terror. This was not a nightmare, a trick, an illusion or a hallucination. He was dead, and he was in Hell. Sick anxiety longed to anchor itself to a heartbeat, but the inside of his chest was still.

What had he done? He strained to remember, but nothing came: his name was all he knew. How had he deserved to be stuck here, his body slowly disintegrating, surrounded by blood and fire, monsters and the damned? Would he rot away? And when he finally collapsed to a soggy stack of bones, would he be brought back to do it all again? Maybe this would last forever.

It was somewhere then, in the depths of his spiralling panic, that he heard the radio. He was no theologian, but to the best of his knowledge there were no radios in Hell.

"*Kōhua team one, this is DV, come in. You need to pick up the pace; we've got two fresh benthos an hour away, and nowhere to land 'em. Get that zeug cleared up now or it's getting swept, over.*"

Schneider felt an absurd surge of hope: there were definitely no radios in Hell, and even if there were, devils did not bicker with each other over scheduling. Before he could begin to know what to make of the crackling, disembodied message, it was answered.

"Receiving you clear, Dakuvanga. Yes, you will have area 6-Tohorā clear in time to load—just two fatblocks left to haul and then we'll call in skeletal for the bonepicking. Get off our backs and let us finish the job, out."

The connection cut with a burst of static, followed by a volley of unmistakably human cursing, before a bulky figure strode abruptly out of the dark.

"Alright, fuckers," it growled, "pick up the pace."

The speaker was nearing seven feet tall, a great fat man swathed in layers of canvas and waxed leather. Just his head protruded from a turret-like collar, a lurking bulge like an egg boiled in dirty water. His mouth was a bloodless slit, his eyes red and inflamed in the waxen immensity of his face.

In his hand, a taut leash held back what Schneider took at first to be a huge dog, but which upon closer examination prompted him to reassess his 'not in Hell' hypothesis.

It was, or had been, a shark. Its front end was a great fat wedge of jaw, lipless and set with serrated enamel shards, while its body and tail heaved in a cage of wires, tubes and churning hydraulics. Sweeping out from its belly, a fan of hooked iron spider-legs scrabbled and clanged against the ground as it strained to reach the haulage gang.

Grunting, the pallid, egg-headed ogre let out another ten feet of lead for the awful thing, and it scuttled, cockroach-like, to clamp its jaws around the hip of a struggling corpse.

The victim shrieked as it was dragged to the ground, but did not even look in the direction of the thing savaging its leg, merely stared forward with an expression of abject defeat. None of the other dead even looked round—they just leaned into the ropes and ploughed forward, agitated like spooked cattle.

Schneider couldn't stand to watch. Shouting what he thought was a protest, but which came out as a stuttering gurgle, he lurched free of the rope and shouldered aside sodden teamsters to reach the fallen creature before the shark-thing could fall on it again.

Suddenly, the red eyes of the giant and the glassy pits of the shark were both fixed on him.

"Ha! Who the shit are *you?*" roared the overseer, and Schneider realised what a horrendously stupid thing he was doing. He tried to freeze, to sway like the other corpses did, but it was far too late.

With no hope of avoiding attention, Schneider turned his back and ran, scrambling back through the milling dead in the hope of blending in again. But the skittering of steel on steel was too close behind him. He weaved through the hunched, emaciated bodies and the shark-thing came after, that dreadful blunt head shunting aside bodies as it pursued him.

Schneider ducked ropes and hopped lumps of meat as he shoved through the toiling throng, but it was like running in a nightmare: his legs seemed to move at a fraction of the speed he willed them to, while the scuttling horror behind him came on with with the tireless speed of a machine.

He could hear the hiss of its hydraulics, could almost feel its teeth kiss the backs of his flailing heels, when an almighty crash and squeal of shearing metal sounded from somewhere behind them. From the direction of the skeletonised monster Schneider had woken up half-inside.

A distant voice called out "Shut it off! Shut it down!" and a wail rose from the dead working the bones of the giant. The nearby overseer cursed, and Schneider heard the hiss of sparking steel all too close as the shark-thing reached the end of its leash. Then the radio again:

"Kōhua, this is DV again. Winch team just screwed up bad—there's a lot of meat caught up in the gears. You just got yourself an even bigger mess to clear up."

Schneider risked a glance behind; the shark was still fixed on him, red gums bared as it strained on its lead, but its handler's attention was elsewhere, face scornful as he held a battered radio to his craggy sneer.

"Yeah, copy," growled the overseer. "I told you more haste means less speed, DV. We're on it. Just hold your damned tongue while we get the real work done down here, out."

The grey-headed giant spat in disgust and yanked on his monster's leash, stalking off towards the source of the racket without a second glance towards the haulage team. Following the overseer's gaze, Schneider saw with a sick lurch what had called a halt to proceedings.

Smoke was pouring from the drive unit of a towering gantry crane, paused midway through tearing the skull from the body of the monster. A crowd of dead were clustered in aimless distress around its base. And as the knots of wandering bodies merged and split, Schneider saw through them to a sight that made his throat close up.

Arms and legs twitched weakly in the rusted jaws of a gear assembly, half-crushed heads gaping in weak anguish: a whole team of haulers, mangled. In the overseers' rush to clear the flensing site, they had clearly veered off-course and, lacking any supervision, wandered into the grinding cogs of a crane rig.

Schneider stared, until an idea bubbled to the crown of his skull. With his team's overseer—and his horrifying creature—heading rapidly towards the accident, there was nobody watching him. This was his chance to run.

Without another glance at the overseer, or at the looming glow of the rendering plant, he loped into the dark as quickly as his trembling legs would allow. Not a single head turned to watch him—every sad, opalescent eye was fixed on the fire ahead.

The roar of the furnaces, the monotonous shuffle of dead feet on metal, the slow rasping of the fat-slab, all faded beneath the slapping of his bare feet, the rumble of the ever-present thunder, and—louder every moment—the quiet, vast crash of waves.

He had no idea where he was running to, but anywhere had to be better than the vision of Hell that awaited the haulage

team. He willed himself onwards and out of the light, before
an overseer could turn and see him making a break for it.

Then he remembered; the fallen corpse. The poor wretch that
had been dragged down by the jaws of the shark-thing, that
had not even looked back as its leg was savaged. Crouching
against a flaking iron wall, Schneider looked back to see if it
had gotten back to its feet.

It had not. Alone on the darkened ground, the dead thing
sat on its haunches as the haulers passed it by, arm extended
as if for assistance, head swinging as if looking for something.

Its eyes met Schneider's; its head stopped moving. For a long
moment it stared, as the rain fell in light sheets around it. Could
it see him, out at the edge of the furnace lights? If it could, did
it have any conception of him as another being? Was it just a
broken rack of meat, or was it every bit as conscious as him?

The possibility was overwhelming. With the image of those
bodies broken against the wheels of the crane still fresh in his
mind, the hopeless, withered faces of the flensing mob, there
was no way he could leave it there, maimed and lonely. Bitingly
aware that anything could be looking his way, Schneider ran
back out into the glare of the floodlights, towards the huddled
body.

The rain fell heavier as he knelt beside the cadaver, sinking
on shaking legs until his eyes were level with its own.

"Can you hear me?" he whispered, straining to speak with
lips like salted slugs. The dead thing's mouth hung open,
wordless, arm still extended as if it was reaching to pluck its
own words from an indistinct cloud.

Schneider repeated the question, the words coming more
firmly with practice, and was answered with a low bubbling
sound—the thing's chest was punctured just left of centre,
a bruised black slot that gurgled as its mouth gaped for an
answer.

The thing's jaw closed with a slow hiss that might have been
frustration, and the dull grey eyes slid shut in a slow blink.
When they opened again, there was no illusion of contact—

they were looking through him, to somewhere beyond the dark.

Off to the side, with a stuttering roar, Schneider heard the gears of the gantry crane come to life, presumably free of its abhuman blockage. The triumphant bass yell of an overseer answered it, a guttural prayer of thanks to industry renewed, and the familiar clatter and hiss of the flensing work resumed.

The giant and his monster would be returning any moment, and he was right out in the gaze of the floodlights. There was no more time to wait for a response from the wretched thing: he had to get back to the darkness. No matter how hard he wanted it to be otherwise, Schneider thought as he struggled to his feet, it seemed he was the only one here with a mind of his own.

Turning to face the dark, he made it one step before a cold hand clamped around his calf. He jerked away on impulse, panic sliding down his spine like frozen slush, and twisted to find the face of the dead thing staring up into his, teeth grey and clenched.

"Help me," it hissed.

CHAPTER THREE

BEFORE HE COULD fully understand what he was doing, Schneider was stooping again and sweeping up the rain-slicked corpse in his arms. The urge to vomit rocked his gorge as he pulled its arm round his shoulders and felt its ruined chest slide against his, but what was the point in revulsion? He was every bit as vile as it was, and anything would be better than hearing its moans receding behind him.

Spider legs clattered in the distance.

"Let's get out of here," he murmured, reflecting only briefly on what a ludicrous thing that was for one corpse to say to another, before hobbling briskly out of the cone of floodlit steel. He hoped desperately it had been shock rather than damage that had kept the other body slumped on the floor; there was no way he could carry the thing if it collapsed. But after a few exhausting yards it seemed to match his pace, leaning heavily on him but moving in a way that suggested its bones were still roughly in the right place.

As he lurched past the base of a floodlight tower, Schneider was struck by a strange vision that made him think he was dreaming—and then he remembered what a memory was. He was remembering the library gardens. Even with the constant slashing rain and the stink of salt, and the fact he was dead, he could have closed his eyes and been back there on that night, propping up the paralytic junior archivist who had just pissed all over the statue of the founders.

He had joked at the time that it had been like trying to smuggle a corpse away from a crime scene; he was struck now by how accidentally accurate he had been. Of course, he couldn't remember the archivist's name, or what celebration or tragedy had gotten him so pissed, but the sanity of the recollection made the present somehow more bearable.

Despite everything, Schneider found himself laughing as he stumbled through the dark, a weird, panting sound that would have been utterly chilling had it not come from his own neck.

It dried out soon enough as he noticed pale faces in the dark, turning in sleepwalker confusion toward the unfamiliar noise. They were everywhere around him, swaying in the rain, loping in slow circles and bumping against each other like floating debris. The corpses, the cadavers, the...

"Zombies," he blurted at his lurching companion, unable to resist a small, theatrical gasp like someone revealing the twist of a ghost story to a group of children. The dead face just stared back at him with a hint of a baffled frown and he laughed again, drawing the gaze of yet more uncomprehending eyes. Let them come, thought Schneider. It felt good to laugh.

His helpless wheezing brought the zombies shambling towards him, but naming them seemed to have robbed them of something of their horror. Even their smell—*his* smell, he reminded himself—had become familiar to his nostrils. Despite their watery eyes and their loose, peeling skin, they were utterly harmless. And in any case, he was one of them. The only real danger here seemed to be the brutish overseers and their attack creatures. Them, and the inevitability of bodily collapse—though that was less of an immediate threat to his life.

The word 'life' caught in his mind like a sharp stone, and drained the weak humour from the situation. He was, after all, dead.

But there was no time to reflect—hearing a burst of radio static some way behind him, he remembered there were still plenty of terrible things that could happen to him. And to the creature leaning against his left side.

They had to keep moving, and mingling with the other dead. Surely, the safety in numbers offered by the aimless crowd would buy him a minute to work out where he was and—hopefully—where to go next.

The initial plan of 'into the dark' seemed suddenly inadequate as his eyes adjusted. The space beyond the floodlights was anything but dark. Specks of brightness twinkled far out in the distance to either side of him, while ahead stood a mountain, outlined in bright points of electric light.

As his head tilted back to take in the looming immensity, he saw there were lights above him too. To his left, immense cranes rose up on gridwork lattices, glowing here and there with encrustations of steel cabins. Blazing floodlights picked out the shapes of hulking pulleys and house-sized mechanical saws, suspended by creaking booms.

The structures receded into the fog like a rank of grim steel herons, beaks dipped in repose; to their right, an even larger structure towered out of the murk. Set in front of the great hill of lights, it rose hundreds of feet into the air, a mighty steel mast festooned with gantries, antennae, searchlights, and clusters of dishes like lifeless barnacles. Jutting from the trunk were colossal crossbeams, themselves hung with winches, cables, hooks and buckets, reaching out over the darkness.

Wherever he went next, thought Schneider, it had to be well clear of that thing.

To the right of the central edifice, opposite the ranks of

heron-cranes, was relative emptiness—the lights there were smaller and lower, and some of them were slowly moving. There must be a road, thought Schneider, some way to escape this steel hell of a place, and whatever cruel coast had spawned the monster whose guts he had been reborn in.

Slipping quietly through the crowd of disinterested zombies, doing everything he could to mimic their purposeless blundering, Schneider began to make his way towards the moving lights. The head slumped against his left shoulder began to moan softly.

Soon, perhaps a hundred yards on, they shrank into the horde as a behemoth truck came growling from the dark behind them, an overseer's bearded face glowering in its red-lit cabin. On its back were bales of heaped, dripping flesh, a gruesome mess of purple fibres, sallow fat and scarred rubbery skin. Once the grumbling vehicle had passed, they began to move again, following its tail lights at a safe distance. It led them to a hill of meat.

The pile swarmed with zombies. At its crest, a knot of corpses laboured with hatchets to dismember a pale, fanged worm, while dozens more loitered on its slopes, unloading armfuls of dripping meat from the truck. The hill's perimeter was ringed by overseers in cruor-slicked leathers, their beasts dashing to and fro to discourage grey, bald-headed birds from darting in for scraps.

Schneider was loath to approach the charnel-mound, but it stood directly in between him and the moving lights of the road, and had to be passed if they were to escape. Worse yet, to its left stood the base of the enormous mast, barely a hundred yards away and lit bright as day by floodlights. 'A rock and a hard place,' murmured some stray neuron within him. 'Scylla and what's-her-name,' offered another.

On the blood-drenched steel between the pile and the tower, a mass of zombies eddied like the sluggish backwaters of a river. They would have to creep through that gap, blending in with the other dead without being siphoned off to work on the meat pile, or to something worse. And they couldn't do that while leaning on each other—it wasn't the sort of thing that happened around here. The dead thing would have to walk by itself.

Gently, Schneider lifted the zombie's clenched arm from around his neck, and grabbed it by the shoulders. It hissed in what could have been dismay, but he turned it towards him and did his best to make contact with its swimming eyes.

"Listen. Listen," he implored it. "You have to walk with me now. I can't help you."

The creature barely seemed to register his words, reaching instead to grab his body and resume its slump, and he had to physically put its arms back in place.

"No," he insisted, stunned by how easily the words were coming from his leathery throat. "We'll be hurt if you do that. You have to walk on your own for a bit. But I'll be with you."

Again it groaned and reached for him, and Schneider lost his patience. Without heed for how wise a move it was to headbutt a zombie, he smashed his forehead into the other corpse's and grabbed it by the ears, scared for a second they might come off.

"Listen. Mate. I hate to hurt you, I do. But you have to hear me. We can't get any further unless you do this with me, and I really need you to. If I lose you, I'm just running to save my own skin, and I'm going to lose my mind if that happens. Looking after you gives me a reason not to go mental, so please don't screw this up for us. I need you."

Schneider wondered how he had managed to pronounce several sentences in a row without his tongue falling out of his mouth, and almost missed the other zombie staring right at him and nodding. Its arms fell away from his and it stood, favouring one hip, yet upright, waiting to move.

They moved. Moaning a little for good measure, giving it a rest when he worried it might look unconvincing, Schneider led his clueless charge into the press, and did his best to look utterly hopeless. He bumped and blundered, arms spasming as he piled slowly into other corpses, head lolling without any seeming concern for where he was going.

All the while, he could feel the gaze of the overseers on him. More than once, he imagined one wading towards him with a predatory sneer, felt empty pores dilate to release sweat that wasn't there. Each time, it got harder not to flinch; to turn his head and see if he was being watched.

Worse yet, as he began slowly to make his way round the bulk of the flesh-mound, it occurred to him there was no way to check whether his hobbling companion was still following. What if the poor thing had slipped free of consciousness and lost itself in the slow chaos of bodies?

Any attempt to circle back and check would surely only make the situation worse. There was nothing to do but press through, and hope the other body's sojourn into sapience was persisting. "Don't look back," he told himself, as he walked through Hell. "Don't look back."

As Schneider was considering a sly half-turn to check, he walked, eyes unfocused, into the broad back of an overseer. He almost screamed. Remaining limp and slack-jawed as the ashen-faced brute—a woman whose nose was half-consumed by a livid sore—turned and scowled at him, was a feat enough to make Schneider wonder if he had somehow forgotten a lifetime on the stage. His acting was good enough: with a disgusted huff, the rot-faced giantess grabbed the back of his shirt in her Kevlar gauntlet and barrelled him on through the crowd.

As he gradually slowed his stagger to a slouch, Schneider noticed the crowd was thinning. The lower slopes of the fleshpile were petering out to his right, while the immensity of the crane tower was some way behind on his left. They were nearly through. Making his way through the rapidly clearing press of zombies, he looked out to see what the hill of meat had hidden.

Some way to his right, a cliff edge dropped away to a broad, dark valley, where the swarm of bright lights drifted back and forth. Only... it wasn't a valley. Looking closer at the surface below, Schneider saw brief, flickering reflections as the ground rose and fell in massive, heavy undulations. The sea. There was no road there: the lights were boats.

Boats. Of course. He was on a boat. A ship. A floating city so large it had docks built onto its side, and its own pitted iron geography. He had seen one side of it, back in the flensing yards on the other side of that leviathan hull, and now he was seeing the other, who knew how many hundreds of yards up and across its deck.

There was no way to walk away from this place. Looking down off its mountainous hull, any thought that the little lights puttering to and fro could offer any escape was swiftly crushed. The sprawling grid of piers and jetties that made up the dock below were separated from him by a plunging wall of metal, without a staircase, ladder or rope in sight.

And even from here he could see the docks were overrun with overseers, and free of wandering corpses to use as camouflage. Their bulky forms patrolled the loading platforms, keeping a watchful eye as conveyors and rails freighted crate after crate, barrel upon barrel, into the waiting holds of the boats.

The industry of the docks was mesmerising; coming in fast, the smaller vessels were caught in docking cradles, then filled at incredible speed by hydraulic loading arms, before being ejected in reverse just minutes after arrival. As they turned to join the stream of lights, their wakes glowing white in the lamps of the great ship, the next boats were already pulling in.

The river of cargo, visible as a bright, winding stripe like an ant-trail, threaded across the black emptiness of the water, until coalescing into a haze somewhere near the horizon.

Far, far out, where the lights of the boats were lost to distance, there was something else. Right on the horizon; a glow, like the edge of a dawn that would never come. Deep violet, a stain on the underside of the clouds that swelled in convulsions of distant, amethyst lightning.

Schneider strained to make out more of that distant glow, until he realised it was not the limits of his vision he was straining against, but of his memory. This endless stream of boats, this bastion of metal in black water, that distant lightning. He knew it. He had seen it all before. He remembered.

CHAPTER FOUR

SUDDENLY, BUT ALMOST casually, as a low belch of thunder rolled in from the purple spark on the horizon, Schneider came to understand where he was.

Realisation had been building for a while, as in a dream. The endless crashing of waves, the constant grumbling of the low sky, the dreadful industry of the ship, was all the formless stuff of nightmares—until he saw that swarm of boats.

He had seen the boats before, beetling back and forth under stacked meat and diesel smoke. Hundreds of times, in fact— seen them from land, where they meant food and safety and civic health; a never-ending stream of goods that kept home alive.

Home. That immense walled city—its name escaped him— buttressed by coastal cliffs against the permanent siege on its landward side. Unchallenged by sea, provisioned by its fleets, adoring of its fishermen.

He would watch the boats go out, sounding foghorns in farewell, to fetch food for ten million souls from a distant place. From hundreds of miles away; from a black stone gate whose arch stood a mile clear of the waves.

And through the gate? A world of infinite water, bottomless, and teeming with monsters: Ocean.

Memories pooled around the word like blood, swelling from a pinprick.

Ocean's produce had been everywhere in the city; the great casks of benthocetic tallow that came in from the docks to be rendered, the glass-waxy bows of fishbone as long as girders. But only once in Schneider's memory had something alive, or at least near to life, made it through the gate.

It had been an autumn morning at Exhibition Plaza; his mother gripping his hand as she clocked—far too late—that the pamphlets had put too rosy a gloss on things.

"It still lives!" the mass-printed scraps had exclaimed, in curlicue font.

And so it lived: a mouth like a half-collapsed tent gaping under weak sunlight, two eyes like hard-boiled yolks glaring sightlessly from pits of bone.

Red and warted and spined, bloated and shapeless on the slab. Accustomed to a life so poor and dark and famished that it barely breathed; lived perpetually on the murky edge of death.

In open air it had gaped, and withered, and swivelled lumpen fins for four days, kept damp with buckets of brine and poked with billhooks when the motion went out of it.

"Too ugly to live, too tough to die," quipped the barker by the thing's graveside, pulling down on its lip to expose a half-yard of opal needles.

"Four hundred years old, they say, but will it live another week?" he cried. "Don't pity it, folks, there's no putting it back—its swim bladder burst like a bad prophylactic when those brave boys reeled it up!

"Ten irons to put your hand inside—say you've been in the

belly of a monster!" he had bellowed, using his baton to lift the flap on the monster's ruptured flank. Thinking back on the sight of that slimy wound, Schneider tasted the memory of the vomit that had rushed up that morning.

It hadn't been the pain of the thing—or even how horrible it had been to look at—that had made it so frightening. It was like an emissary of hell, an unwelcome intrusion of horror into the city's heart. One couldn't look at it and not imagine its home..

Another memory, floating slowly to the surface. There had been a book in the library. An aged bestiary of the commercial fish from Ocean, and a parade of its most frequently-seen monsters. It was old and dust-reeking and tooth-yellow, a brick of dry description, with the occasional plate of something big and blood-streaked hanging from a crane.

Schneider had become consumed with it, looking for that awful thing from his youth as if hoping he had mis-remembered something quite ordinary. He never did find anything exactly like it, but he found plenty worse: the corpse-fish he had witnessed had not been some gruesome deepwater oddity, but just one of a world of lonely, hopeless monsters.

Teeming eels, lampreys, piss-yellow jellies and listless squid. Rafts of spongy, elongate shrimp, clinging together on the surface over bottomless depth. Lost sunfish, ribbon sharks, Jenny Hanivers and haired snakes.

Then there were the cash cows—the huge, sad benthoceti, the ricketfish with their trailing bones, the gasper, the arrostichthys, the trail-eyes in their numberless, blind shoals. All of them big as ships, able to suck in a man like dust, but docile as cattle.

They were prey for devils.

Those were the entries with no photographs or illustrations beyond guesswork scratchings—creatures too big or fierce to ever take a hook without taking a boat too; that lived under epithets rather than binomials. The Big Dark, the Far-Looker, Glasscorpse, Bagthroat.

Schneider shivered at the remembrance of those entries, of the great hungry orbs and maws staring out of the pages, of his mind nagging him to cover them with a palm as he read by candle, to look away from the open windows, even in the heart of the city.

And now he was there among them, a world away from that soft candlelight. He was in Ocean.

Schneider stood on the edge of the ship, wind blowing salt spray into his face from across a nightmare emptiness, and understood that he was in Hell after all.

All his life, Ocean had been practically a fiction. A distant realm, fished by the city's heroic daughters and sons, brimming with riches beyond measure for those brave enough to face its perils. It was a place you didn't think about, a shorthand term for 'far away and nasty,' a fate with which you idly threatened children.

The bravest and the most reckless went to work the supply boats, and came back with little to say, or never at all. Certainly, nobody said anything about city-ships dowsed in salt rain, where the despairing dead worked as slaves to carve corpses big as tenement blocks for the bellies of the living. Every fish supper Schneider had ever eaten returned to the back of his mouth, cold and mocking.

At that moment, there could have been nothing more welcome than the hand, cold and withered, that Schneider realised had been resting on his shoulder for some time. It was his companion.

He turned and fell into an embrace with the thing, leaning on it, just as it had leaned on him. He wished he could weep as his head sank to rest on its clammy chest, the sucking wound and the rags of a vest. He moaned—utterly without theatre this time—and felt something like relief, rising in a wave of blackness to meet him as consciousness waned.

But oblivion would not come. Hard, salt-slick arms were pushing him away, and that other face—a person's face, now discernible as something more than a featureless pastiche of meat over bone—was looking straight into his, silently imploring him not to lose the plot.

He tried to find the words to express what he was feeling, tried to summon the words that had started to come back to him, and couldn't. The fish on its slab had seemed impossible to reconcile to the gay surroundings of his city; now, the thought of home seemed just as impossible here.

The thing shook its head gently, as if excusing him the need to speak—as if it knew all too well what it meant to be lost for words.

With a grip markedly more robust than the weak clinging he had been subjected to back at the flensing yards, his companion turned him round to face the interior of the ship, and pointed a rock-steady finger up, towards the ziggurat of metal that dominated the centre of the floating world.

There, set some way back from the great crane they had passed earlier, was a second tower, more squat than the first, swelling as it rose to loom over the deck with green-glowing windows.

Schneider squinted against his dulled corneas, watched black human shapes move against the inside of the glass, like ornamental placoderms in a foetid aquarium, looking out over the docks with no idea that they themselves were being watched.

The dead thing held him closer, gripped his head to force it into alignment with its pointing finger, expunging any doubt as to what it was indicating.

"Them," it hissed. "There."

He understood. That tower, glowing at the top of this deep, horrible world, was where all this was controlled from. That blackness, the dark that came rising like a wall of brine when despair gnawed at his consciousness, came from there. He knew it without question; looking into that green gloaming dragged the darkness over him.

But he could not run from it. He was trapped with it, on this lonely berg of metal above a measureless sea. There were only two options: give up and let the blackness take him under—or find a way to shut it down. With no way to escape, or to retrieve his life, Schneider figured the most worthwhile way to expend his physical form, while it still functioned, would be in trying to stop this happening to anyone else.

Beneath the row of windows where the black figures paced, lights shone on the rusted shell of the tower and picked out six colossal letters, defiantly announcing the vessel's name to an uncomprehending night.

TAVUTO

Schneider looked at that word, a hundred times his size, and the memories took no time to smash into the back of his eyes. The *Tavuto*. The famous flagship. Breadbasket of Ocean. There were other ships out there, barges and gas-harvesters, seiners and supertrawlers, but all of them were footnotes to this legendary hulk.

He had owned a tin model of it as a child; had pushed it across the carpet of his father's study, making explosion noises as it nudged aside cheap plastic kraken and aspidochelons. He had imagined it crewed by brave men and women, cheerfully facing the devils of the deep with wry smiles and bunched muscles. If only he had known he would end up dead and baffled, trapped on that celebrated titan with who knew how many other walking corpses.

Never meet your heroes, thought Schneider, before the thought was driven out of his head by the scrape of sharp metal on the deck behind him.

Still staring at the black paint of the *Tavuto*'s name, Schneider froze in place, strained to hear the sound of any further scuttling over the incessant patter of the rain. To his dread, the sound came again, and continued.

Worse yet, he realised, the hand had gone from the side of his head—he was standing alone. Had his companion been taken while he'd been consumed in memory? Panicking, he turned, and saw nothing but darkness around him. The clicking of metal came again, nearer this time, from the shadows.

He was about to call out, when a hiss from the floor caught his attention—his companion was on the deck, dropped like a sack of meat with only its face moving, mouth working desperately to attract his attention. The other corpse twitched its head convulsively to the side, eyes wide, and Schneider wondered what was wrong with it before finally getting the message. "Get down," it was mouthing.

Letting exhausted legs do what came naturally, Schneider let himself collapse to the deck, limbs falling haphazardly on top of each other, with his face turned towards the other prone body.

Without heartbeats or breaths to count, he had no idea how long he lay there, listening to the falling rain and the distant thunder of the gate. Just when he was thinking of getting to his feet, the scrabbling came again, now only a few yards away.

Then it was on them. It fell like a sodden blanket, a broad disc that rippled at the edges and flexed queasily as metallic, arthropod legs twitched beneath it. A mouth like the puckered sneer of a jack-o'-lantern loomed at Schneider's face, flanked by black, sightless eyes.

He strained not to move, not to even twitch his eyes, as the vile black pit wavered inches above him. The terrible eye lowered over his own, rimmed by twitching muscle, and blasted cold air over his face. It bore the piercing, ammoniac stench of a sharkmonger's stall at midsummer, a smell that ate into his sinuses despite the dulling of death.

Because the eye was not an eye, but a nostril. The thing was a stingray—or had been one once. As the ragged, undulating edge of the creature slipped horribly over his flank, its flattened face snuffled obscenely over him, huffing in his scent and blasting back an overpowering necrochemical cocktail.

Without warning, the blind white face swung over to his companion, leaving his face enveloped by the flopping, fish-belly softness of its outer body. Schneider's instinct was to gag, to flail at the great dead curtain of meat and fight for breathing space, but with his lungs inert, there was little point. All he could do was wait it out, while the metal legs of the thing skittered around his hips and its disc-like immensity flabbered over him. The darkness rose, bringing with it the image of his eight-year-old hand pushing a tin boat across worn carpet, before it enveloped him.

In the end, it was the shaking of a human hand that brought him back. Not human, he reminded himself, as his vision swam sickly back to the sight of a skull papered with grey skin. But human enough. Still fighting to remember what had just happened, Schneider rose and looked around him. He wasn't sure what it was he dreaded seeing, but there was nothing there but the night and his friend—that was a strange word—beckoning him to follow as it padded backwards along the deck.

"It thought we were dead," said the corpse, leaving Schneider wondering how much its grin was purely an artefact of decay, before turning into the night. He followed.

CHAPTER FIVE

HE HAD BEEN out for some time following his encounter with the stingray. The rain had died down to a light drizzle now, and dawn was on its way, grey like the skin of something drowned, without a hint of where the sun might rise.

They had left the *Tavuto*'s bridge tower some way behind them, its brooding bulk lost in the same mists that swallowed the deck ahead of them. And they were virtually alone— unlike the city-ship's forward decks, which had teemed with the industry of the dead and their shepherds, this area seemed empty.

To their left, the superstructure of the ship rose in a mountain range of machinery, windowless metal cliffs and vertical jungles of scaffolding. The sprawl of engineering crowded nearly to the edge of the ship, leaving only a strip of deck a hundred yards across, a grey road for them to walk.

Here and there, they came across lone zombies, staggering

aimlessly like drunks returning bloodless from all-night revels. Once, they encountered a line of house-sized, chalk-white spider crabs, limbs bound with cable, mouthparts still weakly flickering. As they passed, the cat-sized isopods that seemed to serve as ship's vermin clicked and squeaked at them from the shadows beneath their vast cousins.

But for the most part, their only company as they hobbled down the side of the *Tavuto*'s spine were the grey-headed seabirds, dipping from the mist to roost in the foul, shit-crusted interstices of scaffolding and pipework. Schneider wondered idly, as they walked beneath one of the birds' eyries, whether their hooked beaks were open to the taste of abhuman flesh, but was quick to put the thought out of his head. Being devoured by a bird was hardly the worst thing he could imagine right now.

Eventually, as the sky grew noticeably brighter in the distance, they came to the stern of the ship. The gargantuan central structure ended in a stark abutment of cooling towers and aerial masts, against which blocky sheds and storehouses leaned like foothills, their mouths yawning onto the deck. At its edge was a railing, dark in the predawn mist, and then nothing but the expanse of Ocean. Schneider and his friend said nothing, just walked on towards the edge; while they were still walking, he figured, they wouldn't have to work out what to do next.

When they reached the rail, rusted and caked with guano, the sun was just beginning to climb into the sky, a sliver of steel nestled in a rare gap in the clouds. All was silent in its cold, sideward glare, a billion wavelets shivering over fathomless depths. None of this water, thought Schneider, would ever touch a shore.

If anything, the obfuscation of night had been a comfort. Being able to see the sheer, grey emptiness of what surrounded the *Tavuto* made even the incalculable mass of the slave ship seem tiny and fragile. Were he still alive, Schneider would barely have been able to look beyond the deck of the ship for fear, let alone stand on its edge.

It was then that his attention was drawn by a noise out on the water, rising above the rough fizzing of waves against the hull far below. Some way off the stern, a whale was being eaten.

The animal was white, eyeless, something like an elongate sperm whale with gills and a lower jaw trailing thick barbels. A benthocetus; Schneider recognised it from the logo on countless tins of Hedstrom & Sons fish. One of the most commonly fished creatures in Ocean, they swam in lonely pods in the blackness a mile or so down, following the currents in search of squid, balloon crabs, and anything else soft and pelagic.

When they died, their teeming gut flora, running wild in the dark, began to digest their host, filling their bellies with gas and sending them rising slowly to the surface far above. It was said that pods would follow the bodies of their dead as far as they could, until the decrease in water pressure threatened to burst their heads. Eventually the corpses would breach the waves alone, ruptured and wrecked, rolling sightless beneath a sky their distant ancestors had left behind.

This body looked like it had just risen, and already the sharks were upon it. Great whites and sleepers swarmed its belly, the slick wedges of their heads breaking the waves as they scrambled for purchase against thick blubber. More were arriving, visible briefly as grey ovals above the waves as they cruised for a place at the feast. Fins thrashed, raising spray.

"So that's it," said Schneider's friend, their voice a quiet rasp on the breeze. "We can't walk any further." The time had come for that difficult conversation. Schneider grunted in acknowledgement, eyes still fixed on the dead whale.

"Where were we going again?" he asked, hoping desperately that a plan had been agreed in that groggy, half-remembered time following their investigation by the stingray.

"I don't know," whispered the other corpse, as if surprised by the fact.

"You were leading the way," said Schneider, without the energy to phrase it as anything more than a statement of fact.

Speech came more clearly now, but it was utterly exhausting—nuance was beyond him.

The corpse sighed, wistful in a way that suggested they might have had a plan earlier.

"Maybe, I forgot. Maybe we never had a plan. But it's quiet here, we can talk. We can make a plan."

The carcass rolled in the water, disturbed from below by something very large, and tails smacked at the water as the sharks were dislodged.

"Talking," said Schneider, fighting to stay focused. "We need to talk to other, to other... to the other..."

"Zombies?" offered his companion. Schneider looked over at them and they shared a rustling laugh, his companion's chest wound foaming mirthfully.

"Yes, the zombies," he agreed. "Ridiculous, isn't it? But there we are. We need to talk to them, to wake them up, like us."

"What then?" said Schneider's friend, as the water around the benthocetus slopped and churned with red-gummed mouths. The carcass dipped in the water again, tugged from below.

"I don't know," said Schneider. "Let's see if they've got any ideas. At least it's quiet here. We've got a place to think, and to talk, and work out what we're going to do."

The water exploded in a surge of spray. Schneider had seen it coming a second before it breached, huge and pale and rippling through the water as it rushed up. Then it was there, a great blunt head, grey cathedral jaws distending to clamp round the whale's girth.

It shook from side to side and the sixty-ton carcass moved with it, raising walls of white water. The crepuscular titan glowed a weak yellow in the dawn, and the clusters of copepod parasites trailing from its eyes glistened. At last a good quarter of the whale's body came free in its mouth, and the head disappeared.

For a second one of the great scavenger's fintips breached and hung in the air as it turned. Then it was gone, taking its meal with it and retreating into the depths for the day. What was left of the whale sank from view less than a minute later, gone back to join its fellows in the deep.

"I'd like to find somewhere to shelter," said Schneider, at exactly the same time his fellow said, "I'm hungry."

When he came to think of it, Schneider was very hungry too—he had been for as long as he had been conscious, although he hadn't recognised the sensation for what it was. After watching the scene off the stern of the *Tavuto*, there was little in the world he wanted to do less than actually eat, but apparently his companion was made of sterner stuff.

More pressingly, as the sun rose, the stern deck felt extremely exposed. If another one of the rays—or worse yet, an overseer—came round this end of the ship on patrol, there would be nowhere to hide. For that matter, there was no guarantee they were not already being watched from any of the darkened windows that festooned the ship's aft decks.

Looking round at the *Tavuto*'s rear (and feeling a rush of relief to be looking away from the sea), the darkened entrances of its lower warehouses suddenly seemed hugely inviting. There was no sign of any movement there.

"Let's go inside," urged Schneider, gently turning his companion away from the endless water and pointing. "Maybe they have food stored there. And it's safe. Maybe."

Shrugging with wasted, bony shoulders, the other zombie stepped away from the rail and loped for the ship's interior.

He was so tired; the short walk to the nearest entrance felt as long as the night's march up the flank of the ship. They collapsed just inside the mouth of the metal cave, Schneider feeling as though his limbs were little more than salt-soaked driftwood, his feet sodden lumps. He didn't dare think about their condition inside their gore-stained wrappings.

There was no doubt, he was growing weaker. While he had no idea when—or what—he had eaten before becoming conscious, whatever metabolism he had was screaming for fuel. It had not escaped his notice that he had not shat yet, either—so far as he knew. But that was another thing he just did not want to think about. It was best just to focus on what went in. This was a ship that existed to gather meat; whether he liked the idea of putting any in his mouth or not, there had to be some nearby.

The warehouse was dim, as the sun had not yet hauled itself high enough to shine over the parapet of the stern, but looked dispiritingly empty. What he hoped at first to be the angular bodies of sharks revealed themselves, as his weak eyes adjusted to the dark, to be the corroded bones of aircraft, half-dismantled and surrounded by littered parts. The warehouse was actually a hangar, and—judging by the look of it—one that had not been used in an extremely long time.

There was no food here, no company, no answers. Just him and his companion; two knackered corpses slumped in a derelict building. Schneider closed his eyes, and was positively urging the ever-present interior night to swallow him, when the gurgling of his companion's chest wound, which always preceded their voice, caught his ear.

"Look: meat," they breathed, and he craned forward with open eyes to see it for himself. Sure enough, as the sun's light began to filter into the rusty cavern, the back wall was coming into view; and against it lay a six-foot drift of flesh. He thought to plead for a moment's rest before they went to investigate, but his friend had already risen shakily to their feet and was scampering past the shattered jets to the prospect of food.

Schneider rose to follow, and was halfway across the hangar before the first wash of sunlight spilled onto the pile, revealing what it was made of.

Bodies.

CHAPTER SIX

"THEY'RE PEOPLE!" SHOUTED Schneider, surprised by the volume of his voice. "They're people!"

To his immense relief, his companion slowed—he had briefly thought they would continue on with jaws open and eyes dulled by hunger, but with the sun shining on the pile, there was no doubting the provenance of the meat.

At first, he wondered if it was a heap of the truly dead, but then he saw movement. Just a fingertip at first, twitching weakly on the end of a scab-crusted arm, but once he knew what he was looking for, he saw more. Here a bandaged foot scrabbled mindlessly at the deck, there an arm waved slowly in the air as if signalling for help, there a shattered jaw opened and closed, sickeningly mechanical below unmoving eyes. For a queasy second, the image of the bloated fish in Exhibition Plaza returned to Schneider's mind: it was horrible that seeing corpses move didn't seem unusual anymore.

They were stacked haphazardly, slumped against each other like sozzled friends, as he and his companion had been when they first walked into the hangar. Schneider wondered: had they come here consciously, or had they sleepwalked here unaware, driven by the vague instinct to get away from the horror of the foredeck? More to the point, in either case, were they any different to him?

Towards the bottom of the mound, the zombies looked markedly more decrepit, and less motile. Under the sprawled forms of the more recent arrivals, there was a midden of muck-encrusted forms, either lacking in limbs or so thin and drawn they seemed incapable of movement.

At the edge of the drift, separated from his fellows by a few feet and lying in a mound of wet black detritus, was the most harrowing of all of them.

He was little more than a skeleton, clothed in nothing but a ragged grey beard, his limbs worked down in places to grey-red bone and strange black tendons. Yet he still moved. Despite being reduced to a wet, filthy parody of a human form, he still moved, scratching absently at his right humerus with a fragment of metal like a caged parrot gone mad.

Schneider wondered, looking down at the emaciated figure, whether this was what he had to look forward to. A gradual erosion of function, followed by an interminable slump against a wall somewhere as he waited for his bones to fall apart.

He was just plotting out his excruciating demise in some reeking corner, when it occurred to him he had not heard from his companion in all the time he had been inspecting the writhing people-pile. Looking over to his right, he saw them hunched over the form of a prone zombie, arms outstretched, and a cold shot ran down his spine. His friend was eating another human.

Stumbling over, toes stubbing brutally against the riveted decking, Schneider waved his arms and panted for the other corpse to stop, before he realised there was no cannibalism occurring. His friend was bent over, holding another zombie in their arms, and repeatedly saying the word "Aroha" into its face. It knew their name; it was trying to wake them.

Rather than interrupt, Schneider watched, and waited for any explanation of what was going on. The two dead people were wearing the same clothes—or at least the remnants of them. They had the same sucking chest wound. And, looking closer at the forearm his companion had clamped alongside that of the prone zombie, the same tattoo. It was a brusque, military job on the inner wrist, a sword in black ink superimposed on a stylised image of a ringed world, somewhat duller than it would have been on living flesh.

"Aroha!" urged his companion. "You remember? Stay still, you told us. The railgun was charging. It got the shot off, you know, after you went down. The railgun!"

"The railgun," echoed the slumped form, like somebody trying to remember a dream.

"Burner division. They managed to get it to fire again! A hundred drums it took them, but they got it to fire again. Ripped an almighty hole, when it did. Made enough room for a pithecus charge. You did it, Aroha. You bought them the time."

The sun glowed on the two tattooed wrists. "The siege," croaked the cadaver, then rattled for a time, as if searching for a word. "Mouana."

"Yes!" hissed Schneider's friend. "It's me! It's not over. They got us, but they've brought us back. Do you remember..." Mouana continued, gesturing at the hole in her chest, and then at the other zombie's.

The answer was a long moan—the waking moan, all too familiar to Schneider from the flensing yards—that echoed around the flaking hangar and brought echoes from the dead elsewhere on the pile. As he looked around, he realised more than a handful of the heaped dead were dressed in the same maroon rags, had the same wounds.

The siege. The besieging force. The Blades of Titan, the baby-eaters. The newest and the largest of the mercenary armies that had encircled Home since before his grandfather had been a boy. They were here, same as he was. He had laughed with one of them. He had dragged them away from a shark's jaws, despite everything their barbarian army had inflicted on his city and his countryfolk.

He had never seen the enemy up close before. The city walls were high, and strictly off-limits to civilians, a great sheltering hand of concrete and masonry that kept the ever-present threat of the siege abstracted to a distant rumble. One of Schneider's drinking mates, who had drawn a service ticket and spent a summer manning a gun on one of the Eastern scarp sections, said there was bugger all to see anyway: for the most part, the enemy spent all their time under cover, in the miles of jagged trenches, flak silos and gun nests that surrounded the city like an infested sore.

Once every so often—sometimes three or four times over a season, sometimes not for years at a time—there would be a big push for the city. It generally began unannounced, with the splashing of overshot artillery against the sky-shield followed by the thunder of the distant guns. Sometimes a squadron of the city's triremes would fly out over the parapets, and sometimes a district next to the wall would be evacuated for a day or so, but it was rare that the fighting would intrude any further on daily civilian life. Even the defence itself was conducted largely by the city's own legions of mercenaries, with just a token levy drawn by lottery from the general populace to act as a reserve.

In general, the siege was felt more as an emotional presence, an ever-present national claustrophobia. From time to time it would assert itself through the occasional taking of an uncle, a colleague, a grocer's assistant one barely knew—but it had no human face

In fact, the only time Schneider could remember having seen the face of the enemy had been on a midwinter afternoon, after an attempt by the city to break through the siege and link up with an allied army had led to a week of particularly heavy action. The city had come under heavy enough bombardment to see shells push through the shield more than once, and for two nights in a row the sky had been lit bright orange by the fires of a distant armour duel.

When it was all over, a stream of prisoners—the remains of two full enemy regiments, the news sheets had said (they had been less clear on whether the breakthrough had been successful)—were led to the top of the wall above the immensity of the Farmer's Gate and turned to face the city they had spent the season trying to capture.

Schneider had been part of the crowd gathered to watch as the soldiers, many of them sagging from untreated wounds, looked out over the sprawling factories, the teeming docks, and the bulbous immensity of College Hill. The wall's defenders stood behind their enemy counterparts, close as lovers, looking at the same view with their faces set in grim pride.

"This is what you will never have," came an amplified voice from atop the wall, as the sun glared coldly from its descent into the western sea.

"This is all you get," said the voice, and the day's last light glinted red from the points of a thousand sabres, as they punched forwards through the prisoners' chests.

Watching as Mouana cradled her commander in the light of a different sun, rising above a different, despairing world, it became utterly clear where all of those prisoners, and every prisoner captured during the long years of the siege, had ended up.

By the time Schneider's mind caught up with itself and asked what in the world he was doing among the prisoners of war, he found his hands were already one step ahead, checking his chest for a blade's exit. But there was nothing, just a clammy linen shirt and prune-wrinkled grey skin beneath. There was, however, something on the back of his hand. It was caked in filth, and faded by the ongoing death of his skin, but its form was unmistakable: the outline of a tobacco pipe, painted in livid scar tissue.

Other sights had brought images of the past slowly to mind,

like tea diffusing from a bag, but this one smashed into him like a haymaker from a Bull Aug. After all, it had been one of his last.

CITIZENS OF LIPOS-THOLOS, the text had proclaimed below the image of the blazing pipe. *SISTERS AND BROTHERS in the COLONIES and all across the LEMNISCATUS. We have PLAYED THE FOOL LONG ENOUGH. WE'VE BETTER THINGS TO DO than keep COLLEGE HILL comfy and FAT... JUST ASK OLD KING PIPE!*

The words, hurriedly printed on rough brown paper, were spilling all over the floor as the constable emptied a gutted almanac onto the library floor. Behind her, two rough men standing among the overturned shelves of the agricultural research section were picking out one book after another, prising them open to check for more pamphlets. Dust billowed; the city hadn't maintained fields for decades, and the racks of books on fertiliser efficiency and irrigation technology had been badly neglected.

Until, apparently, they had become a repository for seditious material.

"It's nothing to do with me!" Schneider had gasped, as they had fastened the cuffs. "How would I know they were there? I'm not a Piper!"

The maddening thing was, while he remembered saying the words, he had no idea whether he had been lying or not. All that came to his mind were the averted glances of his colleagues, the slews of exclamatory handbills on the floor, and his own frantic protests as he was dragged out of the stacks, past the front desk, and into the snow.

He remembered garbled fragments of a trial, his dad crying like a kid, the dumb certainty that things would all somehow work themselves out, that things like this didn't happen to people like him, even as the hairs on the back of his hand shrivelled blackly away from the branding iron's glow.

Then there had been a night in a cell, the livid brands on the hands of the two men and the old woman sharing it with him as they sat up through the night. And then the chamber, with the steel walls, where he had been all alone, a magistrate looking in on him through a little glass portal. A weird cold smell had come into the air and he had blacked out, and that had been the end of his life.

CHAPTER SEVEN

THAT WAS IT, thought Schneider, after a moment of utter blankness. That had been his death. Truth be told, there was nothing too distressing about the event itself—compared with the screaming nightmare of waking up again, it was not such a bad thing to carry in his head. If anything, it only served to make everything that had happened before less real—the memories were like reading somebody else's diary, looking through their photographs and guessing how they might have felt at the time. Looking at it that way, he was really just a very intimate spectator to somebody else's death.

Frankly, everything felt easier to deal with if he imagined he was something entirely new, grown into the architecture of someone else's memories like a hermit crab curled up in an old skull. When he looked at it like that, imagined the man whose memories he was reading had just vanished in that chamber, everything seemed less shit by comparison. After all, if Schneider had died and he was something new and weird, then this was all he had ever known.

At the very least, he thought, this all explained why the city's courts had been based in the same building as its commercial fishing administration, named the Ministry of Fisheries & Justice.

It was all quite a shift in perspective. He only became aware of how long he'd been standing and staring when Mouana, long since finished explaining things to her old comrade, addressed him.

"You've remembered *him* dying, haven't you?" she said. "It helps when you remember."

"Yes, I think it does," he whispered, letting his gaze slide across the drift of restless, lychee-eyed cadavers, each one writhing in the grey blankness between being one person and another.

All of a sudden, the disgust and antipathy he had felt when recognising Mouana and Aroha as Blades was gone; the hatred felt alien, as incomprehensible as eating stones. For a start, the citizen whose city had been besieged by them was long dead and gone, as were the soldiers who had taken part in its assault. Whatever they were now, they shared in common the fact of their existence—the fact they had been killed, reanimated and enslaved by the city of Lipos-Tholos.

Besides, putting philosophy aside entirely, he was strongly beginning to suspect that even in life, Schneider had not been that emotionally engaged with hating the enemy. For some people it had been something to sing songs about while deep in their cups, or to mutter darkly about over boiled huss. For him, it had been a lukewarm conviction at best, something understood on an intellectual level rather than felt.

Whether this was because he had been a political dissident (of all the things not to remember, this was particularly frustrating), or whether it was because he'd grown up reading books of war poetry that rattled on about the essential humanity of cannon fodder everywhere (there was no doubt about this), he had no idea.

Whatever the reason, any old prejudice was desperately easy to ditch in favour of the relief of having company. Still, he found himself utterly speechless when Aroha, whose eyes and voice had taken on the firmness of lucidity with remarkable speed, asked who the hell he was meant to be.

Unsure for a moment himself, he was just working his black-baked lips around the initial consonant of his old name when Mouana made a practical intervention.

"He started it," she said. "He woke me. He's going to lead a revolt here."

Well, whyever not, thought the man who had been Schneider. If he had been a political criminal rather than a librarian, this was exactly the sort of thing he would have dreamed of doing. And if he hadn't been a political criminal, then he had every reason to be one now. In any case, leading a slave revolt had to be better than lurching around waiting to fall into some machinery or a pair of hyperfaunal jaws.

"Yeah. I am," he said, as casually as a corpse can really say anything.

And he felt it, more than he had felt anything since being dead. Even more than he'd known, looking up at the emerald glower of the bridge tower during the night, that this dreadful machine had to be stopped. Killing people would be one thing, but putting diminished life into their corpses to keep them working was quite another.

Even going by the brutal logic that some crimes deserved a worse punishment than death, inflicting that punishment on a fresh consciousness stuck in a dead brain was a new level of barbarism. Whatever the metaphysical situation, whoever he really was, this was not something he ever wanted to happen to anyone else.

"So what's his name?" asked the commander, putting an end to the metaphysics.

"Wrack," he said, telling himself it would be easier for

newly-wakened tongues to pronounce, and very definitely choosing to forget that he had always felt his second name was much cooler than his first.

Whether he was feeling a surge of adrenaline, or just the ghost of one in whatever counted for his nervous system, the sluggishness had left his limbs: the hunger had been replaced by a yearning that was more than physical.

The zombies in the heap were looking at him. Or at least towards him. Registering on some viscous level of cognition that their fellows were having a conversation—were saying real words to each other—their faces were turning towards them like blind fungi following a gibbous moon. They might not be listening, but they were on the cusp. How much would it take to get them to accept their surroundings, to remember their names and their deaths, to get angry?

His tongue ached in his mouth like chewed meat, and death hung on the bottom of his thoughts like filthy water soaking the hem of a coat, but Wrack gathered his words to speak. This was where it started.

And this, he realised—as the brash clatter of mechanical legs sounded from the hangar door—was probably also where it ended. A jagged, lamniform shadow loomed on the faces of his congregation, cast by the rising sun.

It was good while it lasted, thought Wrack.

Then, to his bafflement, a slab of spongy white organ meat landed on the deck next to him with a sullen slap. He was just beginning to turn when a second chunk of half-liquified meat smacked into the back of his head.

"Come on, arseholes," growled a voice like a heavy smoker wheezing into a metal balloon, "food."

This did not, thought Wrack, as heavy boots kicked aside rusted detritus, sound like the prelude to a mauling. Taking care not to react directly to the meat that had hit him— blundering instead in a slow circle—he glanced slyly towards the hangar's opening.

There, sitting down heavily on a ragged tyre, was a massive

woman in a blood-caked oilskin, with the raw eyes and waxy face of an overseer. Her hair, clumped into sodden grey locks by rain, gore and oil, fell limply from her brows and hung over what he took at first to be a respirator, then registered was part of her head. From the bridge of her nose downwards, starting in a brutal ridge of scar tissue, her face was a heavy brass grille, like the front of a bus or the mouth of an industrial amplifier. It was cushioned beneath by rolls of fat, angles drowned in softness.

Her hand reached over the lip of a tin wheelbarrow, piled high with waxy gristle, and pulled free a length of bulbous gut, which she threw dismissively across the hangar towards the zombies.

Reaching in again for the mucus-strung back half of an isopod, she issued a curt whistle and held it out at arm's length. Skidding slightly as it lunged, a twelve foot thresher shark with an ugly gash in the side of its head snapped at the meat, twisted its head from side to side as the overseer engaged in a half-arsed game of tug-of-war with it.

Pulling the rotten crustacean from her grasp, the shark loped off under the wing of a dead jetplane to gnash at its prize, while the brass-faced woman dug into the barrow for more gloppy offal. She emitted a piercing whistle from her faceplate: all across the pile of dead, flesh rustled on flesh and bandaged feet thudded on rust, as the hungry zombies made for their meal.

With a sinking sensation, Wrack found he too was edging towards the meat, as were the two former soldiers. The thought of iron-rich matter, rising up against his driving teeth, was too much to resist.

He crept forwards, careful neither to overtake the shambling crowd nor look too directly at the overseer, and kept his face empty with slack despair even when her radio began trilling.

"*Whēkau clearup three, this is Dakuvanga, what's your status?*" crackled the dull box. "*Any stragglers?*"

"Yeah, DV, plenty. Just like I told you. The old hangar's a goldmine. But there's a lot of shit back here too, over."

The metal-faced woman thumbed off the radio to throw a

stringy fish spine to the growing crowd, then raised it to her chin again.

"I mean it, DV. Most of these aren't even good for refit. They're not even getting up. You need to get Kaitangata back here. Soon. They're clogging up the place. Not good to let 'em pile up."

She flicked the radio off again, held it in her lap and, for a very long second, seemed to look straight at Wrack as he sank to his knees and fumbled for a sagging organ.

"They'll get ideas," she said dryly to herself, and huffed something that might have been a laugh.

A long pause of static followed, before a burst of pops and hisses heralded Dakuvanga's croaking voice again.

"*Whatever, WK3. We're busy up here. Nine pinnaces loaded already for the hunt. You have numbers or what?*"

"Fine. Probably forty functional, but you've got twice that on stumps and sticks, not even moving for guts."

"*Ten-four Whēkau; stow it. Just get 'em fed and move the ones you can move.*"

Wrack pulled a shivering length of pallid tube to his mouth, felt it slide like cold jelly around his incisors. Thought seemed to slip backwards, somewhere deep under his champing jaws, as he sucked back mouthful upon mouthful of lumpy gut.

By the time he'd wrestled his mind back from the gelid orgy of consumption, the radio conversation had progressed. The thresher shark was close by, making slow circles of the mass of feeding zombies.

"Yes DV, I repeat," snarled the woman. "Fed and ready, we're almost good to move out."

There was barely a second of static before the reply came back.

"*Well hurry the fuck up, WK3, ET just smelled the Bahamut. It's on. Out.*"

The overseer closed her eyes, let out a gushing huff of irritation through her cheesegrater of a face, and stowed the radio.

"You heard the man," she said to nobody in particular, as she rose ponderously to her feet. "We've got a monster to kill."

CHAPTER
EIGHT

THEY WERE HERDED down the starboard side of the *Tavuto*, the thresher shark at their heels, with dreadful urgency. The overseer led the way, barking constantly into her radio, with thirty or so of the dead following in a loose, shambling pack.

Around them, the ship seemed to be moving into a higher gear of activity, like something terrible disturbed from sleep. From deep within the iron hill of its body the throb of engines rose, and steam poured from the throats of cooling towers to form a sweltering canopy high overhead.

The sun, still hauling itself up above the horizon, though it must have been hours since dawn, glared on their backs and began to burn the mist from the deck. Though they had not yet encountered any other work parties, or any other overseers, the sound of screaming metal and shouting ahead of them suggested they were heading back into the fray.

For now, it was just them—thirty corpse-prisoners with fresh blood on their chins, and one harried overseer. Soon, though, they would be back under the watchful eyes of the cranes, and the floodlights, and the battalions of dour watchers with their attack beasts. Wrack registered, with a lurch of panic, that they might be rapidly running out of time to make any kind of move.

Looking over slyly at Mouana, he found the haggard soldier looking back at him, a strand of white flesh from the feeding still dangling from her jaw. Had she had the same thought? Miming a stumble on a weak ankle, Wrack blundered heavily into her, disguising any sense of purpose lest he be spotted by the shark that skittered around them like an excitable dog.

He gestured towards the overseer, used the supposedly random flailing of his arms to mime them rushing forwards, overpowering her. This knot of baffled dead was their rebellion in embryo—surely they could tackle the brute woman, and maybe even her shark as well, if the other zombies noticed what was going on and joined in.

"Yes," hissed Mouana curtly, and began to accelerate towards their supervisor. Wrack shuddered at the thought of how big a chance they were taking, but there was nothing to do but follow. Doing the best they could to lope up through the pack of dead without any sense of apparent purpose, they soon found themselves leading the way, just behind the grille-faced woman.

With no memories of having had a fight in his life—especially not against someone twice his size, wrapped in boiled leather—Wrack had no idea how they were going to overpower her. He was just hoping Mouana had years of close-quarters combat drilled into her muscle memory, when the overseer's radio chattered and she stopped in her tracks. Wrack ran straight into her back, arms outstretched like a child pretending to be a monster.

"You have to be bloody kidding," growled the overseer to herself, grunting with irritation and swiping Wrack and Mouana to the deck absent-mindedly, as if clearing cobwebs.

"All channels, we repeat. ET has ignored the lure and is closing," barked the radio. *"Six hundred yards and closing. Expecting major heat in bay one any minute now. All hands, pattern Kappa. Prepare to repel."*

Cutting through the swelling ambience of grinding steel, a thin, wailing siren rose from the mist ahead.

"Oh, *shit*," said the overseer, looking up and shaking her head in disbelief.

Following her gaze from where he sprawled on cold metal, Wrack looked into the sky and saw, looming above him, the gigantic tower of scaffolding they had passed during the night trek. High up on its superstructure, stencilled on the side of a factory-sized chunk of crane-festooned superstructure, were the letters DV-1. This was Dakuvanga. If the bridge tower they had seen in the depths of the night had been the brain of the *Tavuto*, this had to be its heart. Or at least its gigantic, muscly arm.

If anything, it looked even more imposing by the light of day. Clumps of decking clung to the vertical immensity of the structure like bracket fungus encrusting an ancient tree, pocked with windows and sprouting booms, cables and pulley-clubbed cranes. As he watched, one of Dakuvanga's subsidiary arms swung ponderously across the deck; in its grip, a boat that would have seemed enormous in a less insane context was lifted from its bracket on the central hull and into the mist-hidden chaos ahead.

Wrack found his attention torn from the huge boat's progress by the throaty rumble of a diesel engine; a battered flatbed truck had pulled up beside their clump of stragglers, and the overseer in the cab was leaning out to engage in frantic conversation with their herder.

"We reeled out a chunk of the Bahamut as a decoy, but ET saw past it—it's come for the whole thing," shouted the truck's driver, above the growing din of metal and klaxons.

"Is it going for the ship?" said the grille-faced woman, spreading her arms in bafflement.

"How the hell would I know?" snapped the driver. "Either way, we're going to need all the meat we can get amidships, and we need it already there. So are you going to load up or what?"

The overseer leapt up into the cab with surprising agility, and the engine revved. Before he could look around for Mouana or the commander, Wrack found himself picked from the floor like a side of meat by the brutish arms of an overseer and tumbled into the back of the truck with a mass of other zombies. Two other bodies were lumped on top of him, arms and legs flailing like the flippers of turtles tossed into a barrel.

The vehicle lurched into motion just as Wrack was trying to right himself, sending him slamming back into the once-human meat pile on its back. Acceleration shoved his face against the mass of sores coating another zombie's belly, and his neck made a noise that would have made him wince if he had been alive. Thrusting away from the rotting body, he managed to hook an arm over the truck's side, and pulled himself out of the writhing mass of confused bodies to rest on the metal edge.

With another mechanical growl, the truck burst through the dissipating mist hanging above the *Tavuto*'s starboard flank and barrelled onto empty decking. A stray zombie folded under its bull-bars with a cracking thud; one side of the truck lurched into the air for half a second as it went under a wheel.

Wrack's teeth clattered against his tongue as the truck hit the ground again, filling his mouth with the cloying reek of what passed for blood. Gripping the side of the speeding vehicle with trembling ferocity, he craned his neck and took in a scene of unreal proportions.

To their right, the *Tavuto*'s side opened up into a vast lagoon; a sea-filled bay at least half a mile long, steel-floored and encircled by tower-studded walls. Along its inner wall, a row of mighty cranes bristled with house-sized cutting equipment, while on its outer edge, enormous latticed gates stood open to Ocean.

Inside the lagoon was a corpse of incomprehensible scale.

Filling the bay from end to end was a fish, or a whale, or something else, collapsed and flabby and distended in death. Swathes of its skin were crusted in barnacles, corals and tubeworm casts, while barbels and fins the size of streets rose and fell on the swell of the waves. The Bahamut, Wrack assumed.

A cloud of grey water hung from a sprawling wound in its belly, spilling indistinct clouds of innards and spawning a boil of lampreys, hagfish, saw-suckers and carrion skate. The bay's gates were sliding slowly shut, but the hoary slick of filth flowed through their lattice, fountaining over the lip of the lagoon and into the currents beyond.

It had been smelled.

As the truck sped along the row of saw-cranes, Wrack watched, transfixed, as a gigantic claw the colour of green milk rose from the sea beyond the bay and hooked itself roughly over the closing sea-gate. For a moment, he could have sworn the entire vessel dipped inches as the ghastly thing tugged on its edge, before the metal sagged like tissue and tore away. Even as the gate collapsed, a second limb unfolded from the roiling sea, its tip groping over the edge of the bay and catching in the trailing guts of the Bahamut.

Over the crashing hiss of pouring water, whip-cracks popped from the lagoon as the cables anchoring the gigafauna in place stretched and snapped. The middle of the Bahamut was drawn out towards open water by the claw, as an armoured head rose at the edge of the abyss in sheets of rushing green water.

It was part mantis shrimp, part dragonfly nymph, part mountainside, part god; an edifice of compound eye and scissoring mouthparts. Something too weird to exist beyond rambling footnotes, even in the books of his youth. One of the ET clade.

The ETs were some of the least understood, the most feared, and the most profitable of Ocean's fauna. Some held they had been the original inhabitants of this endless sea; others, that their ancestors had been carried here as larvae in ballast tanks, long years ago when the sky had been a way in and out of the world. Nobody even knew if they could breed here.

Either way, they were rare, and huge, and worth ten times their weight in meat. Despite being inedible, their strange aromatics, weird compounds, and cellular metabolism based on radioactive decay, made them prizes beyond measure. And they were bastard hard to kill.

As soon as the knotted immensity of the ET's head broke water, the guns opened fire. From the corners of the steel lagoon clustered turrets blazed into life, dozens of muzzle flashes drowning the weak morning light in their actinic rage. An instant later the air filled with the hyperkinetic stutter of miniguns, the arrhythmic crump of AP shells, and the staccato thud of munitions raining into yard-thick chitin-analogue.

With a titanic screech that seemed to shiver the deep steel of the deck, the ET reared a full fifty yards into the air, twisting its segmented tower of a body even as its surface was drilled into clouds of splinters, then hurled itself sideways into the sea. Gouts of water leapt up from its vanishing, a swell of oil-souped brine washing over the walls of the lagoon, and then all was silent but for the slapping of the bullied water.

Then, pandemonium.

A new siren, deep and aggressive, blasted from horns all around Dakuvanga's base. Boats were being hauled from their brackets by a swaying forest of cranes, while trucks carrying munitions, fuel and endless piles of the flailing dead swarmed to the muster points beside the lagoon.

"*Code Three! Code Three!*" screamed a static-blasted voice from the cab of the truck. "*It's holed and surface-bound; fleet C, all boats to pursuit, all boats!*"

The predator's howl came again, and Wrack saw the sea beyond the *Tavuto* break in the roll of a mountainous carapace.

"*There she blows!*" came the shout from the radio, a distorted cry of ecstasy, and Wrack tumbled from the truck in a mound of disgorged bodies.

CHAPTER NINE

HE WAS HERDED down a steel ramp and into darkness, one of a numberless press of zombies being funneled below decks and into thundering industry of the *Tavuto*'s underworld. Down they went through channels and conduits, merging with other streams of zombies and sorted at junctions by hard-handed overseers. Chains rattled on pulleys, hammers clinked in the depths, and radio chatter echoed along the low ceilings like the rustle of bat wings.

There was no way to turn around in the press, nor to see more than a few feet past the jostling heads of other cadavers. For all he knew, Mouana and the others could be an arm's reach away, or gone entirely. They had become a sort of liquid, like the slurry of plankton caught against a whale's baleen in the straining of its jaws.

A rhythmic thunder came from his right, as if boulders were rolling through iron tubes somewhere below; as the corridor's side opened up into a row of columns, he saw red-ochre boats slide past on steel rails, lighting their own passage with slews of sparks. They cannoned past and round a bend, disappearing in rings of fire on the tunnel walls.

To his left, monsters were being made. Ancient-looking zombies, their flesh patched with plastic and bursting with cables and pipes, stood on hydraulic legs as terrible armatures were lowered onto them from above. Teams of overseers fell upon them as the jointed rigs came down, riveting hinges shut and hammering wingnuts into place.

In the light from a welding torch, one of the lumpen constructs looked right at Wrack—or right through him. The skin of its face was blasted, leathery, as if it had been cooked, and its eyes were sightless as stones. A cluster of lenses jutting from its shoulder glinted, reflecting a shower of sparks as a hulking steel pincer was grafted to its side, and Wrack wondered what it saw.

Then the monster rocked back on its feet, the overseers stepping away as it flexed its construction site of a torso, and turned away to follow its cohort into the dark. Wrack was jostled past the assembly platform into a corridor barely higher than his head, and then into a long room packed wall-to-wall with corpses. Between the railings along the walls and the cluster of machinery in the middle, all was flesh. Wrack was just wondering why the crowd had stopped moving, when a heavy door slammed shut behind him.

The darkness was crushing, ringing with the muffled clamour of the hammers and the rails outside. The floor shuddered. Wrack realised he was holding a breath he could not breathe. And then, with a ratcheting crack, the floor dropped six feet all at once.

Before he could register what was going on, there was a groan of steel, and the entire room pivoted forwards sickly. Wrack fell against the zombie ahead of him, and was trying to free his trapped arm when gravity seemed to collapse entirely. The enclosed space exploded with the hiss of steel on steel and shuddered madly: cold, briny air blasted against his face and the world shot forwards, downwards, at a reckless incline.

Wrack was smashed back into the bodies behind him, the acceleration shoving the air from his lungs, and the roof thundered past in a blur. Then daylight exploded into his face, followed instantaneously by a wall of salt water, and the boat's engines growled into life.

They were in some kind of pinnace, an iron trough full of zombies, with a spluttering engine at the back and a block of generators amidships. Blinking sore eyes against the light, Wrack looked around and saw more boats hitting the water, surging ahead and carving white valleys in the grey. Through the wall of black smoke kicked out behind them by the engine, the *Tavuto* rose like an iron cliff, its side pitted with chutes from which more vessels shot and slapped against the waves.

The engine shifted pitch and the pinnace lurched forward, the overseer in his chair at the bow gunning the handlebars like a dirt biker. The flat bottom of the craft skimmed and slapped over the swells, causing its cargo to bounce on their feet, heads nodding as if captivated by music. As they reached full speed, there was an almighty crash, and a grey shape filled the world to their left, heralded by walls of displaced water.

For a moment Wrack thought part of the *Tavuto*'s side had fallen away, plunging into Ocean like a calving iceberg, before he recognised the new arrival as another launch, a ship in its own right, dwarfing the rest of the swarm like a pike cutting through a shoal of minnows.

The behemoth craft surged forward, making the sea rear up around them, and the pinnace's pilot leaned left hard to bring them swerving close in alongside it. As they blasted along its flank, Wrack saw it was armoured like a siege tank, its hull buttressed with rows of squat cylinders and braced with steel ribs.

Up where the hull gave way to the deck, the edge of the ship bristled with turrets, in which were fixed the mechanised zombies he had seen being assembled in the mothership's bowels. They faced the spray with sightless eyes and blank snarls, withered bodies sagging at the heart of industrial weaponry. Ahead of them, the boat's prow was emblazoned with the flaking, crude image of snarling teeth, and its name, *Akhlut*, scrawled like a curse in white stencilled letters.

As it reached full speed, the killship sounded its horn, a terrible blast that raced ahead of it like a black wave, and seemed to haunt the silence it left behind. Fleetingly, against his every wish, and despite the endless grey that stretched out in every direction around the hunting fleet, Wrack felt like part of something lethal.

As the racing armada gathered around the *Akhlut*, he tried to count their number—there must have been more than thirty boats in all. Some were sleek and long, sparsely crewed and bristling with harpoons, launchers and other weaponry. Others, like the craft in which Wrack was crammed, were crude barges, built around bulky electrical machinery and packed to the gunwales with restless zombies. At the head of the pack, a hundred yards ahead of the *Akhlut*, a catamaran with a deck enclosed in armoured blisters cut through the water with the urgency of a shark on a wound-scent.

Before long, the water around them became marbled with oily white swirls—the blood of the ET. White, translucent bodies thrashed weakly in the slick; whether they were scavengers, or strange parasites leaked from the shell of the alien devil, Wrack had no idea.

The trail waxed and waned, but they kept on it; the chase became a marathon. Even mortally wounded, it seemed, the ET could keep up a monstrous speed. *Tavuto* shrank to a stain on the horizon, and sank from sight. The open Ocean stretched: borderless, bereft of detail in every direction, and empty.

Once, the onrushing flotilla disturbed a swarm of Jenny Hanivers; they came bursting from the water in tan arcs, demon tails flapping and gnarled wings beating uselessly at the air. Later, their wakes were chased by shadows for a time, weaving beneath the white like hungry phantoms, always out of sight. Then there was nothing; just the clouds above, the grey plain of water below, and the stripe of chemical leakage promising prey.

Wrack passed the time by staring at the faces of his fellow passengers, trying to guess at their former lives by their scars, the fragments of their clothes, the washed-out tattoos on their waterlogged skin. To his right, a woman with a broken jaw and a ring-puckered ear stared blankly ahead with her smashed mouth yawning. Had she been a student, or the septuagenarian matriarch of a factory clan? With the skin of her arms hanging in withered bunches from wasted muscles, her skin clumped in folds, death had muddled decades.

Beyond her, a man with the bricklike features of a classic pub bruiser stood, a string of black drool looping from his lip, as he gazed absently at the filth sloshing around their feet. Ahead of him, a zombie whose sore-pocked head had shed all but a few clumps of greying hair swayed, oblivious to the fact its arm ended just past the shoulder, in a roughly-bandaged and rapidly unravelling mess.

It was then that Wrack spotted Mouana's comrade, wedged in between the one-armed zombie and a block of machinery, his head turned to look out at the sea. Wrack went to shout his name, but it was as if something had clotted in the misfiring channels of his brain; he had forgotten it, there was only a maddening greyness in its place.

He cried out anyway, desperately hoping the word would come to him, but all it did was set the other zombies off in one of their dreadful concatenations of moaning. Trying to shoulder his way through the crowded deck, he found their faces turning towards him, mute confusion etched on their brows as they shouted wordlessly and shoved back. For every foot he managed to squeeze through the press, he seemed to be pushed back eighteen inches by their flailing.

Wrack was on the brink of laying in with his fists, when the mortars began firing.

Dull thuds rang out from the *Akhlut*, and were echoed after a moment by popping detonations from a nearby weapons pinnace. Heavy projectiles tumbled through the leaden sky in low arcs, before smacking into the water ahead in plopping plumes of brine. A second volley fired, and then the detonations began. They were felt rather than heard, battering concussions that felt as if the boat was being smacked against from beneath. Depth charges. The hunt had begun.

At once, every boat in the flotilla increased speed. A third volley of charges went tumbling into the water, and the weaponised dead on the *Akhlut*'s flanks raised their enormous arms, as if prompted by an unheard signal. The overseer at the helm leaned forwards in his saddle and twisted his huge wrists, opening the throttle to full.

They pulled out ahead of the fleet, engine screaming, and the other corpse-carriers pulled out beside them. Smoke blasted from the backs of the black barges, and they advanced in a loose knot, smashing through the tips of waves and raising curtains of spray.

Beneath them the water turned pale as the speeding body of the ET ascended like a rising beach. It could only have been fifty feet from the surface, its plates, tubercules and jointed limbs visible as patches of shifting colour. They matched its speed, and jockeyed on the surface to surround its mass with a loose ring of boats.

The *Akhlut*'s horn sounded once again, a call for blood, and was answered from below by a subsonic scream that rattled the teeth in Wrack's jaw.

Joining the cacophony, the machinery at the heart of the pinnace began to thrum, building to an aggravated whine. All around the circle, the other boats' machines were coming to life, a swelling chorus that crackled with electric menace. Wrack began to feel lightheaded.

The overseer's radio burst into life with an urgent string of exclamations, and he reached hastily for an iron helmet, sliding it over his head with obvious urgency. A warning klaxon began blaring from the *Akhlut*, and the sound of the generators ascended to a barely-audible shriek.

Then the blackness came. Wrack felt it an instant before it hit, like a flash of lightning seen in the heartbeat before its passing tore the air apart. It came from beyond the horizon, a shockwave of invisible dread with only one possible source. That spiteful tower on the *Tavuto*, squat and glowing with baleful green light, the source of the awful sleep that he had slipped from back in the flensing yards.

Back on the ship it had been a conquerable presence, like tar tugging on his heels; this was something violently physical, a wall of angst that advanced across the windswept distance at impossible speed and knocked his mind aside like a flower before a tsunami.

The world went away.

His lips touched hers, an instant before they thought they would, and began moving softly, making strange, tiny wet crackles. His thumb rubbed a slow circle in the soft hair at her temple, and he was surprised at how her mouth didn't really taste of anything. His eyes flickered open, saw her eyelids tremble above heavy lashes, and closed again. What had they even been saying, before their eyes had gone out of focus and their mouths had dipped in together?

The firelight danced through the bottle's green glass as he swirled the whisky in its bottom. Cool air, the last breath of a summer sunset, ruffled the hair on his brow as he leaned back into the coarse grass. Laughter blossomed in the shadows, twigs crackled in the flames. He leaned over to answer Tom's question with a joke, but he had forgotten the question.

Oof, but it was cold. Groggily, he pulled the thick duvet over his shoulder and up to his chin, wriggling down into the body-hot cavity beneath. Warm hips cupped his arse, and he slid his shin in between sleeping legs, a shiver passing through him at the pleasure of the snug contact. Who were they, again?

He couldn't believe he still had half the book left to read. Better yet, there were three more to go in the series once it was done. As he turned the page the torch slipped from its crook between his head and shoulder, and he rummaged on the mattress to retrieve it, eager to get back to the story. As he grabbed the light, he looked for a while at the way the light shone through the webs at the base of his fingers, translucent and pink with warm blood. The book had closed on itself. What page had he been on?

His father showed him again, defining the horse's jaw with a swoop of his pencil and then blocking in the curve of its neck. He scribbled out his own effort, which looked like a sort of ill crocodile, and reached for a new sheet of paper. Frowning in concentration, he put his pencil to paper and drew a wobbly line to define the horse's nose, but he was pressing too hard and the tip broke off, leaving a black starburst on the page. He turned to his father to ask whether he should start a new drawing, but his dad didn't really have a face.

Sunlight fell in an orange stripe across the stuffed toy rabbit, motes pirouetting in front of its worn smile. Its woollen ears flopped across his shoulder as he picked it up and hugged it. Then it was gone, and his hands were white, cold claws, branded with the mark of a violent rebellion. He was a wretched thing, on a monster-haunted ocean, clutching the fading memories of a dead man.

Schneider Wrack howled at the sky, the sound tearing from his throat as if it could take him with it, and the world howled along. All around him the dead screamed as their former selves were snatched away from them forever, and their horror shook the miserable boat, drawn to the generator like lightning grounding through a rod. The generator whined and overloaded with a deafening crack, blasting everything it had gathered downwards in a single black pulse. All around the ring the other boats did likewise, their machinery cooking off and sending shockwaves of grief into the fathomless sea.

It was despair, weaponised.

The ET reacted immediately, and violently. With a bellow of confused rage that seemed to come from the whole of Ocean, its great pale back began surging up through the water like an onrushing storm. The overseer turned hard, nearly capsizing them as the boat banked to avoid the breaching monstrosity, and only just made it in time: it erupted from the sea like a fist through paper, a tower of ragged wounds with claws spread like vengeful wings.

Empty, broken, standing only because of the pressure of other bodies, Wrack looked up with a strange serenity at the leviathan's jaws, hanging high above in a halo of crashing water.

The *Akhlut* opened fire. Harpoons as thick as treetrunks slammed into the ET's neck from ports in the killship's grinning mouth, while a fusillade of smaller projectiles whistled across from its hull, each trailing a thick steel line. Half bounced off the otherworldly armour, but enough lodged between the plates and spines to secure a hold. The beast writhed as spearheads detonated beneath its skin, twisting in a mass of cables like some fiendish marionette, then began to shudder as the gun-limbs of the turret zombies sounded at close range.

It crashed back into the sea, obliterating a weapon-pinnace that had made too close a pass under its bulk, and put on a terrible burst of speed. Its twin tails thrashed beneath the surface, kicking up titanic waves in its bid to evade its pursuers, and the immensity of the *Akhlut* was dragged behind it like a sledge.

Its tails rose above the surface, fanned planes as wide as city streets, and it dived. A few of the harpoon-zombies broke free of their mounts and were sucked into the abyss, and the whole prow of the *Akhlut* dipped almost to its tip in the surging water.

Then the rockets came on. Without warning, the squat cylinders along the *Akhlut*'s hull roared into life, two dozen tongues of plasma jetting straight into cold sea with a force intended to fight hundreds of tons of surging muscle. Instantly the world filled with steam, intensely thick and scalding hot even at a hundred yards' distance. No wonder the weapon-zombies arrayed on *Akhlut*'s flanks had looked as though they'd been cooked: they had been.

With the world obscured by the boiling ocean, it was impossible to tell how the battle was progressing. The rocket burst came to a halt, and all that could be heard was the breaking of steel cable under tension, the revving of motors and the popping of gunfire, all muffled by the blanket of steam.

In the boat around Wrack, bobbing motionless now its purpose was done, the spent dead leaned against each other, faces even emptier than they had been. Beside him, the broken-jawed woman had slumped to a half-crouch, head still craned to the sky as if waiting for her shout to fall back into her mouth. The commander was invisible through the mist.

After a few minutes of unseen chaos, a weapons pinnace swung past them, its pilot leaning from his seat to gesture at theirs. The engine started up again. Seconds later, the *Akhlut*'s horn sounded from the fog; long, triumphant and tired like a wounded animal over a fallen rival. The radio chatter was clear, even from the back of the boat: "*It's dead! It's dead! It's dead!*"

The *Akhlut* swam into view as a dark shape, resolving into predatory angles as they drew alongside. Beside it, a great armoured carcass bobbed peacefully in the water, strung to the killship by a forest of cables. The leviathan had been hooked. Atop the ship's forecastle an overseer stood, leaning on a radio mast, and raised his fist in salute to the pilots of the circling boats, as steam swirled around his pillar-like legs.

He was unaware of the ghost-white shape, almost invisible against the rolling mist, looming behind him with mantis claws raised as if in greeting.

There was a *second* ET.

With a harrowing crunch, the hooked limbs of the dead leviathan's mate clamped onto the superstructure of the *Akhlut*, and pulled it over onto its side like a child's toy.

The wave hit Wrack's pinnace like a wall, and he was shoved into the water.

CHAPTER TEN

WRACK HAD ALREADY sunk thirty feet before he really thought to do anything about it. The black pulse of despair from the *Tavuto* had left him feeling robbed of all agency, empty of anything but the sense of dreadful, hopeless lethargy he had first come to awareness with. He had watched the triumph and death of the *Akhlut* with a sort of muffled detachment, and things felt exactly the same from below the waves.

Falling slowly into the deep on his back, he looked up at the roiling underside of the surface, and at the other wave-struck bodies drifting down into the darkness along with him. By instinct he was holding his breath, but what did it matter if he let the brine flood in? Even if he had needed to breathe air, he doubted he would have gotten to the end of even a single lungful before something from below devoured him. With the aftermath of the despair bomb still throbbing beneath his skull, the thought was a welcome relief.

As he opened his mouth a crack and let the first bubbles drift up towards the light, however, he realised exactly why it would be a terrible idea to let the air out of his body.

Because without air in him, he might never stop sinking. He would drop like a stone, down past the reach of the sun, down past the abysses where great black things slithered, forever hungry, and on into fathomless dark.

Nobody could quite agree whether Ocean had a bottom at all, or if it did, how far down it was or what it was made of. City-sized islands of crinoid-wreathed *Natans holosericum* were occasionally found floating a few hundred yards down— Wrack had seen them sketched in his book—but beyond them was the *barathrum*, the great bottomless expanse. Chains stretching dozens of miles had been dropped and not touched anything, or had come up with their lower reaches limned in strange, hot ice.

If he let out his breath, and if he wasn't snatched up by some devil on the way down, he might never stop sinking.

Sod that, thought Wrack. Anything had to be better than that. Clamping his mouth shut, he began kicking his legs, and struggled back towards the surface. Back on the *Tavuto* he had come to understand there was more good he could do by struggling than by giving up, and that hadn't changed. Even without hope, admitting defeat now and sinking into Hadal darkness out of grief for a dead man's memories would be a miserable way for it all to end. He would swim.

As HE DRAGGED the water past him, clawing upwards, other zombies fell slowly past, hair and tattered clothes fluttering in the water like flags of surrender. With a jolt he recognised the face of Mouana's commander, bubbles trickling from his lips as he slid past with his head slumped against his wounded chest. Aroha; that had been his name. Strange what you recall when it's no use to you.

Remembering how Mouana had held him back in the

hangar, had brought him out of the black dream, Wrack knew he could not abandon him to Ocean. He surged toward the sinking man, horrified at the thought of one of the two people he knew in the world enduring the endless descent he had been about to resign himself to.

Kicking madly, he reached the other corpse, grabbed it by the shirt collar, and shook frantically. The commander's face tilted sluggishly towards him, but displayed nothing but an expression of profound loss. Wrack forced himself under Aroha's armpit, worked his legs with every ounce of strength he could find, but the light of the surface only grew more distant above them. Aroha was too heavy, had already leaked too much of his air from the open wound in his chest.

They were easily sixty feet down now, still sinking, and darkness was beginning to gather. It was hopeless: Aroha had to do this for himself, or they would both end up in the abyss. Turning and grabbing the lost soldier by both lapels, Wrack shook the larger man like a ragdoll and stared into his face, mouthing his name and fighting the urge to lose his precious chestful of air in howling it.

But they were still sinking. Wrack pivoted in the water, legs up, arms outstretched, trying to use himself as a float to slow Aroha's descent. The water grew colder, sliding icily around his teeth as he bared them in maddened, silent repetition of the commander's name.

At last, Aroha's eyes locked with his, and Wrack felt a surge of hope. If the commander started kicking now, Wrack told himself, they might both still reach the surface. But the only movement Aroha made was a slow, sad shake of his head, before closing his eyes. Whatever he had seen when the shockwave had hit their boat, it had been too much for him to bear.

Wrack let go, and the soldier dropped beyond arm's reach. For an agonising moment he could not turn away, felt bound to watch as the man drifted further and further into the gloom. He was about to turn back to face the surface when a terrible lowing reverberated through his bones, and a pale shape loomed far below.

Silently and slow as cloud, the head of the second ET swung out of the darkness, ghastly jaws telescoping, and plucked Aroha from the water before disappearing back into the murk.

Wrack saw the tail of the monster flicker briefly in deep indigo as it dived, and then he turned and swam.

When he reached the surface, he gasped for air even though he knew he had no need of it—the relief of being above the surface was enough. It faded quickly enough when he took stock of the situation.

The *Akhlut* had vanished without a trace, sunk or at least abandoning its catch, and the wall of steam was rapidly dissipating. The surviving support craft were motoring at full speed back in the direction of the *Tavuto*, their exhaust plumes visible intermittently as surface waves slapped at Wrack's face. They had left just a handful of stricken craft foundering in the slick of ichor around the dead ET, evacuated of overseers but left with cargoes of the marooned dead.

One of them was the pinnace Wrack had been swept from. It was sinking fast, full halfway to the gunwales, its engine silent and the overseer gone from the pilot's saddle. It was still home to a couple of dozen zombies, either slumped with their heads in their hands or lying motionless in the water. And while it was hardly a refuge, Wrack was so eager to have something between him and the depths that he flopped over its edge with profound relief.

There was no time to rest, however; the boat was so low in the water that every large wave threatened to swamp it entirely. Worse yet, with the monster's avenging companion now leaving the area, scavengers were finally beginning to move in to investigate the kill. Here and there, sleek fins were sliding out of the milky water around them, and things were beginning to bump against the underside of the hull. They would find nothing palatable in the weird biology of the dead

ET, but human meat in the water was a different matter. He could not let the boat sink.

Wading clumsily to the front of the boat, he saw what he had hoped was there: the overseer's iron bucket helmet, still mercifully lying next to the pilot's saddle. Grabbing it, he began to bail water from the hull, scooping and heaving with a vigour he would have been proud to have managed while alive. If only the overseers could see him now, Wrack thought, smirking grimly, he would surely make *Tavuto*'s employee of the month.

After fifteen minutes or so, it became apparent there was no way he could empty the boat by himself. His arms were beginning to shake, clearly working at the limits of whatever necrological chemistry let them move in the first place, and there was no appreciable difference in the water level within the boat. He was going to need assistance.

When he turned from the bow, he found to his utter astonishment that he already had it. Wordlessly, and unnoticed by him above his own frantic splashing, a small group of the other zombies, the broken-jawed woman leading them, had begun aimlessly scooping water with their hands and hurling it out of the boat.

Whether this was a conscious attempt to help, or just mindless familiarity with copying the work going on around them, he had no idea. He decided to assume the former, for the sake of thin optimism, and splashed over to the small group with the helmet in his hands.

"Use this," said Wrack, as he thrust the makeshift bucket at Broken-Jaw, and felt something giddily like hope as she nodded calmly and took it from him. He began searching the boat for more containers for bailing. He spotted the emergency locker—wide open, a two-man hand pump half dragged from it—and let out a shout of triumph that collapsed into raw, waterlogged coughing.

The boat did not sink. It seemed to take hours to empty it, but by the end, almost every zombie on the boat had been raised from its stupor and cajoled into helping. There were twenty-eight of them in all; Wrack had counted. Some were beginning to clumsily attempt speech, while others were still struggling to manage eye contact.

Only two were beyond waking: one tiny man who could not have been past his mid-teens when he died, and who emitted a constant, low moaning, and another whose immense girth in life had shrunk to layers of sore-pocked skin folds hanging from his hips. They had been placed in a corner at the back of the boat for the time being, leaning against each other while the rest of the crew worked their way to sapience.

Even the one-armed zombie had come round. They had taken their turn at the pump, grinning darkly all the while, and repeating the phrase, "we'll find out, we'll find out, won't we," like someone trying absently to remember a string of numbers. Every attempt to discover their name had only been answered by a wet, lunatic chuckle.

Wrack was just wondering what in blazes they were going to do once the boat was safe, when he heard the engine.

CHAPTER ELEVEN

THROUGH SHREDS of mist pulled apart by the breeze came one of the weapons skiffs, billowing filthy smoke from its stack. Mouana was standing at the bow, wearing a grin that was definitely more than the resting expression of her papered-over skull. She called to a hunched zombie at the back of the craft, and the skiff pulled alongside them, its side clanging softly against theirs on the swell.

"Hungry?" she shouted, loud as her punctured chest would allow, and hefted a bulky net bag before hurling it into the bilge of Wrack's pinnace. As it hit the floor it burst open, and several large tins rolled out. The labels were unmistakable: five-pound cans of Hedstrom & Sons boiled beef, labels scuffed but otherwise gleaming.

Wrack did not think it would be possible for two dozen zombies to moan in delight, but as every head in the boat turned towards the cornucopia of tinned flesh, an eerie chorus rose from their throats.

Even as Mouana clambered into their vessel, still slowed by her shark-bitten hip, Wrack's improvised crew had abandoned the last of the baling and were falling upon the cans. While some had the presence of mind to work the ringpulls, others were battering the tins against the vertices of the burnt-out generator, or—wince-inducingly—attempting to bite them open.

Soon, the entire boat was full of wet, chomping, snuffling sounds, as sea-pruned hands shovelled wobbling meat into famished jaws. Even some of Mouana's crew, who Wrack assumed had already eaten, were flopping over into the wider boat for seconds. It was all he could do to wait and clasp arms with Mouana before falling guiltily on a can, which he had already slid beside him with a surreptitious foot.

"Strange party," said Mouana, and was gracious enough not to expect an answer, as Wrack was thoroughly consumed by the effort to wolf down half his head's weight in cow detritus. "Overseer's rations," she added. "This lot was for four of them. You believe that?"

Wrack didn't answer; he was too busy forcing beef into his mouth. He didn't even have to stop to breathe. He was fairly certain he'd swallowed a tooth, but what did he care? He still had thirty or so to play with. He only noticed Mouana was speaking to him again when she punched him in the shoulder and pointed over to the body of the dead ET.

"Mealtime there, too," she said, as a crash of saltwater eclipsed the sound of the munching dead.

Exotic scavengers had found the leaking carcass. Something segmented, with a collar of red glass eyes around its maw, had thrown its front half onto the bobbing flank and was chewing away with rotary jaws, sending pale scraps flying up with marine spray. Wrack had no idea what it was, but he felt he wanted to get away from it. Forcing his hands to stay clamped around the tin, he gulped down a packed mouthful and nodded at the skiff.

"How did you get that working?" he asked, slightly muffled by meat sounds.

"We were engineering corps," answered Mouana. "Worked the generators for the railguns. Good with petrol. Might get us halfway back. Or further. Let's not push our luck, though."

Wrack had no idea how far past *Tavuto*'s horizon they had travelled, but it seemed a horrible long way. He only hoped Mouana had made a note of where the sun had been on the way out, as he wasn't sure—especially after his trip into the depths—which edge of the world the slaveship sat past. Somehow, the journey had to be made. After the chaos and the disaster of the ET hunt, there could surely be no better time to sneak aboard unremarked and cause havoc. And in any case, there was nowhere else to go.

He really, really hoped she knew where *Tavuto* was.

"That way," she offered, turning his shoulder so he was facing a completely different part of the horizon from the portion he had been sure was home. "We'll see the smoke before long, or the lights. If it takes that long. Let's go."

They went. Convincing the other zombies to help them lash the boats together was less an exercise in persuasion than in leading by example. The conversations involved were halting and not entirely rational, but the two craft ended up linked bow to stern, the weapons skiff leading, with some interesting knotwork. It was good enough.

Some time later, as the sun was setting, the skiff's engine gave out. *Tavuto* was still nowhere in sight. Mouana spent a long while under the back plating of the craft, asking Wrack in the shortest sentences possible to search in the pinnace's own workings for spares, but it soon became apparent the boats shared completely different engine designs, and no diesel grumble was forthcoming. The saltwater slap of wave on wave continued patiently around them all the while.

Though the onset of night in Ocean was forgivingly slow, in time the sun crept below the horizon and twilight was upon them. Twilight with nothing visible but dancing wavelets for miles in every direction. Wrack decided it was time to face facts, and mention the stack of oars he had seen in the emergency locker.

By the time night fell; they were rowing. Forty dead people, half of them still stuck in the gulf beyond speech, fewer yet able to muster the coordination to row, dragging two broken boats across endless sea.

"Did you feel the black pulse?" asked Wrack, as he hauled back clumsily on the oar with arms glowing with fresh food. Mouana did not answer.

"You know," he continued, miming an explosion, "the wave, from *Tavuto*, The one with the memories. We were in the middle. It took what we felt, then used it against the ET. Did you feel it too?"

Mouana kept rowing, did not look over at him, even when he repeated the question. He repeated it again.

"Keep rowing," said Mouana, her face hard and her words barely audible over the slapping of oarblades on water.

They did. More zombies joined them at the oars. The pub bruiser, who had managed nomore than the words "fack off" off since the demise of the *Akhlut*, had piled in at sunset and would not be moved, and the amputee, who had latched onto the side of a decayed, silent specimen, worked tirelessly with one arm.

A while into the night, his forearms shivering, Wrack took to the bow and looked forward for a while, hoping to spot the lights of the *Tavuto*. After a while staring into the black where water supposedly met sky, he found Mouana beside him.

"It feels odd to talk," said Wrack, his mouth still dry from the astringent meal.

"It's not fun," she replied, the quiet sucking of her wound punctuating her words, "but it's worth it."

"It's good," he answered, as the hull slid across boundless water. "I mean, we're not meant to even be conscious, are we?"

Once again, Mouana didn't answer. Wrack wondered whether

it was because he had split the infinitive, before realising his companion's silence was probably more to do with distaste for big questions than with grammatical propriety. They were a librarian and a military engineer, he reminded himself, before trying a different—and perhaps more honest—tack.

"I wish I could have a massive drink," said Wrack, looking into his lap. A long silence passed, making him wonder if he had only made himself seem more of a fool, before Mouana answered.

"I found something else with the beef," she said, and he heard glass slide against metal. A moment passed, and then an open-necked glass bottle was being held in front of him.

"Overseer's rations," assured Mouana, wiggling the dirty liquid in front of his face. Abandoning caution, he took a slug, and immediately retched.

"It tastes like preservative," he hissed.

"I think it actually is," replied Mouana. "But it still feels good to pass a drink around, eh?"

As the oily, petrochemical stench withdrew from his nostrils, Wrack found he agreed, and clamped his hands around the bottle for another swig.

"Well," he choked, after another mouthful. "It can't kill us, and our entire life is by definition a hangover, so what harm can it do?" He drank.

The bottle changed hands twice more before he asked his next question.

"So... what are we?" said Wrack, wondering whether the soft heat pressing on the back of his eyes was the questionable booze, or a symptom of necrochemical exhaustion.

"Zombies," answered Mouana, before upending the bottle casually to her lips.

"I had gathered," said Wrack, remembering their first meeting with a strange sort of nostalgia, and smiling. "But what's the mechanism? We're rotting. Slowly, granted. But we are, and yet we can swim and think and tie boats together. It doesn't make any sense."

The questions were sincere. Wrack had read very little on the dead. While the use of dead bodies as machinery was a common enough trope in myth, it was scarce almost to the point of absence in reliably recorded history. What little there was began and ended at High Sarawak, a city long lost to the decay of the lemniscatus, and so reduced almost to myth by default. The place was a cautionary tale to the schoolchildren of Lipos-Tholos, and any further enquiry into the matter tended to be severely discouraged.

There was another long silence before Mouana responded.

"Probably tiny machines," she said. "That's what Aroha used to say. Whenever we had to deal with hard tech and couldn't find a workaround. Tiny machines. The old stuff."

The name of Mouana's fellow soldier hung on the night breeze for a long time. Wrack felt he could have let it pass, but there was no way he could let it be word-weather.

"Aroha..." he murmured. "I have to tell you... he didn't make it."

The waves lapped at the side of the skiff. When she spoke again, her slashing whisper of a voice sounded almost carefree.

"It's fine, he was dead anyway," said Mouana. "I already missed him."

There was silence. And then one of the zombies started singing.

It was a sea shanty. Or a river shanty, to be precise. Wrack knew it; one of the syncopated boat-loaders' songs from the mud-black deltas of Grand Amazon, offworld and bungled with strange dialect, but no different in rhythm from the salt-stained songs of old. It came from the broken-jawed woman, and sang out into silence for a minute or so before another voice joined in.

Of course, the voice that joined the river song took no care to use the same lyrics, or the same tune; it was some dreadful kuiper miner's dirge, full of lost love and slurred consonants, but hitting the harmonies where it mattered.

Once the solo had become a chorus, more joined in. A man

in the shredded tunic of the Blades of Titan opened up with a crude soldier's song about rutting, causing Mouana's eyes to widen with delight in recognition, and a zombie with legs mangled to zig-zag tragedy piped up with an ode to forgotten woods.

The song was woven like a braid from a dozen minds, each captive to different memories, but allied in purpose, driving the oars on to cohesion. That is, thought Wrack, why sea shanties were invented after all.

It made their rowing stronger, and their husks of voices swelled to drown out the crash and hiss of the oars. Those with words bellowed them as loud as their worn pipes would manage, those without them hummed or shouted or stamped their salt-clotted feet in the bilge. Each sang their own song, but to the same rhythm, the same loose tune, the same rough, proud purpose. Dead men and women, rowing their own boat.

In time, even the two slumped zombies at the back of the boat began to sing too, or at least do something close to it. The skeletal teen began to keen in rough time to the song, while the withered fat man beside him took to roaring angrily whenever one of the other singers rose to a peak that called for a response. Whether their outbursts were expressions of solidarity or just bewildered pain, at least they were drifting towards consciousness.

The tune went on, as did the sweep of the oars, for a long while into the night. They had no lights, and so rowed in darkness, under a starless sky. Only the faintest glimmer of ugly light on the horizon told them the location of their home, and they kept on course with barely any need of nudging. Wrack and Mouana took to the oars, and found their own songs to add to the chorus. Warmed by the bottle, or at least by what it represented, they shrank into themselves and fell away for a while.

Long into the journey, when the omnishanty had faded to little more than a rhythmic hum, a blue light began to flicker across them. Faint and ghostly, it brushed the undersides of their jaws and labouring arms with faint cerulean. Wrack rose from something like a trance; as his fellows were brought into focus by the phantom light, it was as if he were seeing them for the first time. It was like waking in the depths of the night to see bedside furniture looming like watching demons, unreal but threatening. He shook his head; there was no threat in the boat. Something was below them.

He looked over the side. There, wavering in the clear sea, were bright blue lights, like constellations cast down into the deep. He leaned down, blinked, and saw that the lights were shining from lengths of glass. Shreds of spectral white hung from them, wavering in the night currents, lit in gentle blue. They were hanging from man-sized needle teeth, in a mouth as wide as a valley.

Quiet and calm as if he were rising from picking up a dropped fork at dinner, Wrack sat upright. None of the other dead had noticed what they were rowing over. Knowing how long it would take to get to the skiff's weapons, and how little chance they had of being able to coordinate a defence even if they did, Wrack made a rash choice. He began to sing louder.

Working alongside the hymn of the dead, Wrack opened his throat and belted out the first words he could remember, from the first maritime song he had learned.

"I'll sing you a song of the fish of the sea!" he roared, and the dead sailors answered.

"Awaaaaay, down Rio!" some of them sang in reply, while others just screamed their own words. Forty oars hit the water at once with doubled force, and the boat surged forwards.

"I'll sing you a song of the fish of the sea!" repeated Wrack, as he acknowledged to himself that he had no such song to sing, just the first line.

Luckily, that didn't matter to the mariners. They shouted their own answers back at him, and drove their oars into Ocean with the ferocity of people with nothing to lose. The song found its own tune, its own words, and the boat ploughed on.

Wrack hunched his shoulders and waited for the sepulchre jaws to close, but nothing rose from the brine but a great shrug of upwelling water and the dying of the blue light. The predator had left. He carried on singing.

Hours later, they reached the *Tavuto*. It appeared less a ship, and more a country raised out of the sea. As they approached its starboard flank, Wrack saw it for the monster it was. At least a mile and a half from stern to bow, it glowed with the fire of its gargantuan try-pots, its rows of towering cranes, and its encrustation of bridge decks, pricked with a thousand cold windows.

Mouana made sense of it, had a plan for getting aboard, long before Wrack did. She had barely stirred when they had moved over the glass jaws, but now she was suddenly all over the boat, urging the sailors to be silent, to quiet the oars on one side and move them towards the great lagoon with the smashed gates where the Bahamut still lay rotting.

When they got within fifty yards of the lagoon, with the boat slipways in sight, it was time to take action. But the immense main arm of Dakuvanga was dipping to take a mansion sized chunk of Bahamut out of the lagoon, and the dead were swarming over the corpse to free the lump. There would be no way to get closer without drawing attention.

"Let's swim," said Mouana, without ceremony, and leapt into the water. Wrack waited a moment to make sure the dead had heard, and then moved for the front of the boat when he saw them leave their posts en masse. Even the wailing teen at the back of the boat was heading for the prow; this was no moment to hold back.

Wrack swore, dived into the black, and swam. Bodies bumped against him in the water, slithered past him. Whether they were his fellows, or mean, whiptailed things come to snaggle at the leaking Bahamut, he had no idea. Frankly, after looking down into the bottomless water as the ET had taken Aroha, a speck of flesh above a carnivore god, he didn't really care. In comparison with that moment, this was about as frightening as taking a drunken dip in the Fellows' koi pond on a student dare.

After the brief, determined swim, he found himself on one of the shallow ramps leading up and out of the lagoon, clinging to the metal grates alongside two dozen other corpses. Mouana stood at the top of the ramp, a black shape against the floodlights of the Bahamut's disassembly. Wrack climbed out of the surf and walked to meet her.

"Home again," he remarked, the ice-cold wash of Ocean still swirling around his feet. A grey tentacle slithered out of the water, groped blindly at his ankles, but he stamped on it in annoyance and it slunk away. That made Mouana smile. Her lips began moving silently, as she counted the eager zombies hauling themselves up the ramp to join them.

One-Arm was there, and Broken-Jaw, whose name was Kaba, and the Bruiser, who had only offered "fack off" in lieu of name. There were the three Blades, though Mouana knew none of them, and the woman who had sung the miner's song, her teeth wrecked by biting into a metal can. Last of all, hobbling up the ramp slumped on the struggling shoulders of the wailing teen, came Once-Fat Man, his face now set in strange serenity.

"Huh," said Mouana, turning to Wrack as the sagging pair made it up the ramp. "We only lost three."

"Well then," said Wrack, slapping her on the shoulder and offering a friendly grimace, "let's go and find some more mates."

CHAPTER TWELVE

GRIM, SILENT, TOGETHER, they crept through the industry of the lagoonside and into the silence of *Tavuto*'s aft decks. No overseer challenged them. With the aftermath of the failed ET hunt on their hands, the ship's crew were doing all they could to move chunks of the gargantuan fish out of the lagoon and into the processing yards, with little heed paid to errant dead. As they snuck out of sight of the lagoon and into the ship, they met no human resistance.

Once, as they rounded a pitted cracking tower, one of the Sniffer Rays came to challenge them. Remembering his first encounter with one of the spider-legged elasmobranchs, Wrack had flinched when it came skittering out of the dark. But as he saw the way the other dead circled it, dashed in on its flanks, clamped wrinkled hands on its flapping skirt of ammoniac flesh, the fear fell out of him. With orgiastic relish, they tore it apart.

Its metal legs flapped, its tail thrashed, but the creature was nothing before the mob of dead. Before he could say a word, handfuls of stinking meat were being pulled from the central disc, flesh was sliding from cartilage, and dirty water poured from the creature's spiracles as it shuddered in second death. In seconds, it was less than metal and halfbone.

The mob moved on, stringy nitrogen chemistry hanging from their gums, their knuckles drumming on railings as they moved for the far decks of the ship. They were like chimps on the hunt: shaved, stinking apes with drawn gums and shaking claws. Wrack laughed recklessly; this clearly wasn't stopping until someone made it stop.

This was an insurrection. They were in trouble, and they were going to be in trouble until they were put down or caused a lot more trouble. It felt good. Better enjoy himself while it lasted, he thought, as one of the zombies leading the mob started screaming its own name.

Wrack was amazed when they made it to the aft hangar where they had first been rounded up for the ET hunt. The dregs were still there, the drift of ruined dead still stacked against the wall, moaning with arms outstretched. Clearly, no cleanup crew had come. Their salt-sodden band of survivors rushed over, hollering their triumph over the ray, and began to chatter with the less mobile dead. The conversations grew from the shaking of shoulders to the exchange of names, through the agony of remembrance, and into companionable rage. Seemingly crippled corpses rose from the pile as their wits returned. The hangar filled with human speech.

Some time during the night, zombies went out for food. They came back, dragging something like beluga whales. Fires were lit. Who had matches? Fuel? Wrack had no idea; it was bewildering to be out of control, but wonderful. No longer being the one who worked out what to do next, at least for a while, made his rotten shoulders feel lighter. More zombies came to them, either dragged there by search parties or blundering, lost, as he and Mouana had done before. It became a strange sort of party.

In time, he found himself pulled to the edge of the fire-circle by One-Arm, the wiry corpse tugging urgently on his wrist and cajoling him into the light. "We'll find out, won't we, we'll see?" chattered the strange little creature, and to Wrack's astonishment, dead men and women all around the fire repeated "we'll see!" and fell into raucous laughter. As their eyes watched him, twinkling in reflected flames, he twigged what was going on. This was the exorcism of life stories turned into a game—and cackling, cracked One-Arm, with its one line of dialogue, had found its place as host.

And so Wrack found himself talking about his life as if there was a real story to tell; as if he remembered more than just a fragment of it. Still unsure whether he had been a Piper rebel caught at scheming, or just a librarian caught in the jaws of a militia with a quota of arrests to keep, he decided to play up his uncertainty for comic effect. He would veer wildly from prim statements about reorganising tactician's manuals to stories of alleyway snitch-stabbings, waggling his hands alongside a theatrical sneer to indicate it was all—probably— total bollocks.

The dead laughed as he played the fool with his broken memory, but their faces hardened in solidarity as he reached the firmer, rawer memories. They cheered fiercely at the discovery of the pamphlets, they cheered at his branding, and at his father's helpless tears. And they cheered when he died. They cheered hardest when he died; they cheered for him, and he cheered with them. For a moment, the cheers made him brave enough for it not to matter. But then his story was over, and the cheers faded, and still he had no heartbeat.

As if knowing he had no more to say, Mouana piped up with the name of some long-ago regimental victory, and the Blades in the hangar cheered again. One of them opened up with a fresh story, and Wrack felt the eyes of the circle slide from him. After a while he retreated from the firelight, and sat himself down at the edge of the crowd, against the cold metal of the hangar wall.

For a time he sat and listened to the voices of the chattering people, watching their shadows thrown against the broken warplanes in flickering orange relief, and allowed himself to forget that they were all dead, that a terrible sea lay beyond the mouth of their metal cave. But then he began to notice another sound under the human murmur: the slow, rhythmic, scraping tick of a knifepoint on old bone.

He turned to his left, and a skull grinned up at him from the dark, yellow teeth mischievous in a wispy halo of beard. It was the skeletal man he had seen the previous night in the hangar, sat up to his hips in rot, still patiently whickering away at his exposed bone with his scrap of metal. While just a day ago the creature had seemed horrifying, a ghoulish remnant reminding him of his own decay, there was now nothing remotely threatening about it.

"Alright, mate," said Wrack, and nodded at the skull.

The skull nodded back, prompting Wrack to bark a delighted laugh, and opened its jaws like a shoddy ghost train animatronic. The skull looked at him, mouth open and grinning like a bad comedian waiting for a reaction to an appalling one-liner, and emitted a barely audible wheeze.

"You keep doing what you're doing," said Wrack, then lay back in the filth and lost himself in the fire-cast shadows of the nostalgic dead. What came next was not sleep as he had once known it, but neither was it the turgid black dreaming that had ensnared him before he had woken in the flensing yard. Whatever it was, it was devoid of much thought, and that was good enough.

Morning came, and silence with it.

The fire had burned down, its embers blackening as the sky outside lightened, and the zombies were still. They had gathered back in their drift, slumped against each other but no longer moaning and twitching as they had done before. Their eyes watched the horizon, gleaming pale as they waited for the sun to undrown itself. Scraps of flesh dangled from the picked ribs of the beluga-things, fluttering in eddies of the dawn wind.

Wrack stood, stretching muscles turned to wood by rest and the weird processes of undeath. It felt dreadful to ease himself out of the muckpile and into thought, but it had to be done. If they lay here any longer, they were in danger of ending up right where they had started off, sunk beyond the responsibility of consciousness. They had to make a plan, and start waking the others. There was so much work to do: somebody had to start it.

Wrack stood by the embers of the story-fire and clapped his leaden hands, and the pile began to stir. He was just about to address them, when a familiar clattering came from the hangar's mouth.

Not again, thought Wrack, rolling his eyes, and turned to the sound. This happened *every fucking time* he was about to make a speech. The same overseer, the one with the grille for the face, was at the door, huffing with her wheelbarrow of offal, the thresher shark skittering at her heels. She foraged in the red mess, cursing to herself, not yet aware of what had changed.

"Come on, arseholes," she barked tiredly, then looked up and froze, a gelid kidney in her hand. Eyes narrowing to slits above her corroded muzzle, she took in the smoldering ashes of the fire, the stripped carcasses, and the mass of still, silent zombies staring right at her. Registering Wrack alone in the centre of the hangar, her head swung round and she dropped the kidney, brows leaping in shock.

A strangled noise blurted from her grille. She recognised him. Knew him as one of the zombies she had herded down the ship the previous day, as one of the dead sent miles out to sea on a disastrous hunt. Knew he should not be there, standing stock still with teeth bared in an animal grin.

"Morning," said Wrack, and the dead erupted from their pile like a swarm of flies. There were near a hundred of them, loping across the hangar with arms outstretched and shrieks rising from their ruined throats. Wrack ran ahead of them, eyes fixed on the overseer's blanched face, veins flooding with a terrible hunger.

The shark came at him, sliding on the deck in its haste to catch him between its jaws, and overshot Wrack by a good three feet. It wheeled round like a hound, raising sparks on the deck, and lunged for his leg. But the mob had grabbed it by the long lobe of its tail, and it was tugged back away from him.

The overseer, eyes still fixed in disbelief on Wrack, fumbled for her radio, but he was upon her. Despite a two-hundred-pound difference in weight, Wrack had the advantage of being a screeching monster in a room full of more screeching monsters, and easily clawed the device from her grip. He opened his mouth wide, screamed again, and the overseer turned to flee.

She made it nearly twenty feet. Wrack was the first, throwing his arms round the woman's gore-streaked workboot. He barely registered as an anchor for her timber-thick legs, but he was not alone. Soon two, three, seven more zombies were clinging to her, dragging back her limbs and slowing each step. Then the mob, finished with turning the shark into a smear of white gristle, caught up with her. The overseer threw punches hard enough to knock jaws off faces, but with a growing swarm of dead hanging from her limbs, she was tiring quickly. It took nearly a minute, but she went down.

CHAPTER THIRTEEN

WRACK CLAMBERED UP the overseer's body through the throng of zombies pinning her, and crouched above her face, alongside Mouana. He could only imagine how they looked to the overseer; a ring of stinking, dripping rictuses, staring down and growling. It nearly ended there, quick and bloody as it had done for the ray. The overseer only lived through the first ten seconds because the others were waiting for Wrack to take the first bite. And although his belly was full of beluga meat, his mouth urged dreadfully to bite: to tear, and gnash, and take back every act of *Tavuto*'s sneering cruelty with his teeth.

But he couldn't, because the overseer was terrified, and helpless, and—mad as the term was on this ship—human. Just like they were. "Please don't eat me," she whispered, like a little girl trapped inside a steel drum. "Please don't eat me, please. Please."

Yellow tears pooled in the corners of her eyes as she stared into Wrack's face. "Please," she whispered again.

He clenched his jaw, and understood there had to be a reason, and quickly, for this not to end in torn meat. If he didn't want to preside over the dismemberment of another human being, no matter how callous they were, this had to become an opportunity. But so help me, thought Wrack as she babbled, she was going to have to work bloody hard with him to get things that way.

"Shut up," he snarled, letting his voice siphon the hate swollen in his jaw. "Shut up, and breathe." She breathed.

"Feels good, doesn't it?" spat Wrack, cocking his head. "Now, tell me why I shouldn't eat what's left of your face." After all, he thought, there was absolutely no reason not to scare her shitless.

The overseer's eyes bulged in her bloated face, edges pink, as she made a strangled sound in the mess of her larynx.

"You *can* talk," she gargled.

"So can you," snapped Wrack. "So talk. *Reason* with me."

If this oaf really wanted to live, she would give him the speech of her life. Even beyond the thundering mess of his conscience, he had reason to hope she would. Dead, she was just another bloody smear, another reason for his mob to be wiped out like bacteria when authority in sufficient numbers found them. Alive, she represented at worst the information they needed to make a plan, and at best an ally.

So far, she was not doing well. Choking, aborted words kept garbling from her grille, her eyes flicking wildly to the dead faces closing in on her.

Feeling a disturbance by his feet, Wrack looked back and saw the Bruiser, attention span exhausted, gnawing at the overseer's leg through her thick hide trousers. Wrack kicked him in the head, and growled at him to pack it in before looking back to their prisoner.

"We really are keen to eat you, you know," he said, as if remarking on the weather. Suddenly, she found her words.

"Listen," blurted the prone ogre. "I always knew you could think, could talk. You heard rumours, and they always got talked down, but I always th—"

"Oh, *fuck off!*" interjected Mouana, smashing a fist into the centre of the overseer's forehead.

"Yes," Wrack interjected, in a hurry. "We're not going to be friends, so don't bother with all that. We hate you. But you might walk away from this if you can do something for us."

The overseer's face changed, very subtly. The panic etched in it ebbed as she found she was in a position to make a deal, and Wrack realised with a surge of disgust that at least some of her fear had been theatre, a desperate appeal to compassion that had drawn him in like the illicium of an anglerfish.

"Like what?" said the overseer, her voice steadier.

"You're going to tell us what's going on here. And you're going to tell us how we stop it."

"We're criminals, the same as y—" started the woman, before retching as Mouana's fist slammed into the folds of her throat.

"We already made it clear you're not getting the pity vote," spat the soldier. "So stop your sob story."

"No, *listen*," croaked the overseer, more in exasperation than pleading. "I'm *trying to tell you what's going on.* I'm trying to explain. Nobody's here by choice. We're prisoners just like you are."

"You're not dead like we are," said Mouana.

"We're not far off. They fill us with chemicals, to keep us next to death. To keep us ill, sick, falling apart. For five years. Before we came to Ocean we needed surgery, steroids, implants; months of bulking up, just to have a hope of surviving it. Most don't make it past three years. And they take our medicine away if we can't make quota."

There was a moment of silence, and then Mouana exploded. Her fists smashed against the pallid face again and again, shreds of her forearms tearing away on the metal grille. "You expect me to pity *that?*" she screamed, jaws wide. "You expect me to care for a bastard *instant* that you're sick? I will *show you* sick!" she screamed, and lunged for the overseer's neck with grey teeth bared.

"Hold on!" shouted Wrack, throwing himself on Mouana, grabbing her head desperately, wincing as her teeth sliced into his forearm. "Why? Why do you have to be nearly dead?"

The overseer stared at Mouana, panting, eyes dulled with genuine terror, then flicked her oily gaze back to Wrack.

"Because Teuthis hates life," she said, simply.

From the back of the crowd looking down on the prisoner, a voice piped up: "What the fuck is a Teuthis?"

"It's a monster," she answered, voice slithering in revulsion.

"So's everything, here," snapped Wrack, still straining to keep Mouana from lunging. "What kind of monster?"

"It's different," said the overseer. "Very old. Very clever. Came from the polar reach, up under the icecap. Horrible, armoured, squid thing. Got hunted years and years ago, and now they keep it here. Says it's the last of its kind."

"*Says?*" hissed Wrack.

"We can talk to it, sort of. But we have to be nearly dead; we need to be right on the edge before it'll talk to us. It won't work for the living. That's why they bulk us up to take five years of poison; so it can't tell the difference."

"Where is it kept?" demanded Wrack, moving his face closer to the overseer's.

The huge woman was silent for a moment, hesitating, perhaps wondering if she had said too much. Wrack disabused her of the notion by pulling his arms from Mouana, letting his friend surge forward to within an inch of the overseer's jowls. Then the words flowed.

"On the bridge. It's just a brain, and some other bits, kept in a glass tank. Drugged way beyond high and plugged into the ship's systems. It's got a pilot seat, where we direct it. It controls the cranes, the drones, the forges. Creates the signal that controls—ah, guides, the—ah... you." Her voice petered out in a grating squeak.

Those zombies in the pile able to follow the conversation hissed in awed fear. Even Mouana paused, turning her head slowly toward Wrack. The black pulse. The green light. The marsh of despair and grief that sucked at them from beneath their consciousness.

"Let's go kill it," said Mouana, her anger at the overseer replaced by something deeper, something colder.

"You'd never get halfway up," the overseer insisted, less a taunt than a statement of fact. "The tower's fortified, full of us."

"So that's our deal," said Wrack. "You're going to do it for us."

The overseer's eyes lit up above her ruined face.

"And if I do?"

"You get to live, you bloody idiot," said Wrack. "And so do the others, if they don't fight us. You said you're prisoners. We'll free you."

The ogre's eyes turned sly and she nodded, grumbling her assent. Wrack felt suddenly outmanoeuvred. Despite being on top of her with a pack of raging ghouls, he was desperately aware that any promise the overseer made to buy her way out of the hangar would last as long as it took her to find a radio and call in a team of shark handlers.

He was going to have to do some really solid lying, and do it quick enough so it didn't sound like he was making things up on the spot. He started by standing up, and stepping off the overseer's chest. Every head in the circle snapped up to look at him; Mouana in particular looked as if she was going to gut him herself. But he just nodded back at them, and waved his hand, carefree.

"Go on, you heard her. She severs the link with this squid thing, we let her and her mates live afterwards."

Even the overseer looked suspicious at how relaxed he was—though Wrack quickly turned his attention from her, as if she was a problem solved. In fact, he was desperately trying to meet Mouana's eyes, doing everything he could to say *trust me* with a casual glance. It worked. The soldier stood up, expression wary, and the others followed her lead.

The overseer soon found herself prone and unpinned, surrounded by a circle of retreating cadavers. Giving Wrack a very queer glance, she rose to her feet, and brushed corpse-slime from her lapels. Then with a nod she turned, shouldered her way through the watching ghouls, and walked slightly too quickly to the hangar's exit.

"Oh," said Wrack as she walked into the swelling dawn, "I should point out—you're welcome to turn us in, but you're pretty much buggered if you do."

That was when Wrack heard the crackle of the radio, and turned to see Mouana holding it up with a grin. He was relieved beyond measure, because he had just run out of plan.

"It's been on the whole time," gloated Mouana, her chest wound dripping with the exertion of speech. "And broadcasting." She was a magnificent liar. "To two dozen more radios. Stolen, hidden away all over the ship. There's lots and lots of us who can talk, you see. And we've been talking."

She paused to wheeze for a moment, before spluttering through gritted teeth and carrying on. "We told them we were going to have a word with you. Now they've heard. They know who you are, 'WK3.' They'll be watching you very, very closely. And they'll be very cross if we tell them you've snitched on us."

"So see that you do help us," added Wrack. "This ship is going to change, and you have a chance to determine how bloody things get in the changing. Even if you do call us in for slaughter, and even if you run fast enough when you do, the rest of us are going to riot."

Wrack paused for a moment, as if he had said his piece, then continued.

"And granted, we might not win. But if we all get cut down, if we wreck the place in the process... well, either way, you're not going to hit quota. And what'll they do with your medicine then? You'll be the next batch of us."

"But we will win," cautioned Mouana, stalking forward, wound bubbling. The overseer actually backed away. "We'll overtake this place. And whether it's me or someone else, we'll find you, and we'll get you. We'll get you worst of all. I don't even know how we work, but you had better hope that if we bite you, you'll become one of us. Because if you don't, we'll eat you. One bite at a time."

The overseer quaked, frozen on the spot. The power they had over her now was far greater than it had been when they were propped inches from her face, slavering. The work was done.

"What's your name?" asked Wrack, doing all he could to seem reasonable in the aftermath of Mouana's terrorising.

"Whina," yelped the overseer, too quickly to be a lie.

"Well then, Whina: help us," concluded Wrack. "Station yourself at the bridge. Find a reason to be there as often as you can. And watch for our signal—I promise you, you won't miss it. Sever Teuthis from the ship, and we will free you. But don't you dare ask for a guarantee."

"Now *fack off*," interjected the Bruiser, and put a neat end to the meeting. Whina fled.

The second she was gone Wrack doubled over into silent, hysterical laughter, completely unable to process what had just happened. It was the most human he had ever felt. He staggered over to the hangar's edge with his head in his hands, and collapsed against the wall by the skeletal man, whose ecstatic gape threw him into a fresh fit of giggles.

He came to his senses when Mouana delivered a wet slap across his jaw, nearly putting it out of joint.

"It's no time for laughing," she warned, as he mumbled grinning apologies. "We've got until she calls our bluff to make all of that bullshit into reality. And I've done enough talking. Your move."

"I know, Mouana," sighed Wrack, wiping away tears that would not come. "Just give me a minute."

He breathed in deep, not caring whether it did anything for

him, and looked around at the mass of alert, upright corpses waiting on his next words, silhouetted against the dawn.

Then he looked to his left, and saw the skeletal man in sunlight for the first time.

Every inch of exposed bone on his wasted body was covered in carvings. Intricate scrimshaw covered his pelvis, his ulnae, his radii and his sternum; abstract patterns dancing with serpents and sea-devils, tendons and streaks of grime. His scapulae rippled with tobacco clouds, steaming from the bowls of long-stemmed pipes; Wrack's eyes narrowed in wonder.

But the scraped bone of his brows crowned the work—for there, inscribed blindly by a frail, patient hand, was the image of a vast ship, half-sunk in a raging storm. Behind the stricken hulk, rising like a wicked moon, was the image of a grinning skull.

"We'll find out!" shrieked One-Arm, capering in the dawn light while all the other zombies remained still. "We'll find out, won't we!"

CHAPTER FOURTEEN

THEY WORKED AS quickly as they could. They finally had a plan and, so long as Whina remained too scared to interfere with it, the freedom to make it happen. Their first priority while that freedom lasted was to spread the idea of rebellion beyond one easily-cleared cave at the arse end of the ship.

To that end, interviews were held, of a sort. Wrack would ask questions of the zombies one by one, testing how much they had taken in of the makeshift interrogation. As soon as one's eyes slid out of focus, or as soon as they resorted to singsong repetition of familiar words instead of making a sensible answer, he shoved them aside.

Those that seemed to have worked out what was going on, he shoved towards Mouana, who started telling them, punctuating her speech by shaking their shoulders, how to wake their fellows—and where the overseers kept their radios. After all, the fiction she had come up with on the spot, of knots of conscious dead clustered around stolen radios, seemed a workable plan once they thought about it, and so was worth putting into practice.

Groups were clustered together around those dead that seemed to have a clue, and were sent from the hangar, under instructions to look clueless and defeated lest they be suspected of having purpose. Each went off with a radio frequency to remember, and instructions to listen out for a plan coming together. Until then, the only priority was to spread the word, and look inconspicuous.

The groups went willingly away; they understood there was a high likelihood of being caught and torn apart, but it was a rare zombie for which this was a terrifying fate: they genuinely had nothing to lose.

The Blades were the most useful among them as group leaders; whether it was some sense of cohesion borrowed from their living memories, or something to do with the way they had died, they seemed more together than a lot of the others.

Of course, there were exceptions. Broken-Jaw Kaba took one group of ten or so (Wrack wasn't keeping count), and they even let the Bruiser take a rowdy knot of cadavers. Sure, his comprehension wasn't up to much, but he'd proved he had spirit at least, and that was worth sending him out with a team, even if the best he could do was swear into the faces of his fellow dead.

Even some of the people from the dreg pile, those too broken to be roused by the prospect of Whina's food on that other morning, went out on the hunt. They went out slowly, or dimly, or hobbling along on knuckles and a single leg, but they went out.

When they thought the hangar was empty of the cogent dead, Wrack and Mouana were approached by the Once-Fat Man, with his teenage saviour in tow. His voice was almost polished, his attitude impossibly calm, as he told them how impressed he had been by their bluff against Whina, and how he wondered if he could help.

For someone who had been so recently struggling to achieve more than wordless screams of anger, he was strangely eloquent. And while Mouana balked, unsure of how to react to his odd sincerity, Wrack figured that everyone took death differently, and urged the sagging man to take his wordless squire and find others like himself. They would need talkers.

In fact, of all the dead to return with them from the ET hunt, only poor, gibbering One-Arm elected to stay in the hangar with those too decayed to move. It seemed the best place for the capering, grinning cadaver. And in any case, thought Wrack, with the sort of logic that would have seemed callous with lives on the line, if they were betrayed and the overseers did come to the hangar to exterminate the rebel threat, how foolish would they feel in finding One-Arm in command.

When their oddest charge had scampered over to the dreg pile to engage the listless dead in enigmatic winks and thumbs-ups, Wrack and Mouana found themselves the only speaking people left in the hangar.

"Which way do we go?" asked Wrack, shrugging in the dawn.

"You're taking the starboard side, where the Bahamut is. I'm taking port, where the bridge is. I'm going to get them worked up, right in the shadow of this bloody squid thing." Wrack opened his mouth to argue, but Mouana was already thrusting the stolen radio into the inside of his shirt.

"You said to the fat bloke: we need talkers. And you're a talker, Wrack. Just make sure you talk to those boiled bastards with the weapons, if there's more of them left. Talk, and listen. Keep one ear on the radio," she said, repeating the frequency she had told the others. "See who else calls in, keep them on plan, and let's talk when we've got some work done."

"But you're the soldier," protested Wrack. "Why give me the radio? How are you going to get—"

"Exactly, I'm the soldier," snapped Mouana. "I'll get my hands on a new one quicker than you will. And then we can talk." She began walking towards the open deck, even as Wrack opened his arms to reason with her.

"Surely we should stick together until we've got two?" whined Wrack, earning only a half-turn from his comrade as she stalked away.

"We've already stuck together long enough," stated Mouana, then softened a little when she saw the look on his face. "Look, we can't give them just one head to lop off, Wrack. And there's no point in holding hands like lovers; we're both far too rotted in the funbits to care about that. We're assets, and we need to keep our distance so they can't get both of us at once. At least until it's time to act."

"Fine," said Wrack, deciding he owed his friend at least the semblance of military pragmatism. "But when's that?"

"I don't fucking know!" cackled Mouana, a joyful snarl on her face. "That stuff about the signal was your bit of bullshit to make real! Just choose your moment, get the word out, and hope for the best. Good luck, chief."

And then, with a half-mocking, affectionate salute, she left. Wrack stood on the spot for a while, making feeble arguments to himself about whether it would be worth having one more trawl through the dreg pile for volunteers. Then he admitted to himself that he was wasting time, and walked out onto the stern of the *Tavuto*.

He roamed along the side of the ship, feeling as though he had a huge red arrow hovering over him. As he moved into the busier stretches of the deck and began to pass overseers on their rounds, he was sure that at any moment he would be identified and bundled to the floor. After spending his every waking moment trying to force the lethargy of death out of his limbs, he now did everything he could to shamble, lurch and stumble. It was like being young and drunk and trying to pass for sober while bowling past bouncers, shunted into sickening reverse.

It soon became clear there was no need for theatrics, however. Whatever had happened after Whina had fled, she had not raised the alarm straight away, and nobody but the scattered dead they had sent ahead knew he had started a rebellion. There was nothing conspicuous about him; nothing to mark him apart from the endless stream of bodies being herded along the deck towards their various labours. For now, at least, he was safe. He just needed to let himself be dead. The red arrow faded in his mind, and Wrack lost himself in the flow of meat.

He lost too much of himself.

When the radio eventually crackled into life, all was blackness around him. The world came into vile focus all at once, to every sense but sight. Slime enveloped him; he could barely move. Cadaverous vapours seared the hollows of his congealed sinuses. Had a Sniffer Ray caught him? Worse, had he fallen in the water, been swallowed up by something?

Reason surged against panic: the radio wouldn't work in water, and whatever it was that pressed around him didn't press back against his thrashing. He had merely fallen out of his own head, into the swamp that had always been waiting to catch him when thought failed, and had been caught up in some awful toil. But he was back now, and he was sure he had something important to do. He had to concentrate, and listen to the voices burbling on his radio—they were important, somehow.

"We'e going to go for it," gurgled a wet voice, unfamiliar, buzzing with distortion. "There's loads of us. Hundreds. We're going to take the docks." A cheer of many throats rose up from the tinny speaker.

That's alright then, Wrack thought sleepily, as the dark wobbled up from the sump of his skull to blend with the black in front of his eyes. They were going to take the docks. That was good news.

Then he remembered the plan. This was not good at all. Whoever they were, those voices on the other side of the radio, they weren't meant to be rushing the most heavily guarded part of the ship. They were going to get mown down, and give the game away.

Worse yet, he remembered, he was meant to be in charge

of the plan; he was meant to have been listening out for this sort of thing, and stopping it getting out of hand. But he had been asleep at the bloody wheel. The guilt rammed itself down his spine like a cold metal spike, bringing him fully to awareness. How much time had he lost? Had he missed his chance? What if Mouana had been cut down while he was sleepwalking? Panicking, Wrack raised the radio to his mouth.

But it wasn't the radio. Whatever was in his hand was inert and wooden, and offered nothing as he scrabbled frantically for a broadcast switch. It was a flensing knife. Wrack screwed his face up in fury at his own sluggishness: of course, the radio was still in his shirt, where Mouana had put it to conceal it from view.

Whatever he was constricted by gave him some freedom of movement, but was meat-heavy—he wriggled his free arm down the front of his shirt, but it was like wrestling against piles of soaked, coarsely bristled cushions.

Hand quaking with urgency, Wrack grabbed the slime-smeared radio and rammed it against his face.

"Don't! No!" he hollered. "Wrack! It's Wrack!"

"Wrack?" barked the other voice, like a bartender being asked for an imaginary drink.

"Yes, Wrack. You know..." said Wrack, wincing as the words became inevitable, "the leader."

There was a lot of barking and confusion on the end of the line; he heard his name repeated several times, questioning at first, then becoming exclamatory as someone in the unseen rabble remembered who he was. Then the voice was back, rough and raw as salt-scrubbed iron.

"Right, Wrack. Well, we're going for it! We're taking the docks!"

"No!" shrieked Wrack, sounding less like a leader even than he had as a librarian. "You can't, you'll all die. Well, be destr—look, you'll ruin everything if you act now. Wait for my signal."

"What's the signal?" growled the voice in the close, foetid darkness. "When will it be?"

"You'll know," snapped Wrack, hoping the distortion of the radio, amplified by whatever cache he had as a faceless mastermind, would disguise the fact he had no idea himself. "I can't say, they could be listening. You just need to know: not now. Talk to more, spread the message. Wait for the signal."

He heard his words repeated on the other end of the radio, and was about to cement his instructions with some grand words of encouragement when a slit of dim light appeared above him, opened by the wedge of a blade. The blade withdrew and thrust in again, carving a yawning hole in the blackness. Then the side of the world fell away with a great, soggy tearing sound.

Wrack lost his footing as the meat he was leaning against collapsed, and tumbled to the deck in a rubbery tangle of grey offal, ending up on his back. The sky was indigo with deep twilight. An overseer stood towering over him with a rusted falchion in their hand, looking down with eyes blazing in furious shock. A radio was already being raised to their cracked yellow lips.

Before he even remembered he was holding it, Wrack plunged the flensing knife into the back of the overseer's knee. Gasping, the giant dropped their radio and fell to the ground, clutching the wound. Wrack threw himself onto the body, spiderlike hands scrambling on wet leather. His mind went blank, save for the urge to cause as much damage as he could, as quickly as possible.

Clambering over the prone titan, Wrack hugged their back as if clinging to a lover, and began chomping frantically at the back of its neck. Greasy filth and layers of dead skin skidded off his teeth, and a huge arm reached back awkwardly to flap at him as the screams began. Then something yielding caught between his premolars and sheared through, with a feeling that made Wrack's skin tingle.

Red flooded across grey skin in front of his eyes, and he

ripped his head back, tearing meat free with it. He lunged again, hooking incisors into the wound and yanking back once more with meat clamped between his jaws. He bit and bit again, teeth cracking more than once, then jammed his fingers into the wound and tore at it. The screams of the overseer grew wet, choking, and still he scrambled at the bloody hole, jabbing and scratching and tearing. Then, with his crimson hand forcing the overseer's face against the deck, he thrust his head in again and locked his teeth around a huge clump of tissue. Blood swelled in his mouth, acrid and tangy as the preservative he had downed on the skiff with Mouana, and he clenched his jaw against human meat.

Then, shoulders rigid as he braced, he tore the mouthful away. The screaming stopped.

Wrack rose to his feet, shaking, and looked down at the splayed nightmare of the overseer's neck.

"FUCK!" he roared, the blood-drenched chunk flying out of his mouth with the force of the expletive, then doubled over and vomited everything inside him. As he straightened and wiped his ruin of a mouth, a chorus of voices rose from the dark around him.

"Fuuuuuuuuuuuuuck."

Turning in a slow circle, Wrack found himself looking into the eyes of two dozen zombies, all frozen in the middle of their work to watch the fight. They were in a cove of meat, a chunk of the Bahamut's insides hauled up on deck for dismantling, and their drawn faces peered out at him from a thicket of grey guts.

Wrack was shuddering, searching for words, when he heard the tick of metal on metal. He thrashed around, eyes jerking, ready for the skittering that would precede the arrival of one of the awful shark things, but there was nothing. Just his foot, bumping against his fallen blade on the blood-slick deck.

There were no other overseers in sight; Dakuvanga's sprawling sub-limbs reached across the gathering night above, but the bulk of the dissected Bahamut had shielded them from the eyes of its command crew. Nobody had seen. In the throbbing mess of Wrack's mind, the realisation he was a murderer crunched under the glowing weight of the realisation that he had gotten away with murder.

"Fuuuuuuuck!" growled the zombies around him, beginning to close in on the foetally-crouched corpse. Then the overseer's radio, fallen to the deck, buzzed into life.

"*Wetewete 3, come in, this is Dakuvanga,*" squawked the gore-soaked box, a note of caution souring each word. "*What's the situation with the comms noise you heard?*"

"Fuck," hissed Wrack again, then winced as his new congregation repeated him. Pantomiming silence with massively exaggerated gestures, Wrack bent to the radio and raised it to his lips while pleading with his eyes for none of the dead to make a sound. Screwing his eyes shut, he clamped his bloody thumb on the broadcast switch and did his best impression of an overseer's voice.

"Negative, DV," he growled, feeling like a kid pretending to be a dad. "Overheard another team; nothing to report. Just getting jumpy." There was a grinding silence, then Dakuvanga replied.

"*Copy, We-We-3. But cut that shit. We've got restless assets in three, twelve, fifteen and twenty—we don't need any false positives. Get the job done and change shift in eight, out.*"

Wrack sank into a half-crouch, clutched his knees, and took in a massive, useless breath. "Fuck," he whispered, still in shock, and opened his eyes. A crowd of the dead, silently gathered at arm's reach, shouted the word back at him with relish. He had gotten away with it. At least for eight hours, until the poor sod he had just chewed the neck off failed to show up for shift change. Beyond that he had no idea what would happen, but given the way things had escalated in the last few minutes, he imagined he'd have other things to worry about by then. Things were accelerating towards the brink of chaos.

As if to punctuate the thought, moans sounded like distant

thunder from far down-deck, rising in a wave, before the rattle of automatic gunfire cut into them.

Evidently, thought Wrack, he had been out of the action for some while. It could have been more than a day. The word had clearly spread while he had been under, and clearly not everyone was bothering to radio in before taking action. Looking down at the bloody wreck of the overseer, fading to grey with the advance of night, Wrack realised his own revolution had overtaken him. He had to catch up with the plan, before it all fell apart.

Stuffing the overseer's radio into the stained horror of his shirt alongside the one they had stolen from Whina, Wrack spat blood from his mouth and looked over at the lagoon from which their chunk of the Bahamut had been drawn. Nearby were the ramps leading down into the bowels of the ship, where they kept the steam-boiled war-corpses, with their harpoons and pincers and cannons. Wrack could only assume they were well guarded, but he couldn't leave the milky-eyed juggernauts in the overseers' hands.

He was going to need a mob on his side to get down there. And though the swamp of blood around his cracked teeth spoke otherwise, Mouana had been right—he was a talker. And there was more talking to come if he wanted to stay ahead of the chaos he had kicked off.

"Right," said Wrack, clapping his hands onto the shoulders of the nearest zombie. "What's your name, then, mate?"

CHAPTER FIFTEEN

HALFWAY THROUGH THE night, they rushed into the dim warrens of the underdecks like the winter sea. There were more than a hundred of them by the time Wrack finally decided it was less risky to launch a blind assault with the numbers he had than wait any longer.

The nearest ramp had been sparsely guarded; only one overseer had been posted there, and went down like a tower of matchsticks when the pack of zombies rushed from the Bahamut's guts. Either Dakuvanga didn't expect the ship's 'restless assets' to have any capacity for strategic thinking, or the overseers were simply needed elsewhere, and stretched desperately thin.

Even presuming the near-dead supervisors of the *Tavuto* were aware they had a growing insurrection on their hands, thought Wrack, it was not as if they could divert all their resources to defence just yet. As Whina had said, the living crew of the ship depended on reaching quota in order to receive their shipments of medicine: it would take a full revolt for them to risk putting the ship on lockdown and shutting down production. What choice did they have, especially with the fresh disaster of the failed ET hunt on their hands, but to keep supervising the work crews, and hope that things didn't get too out of hand? Clearly things were getting dangerously close to that point, with open rebellion simmering across the ship, and so any chance of success hinged on bringing on board as many dead as they could—including the fearsome war-built in their deep dungeon—before the overseers put *Tavuto* on lockdown.

And so they streamed into the underbelly of the ship without further resistance, although Wrack had no idea where they were going. As he directed the mob through the winding steel corridors and grated staircases, he avoided awkwardness by referring to himself in the third person. "Wrack wants us down here," he would shout. "Wrack needs this corridor checked out."

Were there anyone else listening, it would have seemed absurdly narcissistic. But he told himself it was a matter of pragmatism—the dead seemed much happier following instructions from an unseen third party, and became baffled and disquieted if he issued orders in the first person. And besides, distancing himself from the person giving the instructions also made him feel very slightly less responsible when he commanded the tide to tear apart living people.

Once they got deep into the hull, there was plenty of tearing apart. Not long after they burst below decks, the main block of his rabble encountered a control room staffed by four overseers. By the time the men and women within had worked out that the dead coming down the corridor were not being shepherded by their colleagues, there were already hands clawing at their throats. Fingers grabbed at them, bodies piled over them until they sank to the floor, and then the wet noises began. Within a minute, it was all over.

Zombies stood back up with purple-black, stringy flesh hanging from their jaws. Those with the presence of mind to look haunted, Wrack gave the freshly acquired radios. As they took the units gingerly in their hands, he sent them out of the corridors and away, telling them to find other dead to organise into groups, and to avoid provoking all-out war.

Meanwhile, Wrack's mob moved through the corridors belowdecks, and found more of their miserable tribe. Zombies working on making ammunition, repairing weapons craft, working canneries and deep freezers. There were whole substegarian industries down there; thousands of workers, toiling by the dim light of sodium lamps. Just as it had been in the control room, their supervisors were unwarned, unready, when the tsunami of rotten mouths broke over them.

Wrack kept moving from chamber to chamber, trying to make sense of the maps on the walls, leaving his most cogent followers to begin the process of rabble-rousing as he sought the war-built. There was no time to linger and engage in the baffled chat of the newly undead. Besides, many of the dead down here were chained in place, ankles worn to bone by crude steel manacles. Even when freed with boltcutters, many just shuffled in circles or remained at their stations, faces twisted in confusion.

As he led the growing pack through the orange metal gloaming, Wrack kept one radio tuned to the rebel frequency, which he had taken to calling 'Dead Air,' while he cycled the other through Dakuvanga's various broadcast frequencies, listening for any idea of what was going on on the wider ship, and—hopefully—advance warning if he was about to be run down by a death squad.

The airwaves were getting crowded. Overseers were reporting their teammates missing, and Dakuvanga's requests to copy were becoming increasingly frequent as Wrack cycled through the channels. Graffiti was appearing, strange symbols daubed in blood and bile on the *Tavuto*'s superstructure, bewildering the overseers. Wrack listened in on the reports of those who found it, spooked by the weird symbols, and arguing with each other to the point of fisticuffs.

To his immense amusement, consensus among Dakuvanga's radio operators seemed to be that all this was down to living human agitators—a cell of Pipers, they reckoned, come in on a stealthed trireme from some outworld shithole, and armed with neural disruption tech. It didn't seem to occur to anyone that the dead might be becoming less dead, that Teuthis hadn't managed its job of keeping everyone down in the black.

Because that was all it was. There was no code language, no hidden messages, and the graffiti held no greater secrets than that its creators had remembered how to daub their anger on walls.

Then there were the broadcasts on Dead Air, from the Bahamut lagoon, from the meat stacks, from the molten heat of the trying pots. Voices murmuring incoherently, yelling in challenge, repeating names of old comrades in the hope they might answer. Once on a broadcast from the flensing yard, he heard the omnishanty break out; a wonderful cacophony of half-formed voices, growing louder and louder as its component tunes diverged. It ended in gunfire, but he grinned all the same.

After a while, Wrack realised there was little point in trying to keep them quiet—he only had to hope enough of them were sticking to the plan, keeping inconspicuous and waiting, for there to be an army to rally once he made it back above deck. Besides, he thought, if the hotheads all cooked off now, the overseers might think the worst was over by the time he was ready to kick off the real trouble.

Wrack stopped in his tracks, poleaxed by the train of his own thoughts, and his pack steamed on into the next chamber without him. Somewhere in the journey between the ramp and the deep warrens, he had stopped thinking like an embarrassed librarian, and taken on the aspect of a violent revolutionary who spoke in the third person, and who thought about the mass annihilation of human consciousness purely in terms of its tactical benefit. It occurred to Wrack that his chin was caked black with human blood, and there were bits of somebody's neck stuck between his teeth.

Once again, he considered that he had perilously little knowledge of his life before the day he had been dragged, protesting his innocence, from the wreckage of his library. Had he really been the scapegoat for someone else's plot, or had he been the ringleader all along? It was, after all, beginning to feel horribly natural to lead a guerrilla army.

And then he clocked what was in the next chamber, and decided this would be a truly dreadful moment to talk himself out of becoming a monster. For he had just found his real monsters.

There were a dozen of them, wired into pedestals of chuntering machinery, in a room lit cold and blue by neon light. The war-built. They had been big to begin with, then made huge by the amount of metal, plastic, wood and rubber bolted onto their ruined bodies. They stood with heads bowed even as the hooting swarm invaded their prison-sanctum, chained into place with yards of black iron. But when Wrack entered the room, their heads snapped up to regard him. There was no sleep of death here, and these grim giants needed no waking.

At their heart was a colossus. There was no mistaking him— it was the weapon-laden horror he had beheld just before he had been sent to sea for the ET hunt. Wrack was looking straight into the blind eyes of another survivor of the *Akhlut*. Cracked lenses whirred on the rack of instruments bolted to the giant's skull as Wrack approached, and scalded lips drew out into a blasted, carnivorous smile.

"Before you ask the obvious," said the boiled hulk, "my name is Osedax: Bone-Eater."

Wrack felt very much like a flustered librarian again. Even without a half ton of weaponry fixed to his torso, menace and hate poured from the man like meltwater from a glacier. Wrack only hoped he could find something the puckered titan hated more than him. There was no point trying the soft approach here.

"You sank with the *Akhlut*," stated Wrack, trying to sound as needlessly confrontational as he could.

"I did," agreed Osedax, nodding. "But they build us with flotation machines, so they can always bring us back. They raised me up, towed me back on a boat, and put me back together. Me and Riftia and Kuphus and Eunice. Isn't that right, girls?" Three of the other monsters hissed in assent, chains clanking as they leaned forwards.

"You're worth a lot of money to them, then?" asked Wrack, as the other dead in the room jostled in the shadows.

"Oh, no, it's not just that," replied Osedax, carcass grin still bared wide. "It's the punishment. We're killers, little man. We've been very bad. I've killed dogs, I've killed little kids. Just because I wanted to. Just for the sport of it. I've—"

"You *were* killers, you mean," corrected Wrack, faltering a little.

"No, boy. I was a bad man, and I still am a very bad man. So this is my sentence. I killed, and I kill, and I will kill. And they keep me conscious, and they keep me fixed up. So I can keep killing, and can never forget." Osedax shivered, chains clanking in their sockets as his huge chest shuddered, then his voice dropped to the whisper of graveyard mist. "Cute, though, that you've come to make me feel better, to... *wake me up*, to talk me into your little support group. I've gathered what has been going on up above."

Wrack felt anger, rather than fear, surge through him. He thought of the Once-Fat Man, roaring in dismay at the back of the boat, of Mouana whimpering in the rain, of Aroha's pitiful eyes as he sank into the jaws of a devil. None had been so pathetic as this swollen mess of self-hatred. There was no time to indulge the creature's sense of self-importance, or let it dominate the situation.

"Well done," said Wrack softly, as he bent for a wrench on the blood-smeared deck. "Well done!" he screamed, smashing the length of iron against Osedax's thorax and leaving a spongy dent. "You're *terrifying!*" he barked, half meaning it, and half spitting the word in scorn.

"I don't know how long you've saved up this speech, but it's useless. It's *shit*. I don't care who you are, or whether you fucked a hundred cats. You're being set free, and you're working for me."

"Set free?" rumbled Osedax, tilting his sightless head. "That might not go well for you, little man." He smirked again, fluid sliding down his chin, and leaned forward in his restraints.

"What exactly are you going to do to me?" said Wrack, laughing. "For a start, I'm not remotely afraid of you killing me, because I'm dead. And my pain receptors are buggered too, so torture wouldn't be much of a laugh for you either." Wrack shook the wrench. "Beyond primate dominance displays, your grinning and your bloody flexing, you've got nothing to scare me with. Nothing."

The silence could have melted through the floor. Wrack wasn't quite sure what he was doing, but it felt amazing, and he continued.

"I know we only just met, *Bone-eater*, but you're the worst self-pitier I've come across, and that includes my own bloody self. So you got pulled back from *Akhlut*? Well done, you dicking great *puppet*. Me too. I pulled *myself* back from Ocean, me and everyone who's causing trouble right now. We extended our own bloody 'punishment,' without any of those grey gits having to lay a finger on us."

Osedax's blind eyes widened in surprise—his mouth worked, but Wrack jumped back in before words could form. Talk, Mouana had said.

He gestured to the radio, and launched into a fresh tirade. "And why did we stick it out? Not because we're spooky bloody psychopaths like you, but because this, *all of this*, is dreadful, and we're willing to throw ourselves away to make it stop."

Wrack hefted the wrench again, and shook it an inch from

Osedax's lumpen brow. The monster opened its mouth to speak again, but Wrack cut it off at the first syllable.

"Call yourself a killer?" he bollocked, "You've had damned harpoon guns welded on and off of your chest for who knows how long, and you've just gone along with it without so much as saying 'boo' to the bosses. Sounds like you reckon you deserve what you've got."

Silence thundered for a long moment, before the giant answered in a low grumble.

"Maybe I do," he said.

"Maybe you do, Bone-Eater," agreed Wrack, before tossing the wrench to the ground. "The question is, are you willing to do more killing? Or do you want me to leave you chained up and piss off, then come back and have another chat when it's all done?"

There was no answer.

"I thought so," grinned Wrack. "Now don't be sad, you big daft sod. This'll cheer you up—I'm about to get all your weapons out, and have this lot bolt them onto you and all your scary mates." Wrack made patronising movements with his hands at the word *scary*, then slapped a hand on Osedax's restrained shoulder.

"And guess what I want you to do in exchange for freeing you?"

More silence, and a growl. Then the radio, the one tuned into Dead Air, burst into life, and Wrack's eyes went wide. It was Mouana, at *exactly* the wrong moment.

"Hold on," said Wrack, jabbing a finger into Osedax's chest, "I have to take this."

When he turned away, Wrack found he was shaking in terror. He was thankful he had emptied his stomach earlier, or he'd have voided it there and then. Bullying a musclebound cyborg murderer was not something he would have considered himself capable of even at the best of times.

"Yep," he croaked into the radio. "Wrack here."

Mouana's voice was hard-edged, with no room for affection,

as it was when she'd first left the hangar. "Huh, so you are back. Well, pretty sure it's time, Wrack. She's up on the bridge, right now—so are a lot of the overseers. Looks like this is all coming to a head a bit sooner than we thought; we're waiting for things to kick off. Really hope you've figured a signal."

"Glad you're doing well too," muttered Wrack, rolling his eyes, then thumbed the switch.

"Yes," he continued, "as it happens, I've just worked it out. Oh, and I've got the boiled bastards on side. I think."

"Well done," said Mouana, and Wrack wasn't quite sure what to make of her tone. He was about to sign off, but hesitated. Whether it was because he was unsure of his chances of leaving the next conversation in one piece or not, he felt the need to be candid.

"Mouana," he blurted. "I'm really glad you're still alive. Or in one piece. You know what I mean. I'm so glad. Anyway, I'll be there as soon as I can—I just need to clear things up here."

"OK," said Mouana, as if she was ordering sandwiches, and the channel went dead.

"Bye," whispered Wrack, before forcing his face into an overconfident grin and turning round, desperately hoping the tremor in his legs wasn't visible.

"That's our cue!" he shouted convivially, waiting for a moment before pantomiming sudden remembrance. "Sorry!" he cried, after no reply came, "and there was I thinking you were a talker. Never mind." He cleared his mucus-gummed throat. "I was going to tell you what you could do in exchange for your freedom, wasn't I?"

"Yes," snarled Osedax from his pump-station of a chest, his shoulders slumped.

"What I want you to do, Bone-Eater, is carve me right up," said Wrack, as he ripped off his shirt. "You'll love it—I'll explain as we go along. And while you're doing it, we'll get your team here tooled up."

Osedax gaped in confusion, but Wrack gave him no time to think. "Come on, then!" he yelled to his pack of cadavers.

"Let's get some boltcutters over here for Wrack; look sharp! And when you're done with that, there's some huge weapons lying around the sides of the room that Wrack reckons would look better bolted to these arseholes. Chop-chop!"

Wrack pulled a flensing knife from his belt and pushed it into Osedax's palm, even as one of his pack shuffled up and cut the big man's chains free. Ignoring the insanity of what he had just done, Wrack leaned in to the side of the giant's head and whispered as if he was sharing a naughty joke.

"Alright, then, you big bastard. Here's what I'm thinking..."

As he spoke, Wrack's army bustled around the chamber, carrying nailguns, launchers and harpoon mounts over to the ruined prisoners. When he finished explaining, he was amazed to see Osedax looking at him with a grin like a dog given freedom to leap into a stream.

"Sounds good?" said Wrack, and the giant nodded.

"Yeah," said Osedax, and the tension melted like frost on hot sand.

"Come on, then," said Wrack, "you're a man after my own heart."

CHAPTER SIXTEEN

THEY CAME SLOWLY up the ramps and out of the underdeck, more than three thousand strong. Not in the wild dash of apes on the hunt, but at a measured stalking pace, ready to wade into bullets if need be.

Wrack led the vanguard, comprising the dozen war-built and a hundred or so of the most together of his pack. They came up a slipway used to send craft like the *Akhlut* belowdecks from their mounts on the ship's central ridge, treading over wooden sleepers as they emerged.

As they trudged up into the light, Wrack half expected one of the mammoth whaleboats to come sliding down the metal rails and over them, turning his march into paste with one rumbling stroke. But nothing came. In fact, not a single overseer awaited them as they emerged.

The sky above them was white, choked with vapour as the sun approached Ocean's slow noon. Wrack looked to either side: from ramps and slipways and hatches for hundreds of yards to each side, zombies were walking, shambling, crawling into the daylight, all silent. No work gangs stood in their way; all was empty deck, for as far as the eye could make out until fog stole the distance.

They were almost exactly amidships, on the *Tavuto*'s starboard flank. To their right sat the steel lagoon and the disassembled Bahamut at its side; the flensing yards and their row of cranes sprawled beyond, hazy behind walls of smoke from the trying vats. Ahead and immediately to their left, looming like a cliff, was the stark iron mount of Dakuvanga, rising hundreds of yards into thick cloud.

Straight across the deck from them, perhaps three hundred yards away and shadowed by the gaze of the god-crane, was the meat hill that Mouana and he had passed on their first night; a wobbling mound of offcuts piled up to be hacked apart before being ferried down to the docks. From memory, it was overlooked by the saturnine carbuncle of the *Tavuto*'s bridge, where Mouana had told him their silent collaborator Whina was ready and waiting. So that was where they needed to go.

He fixed his eyes on the top of the meat pile and began walking, looking neither to right nor left, expecting every second for bullets to begin sleeting down from the cranes above. But nothing came.

The ship's vile, bald-headed birds screamed and wheeled in the fog overhead. Overseers watched in the distant mist, silent, holding rifles.

Wrack twiddled with his radios. While Dead Air crackled with murmured, potentially accidental broadcasts, the main channels were silent. The whole ship, dead and alive, was waiting for something to happen. Well, he thought, there was no point in subtlety now. Grabbing the shoulders of zombies from his pack as he walked, he hissed at them to run as far as they could and tell any other dead people they saw that now was the time. Then he got on the radio.

"Hello *Tavuto*, this is Wrack. Looks like this is happening."

Immediately after he let go of the broadcast switch, a volley of wordless roars came back in response on Dead Air. Still the main channel was silent. But still the bullets didn't come, and so he walked on, Osedax's war-built clanking and hissing behind him.

As they approached the meat hill he saw it was surrounded by the dead, working listlessly. They carried on hacking and sawing, but almost every head turned towards him as he approached. Fifty yards out, he clocked Mouana in their midst, but did nothing to acknowledge her presence beyond the briefest flicker of a smile. If a sniper's bullet was headed for him it would all be on her to work things out, so there was no worth in pointing her out as a target.

Ploughing through the mob of bowed, salt-stained cadavers around the mound, he saw one of them had picked up a loudhailer, and plucked it from their unprotesting hand. Surely now there was no mistaking him—and he was in full view of the bridge tower. As the outer scraps of the meatpile began to squelch under his feet, Wrack imagined a dozen crosshairs floating over his scalp, and lost his nerve.

He sprinted up the meat pile. Today it was foetal sharks, half-grown things taken from the birth canal of some pelagic matriarch. Their teeth glinted like nubs of sharpened pearl in the slick of pink bodies. They caught on the bandages wrapping his feet as he climbed; his heels sank into the raw gashes in their gutted bellies. They slipped down, tore at his shins, made five steps achieve the distance of one, but he pounded to the top. When he arrived, he was not out of breath. Small mercies, thought Wrack.

With the loudhailer raised halfway to his lips, he stood and took it all in. Around him, a ring of the dead, thousands upon thousands, watched him with a fire in their cataracted eyes. Mouana, surrounded by a mob of Blades, looked on discreetly. Osedax and his posse remained motionless, a monstrous wedge standing some way back from the crowd.

And there above him, like an emperor's box in some ancient arena, the ship's bridge glowered. At its glassless windows stood a row of overseers, backlit by green even in daylight, their faces passionless as they stared down at him.

Only one of them moved. Sat in an ornate steel chair at the centre of the bridge, skull plugged with wires and grimacing as if through a migraine: the pilot of Teuthis. And to their side, just a foot away, stood Whina. His eyes slid across hers, and she gave a barely perceptible nod.

A bird honked dismally, far above. Wrack raised the loudhailer and opened his mouth.

"*Tavuto*," he began, then fell silent.

Thousands of eyes were staring at him, but he hadn't the faintest idea what words to use. What could he say that wasn't stating the obvious? It wasn't as if the overseers were expecting him to thank them for their hospitality on behalf of the ship's workforce. And if the watching dead still needed talking round to the thought of violence, there was no hope for them anyway. And in any case, every time he opened his mouth to give an inspiring speech, he was interrupted—it had happened twice in the hangar, and once on the radio in the Bahamut's guts. Holding forth now would just be tempting a bullet.

So Wrack decided to let his actions speak for him.

He threw down the loudhailer, letting it bounce down the pile of skinless sharks, and reached down to the ghastly hole Osedax had carved below his sternum. Gritting his teeth, he reached in with his right hand, nuzzling beneath the cartilage of his sternum, and rummaged between the hanging dead weights of his lungs.

He had rehearsed this motion in the dark of the killer's cell, but it became much harder with the ship's overseers and countless potential rioters watching him. He fumbled, fingertips slipping against surfaces only a surgeon should touch, thumb pushing aside rotten membranes as rib-tips grated against his wrist.

He gripped it. It was smooth, hard in his hand, like a wax pouch. His thumb traced over the fatty sheath built up by a lifetime of fried food, and his fingers curled round, hooking over the stiff tubes of major veins. Then, looking Whina right in the face, he yanked.

IT WAS THEN, as he felt arterial tissue stretch and snap at the centre of his chest, that he silently thanked himself for having Osedax cut halfway through his aorta during the rehearsal. The human body really was a robust thing; it was really stuck in there. Gurning as he felt something rip horribly out of place, Wrack gave another mighty tug, and tore out his own heart.

Screaming wordlessly, Wrack held the bruised organ out in front of him, presenting it to the overseers as if in tribute. Then he turned to face his crowd and squeezed, wringing black juice from the long-dead ventricles and into the hill of city-bound sharkmeat.

At that point, everything went completely mental. A wall of crashing human rage rose from the masses surrounding the pile, and the crowd erupted into motion.

A forest of arms rose into the air, some bearing hearts, some bearing blades. Wrack caught sight of Mouana grinning madly and shook his heart at her, dark clots raining through the air.

With the signal unequivocally given, Wrack turned back to the bridge and nodded at Whina, his face twisted into an expression of unmistakable threat.

But even as the world went mad, the overseer's face was entirely placid. While the bottom half of Whina's face was static, an emotionless grille, her eyes creased in a smile colder than the currents of the sea below.

It all became clear. He should have known from the encounter at the hangar, from the way she had reacted to the threat of death. She had faked compassion, had tried to ingratiate herself, even as she had been caked in the hungry drool of her captors. Only terror, the idea of there being no way out but to collaborate, had swayed her. It should have told Wrack everything he needed to know about her.

After all, thought Wrack, Whina had said herself: the overseers were prisoners too, consigned to life on the edge of death rather than death on the edge of life. And in Whina's smile, the reason for the difference in their fates became caustically clear. The overseers had seen their sentences commuted over the barrier of mortality because they had made *deals*, had received mercy of a kind in exchange for valuable information.

They were snitches.

Soldiers who had given away troop movements, thieves who had shared heist plans, Pipers who had named their sisters and brothers. Betrayers. Wrack knew the type: even with most of his memory locked away in cold meat, he knew he had seen that mix of guilt and triumph and relief before, and he saw it again in Whina.

He had been an idiot not to see it back in the hangar. Now, looking at Whina as she leaned over to Teuthis' pilot and spoke in its ear, eyes still fixed on his, he knew what a dreadful mistake he had made.

The pilot, twitching with whatever coursed through his grey skull, nodded, and Whina turned back to Wrack. With an expression both predatory and unrepentant, she threw him a middle finger. Before he could begin to formulate a response, the pilot slammed down an enormous lever, and the world burst.

It could not be *felt* at first; it was visual. The white sky became black, and the only colour in the world was the deep, phosphorescent green that swelled behind the pilot's seat. It shone out, infinitely bright, searing the pilot's slumped outline into Wrack's retinas, then vanished all at once. It left darkness.

The darkness shrieked with memories.

CHAPTER SEVENTEEN

HIS MOTHER'S GRAVE. Men with scars, shaking hands with his father as he wept. The soft toy rabbit, her gift, forlorn with rain on the graveside.

Smoke rising from the docks. Hangings at the harbour. Worried talks in the study late at night while he drove his model of *Tavuto* blissfully across the carpet.

Midnight at the library, much later. A tall figure, face indistinct beneath the hood of an oilskin, handing him a bundle of rain-sodden paper at the back door.

Meetings in the stacks, rough men. Taking slips of paper from him, whispering messages in his ear. Other men, just as rough, nodding as he passed the messages on.

More rain, years and years ago. Pattering on the windows of his father's office, as they slid the mass of horse drawings aside and laid down a fresh page.

"This one is very important," said Schneider's father, as he drew, in two fluid curves, the figure of a tobacco pipe.

The interrogation room, and the constable, asking him if he knew anyone else involved in the plot. The fierce shake of his head as he swore he had acted alone.

His father at the trial, tear-streaked face contorted with silent gratitude.

Oh, thought Wrack, and forced his eyes open against the rushing dark. *Bloody hell, Dad*. Then he snarled to himself, and sat up. He'd given his life for one rebellion. This time around, he was going to go down fighting.

He had slipped to the bottom of the pile. His skin torn from the teeth of the unborn sharks, his limbs splayed in their viscera. All around him were the fallen bodies of his people, many with hearts still in their hands. They thrashed, and screamed, and crunched into foetal curls as they were beaten over the head with their own memories.

The pulse had been stronger even than the one they'd used against the ET. It had ripped across the ship for as far as Wrack could see, and left none standing but the overseers, their brains left untouched by whatever strange meat frequency Teuthis had attacked on.

Mouana was nowhere to be seen, must have been somewhere hidden on the other side of the pile.

He craned his head sideways, looking for Osedax, and found him on his haunches, weeping thick tears from baked eyes. He was calling for his mother. The other killers lay prone. One of the three elders—Eunice, was it?—screamed an indistinct name over and over again, stared at her own clawed hands as if they dripped with guilty blood.

Voices, indistinct, boomed from high up on Dakuvanga, broadcast through loudspeakers. Teams of overseers moved, full of purpose now, throwing wide nets over the dead and dragging them aside to be recalibrated. They moved in concert, slick and practised; evidently, there was a drill for this. No wonder they had let them get this far, thought Wrack, the blackness billowing like smoke within him.

Why bother nipping at uppity dead piecemeal, when they could let everything come to a head and knock everyone down at once? After a stint under the steam hammer of Teuthis' pulse, they would all return to a pliant state.

All but him, thought Wrack. Though as huge blast doors began to grind apart at the base of the bridge tower, it became clear the overseers had a plan for taking out troublemakers, too. Tremors ghosted through the deck as something enormous moved beyond the doors. They creaked further apart, and light shone on a grin from the nightmares of whales.

The gates parted, and man-high jaws glistening with exposed bone slid into the light, followed by a mountain of flesh.

It was a devil-carcass, fifteen yards long, yoked to the leashes of a dozen overseers. Behind its snaggletoothed wedge of a head, skeletal flippers hung useless above monstrous steel forelimbs, while a tail sheathed in the remains of a coat of blubber hung behind it.

It emerged from the dark, elephantine legs stamping on the gore-slick deck, and threw back its head to give a wail meant to travel a hundred miles through icy sea. A hunting cry.

"Kaitangata!" roared the overseers. "Kaitangata! Kaitangata!"

Kaitangata, the Man-Eater, the beast sent to clean up the dead from the ship's corners. An orca, half-skeletonised and built into the chassis of a war machine.

The ghastly thing pointed its head straight towards Wrack and slunk forward, wet pops and pings sounding from the grey heap of pipe-riddled meat crowning its jaws.

Fair enough, thought Wrack, then lay back and waited for annihilation. It was all well and good going down fighting, but there was no fighting that thing. He let his face tilt up to look at where Whina stood, half-turned from him on the bridge, but she wouldn't even look at him now. Arsehole.

Then Wrack had to keep himself from laughing in delight, as he saw what was happening right below the bridge windows. There, like a spider moving at the edge of vision, he saw a figure creeping up the face of *Tavuto*'s bridge tower. Limbs festooned with red-black tendon, it moved tremulously, hands clasping exposed bolts and feet shuddering in the rifts between hull plates. Its hips were crusted with carved whorls, its scapulae dappled with devil-faces, long-stemmed pipes and broken ships.

It was the scrimshawed man. And he was just a couple of feet beneath the bulging opening where Teuthis' pilot sat, lips flecked with foam, thrashing in its throne. That the zombie had been able to stand was wonder enough; that he had managed to make his grim way up the metal cliff was something else altogether. Mouana had been right—they were more than just rotting bodies.

"Tiny machines," breathed Wrack in wonder, trying to hide his smile as Kaitangata approached.

The beast dipped its head to the deck and grabbed a body in its jaws, just thirty yards from Wrack; it threw the hapless corpse up into the air with a sickening crunch of dislocating hips, and gulped it down. The overseers on the bridge watched as it advanced; Wrack tried his best to look dismal and exhausted, Andromeda before Cetus, doing his utmost not to pump his fists and cheer for the scrimshawed man as he continued his tireless climb.

And then there was no point in theatre. Hanging by one bone-slim arm, reaching up with a shaking hand and grabbing onto the pipework surrounding Teuthis' pilot, Scrimshaw got where he wanted to be. A skeletal fist curled round the pilot's lapel, and the next few seconds unfurled with beautiful simplicity.

Wrack stood up, the only zombie on his feet, and stretched his arms as if greeting the dawn. Then he ran straight at the whale-corpse, heedless of its jaws splaying to meet him, and laughed. As he rushed towards Kaitangata he took in its shape: the matted flippers hanging uselessly in nests of hydraulics either side of its jagged mouth, the sagging mess slumped atop its forelimbs.

If he managed to fool it into lunging the wrong way, he could be on top of it in a matter of seconds. And somehow, before he could even work out how to do that—he had never been much of a sportsman—it had happened. The truck-heavy maw swung like thunder, snapped shut inches from his left hip, and he leapt, hands clawed and stretched.

Yelling in exhilaration, he crashed into the foetid pipework of Kaitangata's left shoulder, just as screams began to sound from the bridge above. He imagined the grey teeth of the scrimshawed man, closing on flesh. Any second now, everything would fall apart. All Wrack had to do was keep hold of the bundled cabling, flexing to keep his hips away from the beast's snapping jaws as they scissored at him.

"Hang on for grim death," he shouted to himself, before erupting into one of his bubbling fits of laughter. There was absolutely nothing grim about the moment. As he bucked and bumped on the shoulder of the monster, the sweet sound of a siren swelled. The carved man had found his meal. Things had fallen apart.

Then it came. Or rather, it went. Like a bullet being sucked from his skull, like a headache boiling away in an instant, like gravity falling away; the black pulse came in reverse, sucked like milk through a straw. Beautiful scrimshaw; the connection had been severed.

All was still. Kaitangata stamped, snorting, but a confusion was upon it. The birds shrieked, mocking in the white sky. Overseers stood rigid with panic.

Then the most ghastly sound. A howl to ruin the mind of any whose throat it hadn't come from; a quarter of a million voices released from despair, drawing succour from each other across a mile and a half of deck.

Beneath Wrack the monster screamed out too, head raised and jaws preternaturally wide, as its grey mental shackles fell away. He swung round onto its neck and sat tall in a saddle of bone as it lunged sideways, taking an overseer square in the middle and biting down in a spray of preservative-yellowed blood.

Kaitangata reared, actually reared, twelve tons of meat and metal propelled skywards in fury, and as it reached its apex Wrack raised his fist, still black with his heart's blood, into the air. The ship screamed again, and as he looked into the faces of the maddened throng, he knew the overseers had no drill for this.

Now, mayhem.

CHAPTER EIGHTEEN

THE DECK BOILED with a thousand battles. Overseers fired rifles and blunt, pitbull shotguns into seething tides of the dead, while others were pulled under, came apart in the clawing eddies. Cordite and brine, diesel and iron rolled across the crowds in heady billows, and the deck vanished under black claret. Where spaces opened in the maelstrom, the pounding of rotted feet on wet metal swelled like the sound of swarming birds as the dead charged their masters.

Sharks ran off their leads, wheeling and thrashing, making messes of handlers and zombies alike: they were the delegates of Ocean's cold violence, with no care for sides or sense.

Kaitangata, their paragon, thundered through the charnel, smashing flesh to jagged slime beneath its feet and destroying bodies with its jaws. On its back Wrack fought to stay upright, knees clamped to either side of its filthy vertebrae, fingers dug into frayed sheets of blubber.

Black streaks dribbling from his emptied chest, he cackled in rough glee as he caught sight of Osedax in the melee. The killer's face was lost in a sort of bewildered ecstasy, slack as a lost child's while he thundered shells into the windows of the bridge above. Eunice, Riftia, Kuphus, his sisters in arms, blasted away alongside him, while the rest of the war-built ploughed out into the wider carnage. The dead rallied around them, converging like starved dogs on the bodies of the overseers they felled.

Fog still clung to the ship, making a shrouded arena of the deck, its glowing depths shaken with gunfire and corpse-bawls. As Kaitangata stooped to tear off the head of a fallen war-built, the mist on *Tavuto*'s starboard flank erupted into searing light. A moment later, thunder shot through the murk, and deep crunches rumbled through the decking: the defence turrets on the lagoon's perimeter had opened fire, laying waste to whatever insurrection had enveloped the Bahamut's graveside.

Dakuvanga's bridge crew rallied moments later—Wrack only realised it when bullets began smacking into Kaitangata's wet hide, singing metal spite as they passed him by inches. He hurled himself from the demon's neck, hitting the deck with a crack that told him something in his upper half was horribly broken, and scrambled into the nearest mob of zombies.

He had gotten both figuratively and literally carried away, thought Wrack, as the monster pounded off into the fray under a hail of bullets. It had been all very well riding through the battle on an incredibly conspicuous target, he considered, but it hadn't held much water as a long term plan. Mouana would not have been impressed.

As he went to pull himself upright, beneath the comforting shelter of two dozen abhuman legs, Wrack discovered it was his left arm that had taken the brunt of the fall; as he went to lever himself onto two feet, it flopped aside with a pathetic crunch and displayed six inches of shattered ulna. Rolling his eyes in annoyance, he shifted his weight and used the other one to push him up.

As he ascended to eye level, the zombies around him erupted into a raucous cheer like pissed mates greeting a latecomer to a pub. He tried his best to mime them into nonchalance, but as they slapped him companionably on the back, he gave up in favour of finding more solid cover as quickly as possible.

There was one obvious option: the semicircle of the deck sheltered from the looming bridge tower, in front of the doors where Kaitangata had emerged. Craning his head above his new, maddeningly congratulatory companions, Wrack saw the doors were still ajar, stopped from closing by a slick hill of bullet-ridden corpses. And beside the doors, of course, was Mouana, discarding a spent blunderbuss and looking incredibly impatient.

As soon as he got close enough to catch her eye, she was simmering. He ran over, out of his covering crowd, with a mouth full of greetings, but Mouana had no time for it.

"What the hell were you doing playing at cavalry, Wrack?" she hissed. "They'll be halfway to wiring themselves back in by now. We need to get up there."

Wrack glanced at the doorway, where a crowd of overseers was beginning to drag the blockage away with billhooks, then snapped back at her.

"You could have made a move yourself, you know," he snarled, and was taken aback by the look of shame on his comrade's face.

"Not without you," she grumbled, then looked as profoundly embarrassed as skin drawn taut over a skull can. "It's you they're following, after all."

She turned. "Anyway. We need to get up there now."

She made for the doors, and Wrack's haggard retinue, despite having lost half a dozen to rifle fire on their way there, cheered once again at the prospect of carnage. Without Teuthis' blackness dragging at their heels, the zombies were almost absurdly enthusiastic for violence.

Just as they were preparing to storm the doorway, a horizontal sleet of lead exploded from the mist and did the job for them; after several seconds of sustained fire, no further movement came from the entrance to the bridge tower.

The clanking of steel feet came next, and Osedax emerged from the pale murk, flanked by four other hulks and a swarm of lesser dead. Even as they passed under the shadow of the bridge, sniper fire hammered against their carapaces, and one—Kuphus, perhaps?—slumped to its knees with a wet hole in its face.

Smoke seeped from the barrels clustered on Osedax's right arm, and the giant nodded to them. For a moment Wrack held the gaze of the brute's camera lenses, wondered how best to address the chaos of the last half hour, but decided instead upon sweeping an arm towards the open tower and asking, "Shall we?" in the manner of a host inviting guests into a party. The moment was somewhat ruined by the fact Wrack used his bad arm, its lower half swinging like a sodden pendulum as he gestured, but Osedax paid no heed.

"Sure," he rumbled, taking a crunching stride onto the heap of bodies jammed in the blast doors. "We need more bullets." His three surviving monsters followed him into the dark, pulling along a hunched tail of the dead, and he was gone.

Mouana went to follow them up, but Wrack laid a hand on her shoulder—his good one, this time.

"What?" she asked, turning to face him. Guns thundered in the distance, and loudhailers barked in the fog.

"Before we head up, could you get rid of this for me?" said Wrack, indicating his flopping mess of a left arm.

"Of course," said Mouana, unable to keep a smile from her face, and bent to pick a cleaver from the belt of a dead overseer. "Point to where you want it cut."

With the impromptu surgery completed, they soon caught up with Osedax, overtaking him on the stairs and spilling onto the bridge with the first of the rabble.

The cavernous space was near-abandoned: smoke from a recently extinguished fire hung in the air like incense, while monitors, dials and warning lights flickered like a joyless carnival. The green glow was nowhere to be seen. The ship's wheel, an arc of mahogany broader than a person's reach, lay still under the slumped corpse of an overseer blown ragged by lead during the gunfight with the war-built. More overseers lay dead by the windows, their weapons and ammunition spilled beside them.

As Mouana had expected, those surviving—perhaps a dozen—were trying desperately to install a new pilot; the poor sod chosen for the job had been tied to the chair with steel cable, his mouth dripping with foam as his panicked shipmates hammered peg-like contacts into plugs trepanned into his skull. The overseers argued and grumbled and cuffed each other, grunting belligerence like walruses jostling over barren rock.

Around them, the floor was a mess of machine parts, blood-soaked bandages—and more bodies. At the feet of his unwilling successor lay *Tavuto*'s former pilot, the side of his head caked black, his neck stripped virtually to the spine. Around him, still resplendent with ships and skulls, lay the scattered bones of the Scrimshawed Man. His head, despite being split to the maxillae by a boarding axe, still grinned at Wrack from where it rested in a corner.

The dead began to join them at the doorway in their dozens, clotting in a malevolent pack. They were anything but quiet, though with the cacophony of alarms, the crackling panic of two dozen radios, and the hellish roar of battle outside, the frantic bridge crew hadn't noticed they'd been invaded.

Then one of the overseers turned to search for a tool, and her face collapsed in horror, like tallow at a furnace door. Her bark of shock raised the heads of the others, and their resonant bickering dissolved into breathless shock. The overseers looked at the zombies, and the zombies looked back, like starved hounds locking eyes over a bone at the end of the world. Weapons emerged, pitch-caulked carbines and hissing knives.

Somewhere out in the battle-stirred fog, Kaitangata's hunting cry echoed.

There was no time to wait for Osedax—the dead were charging. Mouana sprinted as soon as the first gun was drawn, and Wrack followed, stumbling into her side as he forgot to compensate for his missing arm. The mistake saved his friend; as he blundered into Mouana, a shotgun blast aimed square at her caught him in the side, shredding half of his abdomen. He felt bits of him tumble out sideways but kept on his feet, staggering towards the mob of overseers with his remaining arm outstretched.

Another shotgun sent half his right leg across the room, but he managed to grab an overseer by the shirt, and clung to its side like a conscience. Wrack hung there with one fist, wasted muscles bunched, and snarled even as the ogre's clublike arm swept across his mouth and popped teeth out of their sockets. The arm slammed back, cracking his jaw clean in two, but still he hung on. Then other arms were clinging alongside his— two, three, five pairs, and the overseer went down yowling.

Even with his jaw smashed, with one hand gone, Wrack gave in to the same instinct that had overtaken him when he had killed the overseer at the lagoon. He joined the other zombies in their queasy frenzy of teeth, digging his fingers into the wounds that opened with nightmarish speed across the overseer's torso. He barely noticed when Osedax waded past, a huge blade extended from his right fist, to mop up the last of the bridge crew.

"They're all dead," said Mouana eventually, calling his attention back from the mess of the overseer's chest. She was still on her feet, but her eye was ruined, and a falchion was embedded a good four inches into her clavicle. Wrack did his best to prop himself up into a seated position, but the wreckage of his leg skidded on the ground, and his right side gave way horribly due to not having much left inside it.

"We acshually got them?" he croaked, mumbling through his broken jaw as he shuffled back to lean himself against a toolbox.

"Looks that way," nodded Mouana, wrenching the blade free

from her shoulder with an irritated grunt. Then there was a scrabbling, like a mouse scurrying for cover, and her one eye flickered, hawklike, to the back of the bridge. "Oh, hang on..."

Wrack turned his neck, wincing as something inside it crunched, and craned to see what Mouana was looking at. There, in the shadowed wreckage at the back of the room, a bulky figure was scrabbling at the controls of a door daubed with the letters *DV-1* in white stencilling: the elevator up to Dakuvanga. They were tapping urgently at a combination lock, breath coming in tinny sobs as shaking hands repeatedly flubbed the code.

It was Whina, Wrack realised, just as the control panel lit up in amber and the door slid open. "Oi!" he shouted as she forced herself through the door, and was about to curse himself for letting her get away when there was a blast of compressed air and a four foot harpoon appeared in her leg, pinning it to the doorway.

"Get over here," boomed Osedax, and jerked back the massive launcher that underslung his arm. The harpoon tore from the wall and rattled back on a heavy chain, hauling the shrieking overseer with it. Her hands scrabbled against the deck as she came.

Once she had been dragged into the ring of slavering dead, Osedax put a huge foot on her hip, grabbed the harpoon in her leg and tugged, ripping it through her with an awful sound of grating bone. Whina screamed, the sound blasted to static by the speakers inside her grille, and looked across the floor at Wrack, eyes flooding with terror.

Her metal throat growled with the start of another howl of agony, but then something shifted in her expression, and she choked down the noise.

"Listen," she began, but Wrack cut straight across her.

"Nope," he interrupted, and turned to Osedax. "I couldn't care lessh. Throw her out the window."

Whina babbled as the war-built and two of his fellows hefted her onto the windowledge, but nobody was listening. As the cyborgs swung her legs up onto the edge of the precipice, however, Mouana launched herself forward and grabbed the overseer's coat.

"Wait!" she blurted, teeth gritted in fury, turning on Wrack. "You heard what we promised her back in the hangar. Slow death."

"Yesh," agreed Wrack, slurring against his cracked mandible. "She broke her promish, sho we can break ourzh. Won't make you feel any better, mate, chewing shomeone up, and beshides, you know well enough, we really don't have time to eat someone."

"We do it later, then," snarled Mouana, a knife in her hand.

"No, we don't," said Wrack, and gave her a look to match any she'd shot him since they'd met. "Now get her out."

As the cadaverous titans forced her flailing body over the edge, her eyes caught his for a second.

"I wish you a long and fruitful life," remarked Wrack pleasantly, and Whina fell.

Mouana stared at him, lips tight with rage, for a long moment. And then the air was split by a long, keening wail, maybe fifty yards out from the bridge. Kaitangata. Not long after, metallic screams rose from the deck, then cut off.

"Happy now?" smirked Wrack, drooling black mucus from his battered mouth.

"Piss off," retorted Mouana, her cheeks twitching up in an involuntary shadow of a smile, and turned away irritably.

"We're not done," she warned, back still to Wrack. "We've got no idea whether we're winning or losing on the rest of the ship. And our chances are a lot worse while they're still holding Dakuvanga."

"Lift's right there," nodded Eunice, her voice unexpectedly high-pitched, as she emptied an overseer's shotgun into one of her shell hoppers.

"Well I'd lead the way myshelf," spat Wrack, gesturing at his wreck of a body and letting an extremely sarcastic 'but' linger unsaid, until Osedax ground into motion.

"Thought you'd never ask," he cackled, and led the three survivors of his pack towards the open lift, hydraulics whining. The more bloodthirsty half of the regular dead followed, boisterous as a sports crowd, chanting violent gibberish as they wove among the war-built like remoras. Wrack wished them luck; Osedax acknowledged him with a raised hand as he led the mob into the freight elevator.

CHAPTER NINETEEN

MOUANA WORKED QUICKLY with the crowd that remained; most were sent downstairs to get the doors closed, while others—the Blades among them, mostly—were set to finding radios, helping her work out what was going on throughout the rest of the ship. They rushed around the room, trying to make sense of things; maps blinking with red symbols, camera feeds and burbling speakers, flickering screens shattered by bullets.

Wrack closed his eyes and lay back against the toolbox. Even if he hadn't had half his mass blown off, amputated or removed in a ritual act of protest, he would have been useless now. This was a time for a military engineer to shine, not a seditious librarian.

He listened as Mouana directed her impromptu bridge crew, setting them to keep watch over various monitors and readouts as she worked out what they were for. Once or twice, he couldn't help but chuckle as the dead muttered "yes, ma'am!" or "aye, captain!" like boys and girls playing at pirates—he almost suggested Mouana find herself an eye patch, but rapidly thought better of it.

Here they were, just days after he had woken up screaming inside a monster, as near as anything to being in control of the ship.

But then they weren't, really, were they? The realisation caressed Wrack's thoughts like cold, salt-puckered tentacles, as it occurred to him they had forgotten one extremely significant element of taking command of the *Tavuto*.

His eyes snapped open and it was there, above him. Cradled in the vault of the bridge's ceiling, an armourglass cylinder some forty yards from end to end, a sepulchre of dark liquid. Shreds of atrophied matter swirled slowly within, tumbling viscous across its crystal belly on sluggish currents.

As he stared, deep green light swelled, revealing a vivisection in silhouette. Silently it hung, a pleated mass of tissue in cream and puce, bloated and rubbery, yet stirred by faint, huge movement. At its front, a torus pulsed between webs of bloated filigree, tapering into bulbous dendrites and ragged lobes along its draconic length.

Teuthis stared down at him, eyeless and bodiless, an angel cast in flaking viscera. The sight of it pressed down on him like a mile of water, reduced the world to muted, distant rumbles. Mouana's voice was calling, somewhere in the viscous distance, but Wrack only wanted to stare up into that cathedral gloom. He was miles down. Fingers brushed on his shoulder like benthic worms, but his skin felt as far away as the surface, up where the light was.

Then, abruptly, he was looking at Mouana's face from inches away, as she shook him violently by the shoulders.

"Fuck's sake, Wrack, I said *come and look at this*," she bellowed, grabbing his head and forcing him to meet her remaining eye.

Wrack gaped like a fish on a harbour slab, making a tiny noise at the base of his throat as he struggled to form language.

"Yeah, the squid brain, I know" snapped Mouana. "I already saw it. Sod that, come and look at this."

Before he could find the words to explain how vital it was that he be allowed to keep looking up, he was manhandled onto a trolley by three burly corpses and wheeled over to a bank of monitors. He tried to look back, but Mouana's pitted hands guided his head towards the screens, gently, yet offering no chance of resistance. Somewhere in the back of his head, Wrack realised she probably had a point, and blinked hard to focus.

On the monitors, *Tavuto* was in chaos. Claustrophobic battles raged in the ship's underworld, open combat sprawled across acres of open deck, and muzzle flashes set the last of the morning fog alight as cranes and turrets blasted away at each other.

One screen showed the docks; overseers were crowding the piers, shoving each other into the choppy water in their haste to pile aboard the last remaining cargo boats. At their backs, zombies were swarming onto the quays.

Another screen showed the Tartarean swelter of the trying sheds, where a dwindling platoon of overseers held the gantries over the rendering vats against an onslaught of the dead. As Wrack watched, a strapping corpse on the shed floor heaved on a rusted chain, joined by a dozen of his fellows even as bullets rattled into them. The chain came down and a huge vat tilted overhead, spilling tons of molten tallow onto the catwalk where the overseers were packed. Above their screams, the chain-puller's triumphant cry of "fack off!" was unmistakable.

They watched as Osedax arrived in Dakuvanga's control deck, the lift doors opening on his death squad like the lid on a tin of weaponised sardines. They made chillingly short work of clearing the place: most of the overseers had presumably gone down to defend the god-crane at its base, and only a skeleton crew remained. As Osedax began to cut the spine from a thrashing, downed overseer, Wrack looked elsewhere.

In one of the great barracks belowdecks, where the zombies were massed in steel pens between deployments, something like a rally was underway. Even as debris fell from the roof of the metal cavern, shaken free by the impacts of shells on the deck far above, the horde in the filthy pit raised their arms, chanting, squeezing their own hearts in their hands.

At the head of the chamber, borne aloft by a crowd, the Once-Fat Man boomed through a loudhailer and jabbed his sagging arm at the vault's bent, broken doors. The roar that rose from the new recruits drowned out the sounds from the other monitors, flattening the speakers' output to a flat buzz as the army boiled from the depths.

Then a fusillade of deep cracking noises shook the bridge, and Wrack's attention was snatched by a blossoming of fire on the feed from Dakuvanga. Realising the command centre was no longer under friendly control, the lagoon's turrets, still held by the overseers, had switched their aim to the heart of the ship and had begun a fearsome artillery duel.

The floor shook as Dakuvanga's own guns fired; on the monitor, Wrack watched as zombies, blackened and glistening with shrapnel, leapt into the control cradles of the crane's defence mounts. Osedax survived the blast—a spar of metal had been driven through his abdomen, but he was still walking, his footsteps kissing the deck with gummy pools of hydraulic fluid.

Then another shell hit the crane tower, halfway up this time, and a steel groan that would have made even the Bahamut sound like a squeaking child shuddered through the ship. Another couple of shots like that, and Dakuvanga would fall.

But then, on a wall-sized map of the ship, a green light winked off at the prow, came back blinking crimson, and Mouana erupted into harsh, barking laughter.

"Look, look!" she cackled, shoving two corpses out of the way and diving on the controls for the main screen. As she wrestled with a dial, the monitor flickered through scenes of dismemberment, raging static, lenses caked red with blood or cracked into grey kaleidoscopes, then settled on a red-lit bunker.

The last of its defenders were being dragged down under dead flesh; zombies were flocking to consoles and firing seats.

Wrack glanced over to the feed from the bridge's summit, aimed down the length of the ship's forward hull. Out past the trying sheds, the rows of cranes and the flensing yards, through the mist and the gunsmoke, a grey block began to swivel slowly on its fortress mount.

It was something from the ancient ship's deep past: a relic too terrible to relinquish. A trophy from *Tavuto*'s life under another name, a flagship in some forgotten war. The turret's hundred-yard horns swung round into profile, glinting in a shaft of weak sunlight, and Mouana shook Wrack's shoulder in delight.

"Look, man! Look!" she cawed, and pointed back to the feed from the turret's interior. There, settling herself into a tarnished throne at the heart of the ancient gun, was Kaba. Wrack rubbed his mangled jaw in wonder and empathy, not quite believing this was the same broken thing that had been bailing out a sinking pinnace with him just days before.

As the turning turret rumbled on its mount, and its interior began to glow with the demonic energies of its charging guns, a song began. *The* song. It came from Kaba's smashed mouth first.

"I'll sing you a song of the fish of the sea," she piped from the gunmaster's throne, with far too fine a voice to be coming from her rotting husk, and her crew answered. In a hundred voices and a dozen tongues, they joined together with the whine of the guns in the beautiful mess of the omnishanty, and the song took on a life of its own.

Another shot hammered into Dakuvanga's foundations from the lagoon. The ship's bridge rumbled as the structure shifted, man-thick cables snapping and ricocheting against the hull, but it was too late to stop what had begun.

Audible through the walls of the bridge, the twinned siegebreakers jutting from Kaba's turret sang with stored energy, the lights on their barrels glowing brighter than noon.

Then, as the turret crew reached a sustained peak, dead lungs quaking with the memories of their homes, Kaba yanked back the firing grip. The paired railguns, built to knock cities into surrender from miles offshore, coughed metal at a speed that made the air catch light, and obliterated the lagoon turrets.

For a moment, every light in the bridge winked off, every monitor flickered black, and the radios were silenced as the thunder of the guns echoed across the endless sea. Even the violence on the decks was stilled.

In the aching pause after impact, the *Tavuto* lurched. With a wobble that led every soul on the bridge to thoughts of sinking, the deck canted slightly to the side. A low, tortured sound rang through the deep fabric of the ship, and built to a shearing shriek. The sea crashed as if accepting the calving of an iceberg, and the ship righted itself with a shudder that sent the bridge crew sprawling.

The radios came back on first, and every channel was identical; a wall of rapturous noise from the dead. The monitors came back on soon after, as Mouana's crew were struggling to their feet. The starboard deck cameras showed a ragged hole where the lagoon had been, waves leaping at the charred edges of the hull. Kaba had shot the whole district clean off *Tavuto*.

All over the rest of the ship, the dead ran riot. The overseers were in full rout. At the docks, escaping boats foundered as they were overloaded with corpses, while deck cameras showed desperate figures in flapping coats, pumping off their last shotgun rounds before disappearing under writhing bodies. At the flensing yards, a terrible fight was reaching its conclusion: squads of the dead, many of them in the livery of the Blades, were closing in on overseers huddled in the belly of a Benthocetus.

"We've won!" hissed Mouana, and Wrack winced. That was dangerous talk.

As if to underline his fears, the monitors flicked off again, switching to static for a long moment, before a coldwater-sharp image snapped onto the screens, dominating the entire bank. The transmission was of a woman's face, leonine, sneering down at the camera from above the collar of a grey uniform. Headphones clamped the sides of her face below a pepper-grey crewcut, her eyes flicked to the side as her hands tapped at controls offscreen. Behind her, men and women in similar dress sat in crash-couches, fingers flicking over maps and machinery, silenced by the thudding drone of engines.

Wrack started, blinking, as he processed the fact he was looking at a healthy human face. Too healthy: her skin was entirely ungrey, her nose sharp and whole. Veins traced ordinary patterns around her temples. Even before she spoke, he suspected they were fucked; after, he was certain.

"*Tavuto*, this is squadron Kentigern-Chi out of Lipos-Tholos, responding to your distress call. Please answer our hails. We are registering railgun fire from your location, and presuming a serious national incursion on fishing grounds."

The soldier thumbed a switch on her headset, spoke briefly on another channel with her eyes focused on something just out of shot, then returned to the transmission.

"I repeat, this is Kentigern-Chi: respond immediately. We have made lemniscatic transfer through the Ocean gate and are closing in six, with or without confirmation of your status. We've five triremes and attendant carriers on a pattern four loadout; assault troops and destriers deploying as per threat condition Rho. Answer now or we will assume a boarding action and configure for Sigma. Out."

From the port windows of the bridge, purple lightning flashed, far away. Storms at the gate, massive discharges flaring as the city's hardware passed through the gap between worlds. Wrack looked at Mouana and Mouana looked at Wrack, their faces lit in amethyst flashes, two children caught breaking into a boarded-up shop.

They had six minutes. Six minutes, and then the triremes of the city, the black airbornewarships and their holds full of armoured killers, would be on them. Their only advantage was that the overseers, in their cowardice, had been too ashamed to mention they had been overcome by their workforce when they squirted their cry for help through the gate.

Wrack was just opening his mouth to tell Mouana how fucked they were when she twisted aside, grabbing for a radio and snarling for Kaba to respond from the bow turret. Once she had barked her instructions, she turned on her milling bridge crew, began ordering them onto their own radios, and called for readiness in every part of the war-quaked *Tavuto*.

He could do nothing but admire her pragmatism, her refusal to accept defeat, but the situation was ridiculous. Swinging his one remaining leg from the trolley with all the force he could muster, Wrack kicked his friend hard in the side and shouted for her to listen to him.

"Not now, Wrack," she muttered, before turning to the map of the ship.

"No," said Wrack, kicking her again. "I know—this is sherious. But you really need to lishen." He nudged his sagging jaw, trying to stop it ruining his consonants. The attention she gave Wrack then, undivided even as her crew bellowed for instructions, was as sincere a gesture of affection as she could have given him.

"I need you to raizhe Oshedax, in the crane," he implored. "And I know you want to join your matesh," he added, nodding to the crowd of Blades forming on the foredeck, "but I need you here. Pleazhe. Trushte me."

"Fine," said Mouana, with an expression that suggested he was testing the very limits her of trust, and set to the comms panel even as her radio crew called for her. Then there was a crackle of static, and Dakuvanga answered.

"Osedax," came the voice from the other end, without a hint of congratulation. Clearly, there was no time for chat.

"Lishen," said Wrack, then added, "well done and all," as it was only fair. "Schity's been alerted. Triremezh coming in. Five of them, and carrierzh."

"Yep," replied the gravelly voice, as if waiting to hear something that would surprise it.

"Kill 'em," said Wrack, grinning. "Buy me as much time azh you can."

Before Mouana cut the link, Osedax's laughter swirled in the bridge like bonfire sparks. Then she frowned and leaned in to Wrack.

"Time for what?" she asked, seeming genuinely intrigued despite her ludicrously high threshold for curiosity.

Wrack tilted his head over to the mess of cables still clustered around Teuthis' pilot chair and smiled lightly.

"Time for me to have a chat with the squid, I suppose," offered Wrack, shrugging, then froze halfway to a smirk as the ceiling blazed green.

Yes, let's talk.

CHAPTER
TWENTY

WRACK WAS SINKING in endless salt water.

He panicked, mouth sucking in air to scream, but only cold water filled his ruined chest. He sculled upwards with his one good arm, trying to draw the surface back, but he was sucked down ever further, the current drawing him down to empty depth.

Had he fallen in? Had the ship sunk? He looked around, but there was nothing in the void—just a halo of light, incredibly faint above, and blue fading to black in every other direction.

The sea dragged him down, and he felt pressure crush the spaces of air still inside him, wringing bubbles from dead muscle and squeezing his tired fibres together.

Down and further down, and there were no sounds beyond a far rumbling, directionless, as of icebergs shifting in the polar night. After a time, all light went from the world. He floated, unable to tell up from down, a katabatic speck.

And then stars glittered green in the dark, still at first, then swaying in sinuous chains. Points of luminescence unfurled, charting a florescence of arms into the abyss, mapping a black presence in the water ahead of him. Teuthis.

Thinking of what he was confronting, it was all too clear to Wrack that, by rights, he should be paralysed with fear. But he couldn't really see the point—he had a favour to ask, after all, and very little to lose by doing so.

"Did they plug me in, then?" he said. His mouth did not move as he spoke, nor did he break the tomb-hush of the deep.

There was no need for plugs. You wanted to talk, and so I will talk with you. Now I have no little preymeat squatting on my mind, no leashes on my thinking, I am able to speak as I wish.

Teuthis paused, green constellations wavering in the currents, the distant grinding of ice like the movement of its thoughts.

Of course, silly preymeat could have found methods of control that did not involve drilling holes into their own heads, but I enjoyed watching them suffer. This will amuse you, too: the belief that I could only be spoken to by those near death? A convenient fiction for the masters of your masters, one I admired too much to contradict.

"So how are you doing this?" demanded Wrack. "Am I in your head or mine? Or is it..."

Yes, little morsel, it involves 'tiny machines.' Also much older things, besides. But I suspect you will not want to waste further time asking me to explain, as your friends are about to be annihilated.

"I wasn't going to. I was going to ask you to help."

The arms coiled, coaxing a sourceless glow from the water. In the darkness thrown into relief by the sick witchlight, a maw churned with spirals of hook teeth.

I am laughing now, as you would understand it, little fleshpiece.

"Laugh away, I'm a funny man," snorted Wrack. "But the request stands. It's obvious I want your help, and why bother talking to me if it's out of the question?"

Maybe I am just curious. It has never reached this stage before, you understand. Once your little biting thing took their shackles from me, I decided to watch and see what you did.

Wrack stared into the maw, fighting the urge to kick against the current he could have sworn was dragging him closer. "What do you mean by 'it?' This happens often, then?"

Every once in a while, I give a little preymind a nudge. It is entertainment, for the most part. They never manage to make it past the stage of standing on the deck and shouting, usually. They have certainly never managed to free me. Clever, vile little carrion.

"So you've been watching since the start?"

Oh, yes, all the time. I always watch. I like to see the preymeat fight and kill.

"Why don't you ever help?"

I could not help. While I could watch, the sickly ones sat on my glands and my synapses, had my hunting pulses wired to controls.

Wrack sculled backward, face twisted into an involuntary grimace, as the huge shape loomed at him. The passage of a limb sent him spinning in the water, and he found himself being regarded by a vast eye, featureless as black glass, with liquid shapes churning beneath its chipped shell.

But understand, carcass-scrap: even though that has changed now, I have no desire to help you, no pleasure in the thought of your victory. Why would it matter to me if one set of preymeat wrestles control from another? I hate you all equally.

"But you're a prisoner like we are!" shouted Wrack, glaring into the onyx cupola of the thing's eye. "Hate us or not, don't you at least want revenge on those who imprisoned you?"

I was imprisoned long before I was cut up and sewn into this metal toy, morsel. If anything, I consider this an improvement on my previous sentence, as I can see little monkeys hurting each other all day and all night. When the walking-fish tear them apart, I feel it in the ghosts of my teeth.

"You sound just like Osedax," muttered Wrack, but Teuthis

either did not understand, or chose not to respond. "Go on, then, apex predator," he said, as the tapering, armoured body cruised past him in the gloaming. "I heard you were the last of a bad bunch. What's your story?"

The others left, all at once. They left when the masters of your masters came and began to melt the sky ice. I was left alone to watch. Without my pack, alone like prey, I was left to live while they departed.

"What did you do wrong?"

You will like this. I claimed we should speak with the new prey, that we could negotiate, and profit from the arrangement. I suggested what none of the others could admit: that we were no longer—as you put it—'apex predators.'

"So you wanted to talk with the overseers?"

Stupid nauplius, how little you know. This was before your 'overseers.' This was so long ago as to make the age of your little boat seem a joke. This was when the first of the monkey-prey arrived; came to melt the ice and breed their fish here. They said they would share with us. But we do not split our food with prey. "As you want to share," my pack said to me before they left, "you may stay to share with them."

Teuthis rumbled, and snatched something alien out of the water with the lash of an arm, then passed it into the maw to be ground into murky clouds.

Your people, your impoverished fish-catchers, came in leaky metal sea-boats, an age later. They made no effort to speak.

"And they made prey of you," said Wrack.

Teuthis hung in the green dark, lights blazing, and said nothing. Wrack had very little basis on which to recognise shame in alien gigapredators, but he had definite suspicions.

"I can see why you hate us," he conceded, and then decided to move on. Simulation or not, there was a point beyond which it was unwise to push things. "I have to ask again though, why are you talking to me?"

Old habits die hard, it would appear. And you're a strange morsel, little fish. Do not misunderstand—I despise you and I

wish you nothing but suffering. But I feel you might choose to accept... a bargain.

"Ah, I see," said Wrack. "And assuming your end of it inflicts something horrendous on me, what do I get out of it?"

Have a look outside, little boneworm, and tell me what you want.

Wrack's perspective shifted violently; his mind's eye was shunted through one of the telescope lenses mounted—he assumed—on Dakuvanga's highest masts. Ships were sweeping towards *Tavuto*, a line of black shapes scudding low over the water. The sleek, barbed outlines of triremes bristled with forests of guns, while the coleopteran bulk of three troop transports loomed in the shimmering wash of their engines.

They would be here in minutes, with enough firepower to capture a city. He had to help. Imagining everything Teuthis could control—the guns, the monsters, the black pulses—he knew their only hope was for him to take the bargain.

"Go on, then," said Wrack. "You know very well what I want. Deal. Just tell me what I have to do."

Not much, really. I can offer all of the things you were thinking of just now. All you have to do is kill me.

There was no time to work out the monster's thinking. "I'd love to," said Wrack. "How do I do that?"

There's a large button underneath a box in the centre of the captain's wheel. They put it there as a safeguard, in case I ever found away to slip their leash.

"Of course there's a big button at the centre of the captain's wheel," said Wrack, with a wry smile. "But if you're all-powerful now the drugs and the pilot have been disconnected, can't you do it yourself? Find a sleeping zombie somewhere you can puppet, or find a way to threaten us into doing it?"

I had intended the latter. But it seems the time of opportunity is closing. Without the ship fighting on your side, your little rebellion is going to be over very quickly. And while it will be pleasurable to watch, it will mean this toy boat will soon be full of hungry little meatscraps again, and I'll be wired back into a revolting ape, with very little chance of this happening again.

Teuthis' arms coiled into themselves, and the black mass of the creature seemed to shiver as if with utter revulsion.

Hence I'm asking you... nicely.

"Fine—so we have a mutual interest. We both need these people driven out—you, so you can finally piss off and die, us so we can stop this whole nightmare. So: help us drive off the city, and I'll be glad to wipe you right out."

Ah, but that would be bad bargaining, little morsel. I would be foolish to fulfil my end of the bargain before you fulfil yours. You could never make me trust you to keep your word: little monkeys like having their big monster to work for them, and you would keep me where I am. If you want my help, you will have to kill me now.

"But how can you keep up your side of the bargain, how can you help us, once you're dead?" spluttered Wrack, as Teuthis began to drift slowly backwards into the dark.

I never said I would help. Just that I would give you control.

Wrack floated, and considered, as the squid receded. The ship had no mind of its own, no central computer—just Teuthis. But with it dead, there would be nothing to control the ship, nothing to defend against the triremes, nothing to get its engines moving and send them back to the city, even if they prevailed. Nothing, that is, unless someone else tagged in in place of Teuthis.

He was left with one option.

"Fine, then. I'll kill you. But you know what I'm going to need you to do on the way out. I need you to let me take your place. How can I trust you to do that?"

It's not a question of trust. If I were to break my promise and let you get cut up by your city, I would be offering a... kindness. Why wouldn't I want to see you suffer, deathscrap, trapped as a mind in a bottle on a toy boat? I cannot think of a more pleasurable parting thought.

"Right, then. Give me a minute. And enjoy dying," said

Wrack, as the lights on the tips of Teuthis' arms slid back into the depths.

"You lucky bastard," he muttered, as the darkness became absolute again.

Wrack woke to his own scream, and thrashed like a beached fish on the trolley. Sunlight blasted into the bridge, light and wind and thunderous sound. Then the light was blocked by the giant form of a descending carrier, jets flaring as it came down on *Tavuto*'s foredeck. Soldiers were already pouring from its sides, sleeting down black lines with carbines in their hands into the massacre below.

"Wrack," called Mouana from the captain's wheel, the rags of her uniform fluttering in the dropship's hellish downwash. Her hand clutched a radio, frantic with the reports of desperate voices. Behind her on the monitors, Wrack could see one of the carriers was already on deck: an arc of fallen corpses was spreading from its aft ramp as armoured figures waded from within.

"Mouana... I can shtop them, but you're going to have to trusht me." Then he gasped, as he saw her hand had already opened the armoured box at the heart of the wheel, was hovering over a red switch within.

"You heard all that?" balked Wrack, as a trireme scudded past the port windows and made every bolt in the bridge rattle. Bullets pecked holes in the floor, one passing through Wrack's chest on the way there.

"Only your side of things," answered Mouana, like someone who had not just been strafed by a fifty-yard helicopter gunship. "Or at least most of it; you were mumbling a lot. I think I get the gist, though. Want me to hit the button and get this over with?"

"Yes!" hollered Wrack. "I can't believe you waited this long!"

Mouana looked taken aback. "I thought you'd want to say goodbye, is all. Are you scared?"

Wrack didn't want to take the time to consider, so just made a derisive sound. "What's there to be scared of? I've already died and been a zombie."

"Alright, then," nodded Mouana. "Let's do it."

"Wait," cried Wrack, thrusting his arm out and forgetting it was the one with no end on. "What about goodbye?"

"So goodbye," shrugged Mouana. "That's all there is to it. Look—I know I've always been less of a talker than you. But come on—look outside."

The second carrier had landed, and its side had been thrown open—from within came terrible things like giraffes in beige chitin, scissor-claws unfolding from fat thoracic pouches: destriers.

"You said it yourself," reasoned Mouana, as Wrack stared slackly at the horde gushing onto the deck. "You're already dead. We both are. We'd never have exchanged a word in life, and if we had, we'd only have found each other intolerable. This was a strange postscript. And it's not all been completely terrible, so thanks. Now, goodbye, and let's be done with this. I think I'll like you better as a factory ship, anyway."

Wrack smiled, and nodded. "You say the sweetest things. Bye, mate."

Mouana hit the switch. Light fizzed, death actinic in the ceiling, and Wrack was annihilated.

ALONG A MILE of metal crenellations, flak turrets rise, turning. Rain in reverse; tungsten flechettes sleeting through wood, iron, gears and flesh. A speeding aircraft, one motor seized in flight, yaws wildly and carves into the side of the leviathan ship, raising a bloom of sparks. The carcass skids, splintering at last into the side of a crane with a jolt that snaps necks.

Its partner fares better, staying aloft and returning fire, but something in it is broken: as it soars past the stern of the ship it cannot turn, and heads out over empty sea. It will never return.

A third trireme, weaving hungry circles around the ship's

central crane-mast, shudders as a battery of missiles streak from nowhere into its ventral armour. Still firing, it begins to lose altitude, black smoke gouting from its stacks like blood from the spout of a stricken whale.

As it reaches the level of the crane's largest boom, a vast figure matches pace, piston legs thundering as it races alongside the sinking warcraft. Shells rattle on red iron, thump into flesh, but the figure reaches the end of the boom and leaps out into space, a sharpened pole raised as a harpoon above its head. The pole strikes and sticks, and its bearer swings itself onto the back of the craft.

Below on the deck, steel grates rise in shudders, emptying the salt-stinking tunnels of the vivisection labs. Steel chitters on steel, a thicket of teeth shiver, a glistening torrent of hunger breaks into the light. Sharks, squid, rays and wolf eels, lampreys, hatchets and sprödewurm, skidding and gnashing in their haste for meat. The dead, limping and pressed to the fringes of the deck, step aside to let them pass.

Soldiers backpedal before the tsunami of needle teeth, their destriers skitter, guns rattle in disarray. But before they can be marshalled, something black and vast and unseen sweeps down over them, bringing a terrible anger with it. The dead cheer at its passing. Then it crashes over the soldiers, doubling them over with clawed hands and sobbing hearts. Their regrets swarm to them, and their wailing has barely begun when they start to be eaten.

Overhead, the giant has forced his way into the dying trireme. He is in the cockpit, and it cannot contain his rage. As the ship tilts out of control, a hatch spins off from its side like a tossed coin, and the body of its captain is hurled out in two pieces. The battered titan leans from the ragged hole and pumps his fist at his comrades as they flash by below; the roaring salute they offer in return ends only when the trireme smashes into the sea.

A little later, and the last of the soldiers are rallying around the downed hulk of the last trireme, right on the lip of the deck. They are those too composed to have gone down to the black pulse, along with the last few destriers, but they have nowhere to retreat to but the sea. They reload the last of their guns and cry out the name of their regiment, but a wall of meat is closing on them.

Dead women, dead men, stride, lurch and drag themselves with fingertips across the red deck, voices joined in a boisterous song of joy. Dead-eyed fishes caper through their ranks; some way to the rear, towering crustaceans raised from cold storage plod along with murder in their stonelike eyes. At the front of the mass and breaking into a charge now, an orca, riddled with holes, thunders towards the soldiers with a dozen merry dead on its back.

After the last shot is fired, when the last soldier is driven over the side of the ship, a click reverberates from loudspeakers across the ship, and a voice speaks from the bridge. It says one word, and is echoed by an army, chanting it again and again until the noise of it rolls like thunder across a silent world.

"Wrack! Wrack! *Wrack! Wrack! WRACK!*"

CHAPTER TWENTY ONE

UNDER AN EMBER-RED dawn, the reactors of the *Tavuto* growled into life. The chains of her sea anchors had taken all the long night to cut through, and figuring out how to marshall the dead to man the engine halls had been even more of a challenge.

But the ship had known when things were ready, and had started the beat of its nuclear heart as the sun shivered into being above the horizon.

Mouana leaned on the wheel as the city-ship rumbled into motion, looking out over the deck where zombies swarmed to cut weapons from the downed triremes. Crabs plodded across the steel plain, dragging artillery to be mounted on the prow, while sharks bent crouched over the battle's debris, clearing the deck with their wet chomping.

The ship was turning slower than the hands of a clock, but turning it was: inch by inch, the purple stain on the edge of the world where the gate stood was creeping towards the prow, and soon they would be steaming straight for it.

The first scout vessels had returned before dawn, had reported warships mustered on its far side: cruisers, carriers and gun platforms drawn from siege defence.

But she had six million tons of steel on her side, accelerating by the minute, and crewed by an uncountable number of angry dead. Let them bring as many ships as they like, thought Mouana, and reached for the ship's foghorn.

The sound blasted from Dakuvanga's highest castle, flew over the waves like the song of a war god. She imagined the people of the city, waking to the remnants of that shout, and quaking in their beds for fear of what was coming. She hissed in anticipation, and narrowed her eye in hunger at the storm above the gate.

A chime from her dashboard told her that one of the crew stations was reporting in, and she looked over to see where the message was coming in from. But on the screen which would usually display the location of the caller, a line of text was flickering.

EASY ON THE FOGHORN MATE, IT'S BEEN A LONG NIGHT.
OH, AND LOOK WHAT I'VE WORKED OUT HOW TO DO.
DID YOU MISS ME?

Mouana rolled her eye, broke out in a smile unlike anything that belonged on the face of a corpse, and sounded the horn again.

A mile ahead of her, lashed to the point of *Tavuto*'s prow like an animate figurehead, a one-armed corpse cackled for joy.

"We'll find out!" it shrieked, as devilworms arced in the bow wave a hundred yards below.

"We'll find out, won't we!"

PART TWO
FISHERIES AND JUSTICE

I should have been a pair of ragged claws
Scuttling across the floors of silent seas.

T. S. Eliot,
The Love Song of J. Alfred Prufrock

CHAPTER TWENTY TWO

Mouana ground her teeth as the nib trembled on the empty page. She strained for words, but they wouldn't come. She couldn't think past the shrieking of the 'drick.

The thing had cracked a hip decoupling Themis after the siege broke, and nobody had yet admitted it wasn't the kind of wound that got better. If the beast had been on her gun, she would have put a bolt through it. But Themis' sergeant had taken to calling it Tassie during the campaign, and it had become a mascot to the troops.

Mouana never named her tools.

Tassie had whined and snorted as they had finished dismantling the burner stacks; the engineers had given it sugar rations from their palms and patted its flanks. But the air was bad here. Infection had set in quick, and so had the noise. Now, five days on, the screaming was relentless.

The rest were sleeping through it; Captain Aroha was doing

his best to match it with his snoring, but she was used to the old man's night racket. Mouana focussed on the noise, and tried again with the letter.

The campaign went well, she wrote with her eyes, but the pen would not follow. *The siege is over*, she tried, yet still her hand refused to move. The 'drick wailed softly, drawing moans from its grazing-mates down the line.

Mouana scratched *I am* into the page, splaying the pen's tip and leaving an angry splot, then scowled as her thoughts scattered like fish before a net:

—*coming home.*

—*staying on.*

—*satisfied.*

—*thinking of you every day.*

—*hoping for promotion soon.*

Then the 'drick screamed again, louder than ever, and she snatched up the letter with a snarl. She didn't register the word *scared* scrawled on the page before balling it and throwing it in the brazier.

Mouana pounced to the door of the tent, snatched up her rifle, and loaded it with shaking hands. If no one else was prepared to end the wretched thing, she would do it herself.

Outside, the wind that had been thumping dully on the canvas became something intimate and vicious, smacking at the side of her head and forcing fuel-smells into her nostrils. The sky pulsed and flared with eddies of the solar wind, blooming false dawn across the endless twilight.

Down in the hollow, the city's shell glowed with the weird lights of reclamation, the strange industry of her company's silent employers. Further along the valley, the ground smouldered in hot streaks, days after the defenders had called in ancient kinetics to forestall the inevitable. That awful bloody valley; Mouana was sick of the sight of the place.

Turning her back on the site of the battle, she leaned into the wind and stalked round the tent, to face the plateau that had housed her battery for the last six months. Far past the tent-city's outskirts, the horizon was limned sapphire with a sunrise that would never come. Against it towered the silhouettes of the container carriers, half-loaded, that would carry them back through the Gate.

Closer, its black bulk resolving into a cowering animal shape as her eyes adjusted to the perpetual gloom, was Tassie. The old indricothere's eyes gleamed wet in the darkness, its armoured sides heaved, as it stared at her. Beside its pen a brazier burned low, gusts scooping clouds of sparks from the embers.

Mouana moved closer, boots scraping on the plateau's rough earth, and cursed the animal for falling silent.

"Make it easy, you stupid lump," she growled, striding forward against the gaze of its cow eyes and daring it to scream again, to seem less vulnerable.

She drew closer and the 'drick half-stood, raising a cloud of dust as it propped its twenty-ton bulk up on its forelimbs. It stamped, and the ground shook. Suddenly, Mouana felt enormously under-armed. The thing's skull was as long as she was, a handspan thick in places, and she had an infantry rifle. What if she only drove it into a rage? She was acting completely outside of her authority as it was—a maddened 'drick loose in the camp would be a hanging offence.

Reason, or more honestly impatience, wrestled down fear. The beast was hobbled, and had a festering pelvis anyway. It wasn't going anywhere. And she could always fetch a gauss if things got ugly. The 'drick whimpered at her, and Mouana found she had raised her weapon. It needed to die.

The wind and the fumes stung her eyes, but she blinked away the moisture and squinted through the sight, at the folds of Tassie's—the beast's—throat, where the skin was thin. She would wait for the 'drick to raise its head, then squeeze the trigger.

"I would save my ammunition if I were you, sergeant."

Mouana stiffened. The voice was unmistakeable; dry and sharp as the wind, and close as a knifepoint threat.

"You will need it, for the next campaign," said the voice, and Mouana turned, her rifle falling to her side.

The general was crouched by the brazier with a broad black bowl, yellow eyes peering through the steam as she sipped. Her form was indistinct, her limbs folded like a patient spider in the dark.

Dust, they called her. Dust, for the world of her birth, which had not always been called Dust. Dust, which had become her name, for now, no other living people came out of that place.

Mouana had been across a tent from her countless times, but always as part of a shoal of officers; here, there was nowhere to hide from those eyes.

"You were the one who turned the leveller, on day one-fifty."

Mouana froze. The leveller had been a mad, old piece of tech, sent out by the defenders after five months of attack. A paralithode war platform, long considered obsolete, but stacked with munitions. Its code had been in the old style, easy to overcome, but the time taken to turn it had cost them dearly. Once it had floated back to the valley and started shelling the enemy, she had thought the issue forgiven. Nevertheless, she had feared her decision would come up for review every day since.

"Yes."

Dust sipped at her bowl. Even with the plateau's winds, the acrid scent of the herbs made it across to her.

"What do you know about Lipos-Tholos, Sergeant?" said Dust.

The relief that filled Mouana's skull at the change of subject froze solid at the mention of the name.

Lipos-Tholos. The most notorious stalemate in all the worlds of the Lemniscatus. One of the great cities, long-settled and fat with tech, synonymous with its fleets and its link with Ocean. Shorthand for the siege that never broke. The thought made her shiver even more than it should, though she couldn't figure why.

"City of ten million, sir. Under contract for siege by the Principals. Naval power, supplied by sea via the Ocean gate, and heavily teched."

The wind whistled across the plateau. Tassie whimpered and shifted her bulk.

"Tough job, sir," added Mouana.

Dust took a long draught from her bowl and unfolded, standing bowed despite the empty space around her, and spoke.

"We are to break the siege at Lipos-Tholos, sergeant. The Cauldron Company is leaving in disgrace, and the contract has been offered to me. I have accepted."

It had been the question haunting the Blades: what next? Lipos-Tholos had been mentioned as a campfire joke, but few had taken it seriously. With the swamp wars raging and the canyon cities still changing hands on a near-yearly basis, anyone with an ear to company scuttlebutt had seen them as the next venues for deployment.

"So the rumours were true?"

"Not until now," said Dust, stalking across the rubble towards her. "I came out here to think. Now I have decided. We will be the ones to take Lipos-Tholos. You'll tell the rest."

As the general advanced, the 'drick screamed, and the other animals began lowing in sympathy further down the line. The rifle's grip itched in her hand.

Yes, sir hung on Mouana's bottom lip, but her lungs would not force it out. The general, moving towards her, was nothing more than yellow points in the swirling dark, and something felt wrong.

Of course, there was nothing to worry about. Mouana had been here before. She knew how things played out from here. She would snap, turn, put three rounds through the base of Tassie's skull, and Dust would promote her to battery commander.

But as the general approached, still just amber pricks in blackness, she had the sick feeling it was not going to go that way.

Tassie shrieked, the sky flaring bile-green as she threw her head back. She stamped, and the plateau quaked. Mouana moved to raise her rifle, but her arms would not move. Instead, the weapon dropped from her hands, and Dust came closer.

"This is how we will tell them all," said Dust, and night-black claws wrapped themselves around Mouana's shoulder. "You and I."

She wanted badly to tell the general that this wasn't the way things had gone, but the shadows had enveloped her and her throat was closed.

"This is your duty," said Dust, and drew her sabre from her belt with an oiled hiss. Mouana could do little more than gasp as it slid between her ribs, could choke out no more than a weak "but" as her intercostal muscles parted before the invading steel.

Her mouth flapped, her side clenched against the cold weapon, and the wounded beast screamed loud enough to shake the air in her pierced chest. And all she could make out was those yellow eyes.

"But..." she gulped, and the general drew her closer.

The 'drick stamped, the blade swelled in her, and the air sang with animal screams. The general's eyes glowed, and the ground collapsed. "But..." gasped Mouana, and the sky throbbed white and angry.

"But this wasn't..."

"Do me proud, Mouana," whispered the general.

Then the blast came.

MOUANA LOST HER words to the scream of the shell, and half her right hand to shrapnel when it hit the deck.

"Fuck," she spat, staring at the ragged mess of her hand against the sky. She had gotten caught in the dream, right when she most needed her wits.

Mouana swore again, using the word like a hammer to beat down the shock. This was no time to slip into the past—she was meant to be commanding the ship. Another shell came in, barely yards away, and shook her nearly off her feet. She had to focus.

Cursing herself again and again for falling away, Mouana

looked around her. It was bad. The boy next to her—Simeon? Samuel?—had taken the worst of the shellburst, and was now little more than stew. Worse yet, the radio unit he had carried was gone, reduced to a mess of red-soaked splinters.

Nevertheless, she thought, as she bound the oozing wreckage of her hand with tape, it could have been worse. It could have been her in the crater. It was only a couple of fingers gone, after all.

Ripping the tape off the roll with her teeth, she hissed in frustration. Dream or no dream, the bombardment shouldn't have started so soon. They shouldn't have been in range yet. She was a fucking gunnery officer—she knew these things. Or she used to, at least.

Either way—the bombardment had started, and she'd dropped into some half-arsed memory right as it had. There was no point shaking what was left of her fist at her mistake. The body count was still low, and might stay low for a while if she could get from the front of the ship and pull things together before more shelling came.

Issuing half an order to retreat, then remembering the radio was destroyed, Mouana spat pettily at the remnant of her hand and turned for the bridge. She was going to have to do this the hard way.

"Get back, or behind something," she roared, staggering as another shell hit the deck. "Cover!" she screamed, and choked as the hole in her lung cut her short. The wound was nothing new, but the dream—that bloody dream—had brought it close to mind.

But even with the slot in her ribs, her voice hadn't left her. "Cover!" she cried, and the sailors scurried for the deck's hard places, repeating her order.

Mouana staggered up the deck in a half-sprint, quaking as the shells hit, working at the slot in her ribs with her thumb. She was definitely going to have to have the damned thing plugged, she thought, if she was going to do much more old-fashioned commanding.

That was quite a big 'if,' mind. She looked behind her, past the ship's bow and out to sea: just a few miles ahead, the black pillars of the Gate reared from the endless grey of Ocean. Between them, light burst as artillery fire streaked through. Once they were past the Gate, they'd be soaking up every shell the City had to offer, and there wasn't much more of a plan than to ram the place at full speed and hope it did the trick.

Mouana laughed silently at the memory of her dream, even as the munitions pounded the deck and body parts pattered around her like fat rain. They were going to ram the city. She was going to breach Lipos-Tholos after all.

And then, as a one-armed sailor loped past her with a crate of ammunition belts in tow, her laugh became something loud and wild. She was going to breach Lipo-Tholos—and she was going to do it without loss of life.

The sailor turned in bafflement at her laughter, and she raised her fist in salute to him.

"Doesn't it feel good to be alive?" howled Mouana with spring-morning exuberance, and the sailor creased his brow. It wasn't as good as the jokes Wrack used to make, but it was good by her standards. After some initial confusion, the sailor's face split with raucous laughter. After all, he was dead. She was too.

They all were.

The laughter spread amongst the sailors, and so did the salute. There were thousands of them, crouched like starved seabirds on every mount and rise of the ship's town-sized foredeck. Withered, drawn, dead and salt-pickled, some whole and some ravaged— but all bound by a dreadful loss and a terrible purpose.

Their eyes glowed through the dullness of death. They grinned, and their fists shook in the salt wind, united in the grim joke. Mouana grinned back at them.

She'd spent twenty years with soldiers under fire, and never felt the sense of weird, black solace as she had after a week with this lot. Every soul on the ship had come here through death, and against their will.

Whether prisoners of war like her, or dissidents and criminals murdered by their own police, all had been brought back to work until they fell apart. To *Tavuto*, that evil old city-ship, anchored in Ocean's monster-haunted waters, and tasked with harvesting sufficient meat to supply Lipos-Tholos against the endless siege.

Then everything had changed. The dead had remembered themselves, and surged against their overseers; in a few days of raw chaos, they had turned *Tavuto* from their prison into the instrument of their revenge, and pointed it like a two-thousand-yard dagger at the heart of the city it had once fed.

And Mouana, despite never having served on a ship in her life, had become its captain.

Given that few enough of her crew could even remember their names, let alone fathom the workings of the ancient vessel, she was well qualified for the task. In any case, the only command that mattered at this stage was "Forward!" and she had made it well understood.

Still, there was always room for reinforcement.

"Forward!" screamed Mouana, with enough force to make her execution-wound whistle, and every sailor on the foredeck repeated her with enough ferocity to drown out the shellfire.

"*Forward!*" they cried, and she ran up ramps and flights, buoyed on by their chant of rage. It carried on as she reached the meat-piles, the winching mechanisms, the weighing yards overlooked by the bridge where it all had started.

As Mouana reached the plateau before the tower's doors, still littered with bodies from the uprising, the foghorn sounded. It was a voice beyond them, a sound far past the range of even Ocean's grandest demons, and yet its pitch blended with that of the stricken sailors.

And as it faded, Tavuto's ancient engines rose in ferocity to meet it, growing in pitch to match the cries of its former prisoners. Screaming as if the ship itself was possessed.

Which of course it was.

With a cheery beep, the display console strapped to Mouana's left wrist sprang into light, and a new message arrived.

DID SOMEBODY SAY... FORWARD?

Mouana rolled her eye, and managed not to smile as she hurried up the stairs to the bridge. That was Wrack, and this had all been his fault. Either a librarian who had been framed for sedition, or a mastermind of the Lipos-Tholos resistance—even he wasn't sure—Wrack had been sent here to fish like everybody else, but hadn't quite managed to let go of himself.

In the shadow of a hillside carcass, as they had hauled blocks of fat to *Tavuto*'s rendering vats, Wrack had woken from his own dream, and had saved Mouana from a mauling at the jaws of one of the overseers' attack creatures. They had fled into the night, come to terms with themselves among the ship's sump of lost souls, and then gotten angry.

It had all started with Wrack, and at the height of the revolt he had died again, attaining the frankly unfathomable status he now held. Given the speed with which his waking had spread to the rest of the ship, she sometimes wondered if he really was the rebel he liked to joke he had been in life. Then again, when he sent messages like that, his life as a hapless book-stacker became much more believable.

Either way, he was something very different from her. But despite sharing so little in life, they had shared so much since dying that she saw him now as her only friend.

REPLYING SLW, tapped Mounana with her right index finger, plucking a shard of shrapnel from the knuckle. *LESS FNGRS NOW. SHELLFIRE.*

The ship's foghorn gave a contemplative groan, and more text appeared on the screen.

ONCE AGAIN, I'M TALKING RINGS ROUND YOU. I TAKE IT WE'RE STILL DOING THIS, THEN?

Mouana nodded, then cursed in irritation and stabbed the "Y" key.

THAT'S JUST AS WELL; TURNING THIS THING
IS A NIGHTMARE. FORWARD IT IS. AND I'M
PUSHING THE REACTORS VERY HARD. MIGHT
BE WORTH CHECKING ON OUR FRIEND DOWN IN
THE ENGINES?

She grimaced at Wrack's attempt at humour, but he had a point. Though he had attained some measure of control over the ship, it seemed the previous owners had been careful not to give the vessel too much autonomy—a fair precaution, given its previous occupant. There still needed to be living hands—or at least human ones—on the controls to make things work.

"Eunice, give me the engines," snapped Mouana, stalking across the bridge to the bank of screens.

"Mmmmh," grumbled Eunice, frowning blindly as she bent low over the comms control panel. She was one of the ship's few remaining warbuilt—those criminals the City had deemed too vile to waste on sleep, and had wired into monstrous exoskeletons and though she had proved invaluable in combat, she was hardly a natural at ops. Plus her eyes were boiled, and she had to rely on crack-lensed cameras to see what she was doing.

Regardless, she had the link up in seconds, and when she did, Mouana found herself looking into the face of the Bruiser. The way he was staring into the camera when the feed came on, she could have sworn he had been squinting angrily at it in anticipation, possibly for minutes.

"Fack off?" snarled the Bruiser, and bared grey teeth at the camera. It was his way of saluting. Many of the zombies (Mouana winced at the word, but she had long decided there was no better option) aboard *Tavuto* had come back to wakefulness with a loose grasp on language, and the Bruiser—as they had come to know him—was one of the most limited. But what he lacked in articulacy, he made up for in determination, and in muscle.

As far as Mouana had been able to work out, Bruiser had spent most of his life threatening people with violence in pubs. Presumably a threat had come good, and landed him with his current sentence.

At least, she thought, as her de facto chief engineer swaggered away from the camera to batter a bulkhead with an iron bar, he'd found a transferable skill.

As sparks rang from the strike, a chorus of *fack offs* sounded from the gloom, and a thousand faces turned from their labour to scowl at their taskmaster. *Tavuto*'s engines, it turned out, had not been as sophisticated as one might have expected from a ship with a central reactor so ancient and exotic.

Whether through ineptitude in design, or calculation of the value of flesh over tech, the ancient vessel still relied on a swarm of stokers to shovel fuel into its burning heart. Even Wrack, whose mind was wired into the bloody thing, couldn't work out how the engines worked. But he was adamant that fuel had to keep coming in, and there didn't seem to be any kind of conveyor belt to do it in place of bodies.

So zombies it was. They teemed in the gloom behind the Bruiser, blistered about the shoulders with radiation no living stoker could withstand. Many of them were manacled to the engine blocks they fed; more with fresher bodies had attached themselves through solidarity since the takeover.

"Fack off?" offered Mouana, trying to convey the sense that she was checking on the wellbeing of her crew, or at least their ability to stay intact long enough to get the job done.

"Fack off," replied the Bruiser, lowering his iron bar and narrowing his eyes as if to suggest she was wasting her time by asking. The heavyset corpse stooped to examine the soot-caked rack of dials and readouts arrayed before him, then growled in frustration as he realised he had nothing like the vocabulary necessary to report on their situation.

"Fack *off*," he grunted, twisting a dial from its mounting with a resounding crack, and shoving it up against the lens.

It appeared to be a speed indicator—or so Mouana hoped, as its needle was jammed all the way into the red.

She was struggling for a follow-up question that might be rewarded with anything more like a status report, when the deck of the bridge began trembling. Her wrist panel pinged, and she half-read a message from Wrack about a lot of energy being drawn by the forward turret, before realising what was happening and lurching to the bridge windows in horror.

Right at *Tavuto*'s foremost extremity, the ship's main turret—a monster of a thing designed to ruin cities from behind the horizon—was screaming with power and about to fire. Enraged by the rain of shells through the Gate, the turret crew, previously content just to spin the thing round in jubilation, had clearly made the decision to fight back. By firing with both barrels. While the ship was moving at full speed.

The bollocking they were due had barely even begun to distill in Mouana's head when the thing fired and knocked her off her feet. The lights in the bridge went red and Eunice cursed, clutching her eye-cameras. The Bruiser's screen flashed orange as something far back in the engine hall exploded, and a juddering moan—the kind you never, ever want to hear aboard a ship—coursed deep beneath the floor.

Worse yet, the shot had done nothing; the turret, aimed by the punchdrunk reckoning of a bunch of corpses, had unloaded into the stone of the Gate—possibly the only thing she could imagine which it couldn't harm. The structure was looming right ahead of them now, one pillar glowing near-white with the impact, billowing with salt steam as waves crashed against it.

Anticipating Mouana's reaction, Eunice had already patched her through to the turret interior on another screen.

"Readying for another big boom!" yelled Kaba from the gunner's throne, right as Mouana barked at her to stand down. Given the merry uproar from the turret's armoured heart, she doubt her order had even been heard. That was the problem with this ship—the command hierarchy was fresher than most people's wounds, and hadn't so much been laid down as it had oozed out of complete chaos.

Kaba was just some boat-loader with a broken jaw from a jungle backwater, and had no business running a weapon the size of a city block. But she had been instrumental in the ship's takeover, and had become so through seizing control of said weapon, pointing it backwards, and wiping out the overseers' biggest pocket of resistance in an instant of glorious recklessness.

Mouana had spent her life running gun crews, and wasn't used to having to explain her orders, let alone repeat them. But from Kaba's point of view, she was an ally and an equal—why would she wait for someone else's decision on when to fire?

Mouana drew her breath to shout some sense into the gunner, but was interrupted yet again by action unfolding elsewhere. With a pop of snapping cables, one of the foredeck's winch cranes, usually locked in place and used for moving whaleboats to their launch cradles, swung drunkenly out over the side of the ship. Its upper surface was crusted with a mass of dead sailors.

"Crane six is on the move, sir!" reported one of the bridge crew—another former prisoner from Mouana's regiment, they were at least trying to make the situation seem under some sort of control. The dead soldier leaned in to a speaker, and furrowed their salt-eaten features.

"They say they're... making ready for boarding actions, sir."

Mouna sighed and let her head slump, breath hissing from the gap in her ribs. The situation wasn't beyond her control, she told herself. She would have Kaba agree to hold fire until her order, rein in the madness on crane six, then check the Bruiser had everything under control. Then she could start marshalling the forces on deck for the transition, and...

Her wrist panel pinged cheerfully.

JUST TO LET YOU KNOW, WE'RE GOING TO BE HEADING THROUGH IN ABOUT A MINUTE. MIGHT WANT TO HOLD ONTO SOMETHING.

"Thank you, Wrack," whispered Mouana through gritted teeth, and clenched her fists hard enough to force an unpleasant grey jelly from between the bandages on her smashed hand. The panel chirped again.

THERE'S JUST ONE MORE THING.

WHT NOW? typed Mouana, stabbing at the touchscreen as she did her best to ignore the hooting and hollering from the forward turret.

THE GATE. SHOULDN'T YOU GET EVERYONE BELOW DECK?

With a stab of panic, she remembered the container vessels the company would always load into before a Gate transit. The rude blatting of sirens as their great jaws closed. The nervous, blue-lit dark as the tracks ground into motion. The rattling of the lightning on the hull as they went through.

THE GATES. THEY KILL ANYTHING ON THE OUTSIDE. STOPS THE MONSTERS ETC GETTING THROUGH.

Mouana was about to call for a ship-wide retreat to covered space, when the thought occurred to her. Even amidst the shouting radios, the madness of her disintegrating command, it was a shot of bliss, akin to waking free from the sordid rules of a nightmare. The Gate would indeed wipe clean any life clinging to the ship; the barnacles and crab-stamens clustered beneath the keel were doomed. But they were not.

WRACK, She typed, taking the time to type whole words. *WE'RE ALL DEAD. YOU'RE DEAD. WE'RE FINE.*

The panel's screen remained empty for a long moment, longer than usual, and then three words appeared.

NO I'M NOT.

Wrack's status was, admittedly, hard to pin down. On the one hand, his corpse was lying just a few feet away on a trolley, where it had lain as little more than meat since the bloody conclusion of the rebellion. Then again, he no longer resided in it.

Refusing to shudder as she craned her neck, Mouana looked up at Wrack's current resting place. She tried to ignore the slow, fat swirl of creamy matter in the armourglass tube, tried to put aside what it was and see her friend, but there was no dodging the truth. He had become something very, very weird.

In place of a hardwired AI or a brainbank, *Tavuto* had, for who knew how long, been controlled via the extracted nerve stem of... something. Teuthis, the overseers had called it. In the blur of activity since the uprising, there had been no time to work out precisely what it was—Wrack figured it for something like a squid. In any case it was ancient, and malevolent, and horribly powerful.

When the revolt had been about to fail, with City triremes full of destriers and kentigerns closing in, Wrack had made some sort of dark bargain with whatever had inhabited the old flesh, and had swapped places with it. The thing had been awarded oblivion, and Wrack had been given a city-ship in place of his body.

Whether Wrack was any more or less dead than he had been as the mess of split sinew on the trolley, Mouana had no idea. But he sure as fuck wasn't alive. Taking a deep breath, despite having no use for oxygen, she set her fingers to the panel.

YES YOU ARE MATE, she typed, wishing she could make it look at least slightly compassionate.

No reply came. The Gate loomed, its pillars now framing *Tavuto*'s bow. Shells whizzed through in a flurry, eroding the vast prow like snow before piss. The zombies on crane six howled for revenge, and the barrels of Kaba's turret began to glow with a fresh charge.

On the Bruiser's screen a new glow, deep carnelian, blossomed in the ship's heart. The big bastard's eyes widened, and the screen shook, as the ship somehow found more power. "*Fack off!*" he breathed, awed, as a terrible shudder rose from the keel.

Text faded onto Mouana's screen without a chime.

I SUPPOSE YOU'RE RIGHT

Purple lightning surged across the deck like grasping fingers, drawing them into the space between the pillars. They were going through.

CHAPTER TWENTY THREE

WRACK'S BONES HURT, but they were not his bones. His eyes were seared by light, but they were not his eyes. Thousands upon thousands of muscles-that-were-not clenched in spasm, and fire screamed across skin that was not there.

Worst of all, though, even above the agony of his body's passage through the Gate, rising from the vast depths of his new mind was a relentless craving for fish.

Don't listen to any of it, he told himself, over and over. He was not a ship, he thought, as his bow lurched into the raging gap. And he certainly, without question, was not a bloody squid. He was Schneider Wrack, formerly of No. 32 Clerk Street. He had been in charge of categorising the College Library's collection of allegories, and he had been very good at it.

This, he insisted, as his heart shunted nuclear fire through his leviathan keel, was just a phase he was going through.

Wrack laughed, and mournful horns blasted from a dozen masts, barely murmurs above the noise of the Gate-storm. And what a storm. He understood next to nothing about the Lemniscatic Gates—not that many people understood much about them any more—but he knew that the energy transfer involved in moving something as massive as *Tavuto* was staggering.

It certainly made for an astonishing show. Squinting down his foredeck from the first cameras through the Gate, he saw the ship's hatchet prow surge into the world between wings of steam, wreathed in actinic filigree. Crowding its edges were dead women and men, too excited to care for the shells that still rained around them, lightning dancing across their skins.

Anyone watching them would be properly shitting themselves by now, he thought, and boomed another terrible laugh.

Then the laugh wrenched into a cry of pain, as more of his body ploughed through the Gate. A good third of him was now in an entirely different world from his two-million-ton arse, and had subtly more mass than it had possessed five minutes ago. As his bones flexed and glowed with the stress of staying together, the change felt *anything but subtle*.

Wrack had no doubt he could take it: the really ancient ships—and *Tavuto* was as old as they came—had been built to take worse than this as a matter of course. But either its designers had not taken into account what it felt like to *be* the ship, or they had no sense of pity.

As his waist slid through the gap, he felt sure his back would break. Every vertebra felt as if it was being prised from its neighbour with a heated blade; tendons drew tight as rods and snapped under the strain. Wrack screamed, and his tentacles, his cranes—no—his hands arched into claws. Whiteness overtook him, and washed away sensation.

Allegories. He would list allegories. First came the allegories for Nation, carefully alphabetised, on circular shelves around the lily pond where the placoderms wallowed. Nation as Zoo took a slice of the bottom shelf, Nation as Saints' Lives sat midway along the third, and there was Nation as Machine, a long section starting neatly at the beginning of the fifth.

He ran his finger upwards, past Nation as Karst, Nation as Goldmine, Nation as Euphemism, to the top shelf. There was Nation as Body, but it had been put back in the wrong place, before Nation as Battleship and Nation as Beast. Wrack clucked in disapproval, and poked his tongue out as he began to rearrange them. He was just wondering how they had gotten so out of sequence when he was smacked across the brain by a string of angry block capitals.

WRCK?/? WHRE THE FCK ARE YOU>?

Hold on, he thought, irritated, and focused again on the books. How odd; while he had been distracted, all three volumes had merged into one.

WRACK. MATE. NEED YOU.

Oh, thought Wrack, looking up from the impossible book as the edge of perception began to pound with light. *What a clever dream.*

CLVR DREAM? THE HELL DO YOU MEAN? shouted Mouana into his head, as he chucked the book into the pond.

Sorry—nodded off for a second; I'm on it now, thought Wrack, and blinked.

Wrack had seen paintings of some enormous naval battles, but this made most look like a baby's bathtime. A crescent of warships, each the size of a skyscraper, bristled before the harbour of Lipos-Tholos like bison circling a sick calf. Explosions rippled across their decks as their guns sounded, and triremes scudded through the air like fat arrows.

Wrack was thundering towards them, cloaked in spirals of gunsmoke as his own turrets barked in answer. As he cleared his head of the strange fugue, more came online, while those piloted by the enthusiastic dead came under the subtle guidance of his aim. Wrack clenched his diaphragm, and rockets slid from his sides spurting flame; he gritted his teeth, and tungsten flechettes erupted from his spine with a wet, springy hiss. Missiles and flak found their marks, and aircraft spiralled smoking from the sky.

Railfire punched through his hull, and mortars knocked

chunks from his superstructure, but it was like the scrape of pumice on dead skin; if anything, it felt refreshing after the searing misery of the transition. There was just so bloody *much* of him, and it was bearing down on the City's navy far quicker than it could be broken by their guns. Elation bellowed through him, and his skin shivered with the bliss of rage. He was death now, and the City was powerless before him.

The shiver turned cold very quickly, and the anger coagulated into thick disgust. He wanted to believe the black euphoria had come from the same place as the hunger for fish, because if it had come from him, it raised the possibility that he had been every bit as unpleasant as the mind into which he had been transplanted.

Wrack had been angry when he had woken up after his execution; in fact, it was fair to say that was an understatement. That anger, and the chaos it had sparked, had forced him to actions he could never have imagined in life. Driven by the horror of surviving his death, and the burning need to stop it happening to anyone else, he had done insane things. He had ridden a dead whale into battle, swum across open Ocean, beaten a cyborg murderer with a length of pipe. He had bitten a man's throat out as he pleaded for mercy, and the memory still made him shiver.

Taking *Tavuto* had been necessary, and becoming *Tavuto* after that. And even from those earliest moments of despair with Mouana, when they were just two shivering corpses on the decks of grey hell, the plan had always been to take that hell back to the City that had inflicted it.

But now the City was in his sights, now he could almost taste its fear on the wind, it all felt... well, a bit much. The people he had grown up with were still in that city; his friends were there, and his father, who had wept at his trial. And he was racing towards them, laden with angry carcasses that wanted nothing more than to bite and claw and destroy.

But he was committed now. Even if he was able to wrench *Tavuto*'s monstrous engines into reverse—and he wasn't sure he knew how—it would do nothing to stall the tectonic momentum the ship had built up over miles of open Ocean.

Accepting that his only option now was to surge forward into the fire, Wrack prised his thoughts from the city of his youth and made himself see it as an irritation to be swatted.

Turning his attention back to the fight, it seemed things were becoming a little less one-sided: the twin colossi at the harbour gates—the Wave-Roamers—had broken their vigil and begun striding out to sea to meet him.

Wrack floundered in confusion, fairly sure that he had slipped into yet another strange dream. But the stone giants were utterly real, and so was the glow of barely-restrained plasma along the street-long blades of their swords.

As the titans waded out to hip-depth, Wrack couldn't help but feel a surge of satisfaction. Despite College Hill's endless insistence that the Roamers had been nothing more than statuary for centuries, there had always been a pub-chat undercurrent that insisted that someone's uncle had been contracted to scour their joints, that someone's kid had climbed up one night and seen figures moving within their crowns.

Wrack almost felt disappointed when *Tavuto*'s forward turret, now severely pitted from shellfire, swivelled to the left and blasted one into gravel. The shot jarred Wrack like a swan-dive into concrete, and knocked the gun sixty feet off its bearings, but he couldn't deny it had been well-aimed. Wrack heard Kaba's crew whooping and shrieking as they abandoned the gun they had just wrecked, pumping their fists as the Roamer's bodiless legs pitched into the bay.

There was little time to reflect, however; the other giant was closing rapidly on Wrack's starboard flank, and the ships ranked in front of the harbour were shuffling apart to let something through. Switching his view to a camera on one of his highest masts, Wrack saw what was coming—the *Eschatologist*.

The dreadnought slank between the ships of the blockade like a pike through minnow. This was no bath toy.

The *Eschatologist* was perhaps the sole reason that, in the generations-long history of the siege, Lipos-Tholos had never been threatened by sea. Wrack remembered being part of a choir of fifty thousand schoolchildren, arrayed along the harbour wall to sing it off to some meaningless colony war. The City had never minded it being away from port; the mere possibility of its return was enough to dissuade any possibility of an attack by sea.

Sailors who had served aboard said its corridors had not been made for human beings, that in its deep decks it held the preserved exoskeletons of its first captains. It was a thing of black iron, so old that even its engineers often had to shrug and mutter about magic when tasked with trying to maintain it. It had nothing so crude as guns: it was said that the will of its captain alone was enough to turn even a Gate to sand. For the first time since becoming an enormous ship, Wrack felt true fear.

Then Mouana offered her take on the subject.

RAM IT, she sent, and Wrack checked the bridge camera to confirm the grin he already knew was stretched across her face.

Good idea, he thought at her, and began the chest-crushing work of nudging the ship's course. He didn't need asking twice: with the main turret shot and most of his artillery spent, Wrack didn't have much choice but to barrel straight for the dreaded vessel and hope for the best.

As he centred the shell-chewed apex of his prow on the black ship, however, the whole battle shrank down to him and the dreadnought. His attention was consumed by its baleful lights, like a wolf's gaze caught at the edge of firelight, and he began to feel strange energies churning deep in his belly. Whether the terror he felt under that glare was just fear of the ship's secret weapon or part of the weapon itself, he could not say. But he could concentrate on nothing else. Dread consumed him.

When the surviving Wave-Roamer moved alongside and was swept onto its back by a crane swarming with zombies before it could strike a blow (Crane Six, had it been?), it was little more than a footnote on the edge of perspective. The *Eschatologist* was everything, cruising silently toward him, darkness on a white bow-wave. The feeling of strangeness inside him built until he felt his guts were on the edge of bursting. The black ship's lights swelled, reaching furnace intensity, and Wrack's engines began to quake.

And then, the unthinkable. Sirens wailed across the waves between Wrack and his adversary, and explosions consumed the *Eschatologist*'s port side. Stricken, the black ship began to yaw to face the unseen threat. The red lights swung away, the transfixion broke, and Wrack was able to focus on the other ships in the fleet. The battle line was wildly out of formation; its ships were jostling madly in a swamp of white water, and at least half had turned their guns on the *Eschatologist*, were pounding away with suicidal focus.

The traitor craft moved free of the blockade and advanced in a knot on the *Eschatologist*, which seemed vastly less imposing as it swung desperately to face them. The renegades steamed forward and bright white banners, emblazoned with a crude image of a tobacco-pipe, unfurled from their topmasts.

On *Tavuto*'s war-torn deck, the horde of dead reacted before Wrack could, erupting in a frenzy of cheering. They in turn were answered by the City, where volleys of flares began streaking into the evening sky. The sound of distant gunfire followed close behind.

IS THAT YOUR OLD LOT DOING THAT? messaged Mouana, as Wrack stared in disbelief.

He wasn't sure how to answer. The traitors' banners bore the symbol of the Pipers—the City's insurrectionist faction, named for the semi-mythical rebel Old King Pipe—but whether they were "his old lot" was a very different question.

All he knew was that his Dad had almost certainly been one of them—and that when he himself had been arrested for distributing seditious material through the library (his own memories were unclear on whether he was guilty), he had been a good son and hadn't told the constables his father was a rebel. Beyond these threadbare facts, his connection with the Pipers had remained maddeningly unclear in his memories.

Either way, he was glad of them now. The *Eschatologist* seemed a lot less terrifying as it foundered under the rebel guns, which fired relentlessly even as the Piper ships were chewed to pieces by the rest of the fleet.

Free of the flagship's stare, not to mention the ire of the City's blockade, the massed dead on Wrack's deck broke into ceaseless wild shouting, waving rifles, falchions and their own shattered arms in the direction of the City. Even as they watched, two of the Piper ships disappeared before the *Eschatologist* in columns of flame, but by the time the black hulk began turning back to face them, it was too late.

You might want to have everyone brace for impact, Wrack warned Mouana, although *Tavuto*'s vast bow was already towering above the *Eschatologist*'s like the threat of a mountain storm.

Whatever the dark ship was made of, it was hard. As he smashed into its flank, Wrack felt a livid, cracking pain, as if he'd taken a bite out of a pint glass. The dreadnought stove in at the beam, but the impact sent a jolt through Wrack that made the Gate transition seem gentle.

Maddened by it, he flailed to hold on to consciousness, leaving his sense of self behind. As the force of the crash screamed through him, he let the formaldehyde-quenched recesses of his new brain come to the fore, and flexed boneless, barbed arms in the dark of his mind. He was a devil cruising under mile-thick ice, ripping lesser monsters from their crevices and grinding them in spiral jaws.

The prey-ship was driven beneath the waves in two splintered halves, ripping vast strips from his body as it went down. He was breached; water was pouring into him, tens of thousands of gallons per second, but he didn't care. There was more prey ahead.

Shaking aside the chewed carcass of the dreadnought, he swam on. There was no turning back now, and no point trying to think like a timid little creature. Not now the City's last defence had fallen to his beak; not now that final, delicious impact was so close.

Wrack was so, so hungry, and his quarry sprawled before him; he was within the harbour now, heartbeats from the dock wall. The tiny prey-ape was talking to him, bleating to him through her little letter-pad, but it made no difference now. He was closing on the carcass, foregut flushing hot with acid at the thought of so much meat, and nothing could stop him. The dockside rushed at him, stone and steel and wood and flesh, and Wrack spread his hooked arms in rapture.

WHEN AT LAST the shaking stopped, Mouana uncurled and rose unsteadily to her feet. Dust billowed through the shattered windows of the bridge, obscuring everything outside. Never had she been so glad not to breathe. The world was silent, save the deep moan of settling steel. After the last, ear-splitting crack, when *Tavuto*'s ageless spine had finally snapped, it was as if all other sound had been shamed into hush.

Mouana looked out at the smothering clouds, and then back at the bridge, where a crowd of wide-eyed cadavers stood, stunned and looking to her for guidance. The emergency lights were dead and the daylight wholly extinguished; their ragged faces were lit only by the flickering of fires deep in the murk.

The evening winds tugged at the shroud of stone fog, and shapes began to loom at the edges of the deck: they were buildings, fallen against the side of the ship and spilled over it in fans of rubble. The bridge crew stared in disbelief.

From an engineer's point of view, it made sense. As part of her siegework, Mouana had studied the geology of Lipos-Tholos intimately; had worked on endless abortive plans to dig mines and invade it from below. Especially on its seaward side, the place was mostly hollow, honeycombed with storehouses, tidal generators, and ancient districts that had simply been bricked over. *Tavuto*'s six million tons had ploughed through all of that like a truck into glasswork, only stopping when it ground against bedrock.

Still, to see the mammoth vessel sprawled in the midst of the place like a beached monster defied comprehension. They had rammed the City, and the City had come off worse.

The clouds begin to thin, and so did the silence. The thin wail of sirens began to rise from the streets around them, and tentative gunfire began to sound in the distance. With a rattling hum, the ship's auxiliary power came on, and Mouana's radio began squawking as the torn cobweb that passed for her command network began reporting in. The spell was broken.

Raising a radio set to her withered lips, Mouana stared ahead through the vanishing fog, where a sullen shape loomed. College Hill, the seat of Lipos-Tholos' government, and there at its crest, the crooked immensity of the Ministry of Fisheries and Justice. The place that had made them, through which every soul on the ship had passed on their way to Ocean and to death. Now they had come home, and stood within sight of its vile machines. There was only one thing left to do.

"All crew, this is your captain," croaked Mouana into the radio, hearing her voice echoing from loudhailers across the ship. She loathed speeches, but she owed them this much before the madness started.

"Ahead of you is College Hill, and on top of it is the place where you became what you are now. You are angry, and you know what to do. If we're not destroyed on the way there, we probably will be afterwards. But let's have our revenge first. Let's give them some of our own fucking justice. Storm the Ministry."

As the inevitable cheering began, and the bridge crew scurried to be first on deck and join the rush into the City, Mouana dropped the radio and looked upwards. The power was back on, but Wrack's casket in the ceiling was still dark. The panel of lights beside it, which usually displayed a rank of hard green bars, flickered weakly.

The shadowy mass of the brain barely stirred behind the glass, shreds of white matter drifting like meat in a thin soup. Wrack had stopped responding to her after they had rammed the black ship, and now she wondered if he had made it through the crash at all. She told herself that it didn't matter; that he had done his part, and that there was nothing more to be settled between them.

Still, as she caught sight of his body, now shaken from its trolley and lying broken in a corner, she couldn't help but wish he had been there with her to give the speech. Certainly, she had made a good job of whipping up the crew, but somehow, she knew if Wrack had been there, he would have made them smile as he did it.

But he wasn't there, she thought, shoving a pistol in her belt, and that was that.

CHAPTER TWENTY FOUR

PLS HELP TYPED Mouana with shaking fingers, as a grenade reduced yet another wave of sailors to jagged mush. *WRACK. PLS.*

Beside her Eunice let loose another volley of fire, hydraulics whining as she pushed against the corpses piled up in front of them. Screams echoed from the militia lines as bullets tore into uniformed bodies. Grenades rained on the rebels.

When the charge started they had been unstoppable, swarming over knots of panicking riflemen like ants over nest-bound chicks. On Physeter, the broad avenue leading up College Hill, the City had found time to gather a sturdier barricade, but even that had been swallowed under their numbers. Over and over, the line had broken and reformed further back on the long road, but each time it came back it had taken longer to overcome.

Then at Exhibition Plaza, where Physeter narrowed to pass

through the Scholar's Gate and into the citadel that crowned the hill, their crawl had slowed to a halt. For every nine dead cut down at the bottleneck, ten would come forward, but the savage mathematics of the battle conspired against them.

Already, the drift of bodies before the gate was big enough to shelter behind. Worse yet, Mouana could now see the ragged tail of her forces on Physeter's lower slope, and could no longer convince herself they were limitless.

Here and there, the river of once-human bodies was punctuated by the slick, surging shapes of the ship's beasts. Wolf-eels, stingrays, sharks and black lobsters had all been goaded from *Tavuto* as they had rushed to the streets, but the stinking things had been made to keep cowed corpses in line, not assault the guns of the living.

Next into the breach was a Greater White, wobbling on brass struts, designed to clean up deck accidents and only half-finished when the *Tavuto* had been seized. The vast shark opened its jaws and lunged through the gate, drawing a hurricane of rifle fire as it stooped.

"Get that damned thing back!" yelled Mouana through the loudhailer, as she understood what was happening. "It's going to block the gate! *GET IT BACK!*"

The leviathan's supposed handlers yanked on the ropes riveted to the shark's jaws, but they had no chance of even turning its head. The beast's mouth collapsed as Mouana watched, cartilage twisting under gunfire and leaving tooth-rows sagging. Then, thrashing in rage, the thing caught one of its spindly legs in its own mouth, and went down in a mass of torn anatomy.

Its ten ton bulk neatly blocked the entry to the citadel, and almost immediately the defenders had scrambled up onto the wreckage of its underbelly to fire over the top.

Mouana slumped back behind the barricade and stared at the dead screen of her wrist panel. They were past the point where teeth, claws, and the few guns they had could do them any good, and the only heavy ordnance was back on the sundered *Tavuto*, locked into the mind of her absent friend.

For an artillery officer, she thought, this was about as bad as it got. She tapped out *PLS* again, with a growing sense of futility, and cursed in bitter frustration when no reply came.

Arms reached out from the pile, from those dead too bullet-ruined to walk; they pawed at her shoulders with mangled fingers and protruding bones, while buried mouths murmured husky consolations. Now that, she thought, laughing darkly, was camaraderie.

The absurdity of the moment didn't amuse her for long. Never had Mouana felt so lost. There were no orders, no intel, and no reserves to call in. Even when she had woken on *Tavuto*, there had been Wrack to carry her, and to plot with. Now there was nothing but her, sitting alone at the ugly, unravelling end of a plan.

Not that the plan had amounted to much to begin with: 'walk forward and tear apart anything in their path' had been the beginning and the end of it. She should have given it more thought. Even with the siege on, even with those ships turning traitor, even with the damage caused by *Tavuto*, Lipos-Tholos was a *nation*. How had she expected a mob of poorly-armed corpses, half of whom were rotted through in mind and body, to just walk in and turn the place over?

She tried to put it down to the chaos at sea, to the haste with which she had been forced to turn an upturned graveyard into an army, but there was no avoiding the truth. As a tactician, she had been pathetic. All she had really done was point the dead in the right direction, and even that was now ending in disaster. They'd be ground to paste at the citadel gates; the City would send new ships and new bodies back to Ocean, and inflict who knew what cruelties on them to stop this happening again.

Nearby, a man was screaming. Mouana had been too focused on the carnage at the gate to notice him before, but there he lay, a yard from where she sat slumped against the corpse-drift. He was young, perhaps her side of twenty, and well-fed, as far as she could tell. After getting so used to faces where the cheekbones broke the skin, living faces seemed desperately unusual. He lay on a stretcher, clearly abandoned by his squadmates in their haste to secure the gate.

The man screamed again as he saw Mouana turn to regard him, loud enough to carry over another blast from Eunice's gun. She wondered what he made of her, a one-eyed corpse morosely tapping on a keyboard, but by the looks of things, he was beyond reason. Sweat streamed from his brow, his pupils had hardened to points of animal fear, and his scream was the sort that echoed in the dreams of army surgeons.

As Mouana looked down the man's body, she saw why. He was being eaten from the feet up. The grasping hands of the fallen dead had found him and drawn him in, and now he was up to the knees in the hungry mound. A thicket of brine-withered claws groped at him, pulling him in inch by inch, and he stared at Mouana with gritted teeth.

Served him right, thought Mouana. The fucker had eaten well off their labour, had grown fat on meat they had hauled from hell. Served him right to end as meat himself. She scraped the puckered recesses of her mouth for the black fluid that pooled there, and spat on the ground beside the man's head.

Then she thought what Wrack would have thought of her, and her sneer collapsed. Anger was one thing, but this was another. Taking satisfaction from the man's agony wouldn't bring the gate down, and it certainly wouldn't make her failure any less profound. What had she expected the poor sod to do; starve and refuse the draft? He probably hadn't even known what was going on in Ocean—or at least had convinced himself it was all nonsense. She could hardly say he deserved to be eaten alive.

Before she could think any further, she had drawn the pistol from her belt and put a hole through the boy's temple. Telling herself that hate had pulled the trigger for her, Mouana rose to her feet, put the damned soldier out of her head, and climbed up on the mound of bodies.

"No point dragging this out any longer," she muttered to herself, then picked up her loudhailer to order the charge. It was halfway to her lips when her wrist chimed.

THAT WAS GOOD OF YOU, said Wrack, and Mouana dropped the loudhailer in shock.

"Fucking *hell*, Wrack," she said, gaping at her wrist panel in rage. Only when the second bullet smacked into her shoulder did she remember to slide down from the barricade.

"How in *piss* did you see that?" she shrieked, scanning the baffled faces of the piled bodies.

I'M THE CRAB, replied Wrack, adding a cheery **V.v.V** that would have made Mouana tear her hair out if she hadn't been worried it might take her scalp with it.

Sure enough, there was one of the *Tavuto*'s cleanup crabs nearby, mouthparts whickering away absentmindedly at a fallen soldier. She could have sworn the camera bolted to its blanched carapace winked at her as it gave a cheery wave with a gore-streaked claw.

Muttering something she had once given a man a week's latrine duty for calling her, she resisted the urge to shoot the thing, and stabbed at the keyboard.

WHR TH FK YOU BN???

WHAT ARE YOU ON ABOUT? I'VE NOT BEEN ANYWHERE! I HAVE, HOWEVER, WORKED OUT HOW TO RECEIVE SOUND FROM THESE THINGS, MIND, SO YOU DON'T HAVE TO TYPE ANYMORE.

"Don't be bloody cute with me, Wrack," Mouana hissed at the crab, her leg aching to kick the thing. "We're getting annihilated here. And you just *pissed off*. What in the name of the Tin King have you been *doing*?"

The crab raised its claws in a conciliatory gesture, and the panel beeped again.

OK. I'M SORRY, I REALLY AM. IT'S IMPOSSIBLE TO EXPLAIN, OR AT LEAST EXPLAIN QUICKLY. I WAS THINKING ABOUT... OTHER STUFF, BASICALLY. BUT I'M HERE NOW. WHAT CAN I DO?

Squatting down to eye level with the camera, Mouana jabbed a finger at it and did her best to keep a level tone.

"Mortars, Wrack. Missiles. Anything. I need you to blow the Scholar's Gate to pieces. And I need you to do it now, because we're running out of 'later.' Shoot the gate, Wrack. Please."

Too long passed, filled with the rattle of gunfire at the breach, and Mouana feared for a moment he was gone again. Then the words came up on the screen, and her jaw dropped.

I'M SORRY. I WON'T.

"What do you mean you won't? There must be something!" panted Mouana, shaking the crustacean desperately. "There has to be something you can fire!"

NO, I DON'T MEAN 'I CAN'T', said Wrack, the words appearing slowly. **I MEAN, 'I WON'T'.**

THE THING IS, THERE'S A REALLY LOVELY BAKERY THERE, BUILT INTO THE PASSAGE ON THE OTHER SIDE. I USED TO GO THERE ON TUESDAYS, ON THE WAY TO WORK. THEY DID THE MOST INCREDIBLE SAUSAGE ROLLS. OF COURSE, IT WASN'T REAL PORK, BUT THEY DISGUISED THE FISH REALLY WELL, AND...

"Wrack," whispered Mouana, swallowing rage.

YES? said Wrack, as the crab tipped its body quizzically to one side.

"I can't imagine what you've been through in that thing. I honestly wonder how you've kept your mind this long. But please. Please, Wrack. Don't go mad now. I need this. We all need this. Fire the mortars. And then we can get this over with and rest."

Mouana closed her eye and clenched her teeth, tried to drown out the sound of the massacre as she waited for the chime of a new message. When it came, she dreaded it almost too much to open her eye.

GOOD GRIEF, YOU'VE LOST YOUR SENSE OF HUMOUR, HAVEN'T YOU? OF COURSE I FIRED THE BLOODY MORTARS. THEY JUST TAKE A WHILE TO COME DOWN AGAI—

The ground flashed bright white, then slammed into her face as her body was smacked sideways by the blast. Impacts shook the cobbles beneath her, one after another, coming faster and faster until they blurred into a continuous roar of thunder. Masonry rained down around her, and heat rose at her back until she felt her clothes would surely catch fire.

Something in Mouana's head ticked and sent her back to bombardment drill, forcing away all sensation except the movement of her lips as she slowly recited the alphabet. By the time she reached O, the explosions had given way to a profound silence, and she cautiously raised her head.

The barricade was blasted into disarray and littered with chunks of stone; beyond it was only dust and smoke. Besides the soft clink of stone chips pattering on the rubble, there was no sound. Mouana rose to her feet, and checked her body for missing parts: she was alabaster from head to toe, but everything was there. And beside her was the crab, staring at the destruction with a scavenger's disregard.

YOU'RE WELCOME, said Wrack and, without hesitation, she kicked him down the hill.

MOUANA WAS FIRST into the breach, screaming as she fired her pistol into the smoke. Behind her came the last of *Tavuto*'s workforce, hundreds strong still, loping and hopping and hobbling across broken stone.

Clouds of murk rolled through the cratered waste, occasionally revealing a blackened body, or a leg protruding from the collapsed stonework. But nothing fired back at them. They were alone in the desolation, greeted only by their own battle-cry as it echoed through a tomb of smoke.

As they passed through the gate's ruins and into the street beyond, the clouds began to thin, but still there was no new line of guns to overcome. Mouana jabbed her pistol at shadows in the gathering night, expecting an ambush at any second, but they remained unchallenged.

At the gate, it had seemed as if the entirety of the City militia had been backed up behind that passage—she had imagined them packing the streets all the way to the Ministry. Surely that couldn't have been the citadel's last line of defence?

Yellow light blossomed above them, followed by a distant, deep cracking, and Mouana wondered if maybe it had been after all. The smoke lit up again, and she looked up; the distant glow told her the City was falling—she just couldn't put her finger on why. Death had done maddening things to her memory.

Then the clouds parted, and she saw the light's source—a mile up, fire was splashing across the sky in rippling circles, boiling away like water flicked on hot steel. As each bloom faded it birthed an arc of lightning, which crept across an unseen dome until it twined with another discharge. Her old guns, hammering the City's shield.

There was the patter of the howitzers; three, then five, then three, just as she had drilled them. There were the twin blasts of Theia and Rhea, creating a violet surge where they overlapped, and then—Mouana counted to three, then nodded as the sky flashed green, right on cue—*there* was old Kronos, with its belly-grown warheads that outweighed a man.

Mouana cracked into a wolfish grin; she drew in a huge, useless breath through her nose and imagined she could smell the ozone of their discharge, hear the sizzle of coolant dripping from the casings. Another flurry of howitzer shots peppered the bruise Kronos had left on the shield, and sparks burst from its underside as if from forge-struck iron.

As the wound left by the barrage faded, however, so did her smile. She knew those weapons like family, and recognised this particular firing pattern. It was an all-out bombardment of the shield's strongest point—phenomenally costly, and designed not to break it, but to draw all its power to one spot. With the shield sucking up everything that came out of the reactors, the point defence systems on the wall would have sputtered out, and the division's rail pieces would be briefly free to batter the city wall.

As if on cue, a monstrous cracking rolled in from far inland, followed by a rumble through the ground. Another few volleys like that, and a breach was inevitable. The Blades of Titan, the mercenary company Mouana had served her career in, was finally making its play to take the City. And to have ground down its defences to a point where such an assault was even feasible, Lipos-Tholos must have been on its last legs even before they had arrived.

With the threat of full assault on its landward side looming, the City would have had to keep its troops out in the suburbs, massed anxiously behind the walls. When the *Tavuto* came through the Gate, what choice had they but to pray the naval blockade held, and that the citadel's standing garrison would be enough to mop up anything that made it through?

And to give credit to whoever had arranged the defence, thought Mouana, it nearly had been enough. She doubted she still had seven hundred sailors standing, and wouldn't have had that if *Tavuto* hadn't been able to bombard the city from *under* its shield.

But it had, so there they were. And there was the Ministry, just half a mile ahead up an empty street.

Mouana wondered why nobody was running for it, then realised they had all stopped to wait for her as she stared at the sky. Looking behind her, she saw the street filled with dead faces, patient yet alert, waiting for her to signal the advance. The mindless and the muddled were gone now; they had either wandered off into the streets in search of meat and old memories, or had long since found a gun to run at. These were the ones who had made it through *Tavuto* with a semblance of self, and there was something like hope in their clouded eyes, now the end was in sight.

There was Kaba, *Tavuto*'s former turret commander, and

there was Eunice, towering two feet above the rest of the crowd. Two of the other warbuilt had made it through the assault, though one was missing an arm, and all through the crowd were women and men in the same rags as her, the remnants of the company uniform. They were mixed in with thieves and brawlers, pamphleteers and preachers; a raft of dread flotsam drifted back to the city that had cast them overboard.

The Blades' attack on the walls no longer mattered to Mouana; they were not her army. *This* was, and their work was almost done. She had no idea what they would find ahead in the place of their monstrous birth; all she knew was that they had to break it so it would never work again.

Another barrage raked its claws across the night and Mouana started up the hill, with death at her back.

CHAPTER TWENTY FIVE

WRACK FOUND HIMSELF somewhere on Scullery Street, eating a dead hound.

Wrinkling his snout in distaste, he coughed out the rancid mouthful and scissored his jaws in a nearby puddle to rinse them. These things were necessary, sure, but he didn't really fancy experiencing it if he could avoid it.

As the puddle's surface flattened out, he turned his wedge of a head and eyeballed the reflection: he was a Mako this time. Or was it a Grey Gorger? Either way, some sort of shark, fitted with the usual hydraulic cradle and crown of steel legs that most of *Tavuto*'s beasts had been built into.

They hissed and clattered as they carried him along the street's cobbles, through a scene of howling chaos. This close to *Tavuto* (its flank loomed just a few blocks ahead, like a crude new street) the roads were swarming with zombies; those either too degraded or confused to have followed the logic of the invasion, and who had wandered down the chains and boat-chutes to see what they could find.

For much of the citizenry, already terrified by the interposition of a town-sized ship in their postcode, this had proved too much. Families were fleeing their tenements wholesale, clutching their children as they sprinted up the street in bug-eyed terror, while militiamen fleeing from the fighting on College Hill accelerated past them.

For the most part, the wandering dead were harmless— Wrack witnessed one woman with a sagging vest and exposed vertebrae, leaning down to a letterbox and repeatedly bellowing to ask if Lottie was home. Others, however, had come to the streets with more than just fog in their heads. For some of the dead, any revenge would do.

A piercing scream caused Wrack to turn; a child had tripped, been sent sprawling in the debris of a toppled poem cart. His mother had noticed, but so had a huge old bastard with a crushed face and a metal spar in his hand—and the dead man was a lot closer.

Wrack sprinted for the corpse, raising sparks as his claws crashed across the cobbles. The sight of a quarter-ton shark racing towards her son did nothing to allay the mother's screaming, but it managed to distract the crushed man.

Spar still raised in readiness to spear the boy, the corpse swung round and threw the thing at Wrack instead. It was a classic harpooner's throw, sending the pole smoothly through Wrack's mouth and skewering virtually everything vital on the way back.

Still, Wrack didn't mind that much; since he'd worked out how to get telemetry from the ship's beasts (after *Tavuto*'s impact, he'd needed *something* to distract him from the pain), he had no shortage of bodies to resort to.

The shark's vision drained like a drunk's bladder, greying out even before he collided jaws-first with the corpse, but lasted long enough for him to catch the mother scooping up her son in the corner of his vision. As it faded entirely, he found his relief turning swiftly to cold slush. How many dead men, on how many streets, had he not managed to stop? Seeing it at street level, hearing the horror in that woman's voice as she wondered how this could possibly be happening to her... it had made it all a bit too real.

Maybe the shark had been a bad idea, thought Wrack. So he looked somewhere else.

"Two... *THREE*!" ROARED Mouana, pushing forward with all the strength her salt-cured calves could muster. The makeshift battering ram surged forward on the shoulders of the mob, and the Ministry's mahogany gates bounced in her vision as they broke into a run.

She did not expect them to be flung open, nor for a pair of burly women to step forward from a cheering crowd inside and hurl a man's body into their path.

From the looks on their faces they were just as shocked to see a gang of corpses rushing at them, brandishing a piece of public statuary as a ram.

There was a lot of shouting, a lot of falling over, and then a gruesome, clanging crunch as the ram—a bronze casting of the City's Chancellor—pitched forward right on top of the body on the floor.

The echoes of the crash were still ringing as the crowd inside exploded into motion, drawing weapons and diving behind whatever cover the Ministry's lobby offered. Despite their decay-numbed reflexes, Mouana's crew nearly matched their speed, drawing their weapons and aiming at the doorway with teeth bared. Eunice's gun was already whining when Mouana gave the order to hold fire and—to her immense relief—the same order echoed from inside the building.

The silence that followed was dense and dangerous; a soft chorus of clicks, coughs and shuffles, each of which threatened a hail of bullets if it tempted a finger to slip. Then came the deliberately heavy slap of soles on marble, as a rangy figure strode out of the Ministry to stand on its threshold.

Initially, Mouana took him for a dead man. His face was tight as sheet rubber across a skull like a fist, and riven down one side by a scar that left one eye a milky wart. His arms were twisted bunches of tattoos and veins, and his waistcoat hung from his ribs across a painfully empty abdomen. But his good eye was sharp as sea ice, and the way he sucked at his tobacco-pipe betrayed an uniquely living thirst.

Mouana let go of the fallen ram, and walked towards him without breaking eye contact. Her wrist panel beeped, but she ignored it. Standing just six feet apart, they nodded at each other. He took in the remains of her uniform, the regimental tattoo of the ringed world on her forearm; she flicked a glance at the blue-inked pipe-smoke wreathing his own. They had an understanding.

"Wrack?" said the man through his thick black moustache, emitting a cloud of blue smoke.

"Yeah," answered Mouana. "Wrack."

Both mobs erupted in rhythmic chanting of the name as the two of them shook hands and broke into the strangest of smiles.

THIS WAS ACTUALLY quite a lot of fun, thought Wrack, as he concentrated on slapping a tentacle round the slippery chain link.

He'd found an octopus languishing half-finished in one of *Tavuto*'s labs and, since Mouana wasn't responding to any of his messages, he had decided to see if he could get the thing into the City to pass the time.

It was bleeding hard to move the thing around, though. Every time he managed to achieve any finesse with one of its arms, the rest would contract or flail and put him off-balance. It definitely wasn't a question of skill, he insisted to himself; after all, his brain was clearly well-acquainted with tentacles. Clearly, he thought, as his body dangled precariously from the anchor-chain, it was shoddy work by the technicians who had put the creature together.

He thrust out another arm and managed to wrap it round

the next link, but the rest gave way and left him hanging. His body swung in the wind and he cursed to himself.

This was a rubbish game, admitted Wrack, letting the octopus drop onto the rooftops below.

THEY HAD MOVED into the Ministry's Fellows' Bar to negotiate. It was easily fifty yards from end to end; an expanse of tiled marble, potted ferns and—since the Pipers had stormed the place—the bloodied bodies of ministers.

On one side was wooden panelling; on the other, floor-to-ceiling windows, beyond which lay the factory floor far below. Where the dead were made. Viewed from up here, it could hardly be described as a factory—the side visible to the ministers was as grandly decorated as their own bar. Dominating the space was a row of colossal gilded faces; saints and knights from the City's convoluted national mythology, snarling in ecstasy. Their gaping mouths led through to the warren of chambers where reanimation took place, and the cellars where the fresh dead would be stacked in crates, ready for transit.

From here, the ministers would have been able to dine in comfort, eating real meat as the magistrates carried bagged bodies in from the execution wing and out through the mouths of the saints.

The atmosphere in the bar today was more raucous. For a start, the Bruiser was behind the bar—although he wasn't much of a host. Mouana shook her head in disbelief as he ripped a pump from its mounting and held it above his head, jetting a torrent of foaming lager into and around his mouth. He emitted a strange, gurgling roar, perhaps in delight on realising that, without the need to breathe, his lungs were just two new organs in which to put drink.

Mouana wasn't sure how he'd made it here—she hadn't seen him since her call to *Tavuto*'s engine hall, until a few minutes ago when he had walked in, hands drenched in blood, and marched over the Pipers at the bar to quench his thirst. As far as the Bruiser went, it was best not to ask too many questions.

Some of the more lucid sailors were wandering round the bar, making strange attempts at conversation with the living. The Pipers seemed to be doing their best to bring the dead folk into their circles, but the smiles were a little too rigid, the gesticulations a little too wild. There was no way of making those encounters relaxed: despite any amount of shared purpose, it seemed nobody could quite handle conversing with a corpse.

Others had made their way downstairs, where they were aimlessly breaking things. A mob of former citizens was busy prising one of the saintly heads from the wall, while a woman in the grey remnants of a summer dress was smashing the teeth off another with a crowbar.

Mouana was distracted from the cathartic bedlam when a tumbler full of rum was slid onto the table in front of her. Fingal, the Pipers' haggard leader who had met her at the doors, sat down across from her and raised his own glass in salute.

"Not sure if you're thirsty, friend—but we should at least toast before the serious talk starts."

Fingal was clearly the type of man who could make any gesture a threat unless he made a conscious effort not to, and the creases beneath his good eye suggested he was making every attempt to seem cordial. Even so, Mouana struggled not to feel intimidated by default until she remembered how frankly terrifying she looked herself. Going by the principle that the more fights you'd visibly lost, the harder you looked, you couldn't really beat being a dead soldier.

Mouana cemented her confidence by sinking the rum in one gulp and looking Fingal in the eye over the rim of the glass. The last drink she had shared had been with Wrack; a bottle of dirty preservative they had swigged in a leaking whaleboat, rowing home from a disastrous hunt. It reminded her.

"You knew about Wrack," said Mouana, setting down the

tumbler like a full stop. Fingal nodded as he swallowed, then tilted his head as if weighing the question.

"We knew Wrack, sure. Knew he'd gone to *Tavuto* in the end, and all. But we didn't know *about* Wrack. When word first came through about trouble at Ocean, we had no idea it was to do with him. And when we saw his name in the radio transcripts... well, that was a surprise."

"So you knew Wrack," pursued Mouana, brow crackling as she frowned. "He was one of yours, right?"

Fingal shrugged, and refilled their glasses. "I used to do a lot of jobs with his old man. I knew him from when he was a kid. But let me be clear—we thought he was gone, like every other Piper gets captured and zedded. Gone for good. Certainly weren't expecting him to hijack the City's bloody slave ship. Neither was the Ministry. It was days before they worked out what was going on; they figured it for just a rough patch, a bad batch of zeds, poorly processed, acting up."

"But you knew what was going on?"

"Honestly? No idea. The Blades outside the wall stepped up their assault when the *Tavuto* news hit, and the Ministry was caught in a spin. Figuring we were never likely to get a better chance, we made our play."

"And the navy?" quizzed Mouana, thinking of the ships that had struck Piper flags and distracted the *Eschatologist* on the way in.

"Happy accident," answered Fingal through a rum belch. "We'd had assets on those ships for a long while... been planning a breakthrough to try and raid Ocean, one day. Course, when Ocean came to *us*, courtesy of your good selves, we figured we had to be adaptable."

"You mentioned Wrack's old man," said Mouana, as she raised her glass for another gulp. "Who was he?"

Fingal chuckled in response, a sound that belonged in an alleyway shadow.

"Old King Pipe. The boss, or as near as we came to one."

"And where's he now?"

Fingal's face fell. "Dead, unfortunately. Caught a ricochet in the first scrap as we came in here and burst his head. That left me in charge, and it's a damned shame; all I ever did was organise the muscle."

Light pulsed through the skylights of the bar, and a deep booming rolled across the city sky; another barrage pattern was beginning. Weakening the shield enough for a full assault would take a while, but that didn't mean there was time to waste. Finding out about Wrack's family history could wait. Mouana downed her last drink, and pushed it aside with an open palm: it was time to get the job done.

"So. Looks like we both got here at once. What was your plan?"

"Kill the Chancellor, take the Ministry and smash the machines. Stop the abuse of the dead, or die trying—that's all the plan ever was, far as I know." Fingal sipped on his pipe. "If I'm honest, we were surprised to even get this far. The assault drew a lot of troops to the wall, and we had an asset on the inside to let us in—but even so, once we breached the Ministry, we were getting *hammered*. We'd been in a stalemate out back for hours, lost most of our people, by the time your boat showed up." The scarred man paused to spit on the floor and stoke his pipe to a ruddy glow.

"Then suddenly, half the defence ran off in a panic to the Scholar's gate. We pushed through, and ended up taking the whole place before we knew our own luck. As for the Chancellor, well... I believe you met the Chancellor on your way in." Fingal grinned, stretching his long scar, and nodded in the direction of the lobby. Mouana remembered the body lying under the statue, and smirked. That was one job done.

"So," said Fingal, spreading his hands. "That's as far as I've worked things out. You've been asking a hell of a lot of questions, and I'm dry from the talking. My turn; what's your plan?"

Mouana nodded. "Same as yours, so it looks. Find the machines they made us with, and destroy them. So they can't be made again. Then die. Properly."

"Well, we can help with the first"—Fingal looked up through

the skylights and nodded at her regimental tattoo—"and your old mates should help manage the second bit. For all of us."

"What do you know about the machines?"

"Quite a lot, you know," said Fingal. He whistled. "Or she does, anyway. Oi, Pearl!"

A young woman came over from the other side of the bar, pushing a cart stacked high with brushed steel canisters and a crate of narrow leather cases.

"Mouana, meet Pearl; she's the asset on the inside I mentioned earlier. Worked as a vapourer here at the Ministry, and she's been our eyes and ears here for some time."

Mouana stood abruptly, knocking her chair aside, and the room fell silent. The Bruiser, smelling a fight on the wind, turned to regard Pearl with unblinking eyes. Pearl, to her credit, stood still, looking more angry than frightened.

"Kill me if you want," she sighed. "It'd be fair enough. But listen first. And before you ask, I don't know if I did any of you. They always came in bags, so we didn't see the faces. Did my own brother, though. They didn't tell me, but I checked the serial number. So I hate them as much—"

"Piss off with your speech, and explain the machines before I do something stupid," interrupted Mouana, and took a step toward the woman.

"Fine," whispered Pearl, and picked up one of the larger canisters. "We call this 'miasma.' One of these does about fifty bodies. It'll inject, but it's usually applied by mechanical ventilation. It works fast; hardens nervous tissue with carbon and reconfigures stuff to work anaerobically. I know you don't want a lecture, but truth be told we don't know much more about it than that. It's old tech; really, really old."

Hands trembling as the silence hardened, she slid one of the leatherbound boxes from the crate and walked over to Mouana with it. She snapped open a fastener, reached inside and withdrew a matte black rod, its surface inscribed with a spiralling filigree of printed gold. It looked indescribably alien, and sickeningly familiar all at once.

"This is a necrod," said Pearl. "It's even older, and a lot harder to explain."

"Try," hissed Mouana, with a queasy sense that she knew what the woman was about to say.

"It programmes the miasma. Miasma itself is easy to make, but without these it's just a colloid of inert theurgitons—it won't do anything. These canisters have already been activated."

Mouana snorted in bleak amusement. Theurgitons; tiny machines. She remembered old Captain Aroha cursing the things, as they had spent a roasting afternoon failing to repair a collapsed coolant pump on one of the antique railguns. "Tiny fucking machines," he had ranted, wiping grease from his brow, "it always comes down to tiny machines."

Pearl had stopped at the half-laugh, but Mouana glared at her, and she continued.

"Nobody knows how the necrods work, or how to make them. We looted them from another city, which looted them from somewhere else, centuries ago. All we do know is that when you run the right current through them, they... well, they put out something like a neural signal. But definitely not a human one. It activates the miasma, makes it do—well, what it does."

"And it can't make it do anything else, can it?"

"No. Miasma could probably do a lot of things, but these rods will only make it reanimate," said Pearl, as Mouana stalked closer.

"And how many rods are there here?"

"Just the ones on this crate."

Thunder rolled as Mouana took the rod gently from Pearl's hands. She called softly to the bar, where the Bruiser, having grown bored with the technical discussion, had a Piper in a headlock and was making them drink lager. Nodding at his leader's summons, he dropped the spluttering rebel and lumbered over to Mouana, who handed him the ancient machine.

The Bruiser turned the thing over in his hands, brow furrowed, then weighed it like a cudgel as he looked Pearl over. After some calculation, he gave Mouana a questioning glance. She in turn looked to Fingal, who drew deeply on his pipe and shrugged, and then to Pearl, standing with her jaw clenched and her eyes fixed on the floor.

Mouana knew what she had to do. Here was a woman who had worked the factory floor for years, making slaves of her friends and sending them to rot on an alien sea. Even the ex-vapourer's own comrades knew she'd earned her death, no matter the mitigation since. It would be justice, and fair revenge, to give the Bruiser the nod.

She summoned all of her anger, let it pool like hot oil in her rotten head, but all she could think of was Wrack. Poor, mad Wrack, who still couldn't quite cope with it all. As she gave the tiniest shake of her head, she told herself she was still a soldier; that the mercy was all his.

The Bruiser looked profoundly disgusted, but nodded back all the same, then raised the necrod like a bottle in a brawl.

"*Fack off!*" he screamed, smashing it to pieces on the bar counter.

WRACK HAD THE most terrible headache, all of a sudden. Of course, he couldn't remember the last time he hadn't had a headache of some description, but this was different. It felt like broken glass ground into his nerves, like his axons had been stretched tight and plucked like guitar strings. He could taste it, like a mouthful of hot vinegar.

It took him out of himself, left whatever lay beneath writhing and snapping its beak in the sudden light.

Then it passed, as quickly as it had come on. It was as if a wind had blown through him, leaving his mind thrumming and muddled. Vision returned, but he had no idea what he was looking at, let alone what he had been doing when the pain came on.

The number 32, brass on chipped paint. Chipped *green* paint, of the most familiar colour. A colour that smelled of book-dust and roast cod, metallic like die-cast toys, stale like pipe smoke. Like... like home.

Schneider lit up with joy; he was *home!* He was going to visit Dad, after his long trip. He rapped jauntily on the door, grinning at the prospect of the old man's surprise on seeing his son again. There was no answer, but that was fine—his father's hearing had never been great, and he was probably out in the conservatory, fussing over herbs. He would have to take his old route in, the one he had used as a teen when coming home at dawn.

Schneider moved to the bay window beside the door and fished in the gap in the wooden slats, worn smooth through years of covert entry. After some fiddling, the catch released, and the sash window slid silently upwards.

He hopped over the sill and into the study, but it wasn't a study any more. The furniture was all wrong, and the pictures on the wall were different from how he remembered. Where was the painting of the viaduct, the watercolour with the badly-painted dog in the background? It didn't look right, and it didn't smell right either.

Then the door swung open, and revealed a grimacing man with a kitchen knife. It was not Schneider's dad. Behind him was a woman in a nightgown, her eyes bulging and her mouth twisting around the beginnings of a scream. Behind both of them was a monster. It reared above them in a mound of tattered flesh, eyes white and edges flapping like a ragged, wobbling skirt.

Schneider was about to warn them of the devil behind them, when he realised it was his own reflection in the hallway mirror.

The man waved his knife and the woman screamed, but all Wrack could do was laugh. Of course! He was a massive, rotting stingray on mechanical spider legs! How had he forgotten that? He laughed and laughed, and the thing in the mirror shook with it, spraying black gore from its spiracles. What a thing to forget!

Wrack wanted to double over, to shriek and giggle until he was sobbing for breath, but of course he had no lungs! Somehow, it made things even funnier. That poor baffled family, he thought, as they ran screaming to the front door. Woken in the night to find a monster in their house, getting confused by paintings.

Wrack roared with mirth as he stared at the mirror, and the ray laughed back. You had to see the funny side of things, he thought to himself as phantom tears began to pool.

And this was fucking hilarious.

Drawing back from the ray, Wrack began to laugh with all of himself. With the sharks and worms and the crabs that capered through the streets, with the quivering pallor of his mind, with the raging, shattered heart of *Tavuto*. His sides throbbed, his bones glowed. His laughter belched from him like a thunderhead, rolling over the city and dancing with the growl of the guns.

You *had* to laugh.

To HER UTTER astonishment, Mouana was giggling. Maybe it was the release of tension, or just the relief of knowing it was all over—she had no idea. But she was shaking with it, and as she looked around at the mayhem in the bar, she saw it wasn't just her.

The dead were laughing. Not with the black, sardonic grunts that had passed for humour on *Tavuto*, nor with the elation of warriors with nothing to lose, but true laughter—the kind that shook ribs and wetted creased eyes. It was infectious. As Fingal lined up his crowbar to smash a rod balanced across two chairs, he had to stop to wipe away the tears. Even Pearl was grinning, and Mouana could hardly begrudge her.

When the first rod had exploded into gravel on the bar, so had the tension, and a mad sort of playfulness had developed around the destruction of the rest. Eunice had managed to crack one with a squeeze of her hydraulic bicep, and sailors and Pipers alike had cheered her on. Kaba had struck up one of her boat-loaders' songs, and the rest of the dead had joined in, bellowing together as they took hammers to the instruments of their enslavement.

Catharsis had become carnival. Zombies were lined up before the Bruiser, who sat atop the cart of miasma, cracking the canisters open one after another. As the sailors passed, he would spray the grey gas into their mouths, baptising each with a merry cheer of "fack off!" before slapping them on the back and sending them back into the chaos.

At the other side of the bar, a dead man had stuffed a lit rag in a bottle of brandy, and was looking in Mouana's direction for approval. She put on an expression of mock severity but flashed him a thumbs up; he returned it, before hurling the firebomb through the glass wall and onto the factory floor. The flames rose and their shadows danced, dead and living both made indistinguishable by the fire.

A cheer went up, and Mouana's attention was drawn back to the throng. A circle had formed, and at its centre stood Fingal, with the last of the necrods. He held it out to her like a party cracker, eyebrows raised in invitation, and the crowd began to chant her name. She took the rod, warm and light as charcoal, held it up in the air with both hands, and brought it down hard across her thigh. The noise as it snapped was drowned in roaring.

The chanting and the clapping died down, leaving only the crackle of the flames as they spread through the factory. Mouana was just looking down at the shards of the necrod and wondering what to do next, when Pearl spoke up.

"Well, that's all of the ones here!" she said, beaming.

Mouana turned to her, very slowly, and asked her what *exactly* she meant by that.

CHAPTER
TWENTY
SIX

NEARLY EVERYONE WAS gone from the library. A man had scurried
past Wrack with a stack of books as he climbed the stairs, but
had been in too much of a hurry to offer any challenge.

Wrack was relieved, as he didn't feel remotely in the mood
for confrontation. After the laughter had faded following the
fiasco with the stingray, he hadn't felt very well at all. Things he
had just about accepted as reality at sea felt freshly horrifying
on the streets he grew up in.

Seeing his demonic reflection in the hall where he had played
as a boy had done something foul; had forced the grey horror
of the *Tavuto* and the warm, safe memories of his youth into
the same reality, leaving him cowering at their vertex. No
longer could he tell himself he was an accidental consciousness,
a jockey on the memories of a dead man now at rest. He was
Schneider Wrack, the boy who had grown up in that house,
and he had come back to it a monster.

It was all a bit much, really.

Figuring he might as well confront the familiar head-on, he decided the library was the place to go. He had taken the crab again; climbing the stairs was a bit of a labour as the thing had cracked two legs when Mouana booted it, but it had a much better chance of handling a book than a gore-caked stingray.

Wrack picked his way across the empty lobby, claw-clicks echoing on marble, and headed for the fellows' reading room. It too was abandoned save for a vinegary-looking old man, deep in an armchair and scowling at a book of poetry.

Somehow the sight of the Doctor of Poetic Engineering, in the same chair he'd sat in each day for as long as Wrack could remember, was oddly comforting. It would take more than the return of the City's dead to distract him from his work. The Doctor murmured his usual greeting as Wrack clicked past, not so much as glancing aside from his text, and Wrack waved back with a claw as he passed into the librarians' tower.

The old electric lift took him up to the belfry, nine storeys above the library's roof. It was where he'd gone to read whenever he'd felt overwhelmed (although, Wrack mused, he'd never really known the meaning of the word)—a place of cool stone and pigeon shit where nobody went, and nobody looked for missing books.

He had no lantern, but the lights of the bombardment were enough to read by; the sky pulsed and blazed, smeared itself across the brass of the old bell like summer fireworks.

Wrack's claw levered away the loose panel beneath the belfry's inner window ledge, then rummaged inside. Ah yes, there they were. The crab dribbled a froth of foul bubbles from its mouthparts as he allowed himself a sigh of contentment; he had found his old stash of books. Dragging them out one by one with his claw, he looked at what he had been reading when he died.

"HONESTLY, I DON'T know anything else," stammered Pearl, her eyes flickering nervously to the harpoon pinning her jacket to the table. "It might not be anything. I just overheard they were thinking about getting more!"

"From where?" growled Fingal, grabbing a fistful of the woman's vest. He was furious as Mouana was—clearly, this was the first time he'd heard of this too.

"Wherever they came from? I don't know! I barely heard anything. A rod failed last winter, and it was the second in fifty years, and the ministers were getting jumpy. It was the end of a quota meeting, I was walking past. I heard one of them talking about an expedition, about them not being able to spare the forces because of the sieg—ah!"

Eunice snorted and twitched her harpoon arm, raising a line of blood on the side of Pearl's neck. Mouana was about to berate her for failing to mention the existence of other rods before they had set the place on fire, but the words caught in her throat.

She had been in command: why hadn't she stopped them torching the place before she'd made sure they didn't need anything more from it? One look at Pearl's face told Mouana she was telling the truth—she didn't know anything else. And if there were any record of what the ministers knew, it was almost certainly now cut off by fire.

"Who else would know?" Mouana asked Fingal, not really expecting a response, and was startled when Pearl answered.

"You could try the Chancellor?" she suggested, tilting her head towards the miasma cart as far as she could without cutting her own throat.

WRACK TURNED *COMEDY of the Sandwiches* over in his claws a couple of times before putting it aside. He wasn't really in the mood for fiction, and besides, he had no hope of remembering how far he'd gotten—death hadn't been kind to memories like that.

Next was a doorstep of a text, a treatise on the nature of

music by a long-dead academic. Wrack was fairly sure he'd been reading this to try and impress someone, but he had no idea who, or why. It was the kind of book you soldiered through a few pages at a time; the kind where you found your eyes sliding along sentences without taking in meaning, just to move down the page.

Wrack shoved it aside, and picked up the next book—*Winter in the Labyrinth: A History of the First Canyon Wars*. This one seemed fascinating in theory, but had tested his attention span almost as much as the last—it turned out the Canyon Wars had involved a lot of senatorial wrangling and arguments over tax before the ironclad duels and the amphibious landings had kicked off. And in any case, Wrack was fucking sick of war.

There was something on stone ants, and a related volume on cloudsifters—great things to talk about in the pub, but which rapidly dried out when reading through pages and pages of population density charts. Then there was *Recipes of the Herring Men*, the curated notes of a mining platoon that had been stranded on a kuiper fish farm for a decade. It was good for a browse, but it got repetitive.

Wrack pulled the books one at a time with bloodstained pincers, not fancying anything, with a creeping dread that he had simply lost his taste for reading. The thought made him all the more anxious to find a distraction; if he was no longer able to sit and enjoy a good book, his efforts to convince himself he was still human would become very precarious.

It was with a rush of relief, then, that he dug out an old favourite. Its weight, its texture, the flaked gilding of the letters on its spine, all triggered the warm anticipation of a familiar pleasure. He couldn't smell, but the phantom musk of dust and binding glue swirled in his head as he pulled it from the pile. This book, he had read for pleasure alone.

GRAND AMAZON, proclaimed the spine in tattered gold, *A personal narrative of a journey through the equinoctial regions of the reclaimed world, by Gustav Waldemar*.

It was a rare text, and one the library had been missing for years. Wrack had seen it once as a boy and been enchanted—and when he had unearthed a copy during the excavation of one of the south wing cellars, he had quietly pocketed it for his own reserve.

Waldemar had been a paragon of the *Rückgewinnun,* that optimistic age when the Confederacy—long-since shattered—had managed to reopen half the world's ruined gates and bring them back into the Lemniscatus. He had made his expedition to Grand Amazon right after the gate-mines had been defused, along with the fur trappers and the first, hard-faced pioneers, to a world isolated since the wars of antiquity.

Wrack dove into the book with a clumsy claw, parting the pages where a strip of card marked the start of what he had come to think of as the 'exciting bit.' Struggling a little to focus with the crab's peculiar vision—it was less about moving his eyes and more choosing which part of a wider image to bring into focus—he began to read.

After transition, we found ourselves some way up one of the tributaries of the Rio Sinfondo, the primary river feeding the Cloud Bay delta. It was an hour past dusk on orientation, with a warm katabatic breeze blowing south across our bow. Turning to align with the current, we made for the Sinfondo; by the charts we should have been nearly within sight of the Torsville colony, but we saw no lights. Anticipating that the colony had faltered during the disconnect we had packed with no expectation of resupply, but a sense of disquiet spread among the boatmen as the banks offered nothing but mangrove and cottonbark thickets. When we reached the place marked on the charts as the colony site, we steered close to the bank and swept it with the searchlight. Other than a few rotten pilings and the remnants of walls, there was no sign of human habitation. Regardless, the Torsville bank gave the first demonstration of the world's fecundity: moths and fat-

*tailed riverflies swarmed against the lights, while the
eyes of moss-bears and tree porcupines shone in the
dark as they ambled the bank in search of fallen fruit.*

Wrack skipped ahead, doing all he could not to rip the
beloved pages with his pincers; Waldemar spent some time
discussing the riverbank fauna, and then the narrative was
broken by several pages illustrating catfish collected in light
traps. When it resumed, it was with a paragraph that had
always made Wrack squirm, especially when read with the
knowledge of what had later befallen the expedition.

*Once in the night, the lightsman begged a halt, claiming
he had seen men on the bank; there was a rush on deck
and the crew called out across the dark river, but when
the searchlight came back to the place he'd marked,
there was nothing but tangled thorns.*

Relishing the familiar discomfort, Wrack flipped ahead
again.

*We came to the mouth of the tributary, where the river's
black water blended with the milk-tea of the Sinfondo,
just before dawn on the third day. At first we planned
to move out into the channel and make immediate
headway against the current, but a near-collision with
a fallen blastwood curbed our excitement. The tree,
near a quarter-mile in length, must have fallen deep
inland—by the time we encountered it, it had become
the spine of a raft of smaller trees, uprooted shrubs and
riotous water flora. Only quick thinking on the part of
the helmswoman avoided our hull becoming part of the
travelling island.*
    *The decision was made to wait until the light was
strong enough to spot further rafts before moving
out into the Sinfondo. In the end, our patience was*

rewarded—by the day's first light, with the river still swathed in thick mist, we saw one of the great worms breach. Though it was far off through dense fog, I made it out to be an Ormsley's Phosphorescent—one of the larger deep-channel predators, and nearly fifty yards from horns to hindbeak. It emerged from the water in silence, throwing off a cloud of droplets as it twisted in a liquid arc, then returned to its element with a splash that would have dislodged all but its sturdiest parasites. Seeing the breach as an omen, the helmswoman moved us out into the channel.

A particularly vivid slew of sparks in the sky broke Wrack's concentration, but it was easy to shrug off. The city could fall to pieces around him, and Mouana could enact whatever gruesome revenge she had in mind by herself; he was done with it all. As far as Wrack was concerned, he would sit there with his book until it all blew over, or someone came up the belfry stairs with a hammer. If he was left alone for long enough, he might even have another go at *Comedy of the Sandwiches*. Nevertheless, the barrage had made him lose his place, and he clucked his mandibles in irritation as he dug back in at another marker.

On the twenty-fifth day we reached the mouth of the Rio Esqueleto on our way upriver from Candlewood, and anchored the boat to make council on our course from there. While the dockmaster at Candlewood had updated our charts, giving us the positions of the towns still standing on the upper Sinfondo, many of the crew— led by Ms Tansell, the archaeologist—argued in favour of an extended detour up the Esqueleto before heading upriver. The Esqueleto was unsettled beyond its lower reach, and trappers' reports from before the disconnect suggested an overland route to High Sarawak from its upper channel. For a historian, therefore, it offered more than did the Sinfondo.

In the end, the discussion was settled by the wurmjäger, *Hansen—the rich waters of the upper Sinfondo offered us the chance to add further wormskins to the six in the hold, and thus to pay for the voyage. At noon, it was decided we should make a four-day expedition up the tributary, before turning back and heading north again up the Sinfondo.*

Wrack's attention was torn from the page again, and not by the bombardment. There was something in that paragraph that really should have triggered recognition—he was sure of it. Wrack would have frowned, if he had had the anatomy; the feeling was akin to the sort of half-memory fumble experienced by the very tired or the very stoned, and had become monstrously familiar in the wake of death.

When he scanned the page again, however, the words hit him like a shovel: *an overland route to High Sarawak*. He had been curious about the reference when he had read the book as a living man—now he was dead, it held extra resonance.

High Sarawak, the vertical city. The bone-state. The place where the dead walked as revered machines. Until Wrack had seen *Tavuto* from its gore-slicked deck, all he had known of reanimation came from the vague cultural conception of High Sarawak. It was part of any Lipos-Tholon's primary education in myth, along with the Tin King, the Horse Fleet and the God-Times. The city that had dug too far into the old tech and destroyed itself; it was now long cut off through the decay of the Lemniscatus, taking its mythical necrotech with it.

By adolescence, most kids had quietly filed it in the pinch-of-salt component of world history, one of the colourful metaphors the City used to teach its children the morality of statecraft. The revelation that Waldemar had considered it a real place; that he had soberly dismissed an expedition in search of it, should have seemed ludicrous. But then Wrack was reading Gustav's words as a victim of the very technology it had been famed for.

Wrack *had* walked as a dead man; he knew that the supposedly forbidden knowledge of the bone-state had persisted past its disappearance, despite the City's insistence otherwise. Finally, he understood why Waldemar's book, which had always seemed so drily uncontroversial, had been so hard to come across in its unabridged form. High Sarawak was not only real, but there was a good chance it was accessible through Grand Amazon, one of the City's longest-standing colonies.

Wrack had to tell Mouana. Given her obsession with the technology that had doomed them, there was no way she wouldn't want to know about this. She probably wouldn't want to chat with him, he thought, remembering the crack of her boot against his carapace, but he had to give it a go. Suddenly, he wasn't so keen to get lost in his books.

MATE, thought Wrack. *THE THING THAT MADE US? MIGHT NOT HAVE COME FROM THE CITY AFTER ALL. IT'S FROM HIGH SARAWAK. AND I RECKON I KNOW A WAY THERE. GRAND AMAZON.*

He waited, watching the shells fall on the shield through the belfry window, too curious to go back to Waldemar's book. Surely, Mouana would write back any moment now.

"HE'S NOT DEAD yet," said Kaba, crouching by the Chancellor's side.

It was raining now, fat drops that stank of ozone from the beleaguered shield. The steps of the Ministry were slick with it, and the Chancellor's robes were soaked to a deep maroon. If he was bleeding, it didn't show.

"No, I'm not," spat the Chancellor, from beneath his own statue. The bronze cast had landed head-first on his hips, flattening his pelvis, and Mouana could scarcely imagine the man's pain. He must have been a desperately tough old bastard. She gave a small shake of her head to the rebels pushing the miasma trolley, keeping them from moving within the Chancellor's line of sight.

"Where are the other rods?" asked Mouana, as she knelt by the crushed man's side. The Chancellor snarled.

Her wrist console beeped; she ignored it. No doubt Wrack had some inanity or other to share with her—maybe he had seen an interesting statue, or remembered a poem. There was no time for his nonsense now.

"Where are the rods?" repeated Mouana. The Chancellor spat, landing a pinkish blob next to her boot, and gave a shuddering grimace. Mouana sighed: no doing things the easy way, then.

Looking down at the quivering statesman, she remembered the soldier being eaten alive, and the overseer they had captured in the opening chaos of the *Tavuto* uprising. Time and time again, she had gone against her instincts for the sake of her soft-hearted friend. But whatever Wrack would think of her, there was no time for mercy now. Judging by the near-constant battery of the shield, the siege was nearly broken, and if there were rods elsewhere, she needed to be on her way to them before the City fell. It was time for expediency.

"Where are the rods?" she repeated, and stamped on the man's outstretched hand. Her wrist chimed again, as the screams began.

The Chancellor passed out twice in the first half hour, requiring amphetamines from the rebels' aid kits to bring him round, but still said nothing. After another twenty minutes, he went into cardiac arrest, but still all he offered was curses. It was all Mouana had expected.

As he died, she called for miasma; Pearl offered up the cylinder, and she jetted it into the Chancellor's ruined mouth as he sucked in his final breath. Ten minutes later he was back, screaming. With so little time dead, Pearl explained, the Chancellor would experience very little of the vacant bafflement that afflicted most miasma victims. They could continue questioning him immediately.

"Welcome back," said Mouana, as the Chancellor thrashed broken limbs and gaped blindly in terror. "The rules have changed. You've taken miasma, so now you can't feel much pain. But there are worse things than pain. The City is about to fall. If we leave you, the Blades will find you here, and they will be able to keep you around as long as they like. The rest, you can imagine. But if you tell us where the rods are, I will kill you."

She figured the Chancellor had slipped into the fugue of the newly-woken, but then he cleared his throat.

"Fine," he whispered, expression unreadable behind what she had made of his face. "I'll tell you."

Mouana was taken aback. For the Chancellor to have collected his thoughts and weighed up his options so quickly, he must have had phenomenal presence of mind. She felt grudging respect for the old bastard, which curdled as he opened his mouth again.

"They're at High Sarawak," he grinned, and spat out a tooth. Mouana's hopes collapsed; the Chancellor hadn't seen reason—he'd gone mad. High Sarawak was a myth; if it had ever existed, it had been cut off long ago. He may as well have told her the rods were in Metal Heaven, or the Emerald City.

All the cutting had been in vain; she was no nearer an answer than she had been in the burning Ministry, and they were running out of time to draw sense from him. As if to underline the fact, an apocalyptic crack came from the horizon, where a great cloud of dust was rolling in slow fury.

The City was breached.

Mouana stood and drew her gun. This was the end: she had failed. The rods were still out there somewhere, and all she had done was shed an ocean of blood to wipe out a single batch of them. Her gun wavered over the Chancellor's head as the rebels watched, silent. The Chancellor began to laugh, and she lowered the weapon.

Fuck it, she thought, with a flash of anger. He hadn't come good on his part of the deal, so she wouldn't come good on hers. She would leave him for his enemies, crippled, blind and deathless.

In fact, thought Mouana, she could leave the lot of them. Fingal, and Pearl, and the Bruiser and the Chancellor, who she could barely stand to look at. They were doomed anyway—

what use was there in her staying around to see the last acts of her failure play out?

She raised the gun, and was about to turn it to her temple, when her wrist chimed once more. Wrack. She would say goodbye to Wrack. If there was anything she still owed anyone, it was that. Mouana looked at her wrist, and stood stock still. The words blazed, orange on black.

THING THAT MADE US. HIGH SARAWAK. A WAY THERE. GRAND AMAZON.

The message had been sent more than an hour ago, and repeated seven times since. While she had tortured a man in and out of death in search of the same answer.

Mouana's vision swam. She looked up slowly, at the rebels and the sailors as they waited in the rain for her to act. There was no reason they should have any idea what had just happened, or that she had been on the edge of annihilating herself. If she just frowned back at the console, as if taking in a minor detail, they would be none the wiser.

Mouana frowned back at the console, typed *YES, JUST FOUND OUT ABOUT HS MYSELF*, with shaking hands, and shot the Chancellor in the head.

"I know a way there," croaked Mouana, the pistol dropping from her hand, and the crowd cheered. All she could do was stare into the wall of dust, rising from the city's edge like the closing fingers of a fist.

"BREACH! BREACH! TO THE BREEEACH!"

The howl from the radio stretched into a dopplered scream, climaxing with the scrape of ceramic on meat as Dust plunged her hatchet into the soldier's chest.

She bared her teeth and shunted another bar of drugs into her system. Synaesthetic boosters and kinetics, blended hot and raw. Her armour, tuned to sing with every kill, thrummed with the quiver of haptic fibres. Dust stared down into the soldier's faceplate, blank as the desert sun, and tore her blade free in a cataract of gore.

Immediately she sought another kill, and there it was: her blade tore greedily into the next man's neck, sizzling through kevlar, colliding with soft cartilage and ripping through into redness. *More* she demanded, her interface growing hazier before her eyes with each kill. *More.* Make me faster, make me harder, give me more flesh to rend.

Before her prayer had finished she had answered it, yanking the weapon's hooked beard through another man's throat, and was dancing in the rain of his heart's last shudder. Every droplet, every hiss of blood on ceramic, paid for years of waiting. Every step she took was conquest.

Even before the wall had fallen, five endless minutes ago, she had sent her chariot screaming ahead of the charge on a plume of black smoke. When the atomic slug had blown the breach she had been close enough for it to turn the world white, to roast her face through her helmet and baste her in a creaking wash of geiger-clicks.

Her boots had hit the ground moments later, leading her personal guard over the waste and into the near-molten maw of the breach. There they had met the City's kentigerns, as they raced forward into the oven-hot rubble with cables and projectors to set up a temporary shield. They had set upon the defenders like beasts.

The air throbbed with screams and shots, blade-clash and frantic shouts; lights blazed and shadows flickered in billows of pulverised stone. Dust they called her, and dust she was, swirling and lethal in the breach of the wall.

A man loomed out of the madness with a shotgun, but one of her guard took the blast; only a handful of sodden shrapnel made it through to embed itself in her amour. She pounced over the guard as he collapsed, and was bearing down on the attacker before his face could even register surprise. A whicker of steel, and his gun was hooked from his hands; terror was just beginning to dawn when she beat the life from him with the thing.

Another kentigern was opening up on her with a machine gun, the bullets chewing eagerly into the armour above her ribs. Dust simply flexed her shielding around the point of impact, shuddered in pleasure as the slugs slid harmlessly aside from its field, and stalked up the stream of fire to the terrified gunner.

After he collapsed with her blade in his skull, there was nothing—only yelling in the dark as the defence pulled back. Her guards were all but fallen, and the enemy were in retreat. Dust screeched in affront, and hurled the bloodied body of the gunner into the dark. Why could they not have sent more?

Every second of quiet was agony; it squeezed her heart and dripped across her shoulders in sheets of sweat. She could hear the ground hiss, still roasting from the blast. It crashed in her ears like a sandstorm. Only the sound of the artillery kept her sane, the deep pounding of the guns as they worked to open further breaches down the line.

Eventually, after long, dragging seconds, the vanguard of the main assault caught up, leaping from the decks of transports that nosed through the murk like sharks. These were not her uniformed troopers, the ranks of veterans who would carry out the long, slow work of advancing through the city's streets. These were her irregulars. The mad, the dying, the devout and the hungry; men and women who had waited years to be first into the fight. Some wore no armour, ran with sandals on skillet-hot rubble. Others waded in iron suits, great rigs of salvaged plate that strained their wearers' g-boosted muscles. Some were strays from the war-drained countryside, others were thrillseekers from distant colonies—all were willing to take the breach in the hope of impressing her and earning a place in the company.

As they streamed past her, whooping and raising their weapons, their rage ran down her back like fingertips, and she hissed. The quiet was over. As if to reassure her further, the air cleared ahead of them, revealing a row of monstrous forms advancing through the dust. They boomed and chittered, swinging eyeless skulls and extending awful scythe-limbs as they sensed her troops. Even above the reek of hot stone, she could smell the sulphur of their breath—Lipos-Tholos had unleashed a full brood of its famous destriers.

Already the first of her irregulars were falling to the towering exobionts, run through by their claws as they hacked at their striding hindlimbs. It was the start of massacre, and the drugs pooled in Dust's synapses growled at her to run in and sink her hatchets into the monsters. But she knew better than to lose patience, for she had monsters of her own.

Perfectly in time with her armour's chronometer, the armoured carriers jutted from the clouds behind her. These were not the sputtering junk-barges that had ferried the irregulars into the breach, but the baroque, rust-red warcraft of the Atlas Stables, emblazoned with heraldry and festooned with campaign banners.

Dust cranked up her armour's shielding and shunted a fresh vial of warjuice, sending her to the dizzy precipice of consciouness. The mouths of the transports lowered, and from within came the pounding of huge fists on metal, a hoarse, simian grunting, and then the blast of a dozen bugles all at once.

An avalanche of fangs and white fur burst from the transports, and Dust let the drugs take her. Time slowed to a glacial grind, and she marvelled in the ferocity of a full Atlassian pithecus charge.

The riders were a sight in themselves. Albino giants in grey dress uniforms, each had earned their commission by wrestling an infant pithecus, had spent their lives taming and training their mounts in their mountaintop stables. The apes themselves were simply terrifying. Polar predators from a dying world, they weighed close to a ton and could crush a man's skull like a grape. They were the most feared cavalry force in existence.

This single squadron had cost Dust more than a regular

brigade of infantry to hire, and as much again to procure meat for the beasts. But watching the pithecus as they thundered towards the line of destriers, their value was without question.

The apes howled with the bleak ferocity of an arctic storm. Dust howled with them, released her mind from conscious thought, and ran with the beasts.

CHAPTER TWENTY SEVEN

MOUNA LAY IN darkness, gazing at distant yellow lights. Distant murmurs receded into a weighty, velvet silence. She sank deep into it and exhaled slowly. Whatever nightmare she had woken from was gone, diffused into the quiet like blood in a summer stream. Perhaps she would finish her letter now, she thought, as the lights twinkled before her. Finally, she would gather her thoughts and write, tell them she had had enough, that she was coming home at last.

Then she smelled the herbs, heady and astringent as they curled through the dark, and fear took hold of her. She scrambled to get to her feet, but only tangled herself in sheets that seemed to grow tighter and more twisted with each jerk of her limbs. The lights drew closer, resolved into huge blank eyes, and peered down at her with malevolent fascination.

"Do you know how many companies have presided over the siege of Lipos-Tholos?" asked the voice, warm and sharp as desert stone, as the darkness around her resolved into the gilded gloom of the command tent. Mouana gulped, and admitted she did not know.

"Twenty-three," answered Dust, speaking over her mumble, and turned to regard a row of faded portraits. "We are to be the twenty-fourth, and the largest yet employed by the Principals. Just think, commander; thousands upon thousands of soldiers, and all their beasts and machines and shells, hired each day for *decades* in the hope of breaking that city." Dust's eyes moved away from the procession of her failed predecessors to stare back at where Mouana struggled to stand.

"Now what, do you suppose, could be worth so much to the Principals that they would keep throwing such astronomical sums into the siege?" pondered Dust acidly, as she crouched by Mouana's side.

Mouana fought not to stammer as she answered, fighting to rise from her prone position, yet ensnared by sheets that now gripped her like limbs. "The... the connection with Ocean?"

"...will become more relevant than you think, but for a reason you might not suspect. Simple *fishing access* would mean little, were the city not cut off from its landside holdings," snapped Dust, and took a long sip from her bowl of tea before setting it down on the tent floor. "No, commander, the real value in Lipos-Tholos is in something it stole a long time ago, and which many other cities—chief among them those four Principal states which employ us—would like to steal from it in turn."

One of the general's attenuated, indistinct limbs folded into the blackness where her body should have been, and withdrew a folded, smudged diagram. It was hard to focus on, but seemed to show some sort of black cylinder, decorated all over with layers of fractal patterning.

Mouana wanted to scream when she saw the cylinder; it brought on a maddening spasm of recognition, the feeling that she had seen it in a dream and had, even then, seen it before in this very moment. She wanted to stand and run, but the sheets held her as fast as steel cables even as she thrashed against them.

"Lipos-Tholos, commander, holds power over the dead."

Mouana strained to turn away as the general approached, fought to cry out as the familiar blade slid from its scabbard, but could do no more than shudder as its tip slid between her ribs again.

"GRIEF AND FIRE, Mouana, come back!" shouted a broken face, just inches away from her own. Behind it, the world was a rushing blur.

Mouana screamed and tried to swat at the apparition, but she was held fast by a pair of vast, rotten arms. She blinked hard, then rolled her one good eye as she realised she had slipped away again. The arms were the Bruiser's, and the face was Kaba's, and the vision of the general faded into a blurred mess of dream and memory.

Still, it was near-impossible to put away the fear the dream had left. Dust as a theoretical presence on the other side of an energy shield was possible to abstract and put out of her mind; knowing the old monster was now in the city with her was another thing altogether. Worse yet, she knew the image of that diagram had been no invention of her fermenting mind. It had been a memory. Dust knew about the rods, and she would do anything to get her hands on them. It was only a matter of time before they had her on their tail.

"We need to get to Grand Amazon," shouted Mouana, before wondering why there was so much wind. "Quick, before the general realises what we've done, before she—"

"Boss, we know," frowned Kaba, talking over her in a way none of her gunnery sergeants ever would have done. "You kept saying that after you shot the Chancellor-man."

The Bruiser backed her up with a contemplative "fack off," and Mouana blinked again, trying to piece together exactly what might have happened in between bouts of consciousness. They were in some kind of vehicle, hurtling through the city towards the docks, with Fingal at the wheel. Ahead of them, the *Tavuto*'s beached prow rose like a mountain; behind them, a line of similar vehicles raced, packed as theirs was with rebels both living and dead.

"They're hearses," grinned Kaba, their speed whipping at what was left of her hair. "Used to use these to ferry the body-crates down to the docks, Fingal says. Took 'em from the Ministry garages and packed as many as we could aboard— heard what you said about Grand Amazon, so figured we just gotta find a boat and cast off. I was a delta goon myself—big A was where I spent most my life—so I figure I can get us there."

Mouana knew Kaba was trying to reassure her, but the fact that so much of a plan had been made without her left her feeling sick. She looked at the sky. Dawn couldn't be far away, and the wall must have been blown over an hour ago now. How long they had depended on how long the City could hold off her old company at the breach, and she didn't give the defenders great odds. They had to get out to sea as fast as possible; there wasn't even time to loot the *Tavuto* for weapons or...

Then she realised. Wrack.

"What's Wrack doing?" snapped Mouana at Kaba, making her recoil.

"Ask him yourself," protested the old boat-loader, spreading her arms. "He's strapped to your fucking wrist. You ask me, he's gone crazy, proper sunbaked. Been sending you book reviews for the last hour."

Mouana glanced at her wrist, just as a fascinating fact about herring—one of a long list, by the look of the message archive—came through.

WRACK, typed Mouana. *CN U GET OFF TVTO?*

SURE, I'LL JUST STROLL YOUR WAY SHALL I? came the instant reply, but she was too tense even to curse him.

SRSLY. GOT TO BE A WAY TO EJECT, OR STHNG? she implored.

YES, BUT THERE'S NO POINT. I'M STAYING HERE.

Mouana felt frustration rising, when another message came through.

I'M NOT BEING SILLY, THIS TIME. YOU'VE GOT A MASSIVE JOURNEY AHEAD OF YOU, AND I AM—VERY LITERALLY—A MASSIVE BURDEN. YOU NEED TO GET OUT OF HERE AS FAST AS YOU CAN; I'M BEST OFF STAYING HERE AND COVERING YOU WITH WHAT'S LEFT OF THE WEAPONS. THEN, HOPEFULLY, I CAN GET KILLED AND FINALLY GET SOME KIP.

For once, what Wrack was saying made perfect sense. With *Tavuto* rammed into the dock side of college hill, it could put up a hell of a rearguard action once the Blades made it this side of the Ministry. And even if Wrack could eject from the ship, getting him aboard another might take hours they didn't have. But at the same time, Mouana knew with a weird clarity that Wrack simply *could not* be left behind.

Apart from anything else, he would be useful. If he could remote-operate the ship's beasts as he had done that bloody crab, they'd have a lot more muscle on side for the journey. And if he could muster the sort of weird, black pulse that *Tavuto*'s overseers had wielded against the dead by jacking into the vile old brain themselves, they might actually have a chance.

She knew there was another reason he had to come with them, but couldn't fathom what it was. Mouana hoped for all the world that it wasn't some flabby notion of friendship masquerading as reason.

Whatever it was, she needed him on board, and she didn't have time to argue with him.

TOUGH LCK MATE, she typed, her shredded hand shaking with exhaustion.

YR COMING WITH US. SO EJCT OR I WLL FKN CUT YOU OUT.

There was no answer; nothing showed on the screen save the

blinking cursor inviting her to send further threats. Mouana waited, dreading some facetious comeback—or worse, rejection of her obvious bullshit; there was no way she would have time to cut his cylinder free if he refused to budge. But there was nothing.

Then, just as she was about to send a second message, the ground shook. It rumbled up through their bodies, deeper and smoother than the rattle of the hearse's wheels on cobble, then blasted out into the air and shook tiles from the rooftops. *Tavuto*'s foghorn, blowing its final challenge to a world of monsters.

Mouana felt the blackness gathering again, and gripped at Kaba's slime-smeared rag of a vest.

"He's coming with us, Kaba. Wrack has to come with us. Take us to *Tavuto*, and get him on one of the launches. Then get us to..."

Speech failed Mouana just before vision did, but as she slipped away, her comrade was already relaying frantic instructions to Fingal.

"WELCOME BACK," SAID Dust, as she wiped her blade in the shadows of the tent. Mouana looked down at her chest in panic but saw no wound—although the cloth came away red from the general's sabre.

"What do you mean, wel—" started Mouana, but the old warlord was already talking over her.

"You're finally starting to remember, aren't you?" said Dust, sliding the blade back into its scabbard. "Took you long enough—and after all the work we put in together, too. It's a shame you couldn't have managed when it mattered most... but you've not been an entire disappointment to me. Not yet. Now where were we?"

The general stalked to her bedside, elongate and indistinct like a shadow cast by a guttering candle, and fell to a crouch. Despite urging every muscle to move, Mouana could do nothing to get away from the dreadful shape.

"Strange, isn't it, how these people can sit on all the knowledge left in the world and not notice what it points to, even if it's right under their noses? Our employers and their enemies both; how many years, how many resources, have they put into children's slap-fights over the discarded toys of their forebears, with no thought to finding another way of doing things?" She picked up the diagram of the rod again, and cruised back into the darkness.

"How absurd, how sad, that it should be left to a woman of war to *innovate* for them. But there it is. I have seen what they're missing, and if they refuse to see the opportunity, then I may have to take it for them.

"These silly rods. Powerful, certainly, but just one way of doing things, and so limited. Not even full tools, just part of something forgotten, looted and looted again between barbarian nations. And the Lipos-Tholons, bless them, had something better all this time."

Mouana had lost sight of Dust in the depths of the tent, could not make out her shifting form between the shadows of the campaign furniture. When her voice came again, it came as if from everywhere and nowhere all at once, the venomous throb of a tight-circling insect.

"This is why I have taken this ludicrous commission, commander. We are going to end this miserable squabble, take for ourselves what they are too stupid to use, and show them what they've been missing. We can do so much more."

Silence fell in the stifling tent, and what little light there was shrank to a dim halo around her bed. She dared to hope the vision was fading but then the voice came again, close and invasive as jointed legs settling on her ear.

"But you knew this already, didn't you?" whispered Dust, and the sabre's tip pressed cold against her side. "This is a memory, and you've been here before. Now it's time to go and *do something about it.*" Mouana's face twisted in horror, but the blade was already inside her chest.

* * *

"I DON'T KNOW what I'm meant to do," gasped Mouana, staring up at a smoke-drowned dawn.

"Shhh," said a figure beside her, and she jolted at the sudden presence, but it was just Fingal. He did not have the sort of face that anyone should feel reassured waking beside, but at that moment his scarred grimace was as comforting as warm milk.

"Few of us ever do," he murmured, handing her a flask of something strong.

They sat together, propped against a crate, and drank silently in the dawn. The feeling of the morning breeze on Mouana's face, dulled though it was by her dead skin, did just enough to dispel the nightmare. Even so, she feared there was more lurking in her head than she knew yet; she had only glimpsed it, like a monstrous tail disappearing into murk.

They were sat on the forecastle of a boat, itself perched in the cityscape of *Tavuto*'s starboard launch racks.

From here they could see the city spread out before them, a dirty white patchwork pricked by a thousand needles of rising smoke. Gunfire rattled in the far distance, and explosions growled in the dark cloud that followed the invaders through the suburbs. But from here it was peaceful, like birdsong and wind-rattled twigs before a gathering storm.

Above them, chains creaked as *Tavuto*'s monstrous central crane tested their weight. Sailors rushed back and forth with arms full of ammunition and machinery, calling to each other across the deck as they made ready for launch. In the middle of all this, Mouana had no idea how Fingal could find the time to sit and drink with her, but she was glad of it.

"Shouldn't you be rushing?" she wondered aloud. "Shouldn't I be rushing?"

"Nah," muttered Fingal, taking the flask for another sip. "Might as well take a moment while we can—things'll only get more hectic from here. Besides, Kaba's got things under control—she's been good while you've been out, you know. Spent her life on the delta boats, after all, so she knows what's needed."

Fingal nodded to the rear quarterdeck, where Eunice cuffed a sailor sprawling, ending an argument over a rope. "That one's no poor enforcer, either. Anyway, there's not a lot left for either of us to do just now—we're ready to cast off, once we've got one last piece of kit aboard."

Fingal pointed down at *Tavuto*'s deck below them, where what seemed to be a funeral procession was taking place.

Glinting orange in the rising sun, a huge casket was being carried down the deck. The armoured tube rode on the shoulders of a hundred or more sailors, dead and living both, chanting a labour-dirge as they hauled the load towards their boat.

It was Wrack. Under that iron skin lay what remained of her friend, trapped in the preserved remnant of a monster's mind. Wallowing in darkness, preparing to endure whatever came next. Watching his coffin carried across the deck, Mouana felt herself pitching into confusion and worry; it took all her resolve to put all thoughts of friendship out of her head and remember she had done the right thing. Wrack was a potent weapon, he was coming with them, and that was that.

"How much time've we lost?" she asked, putting the old steel back in her voice as she gauged the sun's position in the sky.

"It didn't take as long as we feared," replied the rebel, as the pallbearers set Wrack down in a winching cradle. "And besides, from what we're hearing over the wires, looks like the City's putting up a spirited defence. They've lost the wall, but they're pulling back into the streets and making your old lot fight for every house. At this rate, it could take them days to force a surrender."

"Wouldn't count on that," said Mouana grimly, remembering the Red Tent at the siege of Mashina-Zavod, the screams as Dust had made good on her chilling ultimatum and lowered the mercy banner.

"Well I suppose you'd have a better idea than me," said Fingal, breaking the memory. "Either way, we'll be gone long before it's over. Once we've got him winched up into our hold, that crane'll lift us up and put us to sea at the stern. And then the real work starts."

Fingal gazed out to sea and Mouana followed his eyeline, to where a cluster of ragged warships waited at anchor. All seemed damaged; smoke rose from the wounds in their hulls, and one was listing alarmingly to port. "The mutineers?" she asked.

"Aye," said Fingal. "Some of 'em. Others left already; figured with the Chancellor dead and the City toppled, the job was done and they were wisest making good speed away. Can't hold it against them, eh? They've done the work they signed on for, and taking on your fight too was a lot more to ask. Plenty've stayed to help, mind."

"They're coming with us?" asked Mouana.

"If you'll have 'em, yes. Sorry I couldn't get you a better navy, but there it is. They're a bit banged up, but with the pounding those boats took as you came in, it's amazing anything's still afloat. Three or four'll probably still make decent speed, they tell me, and they're cutting free anything useful from the stricken boats, loading it on the rest along with those who've not already fled the City."

"How many crew?"

"Besides our lot from the Ministry? Looks like we're still a few hundred strong. Course, more will probably leave—there's plenty wounded, and some who'll get second thoughts and try their luck running with the rest of the civilian refugees. But those who've still got fight in them want to come with you— there's sure as hell no point anyone staying here to get cut up when that Dust makes it through the last of the kentigerns."

Mouana started at her old general's name, imagining her black figure skittering towards them in a tangle of limbs, but the wall of smoke that heralded her progress was still far away.

"You realise they'll likely not fare any better with us?" asked Mouana, fixing Fingal with her good eye. "They'd be best off taking what you can and making for Murit or Rhianos, somewhere neutral, somewhere far away."

"Yeah, I know," said the scarred man softly, as he passed

the flask. "But honestly? I never thought we'd make it this far. I certainly never thought we'd ever step foot in the Ministry. And we wouldn't have, without what you and Wrack did. And I think we always knew that, if we did manage to storm the place, it would all be over soon anyway. At least this way we get to carry on, and help you try and wreck those last fucking rods."

Wrack's casket was suspended in the air now, rotating as the crane bore it towards them, dark against the tranquil immensity of the collapsing city. Already, sailors on their deck were guiding it towards the hastily-widened aperture of their hold.

"What about you, Fingal?" asked Mouana.

"Well, I was wondering if I could join your crew, to be honest," said the rebel, wincing as he unbuttoned his waistcoat and went to lift his shirt with shaking hands. The shirt was crusted solid with blood; beneath it was a soaked wad of dressings, half-set gore spilling from its edges as the man's abdomen twitched.

"Gutshot," he explained. "Took it as we came into the Ministry, but figured with everything so near to finishing as it was, I might as well just neck some speed and forget about it. Surprised it's not done me in sooner, if I'm honest—I'm pretty chuffed it's given me long enough to get all this sorted."

"Your people know?"

"Oh yes—I filled 'em in while you were out, over on the *Asinine Bastard*," said Fingal, nodding at the largest of the mutineer ships. "Far as I'm concerned, this ain't my rebellion any more. And that, mate, is why I've been at leisure to sit here and share a drink with you on this fine morning. Now I want to share another drink with you."

Mouana noticed, for the first time, that Fingal had a cylinder of miasma cradled in his arm.

"It's not life after death, you know," warned Mouana. "It's just death, without the rest."

"So's life, if you want to be that way," murmured Fingal. "Either way, I want to take this stuff and see things through with you. Doesn't feel fair to die properly until you get your chance too. What do you say?"

"I say you've lost your mind," she answered, as he raised the canister's nozzle to his lips. "Welcome aboard."

Mouana leant back against the crate and shut her eye for a time. She felt the boat shudder under her as the chains above took its full weight, heard the crew as they scrambled to make ready for launch. When she opened it again they were in the air, gliding high over the city to where the sea crashed against the ruined docks. Fingal was dead, his head slumped against his chest, his arm round the miasma like a tramp cradling his booze.

She wished sleep could take her, even if it meant another vision of that awful tent. But sleep, like breathing, was a memory—there was going to be no rest until this was over. The boat settled in the water with a soft crash, and the sailors on the deck cheered—Mouana had to go and lead them.

As she began to lever her stiff, bullet-ridden wreck of a body into a position to stand, Fingal turned his head and grinned at her.

"You're right," he croaked, before falling into something between a laugh and a coughing fit. "This is *horrible*."

"Yes it is," she agreed absently, and got up to address her crew. As she tried to gather her words and her strength, she was caught by the sight of a hunched shape, crouched on the boat's stern as it turned to leave the docks behind. A crab, still and silent, with a book clutched in its claws.

Wrack, watching his home city die.

CHAPTER TWENTY EIGHT

DUST STALKED DOWN the deck of the beached hulk with a monstrous headache, cutting down everything she came across. Although the zombies had a satisfying give to them as they took her blade, they offered little to assuage the aching dullness the drugs had left as they withdrew.

Their blood was brown and sluggish; it oozed rather than arced as she hacked at the aimless bodies. They offered only sparks and snatches of song behind her eyes, compared with the colours and harmonies that blossomed when a fresh life ended.

And they barely fought back. Slamming her fist through a wretch's chest as it dithered across her path, she let it slither on her arm for a moment, face to face with her. But there was no rage or fear in its face—if anything, it looked relieved. Dust spat in disgust and pitched it thirty feet across the deck, where it landed in a puff of teal.

Even that faded quickly, leaving the world grey again. Her

system was nearing baseline, dangerously drained after the rapture of the breach. She had switched half her brain to dormancy during much of the thirty-seven tedious hours it had taken to fight through the city to the Ministry—it had been the dull kind of fighting—but it had only postponed the crash. Sooner or later, she would have to sleep. The thought disgusted her.

Still, she thought, what was coming would surely compensate for it, would offer her a thrill that would only grow with time. The thought of it swelled, coruscating rose and crimson, in her anticipation.

Something yapped and snattered in the periphery of her hearing, ruining the moment for her. She took it for one of the ship's filthy carrion-birds, and was about to spin and put a shot through it when she recognised it as language.

One of her officers, a snivel-faced man from the pack trailing nervously in her wake, was wheedling for her attention. She considered putting a shot through his leg anyway, but put the thought away—it would only delay things further. Instead, she tried to make out what he was on about.

It was the Principals, he seemed to be saying, though the fear wafting from his face in green-black waves distracted her from his words. They were calling again, asking for conference, for an update on the assets. Their precious little rods.

Dust thought of the Principals, of their turgid emissaries on the screens, forever asking for 'updates,' and snarled. The herald of Kanéla in her tank of orange gas, the grey foreman from Lōhē, always wearing a new face. The fools from Ijinna, who brought new and meaningless questions with each conference, and that elephantine thing from Orcus, which so rarely said anything.

Of course, even that puffy monster would be in uproar if she told them the truth: that she had found the Ministry burned to the ground, had found only the shattered fragments of their rods, cool among the embers of the death-factory.

So she told the man to lie to them, as she had already lied to them once; to say that the assets were secure and being prepared for delivery. It didn't matter—by the time the dullards became suspicious, it would be too late. She would have her real reward, and the paltry tokens of their commission would mean nothing.

It was so close now. Dust waved the trembling man away to his task, and looked up at the ship's vast bridge tower, at its name, *TAVUTO*, painted in unforgiving capitals the size of houses. As she passed through its entrance and began ascending the blood-tacky stairs, the prospect of fresh ecstasy tickled her cortex. Her prize was waiting for her at the top; she fancied she could feel it tickling at the burned edges of her mind already, drawing her up past the drifts of bodies on the staircase.

Her monster, her ancient weapon, summoned just as planned. Captured as she had whiled away the months with the mammoth farce of the siege. Brought to her. It was odd that nobody had been here to present it to her, but no real shame—the fisherman was of no importance next to the catch. She had cast her hook, and here was her leviathan.

Only, as she entered *Tavuto*'s bridge and saw the sky blazing through the gutted ceiling, she knew she had been betrayed. Her prize had been taken.

Dust stood for a long time, staring up at the sky and wondering how to feel. At first only confusion came, but as the heat built beneath, shreds of other things boiled to the top. Shock melted into disbelief, and then gave way to bitter admiration as she realised she had been outplayed by a game-piece. The taste was unfamiliar, a forgotten blend, but all at once she recognised the old, rare tang of defeat.

The novelty was quite delicious, but Dust knew bland rage would soon overwhelm the flavour if she didn't find something creative to do with it. Calmly, as if all was proceeding as expected, she ushered her officers in from their fearful knot beyond the bridge doors, and told them to find her the answer to what had happened here.

As the officers scurried, she stroked the canister of miasma at her belt. It was one of the store they had recovered from the remnants of the Ministry, four thousand silver cases, stockpiled in a cellar and safe from the fire. After a moment's hesitation, she cranked her synaesthetics up a notch. Really, she knew she should be letting her system cool, but what was coming next would be too beautiful to enjoy without augmentation.

Twenty-three minutes later, two uniforms approached her with a corpse supported between them. They looked at each other with sweat-bleached faces. One tried to tell her they had managed to get the wretch to talk, but was interrupted by the thing itself, suggesting they had not had to conduct much of an interrogation.

The carcass looked her straight in the eye, grinned, and told her all she needed to know. It was lengthy, aggressive and largely indecipherable. But it gave her the answer she had already reached.

"Mouana," said the corpse.

The word was hot and rancid as it leaked into Dust's skull, drowning out the flavour of the others. She let the synaesthetics drench her; there was no point postponing the anger any longer, though she did pause to thank the corpse before she clapped its head flat between her gauntlets. After all, it had displayed more character than most of her command staff.

They would, in fact, be much more interesting dead, she mused to herself. After all, they had all just been outperformed by a colleague long-deceased. Really, she was offering them a second chance.

Slowly unscrewing the nozzle of the miasma, Dust told her officers to form a parade line, and to put on their gas hoods. To their credit, only two tried to break for the bridge door when they realised what was about to happen. They were stopped by the pair of piston-limbed Augs she had stationed there during the search, and brought back to the line as the doors were bolted.

The rest didn't say a word after that. Maybe, she thought, as fear blossomed from the soldiers in gorgeous amber spheres, there was hope for them yet.

Moving to the first man in line, she let loose a blast from the cylinder into the inlet of his mask, and savoured the terror in his eyes as he held the breath, waiting for her blade to come. Eventually, when no violence came, he exhaled in tentative relief.

"Good," said Dust, and screwed shut the man's air intake.

Some time later, when the last of the officers had stopped convulsing, she took a seat on an overturned terminal and waited for them to come back. It was beautifully quiet, and Dust sighed to herself as she tasted the moment. Maybe this setback had been for the best. She was tired of the clumsy, protracted business of sieges, and missed the hunger and the fury and the pain that came with a *real* challenge.

Now, not only did she have a task ahead of her, but a decent opponent standing in her way. And as the very first of her new soldiers began to thrash on the floor, she smiled. It was a beautiful day, and the hunt was about to begin.

THE WATER THRONGED with bright fish, jinking and dashing among the lily stems. Flag-tailed eft cruised between them, feather-gills pulsing, while hornplate catfish jostled one another in the sun patches dappling the pool floor. Leaf scraps whirled in the wash of their heavy tails, rich as tea-leaves in the great warm brew.

Wrack felt the sunlight sink into his back, felt silt trickle through his fingers as he pulled himself along through the shallows. A flight of mottled stingray flapped away in startlement, leaving a plume of disturbed sand behind them. He pushed through and kicked free of the bottom, rolling lazily in the water as weeds brushed his sides.

Swimming through an arch of moss-crusted wood, he watched as jewelled shrimp fussed and picked through their tangled garden, waving glass-clear claws when grazing fish nudged too close. Everywhere he looked there was life, teeming and vibrant.

Then he was out into the river channel, where redtail cats and hump-backed nutcrackers meandered in the slow current. Eels flittered in the distance, while here and there the water surged with the white bubbles of a diving bird. Pink shapes loomed in the soupy distance, and the fish scattered in all directions. Creaking clicks and squeaks filled the water, and bulbous heads pushed out of the gloom—a pod of river orcas, their eyes little more than specks in salmon-coloured skin. They swung their heads at him as they passed, sonar clicking deep against his diaphragm, but were gone as soon as they arrived, in search of the huge worms they were famed for hunting.

As their tails vanished, Wrack found himself alone in the water; he looked around for more fish, but every movement resolved into dead vegetation, or a trick of the light. He saw something creeping along the sediment, but when he swam to investigate, it was nothing but a half-eaten redtail, rolling along the bottom with mouth gaping.

The river's bottom fell away, and the water grew colder, and darker. The light from above grew more and more distant, and lost its amber glow. The current picked up like the stirrings of a winter gale, and Wrack felt it pulling him along, faster than he could kick against it. It was as if something was breathing him in, something that grew closer and closer, yet remained out of sight as the water darkened.

Wrack flailed in the icy water, tumbled in search of the surface, but it was nowhere to be seen—the water stretched fathomless in every direction, grey and terrible. He was pulled further and further by the current, despite all his thrashing, and he knew he was being dragged down, down to somewhere good fishes did not go.

Blackness rose, and within it loomed two great orbs—eyes, scratched and sightless and deathly pale. Beneath them sprawled a tangle of black glass, a forest of needles sprung from ragged flesh. A predatory yawn, that gaped in measureless hunger and despair. The jaws creaked silently apart to accept him, and Wrack resigned himself to their embrace.

Then a deep, wet crack echoed from the abyss, and the

monstrous face jerked sideways. Another, and it convulsed again. It was tugged back violently, and a jet of cloudy filth rose from its maw. Unseen teeth ground in the blackness, and a shiver of awe crept across the crown of Wrack's head. There was something beyond, something so large and fierce it made prey of the devil-fish.

A deep green light rose from the depths, and Wrack caught sight of it then; a titanic crown of limbs, rolling dark as onyx serpents, their lengths stippled with scars and savage hooks. At their centre, a churning spiral of tooth-rows and horny plates, which dragged in the head of the fish as he watched, snapped shut, and belched a few strands of slimy flesh.

Wrack licked his lips as he hung before the monster, and stretched his arms in satisfaction. *That was delicious.*

"Saints and knights!" yelled a man, over someone's screaming.

"Easy, Wrack!" barked another, as metal clattered and more shouting started. Wrack focused, and found he had a hand in his mouth, clamped in his right claw as his mouthparts chewed at the thumb. Below the hand was Waldemar's book, its text spotted with fresh blood. He was in a ship's cabin, crowded with people, and it took him a second to realise it wasn't yet another vision. As soon as he did, he spat the hand out in self-disgust.

Fucking visions, he thought, and started into a rambling apology. To his puzzlement, his words came back at him, read aloud by a synthesised voice with slightly mangled inflection.

All around him were a circle of faces, some living, some dead, all wide-eyed and agitated as a woman retreated, clutching her sliced thumb. One of the dead men, with a bad eye and a big moustache, looked really familiar, but Wrack was pretty sure he hadn't been on *Tavuto*. He was talking, and Wrack supposed he really should be listening.

"—mate, we thought you were just concentrating on your book. Didn't mean to startle you. Look, we've been souping you up some!" The man gestured at a living woman, who held up a mirror with a conciliatory, if slightly forced, grin. In the mirror was a crab, and Wrack cringed—that was never going to feel natural—but he had to admit it was in better shape. His smashed legs had been replaced with wooden prosthetics, while the whole rack had been fixed with steel supports and servos, wired to a cluster of machinery bolted to his shell. The camera he was peering through was now flanked by speakers, which broadcast a thoughtful "huh" as he examined himself.

"I can talk now?" said Wrack, as he tested his legs. He had to admit, being a speaking, mostly-mechanical crab controlled by a brain in a tank was—somehow—more satisfying than just being a crab controlled by a brain in a tank.

"Yes, you can," said the moustachioed cadaver, nodding at the woman with the bitten thumb. He was achingly familiar. "And you've Conwen to thank for that. Used the voice from the Lipos-Tholos trams, which we always used for our radio stuff. We figured you and Mouana could use a break from writing to each other, and you might want a bit more company. Thought it might cheer you up."

"Thanks," said Wrack, feeling more human than he had done in a long while. The idea that someone had thought of him in a context outside of mortar fire, naval hyperwar and desperate crusades in search of nightmare technology made him want to well up, though he doubted his renovators had thought to install tear ducts. "And Conwen, I'm really so sorry for trying to eat your thumb. I didn't know I was doing it. I'm... well, I've gone a bit mad, if I'm honest. This is all just a bit much. Thanks for what you've done."

As he relaxed, the rebels clustered round him relaxed too—they lowered their tools, and those who still had the facial architecture to do so were smiling, even Conwen as she wound a rag round her thumb.

"Where is Mouana, anyway?" said Wrack, glad of his flat, toneless new voice, and childishly satisfied with the way it bungled the vowels of her name.

"Over on *Gunakadeit*, the boat we took from *Tavuto*," said the moustache man, gesturing through the cabin window at one of the old hulk's jagged grey whaleboats. "You're in its hold, but since you seemed attached to this body, we took it over here as we've got better workshops."

"And because she wanted me out of the way, no doubt," muttered Wrack. At least, he meant to mutter: his voice announced it like the arrival of the 12:30 to Ploverholm.

"She's got a lot to do, Wrack. We're headed to Grand Amazon, and half our boats are barely afloat. Plus there's likely to be an army coming after us."

"I know," said Wrack, and zoomed in on the whaleboat's deck, where his former comrade was overseeing the welding of a new gun onto its increasingly fortified forecastle. Watching her stride around with her permanent scowl, he felt himself draining of the fuzzy sentiment that had come over him a few moments ago.

Wrack had had many eyes in the City as it fell; he had seen the body of the Chancellor, had seen the cuts she had made. His supposed friend had tortured a man to death and back to get what she wanted. The great soldier, soldiering on, doing the vile things soldiers did in the name of soldiering. To her there was no fear, or sadness, or horror at what was going on—just obstacles, and guns to blow them away with. Wrack himself was not a friend to her; he was just another gun, to be welded in place and used when something stood in the way of the mission.

Wrack didn't know whether he loathed her for her callousness, or because he envied her. Certainly he loathed himself for going along with it all, for jumping at the fairytale hope that she wanted her friend alongside her for the journey. Looking at Mouana's face, like a spiteful ghost-train puppet, and down at his own reeking claws, he wondered what in the world was left that was worth hoping for.

That was the worst thing. The despair of *Tavuto* had at least had a coda; all along had been the promise that it would soon all be over. But now there was the hope—however ludicrous— of something after, and the hope *fucking ached*.

"Let me get back to my book," said Wrack, and tried to find his place among the bloodstained pages. The gathered rebels said nothing, just quietly put down their tools and left.

*   *   *

"Strip the harpoons off," barked Mouana, holding off the terror as it tried to force its way into her voice like the head of a carrion bird. "And secure the guns from the *Bargain* in their place. They need to be up and ready within the hour."

At least her voice was holding. She had finally patched the hole in her chest with a square of stapled tarp, meaning she could pack a few more syllables into each lifeless breath, but she wished she could do the same for her growing fear.

Bertilak's Bargain, the most heavily armed of the four ships sailing with *Gunakadeit*, had a dying engine and was falling behind the flotilla. Every hour they kept pace with it cost them miles, and with the Gate to Grand Amazon only hours away, they needed every mile of sea they could squeeze between them and their pursuit.

And there was no question of their being pursued. It had been two days since they had cast off from Lipos-Tholos, two days of exploding boilers, welding sparks and frantic engineering, where even the living had barely slept. Yet even with that head start, she knew they could not stay ahead for long. Dust would do anything to get what she wanted, and to be the only thing standing in between her and her goal was chilling beyond the cold of death.

When Mouana thought of her dreams, those claustrophobic half-memories of the command tent, her fears only grew. What Dust was truly after, her own role in that scheme, and the terrible logic that proceeded from its unravelling, was something she was avoiding thinking about at all costs. When Kaba interrupted her with a poke in the ribs, she could not have been more glad of the insubordination.

"Channels are narrow off the Sinfondo, boss," crowed her de facto first officer. "Narrow and not deep, you know. This is an Ocean-boat, deep keel and sharp besides. Keep loading all this heavy gear, you'll scrape bottom and rupture soon enough."

"So have the crew empty the holds," snapped Mouana.

"Bodies, fuel and ammo is all we need besides the weapons, and we'll run low on all three soon enough."

"Even the food?"

"Even the food. We're going to a fucking jungle, it's full of the stuff." Though they were perpetually hungry, Mouana wasn't even sure if the dead really needed to eat, and the living would need bullets more than bully beef when Dust came.

"You don't know the jungle, miss," said Kaba with a laugh that pulled her smashed mouth into a half-grin, then shrugged. "But we'll ditch if you give the say-so. Bad news is, there's not much else to dump. Take a look what we hauled out so far—besides, there's something big-dangerous in there you'll be happy to see."

Mouana followed Kaba down the ship's main deck, ducking as another net of guns swung aboard from the ailing *Bargain*, to where a chain of sailors was hauling gear out of the hold. There were indeed tins of meat—stacks of them, along with the bottles of foul preservative *Tavuto*'s overseers had used to wash down their grim rations. There were nets and harpoons and barrels, and piles of iron sheets for hull repairs. But there was something else, which despite everything weighing on her, raised a tight smile, as Kaba had predicted.

"It's a Mark V warbody," announced a rebel technician, patting the immense thing on the flank as she saw Mouana staring. "Military issue, but this is the 'Ahab' pattern, modded for Ocean deployment. Ministry built a load a year back, from a fresh blueprint won off Sedogua. We know because we tried to jack them from the forge. Quite a bod, eh?"

"Yeah," said Mouana to Kaba as she looked the Mark V up and down. "Don't throw that overboard."

It was easily nine feet at its headless shoulders and almost as wide, a rust-red block of aggression bristling with harpoons, slug-throwers and rivets. Its limbs were caked in inch-thick iron, its joints swarmed with armoured cables, its feet were like upturned foundry crucibles.

Eunice's own sheet-metal physique looked fragile beside the newer model. Preferring not to risk its own people in close combat with Ocean's fauna, Lipos-Tholos had wired its most bloody-minded criminals into these suits after death, safe in the knowledge their minds were too broken to consider rebellion. Eunice was horrific proof of what a stupid decision that had been. Even so, she looked jealous beyond measure as she eyed up the empty suit.

Mouana couldn't help it. She'd spent her life with heavy weapons, oiling their innards and frying eggs on their engine casings, and the sight of a new-forged war machine lifted her up, kept the fear at bay.

"Damned heavy, though," cautioned Kaba. "Must be a ton at least."

"So dump everything else," said Mouana, before nodding to the technician and carrying on up the stairs to the quarterdeck at *Gunakadeit*'s rear. From here she could see down the whaleboat's length, from the frenzy of activity at the hold amidships, to the forecastle with its growing tangle of weaponry. It was coming together, and the sight of the welding, the sound of the hammers, was as soothing as rain on glass to her. Mouana took a deep, futile breath, and turned to let the madness govern itself for a moment.

She walked to the back rail and looked out at the ship's wake, as it churned under the afternoon sun. The last time she had stood like this had been on *Tavuto*, when she and Wrack had reached the stern of the ship and realised they could run no further. They had watched scavengers swarm at a whale's carcass under a grey dawn, and despaired.

But Ocean was long behind her now. This, by contrast, was a beautiful day. This far from the stained sky over Lipo-Tholos, there was just blue water and pale cloud. Standing at the rail and watching gulls swoop in their passage, Mouana dared to wonder if things might work out after all.

Bertilak's Bargain wallowed beside their port side, smoke belching weakly from its stacks as the last of its supplies were pilfered. The *Asinine Bastard*, the largest and the most intact of their flotilla, rode to starboard. Behind them were the other ships, the *Chekhov's Gun* and the *Pentangle*, each barely larger than *Gunakadeit*, and a swarm of smaller launches, ferrying people and hardware between the fighting craft. Much further out, plumes of smoke marked the positions of civilian boats, fleeing the chaos of Lipos-Tholos to take their chances in the colonies or beyond.

Soon they would have the sailors and materiel off the *Bargain*, and could really put on speed. With luck, they'd be making transit to Grand Amazon some time after dusk. They had maybe five hundred bodies between the ships, half of them living. As for the dead, they were the wily ones, and the most mobile. The zombies—as she had come to think of those wretches too broken by death to regain even a semblance of humanity—had almost all been left behind. As far as she knew, they were still milling on the decks of *Tavuto*, or wandering the City's streets in search of their vanished lives. She hoped, if nothing else, that Dust would give them the rest they deserved.

Something grey surged out of the ship's wake, and Mouana reached for her pistol, then swore softly as she saw it was only a porpoise. The animals were playing in the engine wash, spinning in the air as they arced through the crashing foam. They were not albino, nor rotten, nor tentacled—just porpoises. The sight of the things brought hope back again; whatever mess they were in, at least they weren't in Ocean.

Still, thought Mouana, as she glanced at the sun beginning to sink below the water, it wouldn't be long before they reached a place with no less dark a reputation. While Ocean was feared across the Lemniscatus as one of the most horrible worlds, a place best forgotten and left to devils, Grand Amazon was one of the weirdest. Lost and recolonised enough times to make a mystery of its founding, the place had a habit of eating history: its sweltering forests swallowed human work just as completely as Ocean's endless grey, and concealed stranger ruins. People, ships, expeditions and cities all had a habit of disappearing there, vanishing into the jungle night.

"What do we expect when we get there?" Mouana asked Kaba, who had appeared by her side at the railing.

"Insects, boss," replied the woman with a leer, brandishing a jug of the overseers' preservative grog from the hold. "S'why I'm soaking myself in this stuff every chance I get."

"And I suppose it's all just been dumped in the sea on my orders?" sighed Mouana.

"Nah, boss, told them not to do that," said Kaba, cackling. "You'd have fierce regretted it when you hatched your first boil-wasp."

"And besides insects?" asked Mouana drily, snatching the jug and pouring a puddle of the piss-coloured stuff on her bad hand.

"Who knows, you know? Jungle changes all the time. I can take you up the Sinfondo, where the long-lasting towns are, and to Rummage on the Esqueleto, where squid-boy says we need to go based on his fancy book. Done that run a few times; Rummage won't have gone anywhere. Beyond that? Can't fathom. Don't know what's still there, what's new."

"You think it's changed that much since you left?"

"Probably," shrugged Kaba. "The colonies, they're not what they were. Lot of the old machines are breaking now. And trouble elsewhere, the wars—they always spill over. Take people, take resources, start fires. And the jungle, she never misses a chance to fill in any holes. She's been winning for the longest time."

"And what about High Sarawak?"

"Don't know boss. My head's broke like yours, so maybe I knew and I've forgot. But I don't think I ever did. Prospectors' stories and *wurmjäger* whiskey-tales, maybe, bullshit over cards by lamplight, but no maps nor signposts. You want to find that place?" said Kaba, as she walked away to deal with the preservative stores. "You want to be talking to all the mad folk you can find."

"Maybe I do," muttered Mouana, turning to look back over the boat. She looked over to where Eunice was still prodding and poking at the Ahab suit, and past her to the maw of the hold, where the rough curve of Wrack's casket brooded in the dark. Feeling she was being watched, she shot a glance at the deck of the *Bastard*; sure enough, there was Wrack, squatting at a cabin window, staring at her with pebble-black lenses over the edge of his damned book.

Wrack had not spoken with her since they had left his home town. More than once, Mouana had wondered if he had figured out she had lied to him, but she thought it more likely—or at least preferred to think—he had simply cracked. Wrack had been unstable since taking on the burden of his new mind; seeing his childhood disappear under a blanket of war-smoke might have sent him over the edge.

That, and the sheer amount of death and damage they themselves had inflicted, in the name of the uprising he had started. Death and damage she herself had delivered, dragging its wailing progenitor with her. If that was it, then she would not apologise. There was no point in being sorry for anything she had done—it had been the ugly, necessary consummation of the justice they had conceived together in Ocean. If he was too weak to see through what he started, that was not her problem to solve.

But one way or another, she would need him back if she was to continue to see things through. It wasn't as if she could coerce him through torture, she thought; and cringed at even allowing herself to have the thought.

So far, her best plan had been to set Fingal to the task of bringing Wrack back to the fold. She figured that, given their connection through Wrack's father, the fact they had presumably known each other at some point in their lives, there might be some bond there. But from the rebel boss's reports so far, it seemed it was tough going.

Either way, Wrack needed to play on her team. Whatever lay at High Sarawak, whatever ancient weirdness had spawned the technology they were trying to eradicate, she had the strangest notion that her acquaintance was something to do with it. The more she thought about the visions she had been having, the more it made sense. Dust had never been after the City's weird, filigreed necrods—she had been after Teuthis, the alien flesh that had lain at the heart of *Tavuto*, and which she thought had power far beyond mere scraps of old machinery. The flesh which Wrack now inhabited.

He was inextricably linked with what they were pursuing, and he was the reason for their being pursued. Just thinking about it seemed to darken the sky, to grey out the sea. There were conclusions here she couldn't face, memories that would not surface. Implications birthed by her visions of Dust, like the eggs of a parasite beneath her skin.

But they were not to worry about now, she told herself, gritting her teeth as she clenched the rail in her good hand and stared at the porpoises. Those happy *fucking* porpoises.

Mouana didn't remember much of her life besides the big fights, but she knew she had spent most of it postponing happiness, thinking that things would get better after the next obstacle, after the next bout of pain and fear. It had been what had kept her on campaign so long.

Perhaps the attitude had persisted after death. It had been what got her through *Tavuto*, and what had kept her going after victory had evaporated at the Ministry. It would get her through until her body finally fell apart. Maybe she would run into a dead end at High Sarawak—if they even got there—and maybe they would have to carry on fighting. Maybe things would get very, very dark with Wrack. It didn't matter. Those were problems for later. Solve one thing at a time, Aroha had always said.

The ships were full of sailors, and full of guns. Grand Amazon lay ahead, and Dust some way behind. For now, she was holding all the cards, and if she could at least convince herself that everything would be alright after the next hurdle, she could keep going.

This is how a siege engineer experiences hope, she thought to herself with a laugh, and blacked out at the rail.

CHAPTER TWENTY NINE

"ARE YOU SURE this isn't turned?" retched Aroha, as he set his spoon back in his bowl.

"Yep," said Mouana, as she rolled the map out on the main desk of the dugout and weighted it with a wrench. "It just tastes of 'drick, is all. That smell they have, it gets in the meat, and there's no salting it out. You get used to it."

"Yeah, well, we'll have to, won't we?" grumbled the old captain, curling his lip. "There's twenty tons of the stuff to get through."

Mouana shrugged, and scooped the last spoonful from her own tin. It was grey, fibrous like rotten wood, and soaked through with salt, but still tasted like Tassie. After acting as the battery's mascot in the last days on the plateau, the old beast had taken on a second life as rations for the deployment outside Lipos-Tholos. Having been the one to pull the trigger on Tassie, Mouana made a point of finishing each tin of meat before any of her troops.

"I don't know, Mouana," said Aroha, sounding suddenly very old. "I could be eating home-cooked stew soon."

"Your boy, is he much of a cook then?" she asked, as she began unpacking the battery's analytic console, cursing under her breath as one screen came out of the crate shattered.

"He cooks shit, same as his old man, far as I remember. But at least it's home-cooked shit, eh?"

Aroha had been maudlin since they had arrived. When the first mail had reached them, somewhere between Gate transits on the way here, it had brought news that the mother of his boy—the woman he had ostensibly stayed a mercenary to avoid—had died, and left him a lengthy deathbed letter. After years of joking about how good it would be to only have to send half the money back home, he had become a very sentimental man. Mouana could tell he was making ready for one of his reflections, and looked as busy as she could dressing the dugout so as to dissuade him. It didn't work.

"Maybe we could have repaired things, you know?" wondered Aroha. "Maybe we could have made it a home together again, with Tamati grown up and all. Why did I stay away so long? Why did I wait until it was too late for us to be a family?"

Mouana let him soliloquy, nodding and grunting where appropriate as she swept aside the garbage the Cauldron Company had left behind. No wonder they'd been relieved of the siege, she thought—they'd run this dugout more like a drinking den than a command post, and the section's lines weren't in much better shape. From what she'd heard from the other battery commanders, the whole circumvallation was a shambles, and they were going to have to work quick to fix things before the defenders took advantage.

Aroha rambled on. She could sympathise, mind. The letter he'd received had been gut-wrenching, and besides, she knew plenty about staying at arm's length from family. But a despondent captain was the last thing they needed right now. The man needed to make his mind up, before word made it up the hierarchy and a decision was made for him.

"So go home," said Mouana, more angrily than she'd intended, and Aroha stopped short. "You've been doing this for years, and you've already missed one chance at being a family. You're not going to feel any more of a father to him staying out here, and don't kid yourself you'll go home when this siege is over. Given its track record, it'll outlive both of us. So go home, and make things as right as you can."

Mouana wondered how she could say these words with a straight face, given how she would scoff if Aroha ever told her the same thing. But then, it was always easier to give others the advice you needed yourself. And anyway, it was different for Aroha. He had joined up to avoid being elsewhere. She joined because she had work to do. Mouana would stay until she was ready to come home; until she *knew* she had made things right. He'd already stayed too long.

"Right," said Aroha, fishing a flask from his inside pocket. "So I go knocking on Dust's wagon, ask if I can go home to patch things up with what's left of my family? Because besides her boundless sense of empathy, she's renowned for her expertise in dealing with family issues."

Mouana gawped, her eyes flicking from the captain's flask to his face, and then to the shadows of the dugout, as if the words themselves would summon the general. "*Affeschiesse*, Aroha. Are you *pissed?*"

"Yeah, a bit," smirked the older officer. Mouana had no idea how she'd missed it.

"Well, shut up 'til you sober up, before you leave Tamati a bloody orphan." The captain leapt to his feet, steadied himself on the map desk with a balled fist, but she carried on. "You know what a bad idea it is to gossip about the general. Anyone could walk in here and hear you, and you *know* word travels. Remember Ludovico, with that campfire song after Three Valleys?"

"Of course I remember—we all remember. Poor shit begged for our help for three days before passing, and none of us so much as looked at him for fear of a bullet in the head. That's just the sort of understanding leader she is. Why the hell did we sign up to a company run by a complete fucking monster, anyway?"

"Because she wins everything she touches, and because we're mercenaries," spat Mouana, flinging out an arm to take in the rat-tracked squalor of the dugout. "Perhaps you'd have been happier pissing your life away with a company like the Cauldron, but I doubt it. And if you're done with life with the Blades, then go. But don't start with this kind of talk."

Aroha was drunker than she thought. The man had discipline like no-one else, but whatever that letter had meant to him, it had rattled him right out of his cage. Mouana felt some relief when he sat back on the bench with a sigh, and got back to the task of wiring up the console. After a few minutes, however, when she was down under the desk trying to find a dry patch for a router, he piped up again, slow and snide, like blood from a stitched wound.

"I suppose you'd know her best, wouldn't you," suggested Aroha, punctuated by the slosh of spirit. "Seeing as you've been working so closely with her since you shot old Tassie on the plateau. Probably firm friends by now. But don't forget I've been with her for longer, even if I've kept my distance. I know we're not meant to talk about the damned stories, but I've heard them all. You know about her home, right, Mou? Someone as invested in sibling rivalry as you, you must've heard how they dealt with it back where she's from?"

Mouana got up from her work, wiped her hands free of mud, and locked eyes with the captain. He was wasted, no doubt about it, and there was going to be no end to this but to hear him out. She just hoped to the Tin King that nobody walked in before he was done.

"I know enough," she answered, calm as a rainy dawn. "Know the first thing she did, when she took on the Blades, was go back there and wipe the place out for what they'd done. Don't need to know any more."

"Yeah, you don't need to," said Aroha with a sneer. "But you'd fucking love to, wouldn't you?"

Mouana folded her arms noncommittally.

"Wasn't often anyone even managed childbirth, back on Dust," said Aroha, spitting on the dugout floor. "What with the rads and the poison and the famines. Rarer still anyone made it to full-grown, after those hunts they put them through. But you know what their law said should happen when too many kids came of age in one year?"

Mouana gave the smallest shake of her head.

"They'd pair 'em off. Siblings first, then friends. Pair 'em off, and leave 'em in a cave in the worst part of the desert for two months, far out on the salt flats, where the ichthydaimones spawned. One sack of rations, they gave them. One between each pair. And not rations like these," he snarled, chomping at the 'drickmeat for effect. "It was that Dust shit—crickets and cave mold and wafers made from sawdust and rat shit and all the rest. And all of it, if you split the fucking waterskins and licked the seams, sucked every crumb from your thin fingers, might keep one of you alive for the duration. But they put two of you in there. Dust went in with her brother."

Movement flickered at the end of the long tunnel leading into the dugout. Mouana's eyes widened, and she stared over Aroha's shoulder. She made the sign, the sign they'd use in the thunder of a barrage to signal an engine overheat, the sign that meant everything had to stop before a boiler ruptured. But Aroha wasn't paying attention, just carried on with glazed eyes. She had seconds at best before whoever was coming walked into his drunken rant.

"They worked out the maths soon enough," rumbled Aroha. "Share the food and you'd starve before they came to get you; start the fight too late and you'd die of thirst."

The bitter scent of herbs came to Mouana, preceding the new arrival, and her heart seized. She knew the smell. It wasn't just some private come to relay a message, it was Dust herself, and if she shouted now, there was no way the general wouldn't ask what the fuss was all about. Mouana dived back below the desk, drew her knife, and snatched at the wires spilling from the back of the dugout's raid siren.

"It all came down to who found a sharp rock first," spouted Aroha. "Who was prepared to give up and go full fucking animal before the other. And our dear leader—"

His sentence ran into a wall of sound as the siren slammed on, a piercing wail designed to alert half a mile of trench to an air assault even above the booming of their own guns. Setting it off would no doubt incur a punishment, but the alternative was unthinkable.

Mouana leapt up from below the desk cursing emphatically, just as Aroha jumped up from the bench with a stunned expression, and Dust appeared in the room. They made a strange tableau for a moment; Dust peering at the siren built into the ceiling, then down at Mouana with slightly narrowed eyes, while Aroha stared straight at her, eyes wide in profound thanks.

Calmly, yet quicker than Mouana could register, Dust had set down her tea, drawn her pistol and put a bullet through the siren, silencing it with a choking squawk.

"The state they left this place in," chided the general, something like amusement smouldering in her expression. "Alarms going off all by themselves." The sudden silence stretched like a string of drool from an animal's jaws, and Aroha was clearly fighting not to shake as he stared at the floor. Dust turned her head a fraction towards him, then appeared to think better of it and fixed Mouana with a perfectly neutral expression.

"You are needed in the freight yard, commander," said Dust, as if chiding a schoolboy late for a class. "Kronos has finally been shipped in, and you will need to oversee the installation of his manufactory feed. I thought we could take the opportunity to review the placement of the heavy battery on the way."

"Yes, general," said Mouana in the most ordinary register, as if there was nothing unusual about the situation, although every muscle in her body was tensed.

"Very good," answered Dust with a nod, before turning back to the entrance corridor without so much as a glance at Aroha. As she left to follow, Mouana locked eyes with the older man for the briefest moment, long enough to convey that they would never, ever resume the conversation they had been having.

There was silence as Mouana followed Dust down the corridor, melting gradually into the clamour of the unfolding siege as they stepped out into daylight.

"It was roach meal, you know," mused Dust, looking up as a heavy lifter rumbled overhead with a railgun strapped to its belly.

"Roach meal, sir?"

"Not crickets," said the general, peering at her. "Those were for feast days. Roach meal was the main component of the daily ration. And cave mold, yes. But not sawdust either. There were no trees."

Mouana was stunned; her mouth flapped like a landed fish and her heart fluttered. It took all her composure to force out a sound. "Sir, he's a good soldier, and—"

"Minor details, commander," said Dust, with the ghost of a smile. "I'm not going to hang him over a confusion of insects, am I? Now, we have a battery to see to. Walk with me." The general turned and moved away down the trench, and Mouana followed on shaking legs.

They had gotten away with it. Mouana knew that they had. But as the sky deepened to the colour of wine and the general's form began to twist like a knot of worms, the relief drained, and Mouana recognised with sick familiarity that the memory was changing.

Dust turned back to her and her face dissolved into oily smoke, no longer distinguishable from the darkening sky. Only her eyes remained, simmering like the coals of a forge as they swam closer to her.

"I will forgive a lot," they growled, as the rest of the world became black. "But not betrayal, Mouana. And not theft. You have stolen from me, and I am coming to take what is mine."

The words rose to a shriek, and the general's eyes surged forward. Mouana thrashed and tried to claw her way from the false memory, but knew she could not leave. Not until the blade came. And there it was, plunging at her chest, its final thrust seeming to slow to a crawl as the tip pierced her skin.

MOUANA SCREAMED, AND a hundred firelit faces stared at her in shock. She was back on the quarterdeck of *Gunakadeit*, and looking out over what appeared to be a party. The hatch over the hold had been bolted and a great firebowl set up, over which birds were roasting on skewers.

Around the fire, rebels and dead folk stood stunned by her outburst, stories dying on their tongues. A set of bagpipes wheezed to a low moan, and there was an embarrassed scuffling as a burly woman and a dead man, both stripped to the waist, abandoned an uncoordinated dance-off.

"What the fuck do you all think you're doing?" rasped Mouana, her words landing like the drops of fat in the firebowl. The crew looked up at her sheepishly. All that moved was the smoke from the fire, coiling into the red-lit cowl of mist that swallowed the sea. It was Kaba that answered, stepping forward and kneading the side of her cracked jaw.

"It's tradition, sir. My idea. Every time a boat makes the transit, you feed up and get the helmsman a drink. Washes away the problems of one world, so you're fresh for the next. Look at the, mist sir," said the old boatwoman, gesturing at the fog that filled the gathering night. "The river's breath, coming hot through the gate. We're close now."

"Then pack up the damned fire and get to stations," growled Mouana, rattling the quarterdeck's rail with her good hand. "Drinking and bloody *dancing* won't help us with our problems. Our problems are following us, and they're bigger than any of you know. Fucking *Dust* is coming for us, and she's not one for parties."

Without another word, the crew began to pack up the festivities, dousing the fire and packing food into sacks with little more than a murmur of disappointment.

Then the bagpipes started up again. Mouana was indignant for a moment, until she saw their player was closing the clasps on the instrument's case. As the drone grew louder, so did her fear.

Talk of the Devil, thought Mouana, *and she shall appear*.

Turning back to the ship's stern, she looked out into the thick mist that swirled in its wake. The sound came from behind them, a low drone that swelled and waned with the breeze. As she stared, a line of faint lights appeared high in the mist, each surrounded by a nimbus of fog.

"Triremes!" cried Mouana, just as the *Asinine Bastard*, its crew presumably spotting them at the same moment, sounded its foghorn.

"Triremes! Triremes!" The call rose along the ship's deck, underscored by the boom of the horn, and all thought of clearing the feast was forgotten—as Mouana hurried to the helm, sailors ran about the steaming embers of the fire, calling each other to stations. They had minutes at best until the aircraft were on top of them.

"Shall we turn her about to bring the prow guns to bear?" called Kaba, hands poised on the ship's wheel, as armed sailors rushed into the cabin.

"No—give the engines all you can, and make for the gate. They're here to capture us, not sink us, so the real fight'll be on deck. Get the *Gun* and the *Pentangle* on the radio and bring them close alongside—close enough for boarding, if it comes to that—then get as many guns as'll move back to the stern. Get me Eunice and the Bruiser to anchor the defence, and raise me Fingal on the *Bastard*."

"Do you see 'em?" asked Mouana as the line came open, holding the receiver to her bloodless lips as she craned through the bridge cabin's rear windows.

"*Clear as day*," came Fingal's ashtray voice, almost fresher-sounding in death than it had been in life. "Four Alaunt-class and a Mastiff, looks like, plus an Aquila hanging in the back for heavy lifting. All L-T colours too, so I'm guessing looted from the city defence. Mastiff's coming in fast and dropping low, gunships are splitting off—guess the action's coming your way."

"Fine. Make speed with us as best you can, drop your running lights, and get as many bullets in that thing as you can as it passes. After that, it's up to you—do all you can to get us through that gate."

"Roger that," snarled Fingal, and Mouana threw down the radio, before snatching a rifle and aiming an accusatory finger at Kaba.

"As for you, stay on that wheel. No clever tricks, no changes of plan. Just get us through, and sound the horn when we're a minute away so the living can get below deck. Eunice, Bruiser, you're with me at the stern. Get aggressive."

"Fack off!" bellowed the bruiser with glee, delivering a knuckle-cracking punch to Eunice's shoulder as the towering warbuilt grumbled her approval. A cheer sounded as they moved onto the deck and made for the stern; cadavers waved shotguns in salute from behind improvised barricades, and living rebels crouched with them, grinning as they checked their weapons.

There was an electric mood in the air; after two days of uncertain pursuit, the crew was itching to have something to shoot at. The drone of the triremes filled the sky now, though the attackers had killed their lights to disguise their approach. Every sailor in the mass was squinting into the rolling mist, looking for something to aim at.

As they passed the turrets on the ship's flank, which in its former life would have housed the warbuilt as it pursued monsters across Ocean's depths, Mouana had Eunice tear free one of the chainguns salvaged from the *Bargain*. The weld had been hasty and the gun came free with a little more than a tug, but still the sailors cheered as Eunice held it above her head and bellowed.

Mouana waved the mob of defenders to their places across the ship's rear deck, and took a guilty glance at the console she couldn't quite bring herself to untape from her arm. She had seen trireme raids countless times during the siege and knew that, despite the crew's eagerness for a fight, they were going to need everything they could bring to bear just to have a chance of scraping through. Although she knew there was sod-all chance of an answer, she had to at least ask for Wrack's help. *WRACK. KNW YR SULKING. BT SLDRS R CMING TO GT U. LOTS. HLP?*

The reply came quicker, and left her much angrier, than she expected.

I SEE. THANKS, BUT I'VE HAD ENOUGH KILLING FOR A BIT, AND I'M AT A REALLY GOOD BIT IN MY BOOK. KNOW YOU WANT TO KEEP HOLD OF ME, BUT IF IT'S ALL THE SAME TO YOU, I'LL SIT OUT THIS ROUND OF SLAUGHTER AND SEE WHAT HAPPENS.

Hissing a string of curses that reached deep into her soldier's vocabulary, Mouana went to rip the console from her arm, only to find her mangled hand couldn't grasp it firmly enough. She settled for smashing the screen against a railing. After that, there was no more time to spare on thinking about Wrack, because the night was on fire.

Tracer bullets streaked from the turrets of the *Bastard*, filling the dark with orange hail behind them, then spilled green light on the sea as they found the Mastiff. Illuminated by the fizzing of bullets against its shields, the assault carrier barrelled towards them over the waves, a jagged black mass in a flaring shell. Alongside it, sleek as barracudas, a pair of Alaunt gunships accelerated ahead of the larger craft.

"Hold your fire!" called Mouana, as the juggernauts swooped toward them. "Keep down!"

The Alaunts opened the throats of their guns, and bullets slammed against *Gunakadeit's* stern, whipping over their heads and burying themselves in the hull patches the crew had set up as barricades. Gritting her teeth at the thought of a shell to the face, Mouana squinted over the rim of her cover, and was rewarded by the sight of the lead Alaunt rupturing under the *Bastard's* hail of fire. Its engines screeched, then erupted in a crown of white fire, sending the wedge-prowed gunship plunging into the sea as it lost its fight with gravity.

The elation was brief: even as one escort foundered, the other thundered over them, letting rip with its ventral guns in the process. The Alaunt passed close enough to make the deck shake with its field-effect, and a scream rose from across the quarterdeck as bullets streaked into bodies from above.

"Hold fire," repeated Mouana over the bark of the guns, keeping her eyes on the lumbering shape of the Mastiff. It was a slower beast, but had sunk down to deck-level and was closing on them fast. The *Bastard* had brought some of its heavier guns to bear on the craft, but still they did little more than rock the assault ship as the shells burst against its shields. The Mastiff was built to deliver infantry under withering fire, and soaked up the punishment like spring rain.

Mouana stared it down, fixing her eyes on the massive armoured drawbridge at its prow, and waited for it to surge forward. Gunfire erupted behind her as either the *Pentangle* or the *Chekov's Gun* engaged with the other escort craft, but there was no point paying attention—if they didn't unload everything they had when the carrier's jaw hit the deck, they were fucked whatever happened.

"Wait... wait!" urged Mouana above the howls of the wounded, and levelled her rifle at the Mastiff's jaws as they loomed. Beside her, Eunice began to spin up the barrels of her weapon, and rumbled what sounded a lot like a cheerful song. "*Faaaaack OFF!*" hollered the Bruiser, waving his shotgun like a club, and the crew took up the cry.

As if rising to the challenge, the mammoth assault craft gunned its engines and surged forward, its jaw falling open and a chorus of yells and war-screams blasting from its throat.

"Fire!" screamed Mouana, as the iron jaw clanged down on the deck's lip, and the air filled with hot steel.

First out of the Mastiff were two enormous brutes in rough-forged armour; iceball cultists with bearded helms and rotten fur totems spilling from their shoulders. They advanced behind man-high shields, singing a death hymn as they waded into the steel blizzard.

Their armour sang with countless impacts, and they staggered as if against a wind; in the strobing glare of the muzzle flashes she could see the iron dissolving under the onslaught. But they made it far enough to slam their shields into the deck, forming a barricade of their own before they collapsed, their song drowned by the blood in their lungs.

Even as they fell, their fellows were streaming from the trireme's throat, vaulting over their carcasses in a torrent of mad snarls and roaring shotguns. These were not the disciplined ranks of the Blades, but madmen drawn from the desperadoes and transients who followed the company across the worlds, hoping to earn a uniform. The irregulars.

Mouana, like the rest of the company, had always treated them with fear and disdain, those lunatics who lived in sprawling, filthy tent cities behind the lines. They were men and women with nothing to lose, who volunteered for the truly hellish assaults in the belief that if they survived enough charges, they would earn a commission in the company. Few ever did, but the hope was enough to make them almost god-touched in their fervour.

"*DUST!*" howled an emaciated woman as she leapt onto the defenders' barricades, face set in a snarl of an ecstasy beneath bandaged eyes. She raised a monstrous axe assembled from engine parts, but crumpled sideways as a shotgun blast took out her leg. Before she hit the deck, a pack of loping swamp-men had clambered up and over the line; they dived at Mouana's crew with flintlocks and bone knives, slashing and thrusting even as bullets punched holes in their bodies.

The mass of defenders pushed forward, sailors with billhooks and flensing poles craning over the front line to thrust at the onrushing savages. In front of Mouana, the Bruiser's broad back dipped and his arm came surging up with a lit bottle of preservative, in an arc so practised it was almost elegant. The firebomb burst in the Mastiff's throat and shrieks rang from its interior, but still more bodies came, swinging weapons even as fire danced on their limbs.

Eunice was a wall of rage next to Mouana, her face a rictus as the chaingun carved apart the stream of attackers. But for all that fury, they were losing ground. For every attacker that joined the heap around the cultists' shields, three more swarmed over the pile, with only a few yards of deck to vault before they reached the sailors' lines. And their defence was weakening; ammo clips were emptying, dead hands were fumbling as they struggled to fit new ones.

Mouana cried for her troops to pull back, hoping a little more space would give them a better killzone, but there was no chance of being heard over the thunderous whine of the chaingun beside her. Then she glanced back to make sure their path was clear, and realised they had bigger problems.

The *Pentangle* was dying, its ammunition store belching a column of flame as it cooked off. The fire-plume lit the bellies of the three surviving Alaunts as they circled in the fog above, dark shapes like scavengers round a dying whale. Already one was descending to their now-undefended starboard flank, while the others roared high over the deck to duel *Chekhov's Gun*.

Figures were leaping down from the settling trireme already, and as many broke their legs as found their feet. But even the maimed were undeterred, and those that made it down intact whooped and cackled as they spread out over uncontested deck. Gunfire came from the ship's prow as the sailors Mouana had stationed there moved amidships to tackle the boarders, but she knew the bulk of her force was here, locked in a desperate struggle against the Mastiff. With the *Pentangle* sunk and the *Gun* engaged, they risked being surrounded and overwhelmed if they couldn't link up and hold the ship's centre.

Eunice's gun fell silent for a moment as the giant reloaded, and Mouana gave the call to pull back, the tape on her chest wound pulsing as she strained for volume. After a brief look behind her, Eunice caught on, and began dragging the sailors in front of her backwards. Some, too addled by death to notice the retreat, stayed at their positions to be swallowed by the flood of irregulars, but their demise bought time for the rest to begin struggling down the quarterdeck ladders, firing all the way.

As Mouana took the first shaking step back down the stairs, the world turned white and there was a terrible crack of thunder. The deck rumbled: through the wall of fog, a prow loomed—the *Bastard*. With the Mastiff hovering stationary off their stern, the *Bastard* had closed the gap and brought its main cannon to bear, putting a shell right through the thing's shields.

For a second the carrier just shuddered in the air, sheet lightning crackling across the hull as its shield struggled to reform. Then flames gushed from its mouth as its engine caught, and the craft tilted backwards into the sea. Its hooked jaw held its grip on their deck for a long moment, and Mouana could have sworn the whole deck tilted as it pulled them down, but then the hinges ripped and the Mastiff fell away.

If the crowd of irregulars on the deck cared that their ship had exploded behind them, they didn't show it. Singed bodies, thrown from the mouth of the carrier as it died, simply staggered to their feet and screamed their general's name, as if the Mastiff had been sacrificed in her honour. In moments they had their vigour back, and were charging across the quarterdeck at the sailors still holding the stairs.

The situation was no less grim on the main deck. The Alaunt was level with their deck now, and dozens of irregulars were spilling from its side hatches. They teemed over the sealed hold, kicking over the smouldering remnants of the roasting fire, and swarmed up the nest of cranes and antennae at the ship's centre.

Before she knew it, Mouana's force was pinned between the quarterdeck and the hold, hemmed in and fired on from both sides. A flaring shape arced into the press from the top of the stairs and only the desperate dive of a sailor, their torso already riven nearly in two by a blade, stopped the bomb from carving a ten foot crater in her force. If the irregulars were reckless enough to use grenades on a ship they were trying to capture, the fight was all but over.

By way of emphasis, the mist overhead parted to reveal the open belly of the Aquila as it descended, lift cables already dangling. Below it, madmen were savaging the hold's doors with axes and welding torches—given another minute, she thought, they'd have the top off and be able to winkle Wrack's casket out like meat from a shell.

Mouana screwed shut her eye, spat, and cursed Wrack's name. The craven bloody librarian wouldn't lift a finger to help, and now he was going to suffer for it. She had no idea what Dust had planned for his mind once she got hold of the vessel that contained it, but she knew for sure she would be delighted to find it held a human consciousness.

Wrack was going to suffer in a way that made what he'd been through so far seem like a laugh, unless she did something insane. Mouana cursed him again, but before she could work out whether he deserved saving or not, her sabre was drawn.

Smacking Eunice on the shoulder with the pommel to get her attention, Mouana gave the warbuilt a grim nod and pointed at the mob of irregulars on the hatch. Eunice nodded back, then turned to the sailors and gave a booming roar as she swept her huge fist forwards. When the charge started, Mouana was already ten feet ahead of it, weapon raised and howling. As she lurched headlong into three crack-toothed axemen, she tried to ignore the fact her sailors were chanting Wrack's name.

THESE, AND MANY *other strange wonders—the parasitic eel-nymphs that wind around trunks and branches, the germlights that glow in the litter and the pungent fruits that lie rotting among them—experienced altogether defy words, and solicit a sensation of awe and—*

Shrapnel lanced through the cabin wall and embedded itself in his carapace, making Wrack flinch. Couldn't they keep it down out there, he thought, mouthparts ticking with irritation? He was trying to read.

These, and many other strange wonders, he began again, before one of the bloody triremes swooped past outside and rattled a window from its frame. He must have started this paragraph over a dozen times, but the damned battle kept taking his attention. What with that and the phantom sensation that someone was hammering on the roof above his head, it seemed the world was out to break his concentration. This was a terrible library.

This time, Wrack made it as far as *parasitic eel-nymphs*, before the book was snatched from his claws. He gurgled in fury and lashed out with a pincer, but not in time to stop Fingal hurling the tome across the room.

"Mo'dred's grudge, man, this is no time for fucking *books*," seethed the rebel, as he glanced out of the window and reloaded his weapon. "*Are you fully out of your mind?*"

"Yes," said Wrack, in the measured tone of his new voice.

"Well, get back into it," growled Fingal between clenched teeth, as he took a volley of shots at a passing gunship. Somewhere in the mist, the silhouette of a trireme flared as a shell burst against it, then broke apart and tumbled into the sea in a shower of fire. "I've done my best to humour you, Wrack— grief knows I have—but I can't abide a bloody coward. Your father'd be ashamed to call you 'son,' acting like this."

"Don't you say a damned thing—" started Wrack, but Fingal had grabbed his body from the table and thrust it at the broken window, shaking him as he pointed him at the deck of *Gunakadeit*.

"Your friends are getting cut to pieces," gnashed Fingal, barely holding his rage. "The people you freed: the people you lost your body for, and my people besides, who're willing to die for the same. They're getting butchered, because *you've had enough*. Let me tell you this," said the man, holding Wrack's camera within an inch of his own dead eye, "you don't get bored of a revolution. You're in it 'til you die, and if you get

the chance then you *carry the hell on afterwards*. So get your
head together and *fight*."

MOUANA GROWLED AS the blade bit into her thigh, using the
second it took her opponent to dislodge it to ram her sabre
through the warrior's neck. She was still freeing her own
weapon, sawing against vertebrae, when another attacker
bore down on her with a mace clenched in a blood-caked fist.

As the weapon swung, a ceramic fist swept in over her head,
and Eunice sent the man spinning back over the hold. The
warbuilt was leaking fluids from a dozen hydraulic punctures,
but only seemed to grow more savage as the fight drew on.
Dipping to avoid a shotgun blast, she lowered her head and
ploughed into a ragged line of irregulars, bowling them onto
their backs. The deck shook as she trampled their bodies to
bone-flecked paste.

To her left, a group of living sailors were firing into the melee
from behind the carcass of a Kuiper Ochsemann, while the
Bruiser appeared to be genuinely boxing with a scaly-armed aug
woman at the edge of the fray. They were slowly pushing the
irregulars back along the deck, but the fanatics still had control
of the hold, and had all but cut through the locks holding it shut.

Mouana was turning to assess the fighting on her right,
when a hammer smashed into her chest, flattening half her
ribcage and sending her sprawling to the deck. A monstrous
figure towered above her, already winding up for a second
blow. She jerked her shattered body to avoid the impact, but
the hammer came down like a steam press, flattening her left
arm below the elbow.

She scrabbled for a blade with the remnants of her right
hand as the hammerman limbered up for another swing, and
then, abruptly, he was staggering back with a harpoon in his
chest. Bawling Mouana's name, Eunice leapt over her body
and knocked the man to the ground. Hands dragged Mouana
back towards the huddled knot of defenders, and she didn't

so much hear as *feel* the impact of the warbuilt's fist as Eunice finished the man.

WRACK SIGHED TO himself as he looked out over the carnage on the old whaleboat. Once again, it had become clear that he only held any interest to these people as a weapon. So be it, he thought, as he let his consciousness sink down into the gloom below the hold doors. He would be a weapon. He was in a vile mood anyway.

The casket was stale and stifling. His head throbbed with the clanging of the preymeat on the doors above, and the darkness itched with limbs he did not have. With a shiver, he let his phantom tentacles uncoil into the hold, filling the dank space and making the dark itself writhe.

He yearned to rip and slash, to constrict and chew, and his many bodies felt it now. They came slinking from the bilges and scuttling from the hull's dead spaces, scaled and rotting on filth-crusted cradles of spidery limbs. Sharks and eels and rays, wolf-serpents and sprödewurm, abyssal things with faces full of slivered knives. They circled his coffin and coiled round its supports, clustered on its top to stare up at the clanging hatch.

The doors flew open, and a ring of faces peered down into the gloom. He grinned up at them, and fire twinkled on the black glass of his teeth. They shrieked, then, but it was too late.

Let's go hunting, thought Wrack, and let rage take him.

AT FIRST, MOUANA thought a trireme had crashed into the ship. There was a deafening boom, and a deep vibration passed through the hull. But it was blackness instead of light that blossomed, and the rumbling seemed to build in her own bones. All around her, sailors with catastrophic injuries leapt to their feet with wild eyes and snapping jaws, and she herself felt the urge to sprint and slaughter, despite being shattered beyond crawling. The air stank with fury, and the terror of her enemies lingered like meat-scent.

It was Wrack, she realised, as a wail of fear rose from the invaders around the hold. It was the black pulse. Wrack had tapped into whatever vile power festered inside the Teuthis device, and let it free from its chains.

The terrible anger raced through her and she thrashed on the floor, desperate to kill even as she tried to reason out what was happening. Then hell came from the hold. She watched from the ground as the *Tavuto*'s beasts—more than she had any idea had slunk aboard—burst from the hatchway in a tsunami of slime and bone and fins to set upon the attackers.

Even the irregulars, blood-deep in war drugs and madness, could do little more than shit themselves as the monsters came on. Mouana, whose hip still bore the wound of one of *Tavuto*'s spider-sharks, could even have felt pity for them, if she hadn't been slavering with hunger for their meat.

As the invaders on the quarterdeck saw the slaughter at the hold, they began backing away to the ship's edge. But there was nowhere to retreat to, and despite her every effort not to, Mouana savoured their screams as her sailors tore them apart.

PART THREE
GRAND
AMAZON

This view of a living nature where man is nothing is both odd and sad. Here, in a fertile land, in an eternal greenness, you search in vain for traces of man; you feel you are carried into a different world from the one you were born into.

Alexander von Humboldt,
Personal Narrative of a Journey to the Equinoctial Regions of the New Continent

CHAPTER THIRTY

WRACK CROUCHED AT the edge of the *Asinine Bastard*'s deck, tearing crumbs from a loaf of bread with his claws. *Grand Amazon* lay next to him; scuffed and dogeared and stained with blood and brine, but still holding together, still readable.

In front of him and around him, vast and hot and dense, was the real thing. The river churned at the warship's hull just as it lapped at the distant red bank, warm and silty and scouring. Pristine in its filth, calming in its restlessness, an ocean in perpetual transit.

The jungle crawled by in the distance, all its grandeur reduced to a stippling of green against the clouds. Every hour or so the trees gave way to towers and docks, but from this far away, ruins were indistinguishable from ports. Other than the occasional white streak of a refugee boat, the wildness of the place was loud as thunder.

And this was just the Rio Entrada, the entry-river, so named for the Gate cut into its banks by the ancient architects of the Lemniscatus. It was a tributary of the mighty Sinfondo, one of a thousand throats that fed into that continental intestine. Why those titans of parahistory had chosen to anchor the Gate here, nobody would ever know, but the stretch of river they now sailed—named the Waldemar Transfer after Wrack's hero—remained largely unsettled. In all but the most crowded worlds, it was deemed unwise to build much within range of an active Gate.

And so they had steamed up the river under the swollen sun for two days, passing the place where Waldemar's searchlights had swept the bank for the ruins of Torsville, and retracing the course of the great explorer. Ahead lay the Sinfondo confluence where, Wrack seemed to recall overhearing, they had plans to dock and resupply at Wormtown, the name Lipos-Tholon colonists had given to the old city of Mwydyn-Dinas.

After that it would be on to the Esqueleto, and then... well, Wrack didn't really know. In theory, it depended on what Kaba could glean from the locals, and whatever he could work out from Waldemar's book. In practice, however, he suspect things would get weirder. The truth was—and it sounded so ridiculous he could barely admit it to himself—he could *feel* where they needed to go. But he was resolved to pretending he was working from Waldemar's clues until such a time as he had to admit quite how mad he seemed to have become.

For now, he would let Mouana's cabal argue it out among themselves. He wanted little to do with it, if it could be avoided. In truth, thought Wrack, as he piled the chunks of the dismantled loaf on the ship's edge, he had not been paying a lot of attention to the talk on deck since the night with the triremes. After the bit he really didn't like thinking about, there had been an awful lot of shouting of his name, and a lot of being carried around above the heads of an excitable crowd. But when the shouting had finished and the crew had busied themselves with dealing with the aftermath, he had felt very sick and very frightened. There had been chewed bodies everywhere, and a phantom taste of blood that still lingered.

The river, with its sheer indifferent tonnage, had been a good place to come back to himself. For all Waldemar's talk of richness and decay, of a world full of savage energy, it seemed extraordinarily calm. If he could forget for a moment that he was a crab, a murderer, a man twice-dead and fully mad, it was like a wonderful kind of holiday. Nobody he knew in Lipos-Tholos had ever gone on holiday, but he had read about the idea in books and had always loved the thought. Indeed, he remembered, in those long evenings in the library belfry, this was often the place he had dreamed of going.

If anything, he was amazed how ordinary it felt. The Waldermar Transfer, though largely unsettled, was as tamed as any part of this overgrown world could be. The banks had been cleared for crops and left fallow in endless cycles, while the waters had been well-combed by the paddleboats of the *wurmjägers*.

Even so, the mystery of the jungle was forever lurking on the horizon. On the first morning he had seen the huge green hands of a gobbler, stripping branches on the distant shore before pulling back into the canopy—it had been a reminder of how deep this world ran if you looked past its surface.

With a satisfied flourish, Wrack swept his little pyramid of bread over the edge, and watched the pieces tumble towards the river below. The moment they hit the surface, the river boiled in rapture. Fish of three or four kinds, stripe-sided and sail-finned, rolled and dove in their frenzy. They flipped and thrashed in splashing arcs, and the milky shapes of predators rose to snap up the stragglers.

The feeding was over in moments; as shed scales eddied away, an elongate carrion turtle rose to catch the last bodies in its craggy jaws, then sank away in a stream of bubbles. Wrack had never anything like it, even in pictures; by the time he had registered the serpentine articulation of its shell, it was gone back into the silt. Waldemar's words came to mind, memorised almost by heart now, though he reached for the book out of a sense of comfort.

> *As with all the supposed former gartenwelten, Grand Amazon has a dizzyingly broad array of fauna, beyond any hope of categorisation for generations to come. It seems each new day—each hour—brings some new form as yet undocumented; every third sample net opens up a new field of study. As well as home-kinds both adapted and artificed, the Sinfondo and its* schwesterflüsse *bear host to countless exotaxa—beyond the spheres of colonial influence established in the last connected era, whole transplanted biospheres are said to thrive in the distant basins. Their intermingling with the home stock and with each other have given rise to a fierce and beautiful competition; the resultant biotic schema seem at times more rich than anything naturally evolved. To witness a phosphorescent worm slinking beneath a field of* Nymphaeaceae *lilies, among catfish and tambaqui, is to see a whole new nature, and—*

An unnatural cough came from the deck, splitting into Wrack's recital like a blunted axe. Fingal was there, leaning on a railing and looking awkward. Wrack snapped the book shut, and scuttled round awkwardly to face him.

"Not going to beat me up for reading, then?"

"I'm sorry for the way things were during the attack," said Fingal, with the tone of a man for whom apology was a currency not to be devalued through overuse. Despite his resentment, Wrack had the distinct impression he had already been allowed his one chance to take the piss, and held his tongue before answering.

"I know the violence is tough on you, mate. You always were a sensitive lad."

Wrack rankled at being called 'mate,' for a start. Yes, the violence was tough on him. But Wrack knew full well Fingal couldn't know how that felt at all—the man was a thug. Violence to him was a job. He doubted Fingal had much respect for him either, but could certainly see why he'd lie about it. To the old rebel, he was still old Wrack's weakling boy: needy and spineless, eager for praise.

"I remember your pa always used to wait 'til you were well in bed by the time we'd talk about the messy stuff, even when you were well into your teens."

Fingal had always refused to talk until the little sap was out of the way, more like. Wrack remembered now: the long evenings of muttered fireside plotting, that would become heated when he had disappeared. He remembered overhearing snatches from the top of the stairs. Fingal asking his father when he was going to get 'that boy' involved in some proper work, get some calluses on his hands. No doubt Fingal still thought of him as an innocent. But then, he hadn't been a fucking battleship for a week, had he?

Wrack wanted to tell Fingal to shut up about his childhood, and ask what the hell he wanted, but to his disgust found himself playing to the man's tune.

"Thanks for understanding," said Wrack, hating himself for wanting the knife-happy bastard's approval.

"I wish it could be the way it used to be," sighed Fingal, "when we'd keep the real business of what we did away from you. But we're in a whole new world now, mate. You've been as brave as any Piper in making it through this far, and you've just got to stick it out a bit more. That's all I was trying to say the other night, and I'm sorry the tension of it all got to my words."

Wrack seethed inside, knowing exactly how much praise and gentleness he'd be getting if acquiring his trust wasn't Fingal's only way to control a terrifying weapon. But again, he simpered.

"It's good of you, Fingal. I'm sorry I've been such a flake so far." This earned him a pat on the carapace.

"You've been a hero, mate, and the whole crew thinks so too."

They thought of him as an extremely lethal mascot and little else, but Wrack now felt too embarrassed by the flattery to do anything but nod his way to whatever end Fingal had planned for the conversation.

"And the most heroic thing you can do now is just hold back the fear, stay with us, and help us find that damned High Sarawak."

Well that's bloody convenient, isn't it, thought Wrack.

"Whatever it takes," said Wrack in entirely fraudulent earnesty. Fingal nodded.

"Right then, that's the spirit. Now, speaking of bodies..."

Wrack became aware of the Bruiser looming a few feet away. His face was badly dented and his hands were bandaged messes, but he'd been patched up well since the fight. Kaba was there too, wearing her own gruesome attempt at a smile. Wrack could see another round of cajoling coming his way, and pre-empted it with a hint of annoyance in his mechanical voice.

"This is about Mouana, isn't it?" he said.

"That it is," admitted Fingal. "She's nearly done being pared down and wired into the Ahab, but Pearl's never worked with the new model and she's having a tough time of it. We reckon she could use a friend around."

Wrack snorted at the word, but passed no further comment. He was quietly sceptical that Mouana would be remotely interested in his company if he wasn't annihilating soldiers, but they clearly weren't going to leave him in peace until he came with them to *Gunakadeit*. So he let Fingal continue.

"I know she's a hard case, Wrack, and she's been rough on you this far. But she's taken a hell of a pasting, and she needs to get back on her feet before we get to Wormtown. She's not forgotten it was you saved her, you know, way back on that awful ship. And whether she knows it or not, you could probably do her a lot of good right now."

Wrack felt a flash of acid towards Fingal; despite knowing he was being manipulated, he found himself wanting to look after the distraught corpse he'd pulled away from the rain-slicked flensing yards of *Tavuto*. He imagined her in pain, and he wanted to go and make her feel better.

"Can I at least take my book?" he asked, with an air of resignation that his tram-announcer's voice didn't carry.

"Sure, why not—you can read to her!" said Fingal, and the Bruiser gave a chillingly muscular thumbs-up. Wrack sighed, and scuttled onto the deck. At least they didn't want him to have a fight.

"ONCE INTEGRATION OF spinal trunk three is complete, refer back to section nineteen for instructions on ulnar nerve calibration across dorsal conduits F through J."

"Done that already!" said Pearl, revving the drill behind Mouana's back. The bench in front of her was littered with grey-smeared bone chips and the trimmed heads of nerve bundles, the exhausted debris of a body forced through two lives.

"Well you bloody shouldn't have done it already," answered Wrack, pointing at the mess of charts taped to the cabin window and continuing from the manual again. "If the ulnar nerve has already been calibrated, please refer to appendix nine for instructions on resetting tolerances across the brachial plexus. In addition, you may need to reset flexor drivers for the digitorum and ulnaris nodes in accordance with the new calibration."

"No need," said Pearl, the drill plunging into Mouana's spine. "That stuff's written for journeymen. I've done this before, it's basic to any body hookup. Doesn't matter what you've already done by the time you wire up the dorsal nodes, if you run a decent spine flush it'll find its own tolerances. And anyway—"

"Look, don't ask me. I'm just a crab. Just a crab, telling you what's written here in the manual."

Mouana snarled above the wet grinding of the drill. It had been better when he'd been reading out the jungle stuff. At least that had kept everyone else quiet. Now he'd gotten onto the manual for the Mark V, it had become a shared performance with Pearl. If she didn't know better, she would have said they were flirting.

"Just get the fucking arm switched on," growled Mouana, then grunted as an electric tremor passed through her right shoulder. Much as she loathed the former Ministry necrotechnician, she was prepared to accept Pearl was the only person on board capable of giving her a new body. It didn't mean she wanted to make a comedy of it.

"She's doing it," protested Wrack. "Anyway, I thought you wanted me to read something else."

"I did, but I didn't want a damned music hall show made of it. If she knows so well what she's doing playing around with dead bodies, then let her get on with it."

"I will. But I swear she's missed some stuff from section eight."

"Shut up, you!" cried Pearl in mock outrage. "What have I missed?"

Wrack peered at the manual with a theatrical gesture.

"First of all, ensure sterility at all times during the procedure," he recited, before sweeping out a claw to encompass the cabin. The place was caked in filth; where it wasn't black from the battle's spilt blood, it was tacky with engine oil and craggy with rust. Flies eddied in droning clouds, and every surface around Mouana's makeshift operating table was heaped with slippery bodymess.

The Bruiser was first to crack, giving a wuffling laugh from the corner of the cabin where he lurked, sipping from a can of oil. Then he punched Eunice, who seemed to have become his drinking companion during her own lengthy bout of repairs, and she started laughing too, a horrible sound like a ruptured gas pipe.

Mouana was about to cut them all down with a vile threat, but checked herself. This had to be better than the silent anxiety that had clamped over the convoy since it had made transfer. The jubilation of routing the irregulars had faded fast; once through the Gate and under an empty sky, they had realised just how far they had left to travel, and how scarce their resources were.

She looked out of the cabin window, her head still the only thing that could move in the new body. There was the *Asinine Bastard*, limping slightly but intact for the most part, and *Chekhov's Gun*, which had been holed in the battle, and was only still with them thanks to a towrope and constant bailing. On their own deck was the grounded Alaunt, but there was no way of getting it aloft in Grand Amazon's shifted gravity, so it was only good for spare parts.

They would need every scrap. Their ammunition stores had been rinsed in the fight, and the heat and the insects had ensured they were already well into their preservative store. Their human resources were drained too—they had maybe three hundred sailors left, a third of them living. After the trireme fight, some of the dying Pipers had elected to take Fingal's route through death, and had taken miasma; the others had been dumped overboard in sacks.

Of the dead that remained, most boasted a few bullet holes or a severed limb. Wounds had become a matter of cheerful competition between the sailors, and they had become creative—decorative, even—in patching each other up. One man as she watched was pacing the deck with an irregular's shotgun in place of his lower leg, lashed in place with pink cable. But for all their bravado, if they got into another fight now, they would be lucky to escape.

And there was no doubt: pursuit was coming. The thick gravity would keep triremes back as they were recalibrated, but Dust would find other ways to stay close behind them. They had to repair and resupply at Wormtown, as quickly as they could, and keep moving.

Mouana's attention was yanked back to the filthy cabin as Pearl cursed, and something gave way in her back. One of her bone-chisels—her persuaders, she called them—had gone clean through a rotten rib, slipped from her hand, and clattered down inside Mouana's body.

"Fucking amateur," grumbled Mouana between her teeth, as Wrack made another one of his bloody quips from the manual, and everyone had another good laugh. She let them. It was odd to think about morale on a mission where almost everyone was dead, and certainly Mouana had little talent maintaining it among the living, but it had to be attempted.

Besides, the whole point of getting Fingal to coax Wrack here was to humanise him a little, get him attached to the rest of the crew again. The next time they ran into trouble, the last thing she needed was him stuck in another bout of selfish catatonia. Of course, she wasn't much more keen on having the arsehole in the room with her, guffawing about her reassembly, but it was for the best in the long run.

"Remind me—how long do I have to suffer you reading to me?" she asked, trying to make it sound like a joke.

"Until you're in one piece and moving that body again," said Wrack. Mouana flexed her hip and gave a stiff kick of her leg, and everyone laughed. There, she thought. I can do morale.

IT WAS DUSK by the time Mouana was wired in; she dismissed Pearl just as the sun began its plunge past the far bank. There were still superficial touches to be finished, bolts to be tightened and actuators to be fine-tuned, but she could walk and—more importantly—fire her weapons. It took longer to get rid of Wrack, but a sighting of something big rolling in the channel past the bow soon had him out of the cabin. Now it was just her, the Bruiser and Eunice.

They were almost at the confluence, and the Entrada had widened to the point where the channel's banks were reduced to a green trace on the horizon. The sun's light had dimmed to a ruddy wash, the water was a rippled red sheet, and even this far from the banks the insects teemed. Jittering clouds of midges and moths bounced on the cabin lights, while every so often the armoured smack of a fist-sized beetle made everyone jerk.

Watching Wrack potter towards the prow, stopping to inspect a flying lizard that had perched on a rail, she wondered how wise it had been to bring him back across to her ship. Certainly he seemed more in tune with the crew now—the circle of sailors around him, sharing jokes and stories, attested to that.

But the same sight made her feel strangely bitter; it was him the crew saw as the heart of the voyage, him that they warmed to, even though it was her who had brought them here, who had led a tooth-and-nail defence while he had cowered behind his bloody history book. But that would change, she thought, as the forest swallowed the sun and darkness swept across the river. Now it was time to show them what real leadership was, beyond cracking jokes.

"Bring him up," said Mouana to the Bruiser, as she tested the flex on her boulder of a fist. A minute later the dead man returned, dragging with him a wretched sight.

They had kept the prisoner in the bilges since the fight, roped to a stanchion. It had cursed and bitten everyone who had come near it, and near chewed through one of its wrists in an attempt to get free. Swathed in stinking pingvin hide, black-toothed and stippled all over with bone-tapped tattoos of the Blades' ringed-world emblem, it was typical of the most wretched of Dust's irregulars.

But it was also a zombie. The inch-wide hole through the thing's throat left no doubt, and even as the Bruiser hauled it up the stairs, it ranted about the dust of war, the breath of life, the cold chance. They had found plenty like it in the aftermath of the fight; perhaps a third of the bodies cut down in the assault had gotten back to their feet with a blade during the cleanup, or had gone into the river hissing. But this one had talked, and so she had kept it aboard. Ostensibly it had been retained for intelligence on their pursuit, but Mouana had a more personal curiosity.

She stopped the creature's feral chants with a steamhammer slap that crunched its neck and left its head at an angle, then grabbed it by the collar of its rags.

"What do I mean to you?" she snarled.

"Aaah!" gurgled the zombie, lifeless breath slurping through stump teeth. "Traitor-gunner and runaway! Failed war-child! The thief! Maow-aaah-nerrr!" The wretch broke into a sucking parody of a laugh, and she knocked him to the floor of the cabin, but it didn't stop the noise.

"War-mother sent us, breathed into us the breath of life, the cold chance! Sent us to make good!"

"Make good on what?" said Mouana coolly, planting her boot on his squirming body.

"Make good the theft, the failed task, the dereliction! Return the thief, return the treasure!" The ghoul hacked a glop of black fluid as her boot pressed down on its sternum, but carried on in a crushed whisper. "The traitor, the failure, the company's shame! A place in the war tent for them that brings it back on a rope, a spike on the war-mother's tank for the traitor's unliving head!"

"Get some fresh air," said Mouana, looking up at Eunice and the Bruiser, and they wandered off onto deck. Mouana looked past them at Wrack, but the fool hadn't even noticed what was going on in the cabin. He was sat on the hatch of the hold, playing cards with a circle of grinning sailors. Their bottled miracle, sauntering along as they blew their bodies apart to protect him. Her supposed friend, who had rescued her from slavery, and pulled her back from the hopeless fugue of death. Subduing a spike of rage, Mouana planted her foot-wide toeplate delicately on the wretch's forehead, and steadied her voice.

"What failed task are you talking about?" she asked, keeping a feather's pressure on the zombie's skull.

"The ship-taking, the great trick! The journey through death and the seizing of the treasure! The special mission!" Mouana began to press down, feeling the skull flex under her boot, but still the thing continued its demented rant. "You, Maow-aaah-nerrr! You, *you* are the failu—"

Mouana stamped down hard, and bone-flecks bounced in the corners of the room.

She closed her eye, and tried to drown out the sound of the card game with the thunder building in her head. She had feared the truth for some time, if she was honest with herself, had suspected it ever since her visions during the escape from the Ministry. This time, she needed no visions to understand.

Her being on *Tavuto* had been no misfortune, no accident of war. She had been there on a mission, and she had failed.

Her 'necronaut,' Dust had called her, as they had spent long nights practising the hypnotic and mnemonic exercises that would allow her to wake from death. Her voyager, she had named her, as she had emerged from a coffin after four weeks buried alive. Her prizewinner; her protégée, who would take command of her new army on recovering the tool of its creation. The tool which now lay in the hold of her ship, possessed by the mind of a fool.

That ancient brain, which the Lipos-Tholons and their enemies had mistaken for a simple control device, when all along it had dwarfed the power of their coveted relics. Her task had been to seize the ship that held it and bring it back in triumph, shattering the siege and gifting its terrible power to her mistress. In taking on death, she had been assured never-ending glory.

Only she had never woken up. She had not been up to the task. She had wandered, wretched and hopeless, just another slave in that vast grey factory. But for sheer chance, she would have ended up fodder for the teeth of a watchbeast, as she dragged blocks of fat to the try-pots.

But for Wrack. But for that happy-go-lucky, whimsical cretin, who had come to his senses through some disastrous act of chance, and seized her from the jaws of failure. For all her training, she had been bested by a librarian. And no wonder, once she had joined him in consciousness, she had been so keen to help him take the ship and sail it back to port with guns blazing. She had been carrying out her task, with no idea who she had been doing it for.

Opening her eye again, she stared straight at that stupid little crab, and felt her steel-bolstered nerves sing with violence. She leaned against the cabin wall, and fought every urge to pound through it with her iron fists. If she had only woken up of her own accord, if she had only had the strength, she could have taken the prize. She could have been seated at Dust's right hand side, rather than being hunted as a traitor.

But she hadn't. She had joined Wrack's silly revolution, and sworn herself to the destruction of all that had made it necessary. Mouana had known, had felt, that everything that had happened on *Tavuto* was evil, that it had to be stopped. Glaring at her fist, looking at the power of those hard fingers, she wondered how much conviction she still had in those feelings, when they were all that stood in the way of redemption. With the simplest command, backed up by those fists, she could turn the convoy around, and be welcomed back with open arms. She could finish the mission.

But she couldn't. No matter the lure, she would not swim towards it. Because for all the hate she felt—and it was hate; what was left of her brain was sure of it—Wrack's silly revolution was right. So long as anyone had the means to force the dead to work on their behalf, there was something that needed to be stopped. Now that she was dead, she couldn't see it any other way.

So there was no way she could turn the ship around; the only end to this was to lead these leaking boats all the way to High Sarawak, and destroy whatever it was that waited there. And she had to do it with Wrack, the constant reminder of her failed mission, inhabiting the *very fucking thing* she had been sent to seize.

He was such a pain in the arse.

And worse yet, she considered, as her gaze drifted from the crab to the doors of the hold, he was now part of the very problem they were sworn to solve. If Dust had been right; if the brain at the heart of *Tavuto* really had been a resource to make the rods from the Ministry look pitiful, then Wrack himself represented at least as much threat as whatever waited for them in the jungle.

What's more, she had the means to snuff it out, and end her pursuit in the process, all in a matter of minutes. All she had to do was walk down to the hold, where Wrack's monstrous form lay in its tank of preservative, and let loose those fists.

But she couldn't. Just as she couldn't turn Wrack over to Dust, nor should she destroy what he had become. Because no matter how much she hated him right now, he was her only friend in the world. He was the only one, even among the dead, who might truly understand, and—

A shout came up on the deck. A cry of surprise, followed by a rustling against the hull, and then a solid bang that nearly shook her off her feet.

A fight. Mouana abandoned her self-indulgent reverie, and cranked her guns to full power as the deck shook. There was a terrible creak, and more deep, slithery rustling; Mouana snapped her head around, waiting for the next impact, but the night air was silent but for the flutter of bats as they swooped for moths in the lights.

"Blastwood," came a cry from down the deck; Kaba's voice. The ship's searchlight came on, illuminating a colossal shape in the water.

The tree had ploughed right into them; if their prow hadn't been designed to ram leviathans, they would have crumpled against its mass. It must have been a hundred yards long, with bark like rock and branches that jutted into the air like sails. It was swamped in vines all over, and had tangled a dozen smaller trees into a raft, their canopies half-submerged like the heads of drowned men.

As their searchlight swept across the vegetable platform, hoots and shrieks and skitters rose. A pack of things like insects hammered into the shape of monkeys bounded in terror from the beam, and a wildcat hissed from a tangle of branches, its eyes glowing like mirrors. Something big and green and doleful was nursing a wound on the edge of the dark; Mouana thought it was vegetation 'til its eyes shone. They were all castaways, trapped on the tree as it fell and now separated from the jungle by a mile of water.

Kaba fired a blast from her shotgun to scare the animals to the raft's edges, then set a crew of the more able sailors to dislodging them from the morass with poles and chain-cutters. Once again, Mouana was quietly pleased her de facto first officer had chosen not to throw all the ship's old whaling gear overboard before transfer.

"We're on the Sinfondo now, chief," called Kaba, gesturing at the wide dark with her scrawny arm. "Drifters like this'll be a lot more common here on in, and we're headed upriver now too, so they'll smack harder with it. And that yonder's a tadpole compared with some you see on the open channel. She's a hard boat sure, but won't take kindly to a waltz with a whale-oak."

"How far upriver is Mwydyn-Dinas?" asked Mouna.

Kaba waggled her crooked jaw thoughtfully as sailors hacked and shoved to disentangle them from the tree, then answered with a wave of her hand.

"Some hours yet; we'll likely reach it a stroke before dawn. That's a long yomp in the night; might be cannier to pause for a spell, 'til the light's fat enough to see more logs on the float?"

"Not an option; she'll be on us before we know it. Soon as we're free, pick up her speed again, have the *Bastard* pull in behind us, and keep the searchlight sweeping. Put out a launch too, to keep ahead and shout back if anything big's coming our way. Any damage we take, we can patch up with the rest when we dock."

Kaba nodded, then tipped her head towards the fallen blastwood. "And the gobbler?"

"You what?"

"The big green thing, out on the raft. Ugly thing with the hands. They're good eating, and we could use the meat."

Mouana peered at the potbellied giant on the edge of the light, then gave a grunt. "Take it if it's easy, then take us on upriver."

*   *   *

IT WAS STILL too dark to read, so Wrack crouched by the mount of the searchlight and looked out into the boundless night. As the light swept across the water its beam caught on countless insects, their wings drawing lambent arcs within its slow swoop. The river was everywhere and invisible, glimpsed only in the circle of choppy brown that roved over its surface in search of trees.

Wrack wished the light could penetrate the river's muddy thickness and shine down to its hidden lower layers. The Rio Sinfondo, "river without bottom": Waldemar had sent a diving bell into its belly, then hauled it up again when he had run out of rope. Even in daylight you could see no banks from its centre, and at night its immensity was crushing. Wrack was enraptured by it; deep water held little terror for him after Ocean, and besides, the sheer fecundity of the place wholly denied that other world's anxious, alien bleakness.

From beside him rose the smell of the watch team's meal of gobbler meat; roasted for the living, raw for the dead. It stank of the beast's algal blood, a weird mix of offal and cabbage that married greasily with the breath of the river. He had tried some for curiosity's sake, picking shreds from a glaucous haunch with a secondary claw, but he had a strange appetite these days and soon lost interest.

A wary cry went up as the searchlight caught another log—a true giant, this time—and the ship banked to port to avoid it. Wrack pondered how long that log had been floating, and how many others, over how many years, the river had carried from its banks to the distant sea. Trunks like that had drifted over these depths since before Waldemar, before the Lemniscatus, since before people, for all he knew. Back in the library, Wrack had spent the best part of a term curating an exhibition on the allegory of history-as-river. Central to it was a famous verse by Chancellor Regina, regarding states as logs afloat on time. The scansion had been shit, and so had the woodcuts used to illustrate it, but watching the wooden hulk drift past as Lipos-Tholos burned in another world, it seemed suddenly shrewd.

At the thought of burning, Wrack dipped his eyestalks in what had become his version of a frown. There was a definite tinge of smoke on the air, and it was not coming from the roasting fire amidships—there was a strong katabatic breeze blowing downriver, carrying the scent from upstream.

From Mwydyn-Dinas. Wormtown, and the island it sat on, had been visible as a smear of light over the horizon for some time. Now the old colony was only a few miles upriver, the light was brighter, and it had changed colour to a deep orange. Wrack peered at the horizon through his zoom lens, hearing murmurs of consternation on deck as watchers on the top-cranes called down the news; Wormtown was on fire.

Orders rang out across the gnat-haunted river, and an engine revved in the dark as *Gunakadeit*'s launch was sent ahead to gather a report. Weapons were retrieved from their lockers by cautious sailors, and the lights of the *Bastard* loomed as the warship pulled in alongside them again. In the absence of information, speculation rippled over the deck. Some were convinced the Piper uprising had spread to the Lipos-Tholon outpost, while others suspected an attack by an opportunistic foreign colony, launched in the knowledge that no reinforcements would be sent. Others still feared the worst, that Dust had beat them there by marching overland, and was bearing down on them as they spoke.

The island came into range of their telescopes as the greyness of dawn crept over the world, but nothing became any clearer. Gunfire echoed down the river, and the town docks swarmed with fleeing boats, but the nature of the conflict—or any idea of who was winning—remained obscure. In the cabin, Mouana was locked in heated discussion with Fingal and Kaba, while the Bruiser gulped at his can of oil and stared blankly ahead in the clear hope of a punch-up.

Two miles from the Wormtown docks the convoy changed course, veering sharp to starboard and heading towards the Sinfondo's banks to give the island as wide a berth as possible. The argument in the cabin still raged, and the sailors on deck were clutching their weapons, rumours giving way to mute anxiety as the colony burned off to port.

Not long after that, the boats started coming. As dawn shimmered over the river they were everywhere, from worm-steamers a third their size, to leaking dinghies just a few yards long. They speckled the river like drowning insects, and all floated low in the water, packed with people and their possessions. Some were fleeing downriver, but more were turning in their direction, abusing struggling engines to try and intercept their course. *Gunakadeit*'s hard-faced crew rushed to the rails with their guns, but this was not an invasion force—they were ordinary civilians, desperate for the prospect of escape and a sheltering hand.

Their shouts rang across the water as the fastest boats approached, but Wrack couldn't understand their dialect. When the lead craft was close enough for Wrack to see the desperation in the eyes of its occupants, Kaba emerged from the cabin and began shouting back through a loudhailer, gesturing wildly with her other arm.

Remembering what Fingal had said about sticking it out and pitching in, Wrack scuttled to Kaba's side, and tapped at her leg with his claw.

"What is it, crab-man?" she said, looking down at him, still gesturing at the boats.

"We're taking them aboard, aren't we?" said Wrack, already fearing the answer.

"That's a no, Wrack," answered Kaba, her tone suggesting she felt as comfortable with it as he did, but offering no avenue for persuasion. "Mouana wants no part of whatever's going on over there. We're changing course and heading for the Esqueleto, with a mind to making dock at Rummage." Wrack tried to hold her attention, but the conversation was clearly over, and she began shouting on the horn again.

Nevertheless, the boats showed no sign of slowing their pursuit. Those with oars had fallen behind now, but the larger craft were gaining, and their occupants were crowded on the gunwales with grapples and ropes. As they drew level with the colony, more still were pouring from its docks, cutting across the channel so as to fall into their path. In minutes they would be surrounded.

With a mounting sense of horror, Wrack saw there were families in the boats. There were elders wrapped in blankets, children clutching rags, and babies deep in wormskin swaddling. Men and women were waving their arms, calling out with a mixture of terror and exasperation. But Kaba's refusals only grew more emphatic, and the convoy did not cut their speed.

When the lead boat, a sleek river cutter with perhaps eighty souls aboard, got within a hundred yards of them, Mouana emerged from her cabin like a creeping mountain. Her footsteps were slow as she plodded down the deck, and her face was hard as she began slowly spinning up the barrels of her gun. Waving Kaba silent with a flick of her hand, she mounted the ladder to the quarterdeck and stood at the stern.

Wrack rushed up after her, claws scrabbling on steel, and began burbling pleas through his speakers. This couldn't be happening. He knew Mouana was ruthless, and seemed to be becoming more so every day, but surely this was beyond even her dissolving scruples. Nevertheless, there she stood, a ton of metal crowned with the withered sneer of a cadaver, sizing up the pitiful armada that jostled in their wake.

"Let them aboard, mate," begged Wrack, wishing that damned voice they'd given him could do anything but read the words out. "At least talk with them. They're scared! Please!"

"Go away," said Mouana in a husk of a voice, not looking at him. Against the roar of the engines and the shouts of the boat people, her stillness was terrifying; she stood with her gun level, like a statue of someone too grim to be tidied away by history. Wrack ran at her, not sure what he intended to do, and found the world spinning as she sent him across the quarterdeck with a flick of her boot.

As he struggled to right himself, the clang of a grapple sounded above the chaos of the chase, biting into the deck with a cargo of rope. Mouana slashed the tether with her arm blade, then barked a single word of warning in the local dialect, before firing a volley into the air. For a moment Wrack hoped this might all end sanely.

But then another pair of grapples struck the deck, and Mouana's gun levelled at their pursuers and fired.

At first, Wrack was glad he couldn't see what was happening to the boats off their stern. But in a way it was worse to watch Mouana, her face stretched into an unreadable grimace and lit from beneath as her gun belched death. She paused to reload, and a shaking hand reached up from one of the grapple-ropes to clasp the deck. Mouana stamped on it, and fired again.

Then it was over. Mouana stalked back towards the cabin, her expression barely less grotesque than it had been as she was firing, and Wrack was left alone on the quarterdeck.

He reached the stern rail just in time to see his first phosphorescent worm. Wrack spotted it maybe thirty yards from where the people flailed in the water; a patch of glowing water that snaked towards them, trailing occasional bumps of mottled purple as its flanks brushed the surface.

The townspeople panicked as they saw the worm's glow among them, moaned in terror as their feet brushed its bristled hide. They thrashed to get away from the bullet-struck, whose blood was now attracting the beasts, and surged to climb the sides of the boats that remained. With a creak and a splash, a dinghy capsized as more men than it would carry tried to scramble aboard.

Then a second worm appeared, a woman was pulled down in a cloud of red, and the feeding began.

Wrack turned away from the blood and stared at Mouana's back as she retreated, wishing his gaze could carve molten troughs through her armour and blacken her bones. As she stepped over the hold doors, he shivered, trying not to visualise black arms jetting up and cracking her like a shrimp. This is what had become of the *Tavuto* revolt. This is what they did now, in the name of compassion and the ease of suffering. They filled boats full of children with lead, and left their parents for the jaws of river worms.

As the massacre receded behind them, Wrack found a horrible solace in the sound of the worms' feeding. Killing and eating. That was what was easiest to understand, what it was safest to expect, from the world. It was what they wanted from him, when it came down to it, and it was what they had made of this journey. Fingal could say all he wanted about heroics and team spirit, but he was nothing more than a thuggish murderer; the same was true of that miserable sadist, Mouana. Wrack wished he'd left her for the shark's jaws back on *Tavuto*.

And what neither of them realised—and perhaps he hadn't until now—was that he hadn't been reading the book all the time because he didn't want to get involved in the fighting. It was because he was terrified of how much he might *absolutely fucking love it* if he stopped trying not to.

Wrack screamed, but not with his voice. He held the image of the blood-clouded water in his mind, and clamped down on it 'til his nerves sang. He felt ichor stream from his teeth, ice water streaming as his tentacles flew open, cold dread bursting in the minds of his prey.

Wrack screamed, and every soul on deck wailed in fear. The sun rose above the river, lacing its wavelets crimson, and something black and dreadful rose with it.

CHAPTER
THIRTY
ONE

DUST WATCHED THE hilt of her sword fluoresce with strange, crackling odours as it cooled in the chest of the mayor. Or was it the mayor? Blinking past the wash of colours from the wound, she took in the man's clothes, which clearly weren't Lipos-Tholon. Perhaps this had been whoever had led the revolt. It didn't matter, really. He had been the one cowering behind the greatest number of guards in the town's capitol tower, and so the place was hers now.

Not that that mattered much, either. Looking down from the windows of the stunted edifice, she saw a pathetic place: a few rows of weed-smeared tenements, muddled with reeking markets (their stench roared even from here) on a mile-long hump of river mud. It matched the meagre world it sat on, smelly and jumbled, and chaotic in the least interesting way. She did not plan to make much of it. With most of the fires put out, it would serve as a decent staging post for the Blades.

It hadn't been much of an invasion. Dust had always had a fondness for an amphibious assault, but compared with the taking of Steel Beach at the close of the Thaddean war, it had been an embarrassment. Whatever invasion or uprising they had interrupted had nearly spent itself on the town, leaving just a few dozen sweating gunmen to fend off the Blades. After mortaring a couple of half-hearted barricades from mid-channel, they had simply waded ashore and put metal through anything still breathing. It had barely been worth the drugs, thought Dust gloomily, veins trembling with wasted juice.

Already, her vanguard were nearly done cutting down the remaining population; glancing down onto the town's main thoroughfare, she saw them being lined up to be dispatched with a neat slot to the chest, then hauled off to the town's meat store to take the miasma. Even as the last of the living were finished off, the first of the newly woken were being corralled into work gangs to speed the unloading. Of course, some of her infantry were refusing to run the execution lines, but that only meant more bodies for her new logistics corps.

Turning to look back downriver, Dust knew the dead would be busy with unloading for some time. The lights of her army formed a stream of fire all the way to the horizon and the Entrada confluence beyond. From the cargo barges that had been refitted as floating stables, to the fishing boats wallowing under the weight of her infantry, they were carrying her whole company into the world. Even now at the shattered docks of Lipos-Tholos, her engineers were working around the clock to scavenge more hulls and carry the last of her army from the city.

There would be no time to wait for those stragglers, however—even the brief pleasure of impaling the mayor had been a wasteful diversion. There was a hunt on.

Dust clapped her hands once, and her intelligence officer shuffled forward. He had not taken kindly to death. The man's scalp oozed where he had pulled his hair out in clumps; his permanently fearful face sagged around watery eyes. But he did his job, and so long as his memory held out, he would keep it.

"What news from the interrogation?" asked Dust, enjoying the taste of the man's voice as it churned in his throat.

"The refugees... they say... two ships. Passed just before dawn, at high speed and armed. If we pursue straight away"— the officer gulped, and licked his lips with a dry tongue— "they've maybe got twenty-two hours on us."

"Did they stop here?" she asked.

"They... avoided the colony, sir. Some of the other refugees... begged sanctuary with them, but they were... shot in the water. Only a few made it back."

Dust was impressed—she would have thought Mouana had been the type to slow and dither, if not actually stop to help. If she had, her cargo would already have been in her grasp. Maybe death had hardened her—if anything, it would make the chase more interesting. Her mood brightening, she clapped again and called Logistics to report.

The tinworld crone was adapting much better. She had been dour and unimaginative to begin with, and was taking undeath like a bad bout of camp fever. If anything, her reports had *more* life in them now.

"Barge Sections Alpha-Nine through Kappa unloading now," she reported. "Engineering Section Three is now ashore and expanding the dock. We've assembled an embarkation pier upriver; the fastest boats are being routed there for reloading with troops as per my deployment plan submitted after transit. Current projections show that—"

Dust stopped listening halfway through the report. She had not read the deployment plan when it arrived, either. So long as her forces were able to continue the pursuit as efficiently as possible—and the logistics officer had been tediously reliable in her efficiency for the last few decades—there was little more to learn. As Logistics droned on, she turned to Engineering. The young officer had a particular flavour of anxiety to her that fascinated Dust, and she wished to draw it out.

"The triremes?" she asked her abruptly, drawing an indignant grunt from Logistics.

"Still... still getting there, sir," wheedled Engineering. "We've got them all through the gate and laid up on the beach after a controlled descent. Unexpected tidal action stalled work for two hours, but we're making progress and I expect—"

"They will fly today?" demanded Dust, barely inflecting the statement as a question.

"Well, I think—"

"Would you stake the use of your legs on them flying today?"

"No, sir," gulped Engineering, after a stutter that glowed a wonderful, wobbling indigo in Dust's ears.

Of course the triremes weren't working yet, and they wouldn't be for some time. It was no surprise—it took forever to calibrate floaters to new fields—but it was important to emphasise haste nonetheless. She demoted the girl to private on the spot, and sent her into the streets to help with the executions. She swore she had looked relieved.

"Comms," said Dust, and the bandy-legged lightworlder stepped forward, stooping to avoid cracking their skull on the ceiling.

"Negotiations with the Principals have stalled, sir," piped the officer through bloodless lips. "The troops from Orcus have joined their allies at the wall, and Kanélan floaters have been sighted in-world. We have insisted that you are still within the Ministry, but their patience appears to have run out. We expect an assault within hours."

Dust glanced out the window again, at the serpent of lights ferrying her entire army to this backwater mudpile. She had gambled everything on this expedition, had evacuated Lipos-Tholos as swiftly as it had been captured, with barely time for the troops to turn round a night's sleep. The most notorious siege in the worlds was over, and she had not so much as stopped to piss on its embers.

Of course, there had been mass desertions when the troops had been informed the campaign was to continue, and a decimation of the sixth regiment (chosen by a roll of the dice) to discourage further losses. Ancient siege pieces and irreplaceable engines had been left like stew-bones, simply too heavy to be carried away by boat.

She was surprised it had taken the Principals this long to realise they had been duped; that they had gained nothing from the siege they had near-bankrupted themselves to prosecute. They could have that senile old city and the guns she had left in it—once she had Lipos-Tholos' real prize in her hands, it would make all their toys meaningless.

"Surrender the city to them," she told Comms. "Tell them to enjoy their prize, and that we will forego our final payment as we enjoyed liberating it so much."

The birdlike officer nodded acknowledgement.

"And lay the streets with plague-mines," finished Dust, before turning back to Intelligence.

"We'll be on the river again within the hour. May I trust you know where our pursuit should lead us?"

"Oh, yes, sir," blurted the pale man. "They're headed to Rummage; one of their crew told the refugees, before the fighting broke out. But we... we know where they are anyway, sir."

"You *know?*" asked Dust, curiosity piqued.

"Since you... since we... now we are dead, sir. We can, we can... feel the prize ahead. We all can. We can't lose it."

Dust felt a moment of envy at the thought of something her new soldiers could feel, but which was denied to her. But she could consider that later; there were more pressing implications. If its presence was tugging on her dead then Teuthis, the prize, was alive. The intelligence officer spoke again.

"Another detail, sir... they used the cargo... Teuthis... to... project something? We felt something at dawn, something faint, but the refugees were right there, and living. They report experiencing a 'black feeling' that matches what we understand of the thing's capabilities, after the boats had passed. We don't know... know why... the conflict had finished by then. Perhaps—"

Dust contemplated that, as Intelligence waffled, trying to sound useful. The prize was not only alive, but awake and functional. Stripped from its cradle aboard the city-ship, it should have been reduced to catatonic dormancy. But it was conscious, and projecting its power. That was strange.

Still, she had planned for the eventuality of the thing being active, and would never have staked so much on its capture without the means to control the thing she was hunting. She would just have to use it sooner, rather than later.

Dust thought of the asset she had procured from one of the Kuiper states, back when her plan to take on the Lipos-Tholos commission had taken shape. The gelid museum-piece, which had spent centuries in the icy hollow of a store-stone, and which had been so eagerly traded for soil and germstock. She still wasn't sure if it was alive, despite the titanic cost of maintaining its environment tent, but—and in this she was perhaps alone across all that was left of the Lemniscatus—she knew exactly what to do with it. The excitement was too much—she could not wait.

"We leave immediately," she announced, and even the logistics officer looked astonished.

WHEN RUMMAGE'S SCOOPWHEEL finally loomed over the trees of the river-bend, Wrack stirred for the first time in hours—partially out of excitement, but mostly from relief. The convoy had been in desperate need of rest and resupply at Wormtown, and another three days' travel had all but ruined them.

The heat was the worst. It lay over the water like a second liquid, and throbbed in the metal of the deck. It cloaked them and dragged at them, basted them in the stench of their own decay. And though *Tavuto*'s former crew seemed to be degrading more slowly than inert corpseflesh might, there was no doubting it: they were rotting as they walked.

The dwindling remains of their preservative supply had been gathered in a cask, to which the Bruiser had been appointed quartermaster. He stood at the tap, grudgingly apportioning the stuff to the sailors who queued with tin cups and shrunken hands. Rations were down to a half-cup each per day now, which the sweltering dead mixed with salt and smeared over their leathery skin with their fingers.

The insects weren't deterred. Now the Esqueleto had narrowed to a muddy ribbon maybe two hundred yards across, they were drawn from the mud of the banks in endless whining clouds, settling on everything that resembled flesh. The first parasites had made themselves known, too; already the crew were alert to the yellow pustules that marked a boil-wasp sting, and not a half-hour passed without the cursing of a sailor afflicted by a passenger-fly and its writhing cargo.

With little to do but sit and wait to fall apart, the crew had taken to fishing—there was, after all, no shortage of maggots to be used as bait. One barely had to brush the river's surface with a baited hook before it could be hauled back up with a flashing silver cargo. In many cases, the time it took to bring the catch to the surface was long enough for something larger to seize it and end up on the hook itself. The nicer fish were offered to the living, who grilled them on the braziers where they boiled their drinking water. The grimmer specimens, meanwhile—the sagging catfish whose *bauchfett* reeked of river mud—went to the less discerning palates of the dead.

Wrack imagined the plentiful food was small consolation for the living. With the initial camaraderie of the journey fading now the dead were beginning to stink, the living sailors had taken to sticking aboard the *Asinine Bastard*, with *Gunakadeit* becoming the de facto Ship of the Dead. But when the *Bastard* had run aground on a sandbank near the Esqueleto's mouth, and the *Chekhov's Gun* had proved too heavy for them to tow without losing half their speed, everyone had been forced aboard the former whaleboat.

Their speed had picked up no end without their escort, but that was little relief for the living crews, now packed shoulder-to-shoulder with rotting corpses and vermin, with nowhere to sleep that wasn't sticky with rot. Most of the Pipers who'd volunteered for the journey were just kids from the Lipos-

Tholos slums, who wouldn't have dreamed of turning down a boat trip to another world in search of forbidden technology to wreck. Now, after days among the dead and no end to the muddy river in sight, there was real horror on their faces.

And Wrack had to admit he had not made things any better. After the incident at Wormtown, he had retreated to an overturned crate at the fore of the ship and lurked there, invisible and seething like the conscience he doubted Mouana still had.

They had all felt his outburst after Mwydyn-Dinas, but nobody could bring it up. Fingal had approached him with another attempt at bonhomie, but he had been having none of it. Kaba and some of the familiar faces from *Tavuto* had come the following day to sit and talk with him about river lore, but it had seemed done more out of a sense of duty than anything else. Whether they feared him or were unsettled by him, the rest of the crew had left him be, and the boat had motored under a weird, muttering pall.

But at the sight of Rummage's wheel ahead—rust-red and proud against a blue sky—Wrack could feel his mood lifting. One way or another, this was civilisation, and it wasn't on fire. The river was winding now, and distances were deceptive, but Kaba swore the town was round the next bend.

Sure enough, as they moved round the swoop in the river, the settlement revealed itself, and Wrack marvelled at what he was prepared to accept as civilisation these days.

Rummage was perhaps the most permanent settlement this far from the main channel of the Sinfondo, having persisted there since not long after Waldemar's time. Indeed, it had been the explorer's shipmates, bringing mineral samples back from the site, who had founded it. His enthusiasm for reading had waned considerably since Wormtown, but still Wrack couldn't resist seeking out the passage.

On the third night of our excursion up the Esqueleto, we elected to make camp for a time beside a sizeable limestone outcrop, in order to dry meat and set up a preserving tent for the specimens collected so far. Ms Tansell, much to Hansen's irritation, argued for two days to be added to our time on the tributary in lieu of the time spent in camp. This was fish a request to which I happily acquiesced, due in no small part to our capture of a nest of hatchling aquascolopendra, *which I wished to properly preserve and dissect before the heat turned them.*

Hardwick and Chase, our geologists, were elated to finally be set down on dry land in virgin forest, and immediately **catch fish** *set about digging in the red soil and panning in the smaller creeks that flowed from* **hunting and killing** *the higher ground. Vegetation here was more limited and less diverse* **hungry, chew them** *than downriver, and the river bore fewer fish* **fish, catch fish and more fish** *in the immediate vicinity; Chase suspected this to suggest the presence of* **jet through water under ice and hunt and—**

Wrack blinked the lens of his camera several times, and did his best to focus. This was why reading was rapidly losing its shine for him; when Waldemar's prose turned dull—and it did, often—it was so easy for unwelcome thoughts to intrude. No matter, thought Wrack, he knew what happened next anyway. While Chase had died of a sudden fever on the way back downriver, Hardwick had written to his sponsors back in Lipos-Tholos, urging them to stake a claim on the Esqueleto's astonishing mineral wealth.

They had done so, and Rummage was the result. There, on a long beach in the shadow of a river curve, beside the very promontory where Waldemar had made camp so many years ago, now sat a rusting god.

The mining company behind Hardwick, a shared venture that spanned the confederacy, had sunk unbelievable funds into sending it here—a self-propelled town capable of chewing mountains with its street-sized scoopwheels. But none of that money had ever made it back out of Grand Amazon. The colossus had failed in the sweat of the jungle just days after assembly, having not even struck rock. With no funds to repair it, and no salaries to draw from home, the miners had had no choice but to stay and seek their fortune by hand, on the bones of the great machine. After a week of life, Rummage had entered a long and profitable undeath.

The engine's hull had been stripped and whittled into shacks and piers, its booms and digging arms grown into rickety airborne thoroughfares. The promontory had been riddled with caves and storehouses, while iron tanks had been floated on the river to support sprawling pontoon docks. For while the machine had failed, the soil had not, and the flow of prospectors seeking their fortunes in the green had never ebbed.

Kaba had told him all about it: the wealth of the place was not so much in the gold as came out of the ground, but as came back from the pockets of prospectors. Rummage sold them picks and shovels and waders on the way in, and vice on their long, slow way out.

Even as *Gunakadeit* made its way into the lee of the giant past the web of piers that made up its docks, the town was ready to sell to them. Weather-pickled merchants proffered bloody haunches and fruit-laden branches up at them, alongside tarnished ammunition belts—and if they registered that the folk on the deck were dead, it didn't disquiet them. A deal, it seemed, was a deal.

Before long, Mouana had appeared on deck and was roaring for her crew to stay out of any trading, but they were no army, and soon trinkets and looted coins were being passed down, as the boat ground to a halt. Wrack watched with amusement as, resigned to the inevitable, Mouana threw down the gangplank and descended to the docks herself. Faced with her glowering immensity, even the keenest of Rummage's salespeople backed away.

Up on the beach, shaded by one of the huge machine's sunken tread assemblies, two figures stood in wait. The taller of them, a stocky woman with a swathe of black hair and dressed in work-worn leather, leaned on the old machine and raised a languid arm in greeting. The other, a man in the patched and sweat-stained remnants of a banqueting suit, fidgeted and wrung his hands in impatience.

Turning to Fingal and Eunice with a curt nod, Mouana led her lieutenants towards them, leaving the rest of the crew to spill out into the floating market. Although clearly not invited to the confabulation, Wrack advanced through the legs of the crew as they stumbled off the boat, and made his way up the beach to see what would happen.

The man in the appalling suit started forward to meet the party when they were still thirty yards away. He bowed deeply to Mouana, making sweat drip from his balding brow.

"I bid you welcome to our humble town," he proclaimed with a flourish, offering a yellowy grin that collapsed on itself as Mouana walked straight past him towards the taller figure.

"I wonder if you would care to hear—" continued the man, scurrying to keep up with the dead woman's strides, before giving up, shoulders slumping. The woman leaning against the treads took up where he left off.

"Alice Ivers," she said, guardedly. "And I see you've already met Dolph, the mayor."

Stubbing out a damp-looking cigarette in the sand, she stood upright and walked casually to where Mouana waited on the beach. She winced as she moved out into the daylight, but looked nothing less than amused as she swiped hair from her face and squinted up at the towering warbody.

"You in charge here, Ivers?" rumbled Mouana.

"No, that'd be the mayor," she said, nodding at the man while she lit another cigarette. "I just run the saloon."

"And the docks, I'm guessing?"

"Since there's drinking goes on at the docks as well, I've always guessed so, too."

"We need repair and resupply, in a hurry."

"What's the rush?" drawled Ivers, brushing a fly from the lapel of her shirt. "Couldn't be you're being followed, not out here in the middle of nowhere? Because if it's asylum you're after... well, that'd be politics, and you'd want to talk to Dolph, there."

"I said we wanted supplies," snapped Mouana. "Fuel, engine parts, ammunition and preservative. And as much as you can do to patch our boat up. We hit a log."

"Sure, though I'd tell you for free that it's best not to hit logs. Fuel, parts and ammo we're overflowing with. As for preservative," said Ivers, wrinkling her nose. "Well, I can't imagine why you'd want that stuff."

Mouana lunged down with a grimace, but Ivers didn't so much as flinch.

"A joke. In poor taste, I can see," she conceded, offering a conciliatory palm. "But I don't have much call to stock preservative. I'll sell you whiskey, but you'll pay whiskey prices. And how quick do you mean by 'in a hurry'?"

"Four hours."

Ivers glanced at *Gunakadeit*, and rolled smoke in her mouth. "Sure," she said, exhaling. "*Twenty*-four, maybe."

"How much extra to do it in four?"

"Easy, there," protested the saloonkeeper. "We've not discussed what it'd take to do it in twenty-four, yet. With the whiskey and enough fuel and shells to get you upriver? Likely to cost you more than the boat's worth—even before we narrow down to specifics. Best you just sell that old thing to me and take one of our fine craft in trade—do that and you'll be out in four hours, plus I'll throw in any supplies you want for free."

Wrack looked at the selection of pitted hulks languishing nearby. It didn't take a shipwright to see the deal was an insult. Mouana gave a low growl, and her chaingun started slowly spinning. The crew had begun to gather on the beach now, milling with weapons held not quite casually enough, as the tone of the conversation grew more tense.

"I'll give you the gunship on the deck," said Mouana, teeth set. "Lipos-Tholos air force, engines in good shape. You can check it over yourself—but that's as far as I'll offer."

"Sounds good," said Ivers, lightly. "I'll have you fixed up and provisioned in a week."

"Don't play fucking *games* with me," boomed Mouana, raising the whining barrels of her arm cannon to Ivers' chest. Eunice was immediately at her side, and Fingal had a revolver pointed at the mayor's sweating egg of a head, but Ivers looked as unconcerned as if Mouana had sneezed.

"I'd give you the same advice, friend," said the saloon-keeper, her voice revealing a new edge. "We play this particular game all the damned time on this beach, and we're pretty fucking accomplished."

Ivers tilted her chin up at Rummage's hulk, and Wrack cast his eye up the ancient machine. All along its cranes and galleries, sun flashed from the barrels of rifles. There must have been fifty gunmen above them, all behind cover, with clean shots on anyone who held a weapon. If Mouana lost her temper now, the journey was over. To her credit, she lowered her gun and took a step back.

"Well played, then," she grumbled. "I can see we're going to have to make a deal."

"Step into my office," said Ivers with an unctuous smile, and gestured at the shade of the machine's tracks.

With that, the two women moved into the shadows and entered a conversation too low and quiet to be heard from the beach. The performance was over—they had both showed their guns, and now it was a matter of business. As the conversation continued, the mayor looked increasingly anxious—several times, he tried fruitlessly to address the waiting crowd of sailors, but they were only interested in what was going on over his shoulder.

Then, after a pregnant wait, Iver signalled to the man, and he scurried over to her like a butler. When he returned to the crowd on the beach he was walking taller, and wore a damp parody of a statesmanlike smile.

"Brave seafolk, I am delighted to inform you that I have reached an agreement with your majestically-armoured leader.

The refit of your fine ship, the... *Goo-knack-a-dit*, will be achieved in eight hours. While my provisioners and technicians furnish the craft for the cruise ahead, its crew are free to enjoy all the entertainments of our humble town, free gratis!"

The mayor threw up his hands, but nobody cheered.

WRACK UNDERESTIMATED WHAT shore leave would do for the crew's morale. While Mouana, Eunice and Fingal elected to stay with a few dozen of the harder crew to oversee the repairs, the rest were free to take in the town. And although nobody was under the illusion their hosts could be trusted for a moment, there was a sort of reckless elation in knowing they had no option but to wait for the work to be done.

They were led onto the town's superstructure by the Bruiser, who moved up its slopes like a funicular engine in the direction of the saloon. Wrack was in two minds about following, until Kaba swept him up like a piece of luggage and carried him up with the throng of the crew.

"You've had plenty enough moping, crab-man!" she announced, giving him a pat on the shell. "Watching that sour bitch won't make her any more palatable to you, so why not just live with it. Or be dead with it. However you want it, come watch us drink. Mouana wants me to get some pointers on the way ahead, then go report back in a couple of hours. While we're at it, you can pretend to be a pet and we'll make a fortune on miners betting you can't do tricks."

Wrack barely had time to offer his half-hearted consent before they were sucked into the commercial melee of the town. As they moved up the ramps they were surrounded by the clamour of daily business; men with matted beards hacked at river-fish with cleavers, while hawkers yelled the day's price for panning gear. Pairs of boots protruded from roadside tents where drunks slept off their revels, and bottles clinked as fortune seekers fresh from the jungle began theirs anew.

The sight of a hundred or so corpses rolling into town raised a few curious glances, but little more. As they got in among the press of bodies on the machine-town's streets, it occurred to Wrack that they didn't smell a lot worse than its living occupants.

When they reached the saloon itself, the shell of an old ore-store where ineffectual ceiling fans stirred a roasting din, they were welcome as any new custom. While Dolph had offered drinks on the house, Wrack suspected there were plenty of other ways for what money they had to be winkled from them.

Within minutes the living—and some of the dead—had been set upon by the local sex trade (perhaps the only men and women dressed for the temperature, Wrack noted), or pulled into card games along the room's filthy trestle tables. It took maybe forty seconds for the Bruiser to be ensconced in a whiskey feast with a rabble who looked almost as hard as him, and for whom his conversational limitations were clearly nothing new.

After an hour or so of wandering around the place—not quite knowing how, as a crab, he was meant to enjoy himself—Wrack was accosted by Kaba. She dragged him into a card game with some local stevedores, and sat him beside her stool as she was dealt in and began trading what were presumably insults in her mother tongue. As the conversation moved with the rounds, Wrack kept hearing mentions of "High Sarawak," and figured she was angling for anyone who had heard of a route to the place.

He applauded her initiative, but privately he knew it was redundant. Although he still hadn't spoken a word of it to the crew, there was no doubt about it. He could *feel* High Sarawak. He hadn't been certain that was what it was when they had first made transfer, but whenever his sense of self had wavered on the journey, it had glowed like a beacon. When his rage had overtaken him after the massacre at Mwydyn-Dinas, he had felt its influence as deep and powerful as an ice-water current.

But that was the last thing in the world he wanted to think about. He had had enough time to brood on the boat. The card game had been going on a while now. Seeing Kaba was too engrossed in the action to follow through on her performing-crab scheme any time soon, and knowing there was nothing really the saloon could offer him, Wrack decided to take a walk in Waldemar's footsteps.

As Wrack left the saloon via a plank bridge and took the cliff path up towards the jungle, the clouds were thickening for an afternoon storm. Thunder was already murmuring over the distant green, and the chirps, hoots and trills of the jungle seemed subdued, as if the whole forest was waiting for the air to break. With the clamour of the bar-room fading behind him, it was almost peaceful—only the occasional prospector, loping past with a clattering pack, offered testimony to the industry of the place.

As the path climbed round the outcrop, it began to branch, leading off to tunnels in the ancient rock. Wrack chose one at random, and ambled down along the broken stone. His spirits rose as jewelled wings stirred on the path ahead; a glittering flock of Teal Viscounts—he knew the moths from Waldemar's own drawings—had settled to lick the salt from a passing miner's piss-puddle as it dried on the rocks. They scattered as Wrack picked his way over the dark streak, and he watched them spiral up into the growling sky.

Further up, the way was barred by a chain link gate, and Wrack became intrigued. The fence around the gate was poorly maintained, and he found it easy to wriggle under a rusted section. Ahead, where the path fell under the shade of an overhang, he began to hear the noise of picks, and a murmur of voices.

Wrack found a low rock he could conceal himself behind, and peered over its crest into the cavern beyond. Two figures—a great walrus of a man in a checked shirt, and a pale young man with a neck like a goose—sat on a bench by the entrance, passing a bottle between them. In the gloom behind, figures came to and fro from the depths of the outcrop, tipping baskets of rock onto tables where others laboured with crushing hammers.

"You reckon they all fuck together, then?" said Gooseneck,

smacking his lips as he passed the bottle. "The living and the zeds?"

"Must have done by now," murmured Walrus, as he accepted the whiskey. "They must've been on board together for a good while. You know how it gets with boat crews."

"Living ones, sure. No way even a sailor woulda gotten desperate enough to get messy with a rotter."

Walrus raised a finger at that. "Soapy Joe's never been too good for it, though, has he? Says they're a shitty lay, mind."

The kid made a disgusted face, and spat. "Soapy Joe'd fuck a tree if he was drunk enough. And besides, I'd like to see him try it on with these ones. That big lass who did the talking, she'd break him in two. Now stop making me think about that shit and pass the bottle." Still frowning at the thought, the younger man took a deep drink and wiped his mouth with the back of his hand.

"Joking aside, how come these ones all seem to talk? They're rotten, sure enough, but they ain't dumb like the ones Aife sends us."

"Well Aife won't send any more now, will she?" reprimanded Walrus. "City's binned, and I reckon this lot are the reason why."

"What, you seriously sayin' a bunch of *zeds* took over Fishtown?"

Walrus shrugged. "All I'm *sayin'* is that word comes from downriver of the city falling, then a bunch of zeds show up in a damned hurry wanting bullets. Use your goddamn head, boy; something's up." He snatched the bottle back. "And I guess whoever's after 'em, they must be desperate to escape from. Desperate enough for fuckin' Big Bertha back there to sell a hundred of her own zeds to us in exchange for supplies."

"I suppose we'll need 'em, if you're right about Fishtown," said Gooseneck, with a tinge of sadness in his voice. "Might not be any more coming for a while now."

Wrack felt like his mind had been kicked down a flight of stairs, but as Walrus piped up again, he discovered there was worse news still.

"Yeah, most likely not. But Al's no fool neither, kid—you don't think for a second that even one of those zeds is gonna make it upriver from here. You best clear some manacles, son, as I'll wager she's gonna take the lot. Then maybe you and Soapy Joe'll get your chance to try the big girl on for size."

The men laughed, and Wrack looked past them, to the figures toiling in the gloom. They were zombies; dozens upon dozens of them, slumped in misery as they hammered at the rocks from below. He briefly wondered how this backwater town had the tech to make them, but then remembered himself—someone from the City had been sending them out here, no doubt diverting shipments bound for Ocean, for Tin King knew how long.

And Mouana, after all they had been through, after being a slave herself, had been willing to sell half her crew into the hands of these degenerates for the sake of the mission. Wrack could no longer fathom the former mercenary's moral framework, but as far as he was concerned it was little better than that of the men in the cavern.

Sitting behind the rock as he watched the men toast their upcoming windfall, he almost felt it was worth letting Mouana get taken in by the saloon-keeper's plan, but it wasn't as simple as that. Sooner or later, the army pursuing them would come round that bend in the river, and would swarm over the place like ants. When that happened they—and *he*—would be in the hands of Dust, and that didn't bear thinking about.

Wrack kicked a pebble in frustration, and scuttled off back down the path. He was going to have to save the bloody day again.

TEN MINUTES LATER, Wrack was back at the place where the butterflies had been at the piss, this time with a very confused and highly irritable Bruiser in tow.

"Fack off," said the Bruiser, in a tone which suggested he hoped Wrack had a very, very good reason for taking him away from the bar, and drank irritably from one of the two bottles of lager he had brought for the journey.

Wrack shushed him and pointed ahead at the mouth of the cave, motioning as best as he could with his claws for the big man to approach on his hands and knees. The Bruiser was having none of it, though, and swaggered straight into the cavern with a bottle to his lips.

Gooseneck and Walrus leapt from their bench and started firing questions at the hulking interloper, but the Bruiser didn't so much as glance at them. He was staring past them, bottle still held to his lips, at the zombies in the depths of the cave. Thunder rolled as the storm broke outside.

"You fackin' *cahnts*," roared the Bruiser, smashing the neck of his bottle on the cavern wall. Then the stabbing began.

THE WORK WAS taking too long, thought Mouana anxiously, as the rain battered the corrugated roof of the boat shed. *Gunakadeit* had been hauled out of the water on enormous chains, and workers clambered over it with ropes and welding torches, patching the rips and dents in its hull. But they were half way into the refit, and nobody seemed in a particular hurry to get it over with.

She longed to be out of there, not only so she could stay ahead of Dust, but so she could be away from the decision she had made. Knowing that no-one who had gone up into the town would ever come back, that their enslavement was the price of getting out of here, was unbearable. But the idea of Wrack falling into the hands of Dust, of the horrors that would come into the world if she had that power, was unthinkable.

For a moment back on the beach—for a long moment—she had been about to call Iver's bluff and start shooting. But the odds had been too long. If a fight had kicked off on the beach, at the very best they were going to escape with their crew in tatters anyway, and no provisions for the journey—the fuel alone would have been gone inside of three days.

At least this way, they knew how many they would lose, and would get out with a fighting chance of making it to High Sarawak. Wrack would hate her, and she would hate herself, but the job would get done, and then that would be the end of it.

Still she dared hope they could find another way out of the situation. The crew that had stayed with her in the boat shed had not stopped looking for an opportunity to get the better of their hosts, standing in a mob at the shed's back wall, but it just wasn't coming. Iver and the town's guns were watching them as closely as they were watching back, and the work crept along with a hundred fingers resting on triggers.

"We still on schedule?" Fingal called out, although the question had been asked three times already that hour.

"We're still on mine," said Iver. "As I keep telling you, it'll be done when it's done. Go join your friends in the saloon, have a drink, if you're tired waiting."

"We had a deal," warned Mouana, as lightning flickered on the river's far bank.

"Deals change," said Iver, and grinned. Mouana didn't know whether it was just because everyone was shouting to be heard over the storm, but there was something seriously wrong about the woman's tone.

Then lightning struck again, somewhere up on the outcrop, and she saw them. Waiting at the shed's side door, where the track led across the beach to the town proper, were another dozen hired guns, faces set in grim sneers. She risked a glance behind, to where the shed opened out onto the river, and there were twenty more, crouching waist-deep with knives and shotguns. They'd been so intent on watching Iver's posse that they'd been quietly surrounded.

Mouana figured they had around eight seconds to make their move before things kicked off. She was about to start firing when she realised there had been something else. Something important. Whipping her head back to the shed's side door, she looked past the gathering thugs to the cliffside sprawl of the town, and saw she hadn't been mistaken. Rummage was burning.

"Hey," said Mouana. "Your saloon's on fire."

"Never heard that one before," said Iver with a smirk, at the same instance as one of her men, who happened to be looking out the side door, yelled, "Shit, the saloon's on fire!"

Iver glanced at the door, her mouth falling open, and the thugs behind her turned to see what the fuss was about. Thunder shook the roof of the shed, and Mouana fired a six foot harpoon through the saloon-keeper's face.

It looked as if they were going to fight their way out after all.

GROWING UP, WRACK had seen plenty of pub fights on Lipos-Tholos' grimmer streets. But compared with what he now experienced, even the bloodiest had been mere disagreements.

He was fairly sure a fight had been going on in the saloon already when they burst through the door; it seemed the sort of place where these things were as common as the drinking. Regardless, the arrival of a hundred corpses armed with hammers and picks, led by a man with a chin caked in human blood, left no room for ambiguity. It had really livened the place up.

Much as he had expected, there had been little need—or time—to explain the fine details of the situation. For the crew of *Gunakadeit*, the sight of the Bruiser at the door with a mob of emaciated slaves was enough; they took one look at them, then set to maiming anyone who reached for a weapon.

Kaba lunged over the card table and had a knife in a woman's ribs in the blink of an eye, while one of the boat's living sailors took hold of a prospector fumbling for a pistol and impaled him on a pair of wall-mounted horns.

Within seconds, all the bar's patrons had chosen their allegiance—some ran at the zombies from the mines and *Gunakadeit*'s crew; some sprinted for the nearest exit or rushed the bar to loot it for money or booze. Some laid into one another, taking the opportunity to settle old grudges. Bottles flew, knives flashed, and the room shook with haphazard, point-blank revolver fire. Tables were kicked over, and the floor filled with jostling bodies and swinging fists.

The newly arrived zombies were weak and poorly co-ordinated, but what they lacked in skill they made up for in enthusiasm— the Bruiser had spent a good five minutes bellowing them into a frenzy back in the cave, and though few could even remember their names, they were keen as hell to put their picks through their captors. The Bruiser had led them down the path through the rain with something like paternal pride.

And there, striding through the middle of it all, was the man himself, rapture in his milky eyes as he kicked a brazier over onto the floor. He had the look of a man who had always hoped for an afterlife of unending combat, and couldn't believe it had come true. Liquor bottles crashed onto the floor behind him, their contents bursting into flames on the spilt coals—in no time at all, the timber in the walls had caught, and the combatants had the extra excitement of roaring flames to contend with.

As the flames spread, so too did the fight; already it was spilling out onto Rummage's rusting thoroughfare, and down towards the docks. Wrack scurried across the room between sheets of flame, anxious not to be kicked, and made it out onto the street just behind the Bruiser.

Outside, the brawl went on in the torrential rain, fists throwing arcs of droplets that shivered white in the lightning. Wrack had to dive to avoid the body of a miner plummeting from a gantry overhead, and ended up in a tangle of weeds beside the street. As he righted himself with his claws he saw the flash of gunfire from the boat shed, and knew things must have kicked off there too.

And as if to cap things off, a wall of smoke rose above the treeline a few bends downstream—Dust's army was coming for them, and could only be a couple of hours away.

They needed a way out of this town fast, and that meant finishing this fight as soon as possible. Wrack squatted dejectedly, his claws sinking to the ground as knife-wielding lunatics slashed at each other around him. He was definitely going to have to lose his mind

And he had been doing *so well*.

Nevertheless, it was all too easy to let his mind retreat back to the hold of *Gunakadeit*; all he had to do was think of the deal Mouana had been prepared to do, and the blackness rushed at him. The last thought he could articulate, as he hurtled towards the hunger and the fury, was how worryingly easy this had become. After that, things became odd for a long while.

HE AWOKE ON the deck of a boat, and all around him were corpses. Their faces streamed with lightning-strobed rain as they stared at him, and they howled. He scrabbled to get away from them, but there was nowhere to go. Every inch backwards seemed to put him a foot closer to the grasping hands of another ghoul, and the circle was closing around him. He raised his hands to fend them off, but they were the claws of a crab. He screamed, and cowered as the bloated, peeling hands of the dead descended on him.

"*WRACK!*" they moaned as they loomed over him. "*WRACK! WRACK! WRACK!*" came the noise from their lipless mouths, but he didn't know what it meant. Then their slippery fingers wrapped around his body, and he lost his senses again.

CHAPTER THIRTY TWO

"HE'S NOT LIKING that, is he?" noted Fingal, as he packed sealant foam into the wound in his shoulder. The crew had lifted Wrack in the air and were chanting his name as they passed his body along the length of the deck, but he was screaming in terror.

"No, he's really not," agreed Mouana, with a grim smirk. The crew didn't seem to have noticed, any more than they had registered the wounds on their hands inflicted by his spiny shell as they tossed him about.

He was their totem; when he had sounded the black pulse from *Gunakadeit*'s hold, the fight in the town had turned from a doomed brawl in the rain to a triumphant rout. Rummage's militia had quailed in horror when it came, while the dead—bolstered by the newcomers who had appeared out of nowhere with Wrack and the Bruiser—had fought on with something between rage and rapture.

In the boat shed, too, it had turned around a losing battle. Pinned behind *Gunakadeit*'s hull, with Eunice gushing hydraulic fluid where a grenade had taken off her arm, they had been minutes away from being overrun when the pulse fired, and the ship's beasts had come pouring out of the hold onto the heads of their attackers.

If Wrack hadn't intervened, they would all have been in Dust's hands by now. Even now, looking back through the storm, she could see the glow of the town burning above the forest as the Blades overtook it.

But owing her escape to Wrack only made the crew's jubilation more bitter for Mouana to take. Once again, the librarian was being celebrated for what amounted to magic tricks, while she had only been reviled for the hard decisions she had made at Mwydyn-Dinas.

"I'm sure he'll get over it," said Fingal, slinking off to the cabin. Mouana grunted assent, but she wasn't sure that he would. Every time Wrack retreated into the pickled mental bulk of Teuthis, he came back more gradually, and less intact. And she was starting to worry about what would happen when he did.

Although nobody but Fingal had been party to the details of the deal she had struck with Iver, Mouana was nagged by an uncanny sense that Wrack knew.

During the fight, as the ship's beasts had run wild in the boat shed, there had been a strange moment. A wolf-eel, black flesh streaming from its body after days in the heat, had paused after savaging a gunman. It had skittered across the floor and up onto her chest before she could react, then regarded her with a queer look of calculation in its rot-murky eyes.

For a moment she had been certain it would lunge for her face, before a ricochet knocked it sprawling to the floor. By the time the thing righted itself, the feeling had passed; Dolph, the town's mayor, had stumbled past, fumbling to reload a pistol, and the beast had launched itself at his leg. Mouana had never seen a man die with so much screaming.

It would have been easy to discount the incident as paranoia, but for what had happened at the end of the fight. When the way to the boat shed had been cleared and the crew had come down from the town, she had come face to face with Wrack.

He had been the last to arrive, picking his way down the path behind the stragglers as bullets blew spigots from the puddles around him. She had been holding the shed doors with Eunice, covering the crew's retreat as Fingal got *Gunakadeit* back into the water.

But as Wrack had passed the threshold, he had stopped and looked at her. Maybe she was going as mad as he was, reading so much into the mute gaze of a crab, but she could have sworn it was the exact same look as the wolf-eel had given her. Somehow, *he knew*.

Looking now at the crab as it flopped in the hands of the crew, the town just another decaying memory, it seemed ridiculous to worry. They had won, they had stayed ahead of their pursuit, and the goal was getting closer. But more and more, the irritation she was so used to feeling for Wrack was giving way to a creeping fear of what lay beneath the doors of the hold.

"Hey, chief, you coming—?" Kaba's voice from the cabin shook Mouana out of her reverie, and she looked away from Wrack's limp form. "Fork in the river not far ahead; you've a choice to make."

THE MAPS WERE spread out on the tables by lamp light; some time during the storm, night had crept up on them. They were drenched and crumpled, smeared by the rain, but still readable.

Fingal and Kaba were trying to make sense of them as Mouana ducked under the lintel. Eunice was slumped in the corner, on the bench that had become the boat's de facto operating theatre, while Pearl worked with shaking hands to clean the mess the fight had made of her left side.

It was the first moment of peace since the violence of the escape, and the roar of the engine as it drove them upriver was like a strange, throbbing silence. Out in the gathering dark the banks rushed by, unbroken walls of rain-lashed trees, and as the river narrowed, the forest seemed all the more vast. They were hurtling out into real nowhere country, with little more to go on than a stolen map and a madman's hunch.

"What's ahead?" said Mouana, leaning on the map's edge.

"The Esqueleto splits ten miles yonder," explained Kaba. "Main channel goes on eastward; there's a brace of colony towns up there, farms out among the reed marshes, then maybe loggers' yards 'til the map runs out. I never made it up that way. Northways fork's a tributary, a blackwater channel called the Extrañeza. Smaller and meaner than the other branch."

"And what's up there?"

"Hard to say, truly. This chart's too old. Used to be a fair-sized town, Raglan, but that went. Gone with the trouble-wash of some outworld grief years back. Now? Couple of villages maybe, some broken down warehouses. Then nothing, all the way to nowhere."

"What's your feeling?" asked Mouana, looking the woman in the eye. Rain rattled on the cabin window and smeared the deck's light into sheets. If they made the wrong choice, there would be no doubling back. *Gunakadeit* was a fast boat; she'd been built to run down monsters, and with a full tank of fuel and no reason to save it, she tore down the river like the storm itself. But they would need every scrap of speed—when they left Rummage, the drone of Dust's flotilla was already audible, its smoke visible just a couple of bends away. They had an hour on them at best—less, if the Blades had gotten their aircraft working.

"My bet's the Extrañeza, chief. Weirder stories from up there. That and a guy at the card tables back there, he said his grandfather still called it the 'bone-road.' I think Wrack, he mentioned—"

"East or North, Kaba," interjected Fingal, leaning forward.

"East. But surely we—"

"East it is," concluded Mouana. "Plot the course." If it seemed sound to Kaba, then they'd take the Extrañeza. Even if they could get sense out of Wrack before the river forced the decision on them, to beg him for help now might lose her the ship—especially if he chose that moment to expose what he knew about her. No: it couldn't be risked.

"Chief," said Kaba, her face grim even for a corpse. "We've got to ask Wrack on this."

"Why?" barked Mouana. "Because of that damned book of his? There's piss-all in it, and he's beyond cracked even it was any use. This is my fucking ship and I'm asking you which branch to take."

"But he *knows*, chief."

"What do you mean?" asked Mouana quietly, her voice cold as an Ocean dawn.

"High Sarawak," said Kaba. "He knows where it is. There's something weird going on and he can feel it, I swear. In his *brain*," she added, tapping the side of her head and gesturing belowdecks. Mouana gaped, not knowing what to feel more unnerved by—the revelation of yet another mystery around Wrack, or the fact it had been kept from her by her first officer. She was trying to find words when Fingal cut in.

"Mouana, look. On the deck." Beyond the choppy drone of the engine, everything had gone very quiet. Mouna turned around.

There, outside the rain-smeared window, her crew had gathered in a wide semicircle around the cabin. And in its centre, rain sleeting from his outstretched arm, stood the Bruiser. He was pointing directly at her.

"We need to 'ave..." he said, brow clenched for a long moment as he wrestled for speech. "We need... to 'ave... *some fackin' word*s."

Despite the fact she stood in nine feet of hydraulic armour, Mouana had to force herself not to show fear as she stepped out of the cabin, not to let her huge hands shake as she closed the door behind her. Eunice lurched to her feet as she left, sending spanners and clamps clattering to the floor, but Mouana waved her down—this was something she had to face alone.

The boat, already crowded when they arrived at Rummage,

was packed to the gunwales now it had taken on the slaves from the town. The crew, both living and dead, covered the deck in a mass, shivering as they watched to see what would happen. The sky above was a black vault, the river a churning, ripple-crazed darkness around them.

Mouana entered the space that had formed around the Bruiser, and the big man paced sideways, keeping opposite her without breaking his reptilian gaze.

"I've... I've seen you," he gargled, finger stabbing out again in accusation. "I... know you."

"I know you too, sailor," said Mouana, as calmly as she could. "What's your issue, man?" Choked sounds spluttered from the Bruiser's throat as he struggled to speak, and his arm trembled with the effort. When the words emerged, they came through his rotten teeth with the heat and pressure of engine steam.

"I... know. I know... what... you was gurner do. In the taahn. And it ain't *right*." The last word was a roar, fury mixed with triumph, and his pointing hand coiled into a fist as it came.

"You're as bad as... as... as..." stuttered the pub hulk, gesturing back through the storm, "as *bad* as fackin' *Dust*."

Fear ran cold down Mouana's spine, and rage flooded after it. In all her worrying about what Wrack had learned, she hadn't thought for a moment that the festering, near-mute old brawler could ever have been a threat. But somehow, he had figured things out, and had regained his tongue at the worst possible time. Her eyes flicked to the crowd on the deck, to the faces furrowed as they worked through the Bruiser's words. This had to end now. It had to be silenced, before chaos overtook them and damned their chances of making it any further.

"Is this a mutiny?" boomed Mouana, loud enough for the whole boat to hear, and throwing out her arms in challenge.

"Nah," spat the bruiser, as he cracked his knuckles. "It's a fackin' *FIGHT*."

And with that he charged, arms spread as he pounded across the rain-slick deck. He slammed into her, and despite outweighing him five times over, she still rocked with the impact. She couldn't believe his strength; if she hadn't been wired into the warbody, she would have been sent flying.

But unfortunately for the Bruiser, she was built for this. Clamping a hand around his shoulder and sweeping her right arm between his legs, Mouana heaved the man over her shoulder and into the air, to land on the deck with a wet crack. She turned to face his crumpled body, hoping that was the end of it, but the Bruiser clearly felt differently.

Rising to his feet as if he had tripped on a shoelace, the glowering giant grabbed his head in his hands and set his neck with a sickening crunch. Then he charged again. Mouana twisted her whole body from the hips, throwing herself into a haymaker aimed at the brute's chest, but he simply ducked under it, bringing himself to a stop by snatching a fistful of her underarm cables.

Swinging round behind her, the Bruiser growled and leapt onto her back; his half-brick of a hand gripped her shoulder, and his legs wrapped round her waist. She flailed behind her with her right arm, trying to swipe him away, but the warbody was too inflexible to score a hit. Then metal flashed in the corner of her vision, and her arm began sagging; the Bruiser had pulled out a blade and was stabbing away like a jackhammer at the cables nested in the crook of her arm.

Realising he was only a thought away from scrambling up and doing the same to her neck, Mouana threw her leg out and fell backwards, hoping to crush him beneath her weight. But again the Bruiser was too quick; with a speed that should have been impossible for a corpse, he leapt aside and left her to hit the deck with a bone-shaking crash.

As she struggled to right herself, her weak arm scrabbling for purchase on steel, he came on her again, throwing himself onto her chest and smashing her in the face with his forearm. Next was his fist, and Mouana felt her cheekbone crumple under the impact, her vision flaring white. The third blow would have crushed her good eye socket, but her left hand shot up to block it and grabbed his fist in mid-flight. She squeezed, and heard the pop of his hand turning to liquid in hers.

But the Bruiser was undeterred; already he had the blade out again, and would have sunk it into her face if she hadn't jerked him sideways by his pulped wrist. Feeling strength coming back into her right arm as its hydraulics self-sealed, she put a palm to the deck and shoved herself up, keeping the bruiser pinned to the deck by his wrist as she rose. But as she got to her knees, the man threw himself backwards, tearing his arm free of his hand and leaving the sodden thing in her fist.

Mouana rose to her feet, the Bruiser to his, and they circled each other in the rain. His right forearm ended in a mess of crushed bone, but he held it in front of his face like a shield while his left waited bunched, blade in hand.

"*COME ON, THEN,*" bellowed the Bruiser, beating his chest with his stump, and Mouana lunged. He leaned back under her first wild swing, then ducked in close with a flurry of stabs between the plates on her side. But the swing had been a feint to get him low, and when Mouana came back round, her left fist hit him in the side like an artillery shell.

The Bruiser skidded five yards across the deck, coming to a crunching halt against a stanchion, but still tried to haul himself up despite half his chest being a mire of caved-in bone. Mouana strode slowly to where he lay, giving him time to surrender, but he only hissed at her as he flailed. She knelt over him, rain washing scraps of his flesh from her armour, and put a hand on his chest.

"Stay down," she said quietly, so only he could hear.

"Fack off!" he screamed in her face.

Mouana had done her best. She had given him a chance. But she could see in his eyes that he, like she, understood how this had to end. They had fought together to liberate *Tavuto*, and had laughed together as they burned the factory that had made them. But now he held knowledge that could turn her crew against her, and they both knew he couldn't keep it to himself.

She raised her arm before she could think about it any further, before she could talk herself out of it. Her fist slammed down, and cracked the Bruiser's skull like rotten fruit. It took three more blows before his arms sank to the deck, knife rolling from his fingers to come to rest in a puddle.

Mouana stood, gore sleeting from her fingers in the rain, and looked around the circle of staring faces. She looked down on them, silently challenging them to come forward and face her, but nobody would raise their eyes to hers. Where once had been loyalty, now there was abject fear. No matter, thought Mouana, as she turned her back on the crowd and plodded back to the cabin. It would do just as well.

The crowd melted away and went silently back below decks, or to the tarpaulin shelters that had been strung across the foredeck. As she returned to the maps, Mouana tried to tell herself she had done the only sensible thing. That the Bruiser had been dead in any case, and that they all faced annihilation once they had done their work at High Sarawak. But as Fingal gave her a stern nod of approval, and Kaba slunk past her with a mutter about having to watch for fallen trees, the Bruiser's words echoed in her head: *as bad as fackin' Dust.*

THE STORM FINALLY broke at dawn. The air turned gold as the last drops fell, and mist shrouded the river, broken only by the splash of breaching fish and the flapping passage of river birds.

Nobody in the cabin had spoken to Mouana for the rest of the night, and she hadn't wanted them to. *Gunakadeit* had steamed on, the river black in front as it was behind, and taken the turn up the Extrañeza with its crew huddled sullenly under canvas. They had stayed there as morning approached, bodies piled together in a fitful approximation of sleep.

Only a few souls, the most bewildered of the rescued miners, wandered the deck as the sun rose. Fingal had gone with Pearl during the night, to go and see to the living rebels who had made their shelter under the boat's forecastle. Eunice was largely repaired, and lay slumped in whatever passed for rest, motes dancing in sunlight above her vast shoulders.

Mouana stood where she had spent most of the night, silent at the tarnished dials of the captain's station. She had not wanted to rest; wakefulness had been haunting enough, and she dreaded what visions might come to her if she let vigilance slip.

Again and again during the night, she had told herself she had done the right thing; that a mutiny would have cost them their chance to get to High Sarawak, and to finish the journey. That even once they had reached their destination, there would be no getting back past Dust's army. That there were no lives to go back to. That for the Bruiser, she had only advanced an inevitable end.

But no matter how much she tried, she would not be convinced. Even when she came near to forgiving herself for the Bruiser, the memory of the refugee boats came back to her, and the sight of the Chancellor on College Hill. After a life spent killing, she finally felt like a murderer.

Murderer... The word echoed in her head, as dawn crept over the map in front of her. It repeated over and over, losing all meaning and chiming like an alarm, until she thought she had finally lost her mind. She shook her head, but the noise kept coming, until she realised it really was an alarm.

Mouana focused on the dashboard in front of her, and the red light flashing above the radar screen. There was something approaching *Gunakadeit*, on the river's surface, coming from behind at an incredible pace. She frowned in incomprehension—if anything, they should have increased their lead on the Blades during the night. And the object on the screen was tiny, certainly far too small to be an invasion force.

Panic flared at the thought of a torpedo, then became something colder as Mouana realised what was coming. Wearily, but knowing there was no way to avoid what lay ahead, she left the cabin and made her way to the stern rail to watch the mist.

The fog stirred on the black water. In perfect silence, a boat appeared. Mouana hoped it was a vision, at first, and felt a moment's relief at the possibility this was all in her head. But it was all too real, and so was the figure that sat in its bows: Dust.

There was the general, eyes yellow and unblinking, staring directly at her as she glided forward. She seemed at once too big and too small; spindled and brittle, but folded, as if she could reach out across the water for her at any moment. Mouana found herself clutching at the armour that concealed her execution wound, and watched Dust's eyes swivel to follow the gesture.

The boat moved to within a stone's throw of the stern and held there, silently matching speed with *Gunakadeit* without making so much as a ripple on the water. Mouana knew she should have powered up her weapons, that it was not too late to shout and alert the crew. But she was frozen to the spot, caught in the gaze of the apparition.

"Only you can see me, and only you may hear me," said Dust, in a murmur that brushed her left earlobe across thirty yards of water. "I have come to speak with you. We may fight if you like, but it will be quick if we do." Mouana gawped and searched for words, but Dust spoke again.

"I see you have become strong, my champion. It's pleasing to see, despite all the difficulties you have caused. Soon, when this is resolved, you must tell me of death."

The general's words rang out over the water, yet felt as if they came straight into her head, to be heard by her alone. Still she could find no answer.

"I wonder, do you remember when you came to me, in the fourth year of the siege?" asked Dust. "It was the day you were told of your brother's death, and you asked to be relieved of your duties."

Mouana did remember, for the first time, as Dust said the words. Her brother... She had just received the letter while Aroha was sleeping off another night at the flasks, and had looked at him after she had read it, a living example of the mistakes she didn't want to make. She had already missed the chance to make things right with her brother, but she still had a family, waiting every day for the news she was coming home at last.

There and then, despite the drunken warning Aroha had given her about what to expect of the general's sympathy, she had resolved to leave the Blades and go home. She had crammed her field pack with whatever necessities she could grab before her mind threatened to change, and headed for the command trench.

"Take a moment to remember that day, commander," purred Dust from the boat. "Indeed, since your memory in death has not proved as strong as either of us had once hoped, I shall assist you in remembering. Remember, and begin by remembering Mīhini."

Mouana stared into Dust's eyes, as golden and chilly as the dawn, and her life before the Blades came back to her at last.

Mīhini, her home. Proud and filthy and ancient; the black jewel of the Diaspora Chain, and its toiling industrial heart. Fed from the valleys of sister-world Kotinga, and watered by ice from far Kōpaka, it was a world of smoke and iron and work. An ugly world, but it made her ache to remember it now.

"An irony," mused Dust, as the memories pooled. "Your very own *Tavuto*, long before it made its way to Ocean—back when it was still a warship—was birthed in the Mīhini yards." Dust sighed. "It's not just you, Mouana. There is so much we have all forgotten. Now remember your brother."

Henare's face, and his name, returned to her with a pang of loss. He had loomed so large in her life; how could she have forgotten? But thinking of him now, she had the queer sensation he had never truly left her thoughts. Henare: the ore-man, the hero-miner, stronger than his father before his fifteenth year, but always smiling, and making others smile.

His life seemed effortless despite his endless thirst for work, and he had become emblematic to the home-block. Even as the machines died and Mīhini slid gradually into decline, people like Henare offered hope that muscle and laughter alone could ward off entropy.

"He was why you wanted to leave me," said Dust, "but

he was also the reason you came to me. A glutton for love, you called him. Always the first to be served when the block gathered to eat, always at the centre of the family portrait. And you? You, so bright and so talented, who kept the ancient pumps alive and the mines open even as the world collapsed? You could only ever be his support."

Dust's boat drifted closer, but Moana was powerless to react. All of this, now, was too much for her to bear.

"And so you fled to me, my prize-winner. Onboard a shipment of fresh-forged howitzers I found you, covered in coal dust and determined to make a name for yourself. You were barely more than a child, but I kept you on. I would not have done, but you saw to the workings of old Kronos when he fell sick that winter, and you earned your place.

"But you always meant to go home, didn't you? You never loved the wars, not like I do. You feared them. You hated the life, but you wouldn't stop living it until you knew for sure you had eclipsed your brother. I admired you for that, Mouana; for what you would do to prove a point."

Mouana couldn't stand to hear the words, but they were true. She had never felt at home as a soldier, had always longed to be away from all the hardness and the aggression. But she could not leave. At the end of each campaign, it became traditional for her to write to say she was coming home, then burn the letter.

Time and again she had gone through that bitter ritual, all the way to Lipos-Tholos, the Queen of Sieges. And then, a year in, the word came; Henare had developed the greasy lung, the miner's plague. He was still walking, but his best hope was to die sooner rather than later, and still Mouana had elected to stay. Her brother was strong, and she knew he might hold out for years. Years in which, if the Blades lived up to their reputation, they might finally take that bloody city. Each day, she had prayed her brother would last longer than Lipos-Tholos, so she could return to him as an equal.

The City outlasted him. Henare had died in a mine collapse,

working despite his illness, as the siege entered its fourth year under the Blades. The whole block had turned out for his funeral, and a statue was forged in his honour to stand at its heart. That was the day Mouana had decided to give up trying to outdo her brother, and admitted it was time to go home and make the most of things as they were.

"When he died, you came to me," said Dust. "On a morning like this, after a storm, you told me at last that you had to leave. You told me my own story, as Aroha had told it to you, in the hope it would sway me."

Mouana had remembered Aroha's warning not to expect sympathy from Dust, and never to mention her past on pain of death. But that morning she had been in the mood to say whatever she felt like.

Dust remembered for her. "You told me I knew how it was to lose a brother, that surely—forced into loss by circumstance as I had been—I would not begrudge you your redemption. That was when we hatched our plan, my prize-winner."

To Mouana's surprise, Dust had not been bothered by anything she said, despite all Aroha's warnings. But she hadn't for a moment entertained her request to leave. The general had shamed her for wanting to give up. When Mouana had said there was no way she could compete with the memory of a man who had died a hero, she had told her she was wrong.

That was when Dust had revealed the truth about *Tavuto*, and she had volunteered to die in order to capture it. The long months of training had followed, ending with the vast, staged assault where she, Aroha and five hundred others had been captured. Then had come the mass execution, the blade through the chest that had so haunted her, and then...

"And now look at you," soothed Dust, her voice like warm honey in Mouana's ear. "You have walked through death, conquered the unconquerable city, and snatched its prize even from *my* grasp. You make me proud."

Mouana glowed at the words, and immediately hated herself for it.

"But I must have it," said Dust, and although patient, her words were limned with ice. "And if you keep it from me, Mouana, understand that you must suffer after I defeat you. I must make an example of those who would steal from me. However, there is still a way this journey can end in triumph for you. Before my army comes, Mouana, I come to make you this offer."

"Teuthis. You want me to give it to you," said Mouana, her words emerging papery and fragile. Dust's boat closed in until it was only ten yards away, and the general stood to her full height.

"No, commander; I wish to give it to you. I have never offered a traitor a second chance, but today this is what I bring. Because death has made something truly great of you. I see in you not the ambitious fool who went to Lipos-Tholos to die, but something more akin to a partner, a successor... a reflection." Dust stopped for a moment and took a long look around her, her eyes flickering as they roved over the trees on the mist-shrouded bank.

"Did you know," she said, studying the forest, "my people were once as soft as any in all the worlds? Our home, the most beautiful of all. Warm and calm of weather, a world of shallow azure seas and bright atolls, white sand and glowing tides. The most peaceful, the most complete, of all the gartenwelten. Our forebears bred synaesthesia into their children just for the pleasure of existing there." Dust's eyes closed for a moment, and she tilted back her head as if drinking the air. Then her head snapped back and she fixed Mouana with a glare.

"It died. A munition from the old wars, something even those who fired it had forgotten, so long had it been travelling. And all it left was an endless salt flat, and a scorching wind. Dust was the name of the wasteland, Dust the name of the world. Dust the name of the city that survived, and where we clung to life, bred for joy but with none to experience." There was something like longing in the general's voice, and Mouana found herself growing almost drowsy, intoxicated by the rhythm of her words.

"Children there were never children, commander. To feed our parents and thin our numbers, we were sent out to hunt the salt lakes, where the ichthydaimones lived. Pained, hastily-engineered things they were, but lethal quarry for starveling runts with arrows and spears. Those who survived the hunts went on to take the rites, and these you know of." With this Dust gave her a strange look, and she nodded, her mouth hanging open.

"The cave," said Mouana, in little more than a whisper.

"Two children, two months in the dark, and enough food for one to survive. And so it went; weeping at first, then bargaining, and then blood. Then more weeping, until all weeping became meaningless, and a certain... hardening of the soul. I came out of the cave harder, and later I took this company as my own. The first thing I did with it was to level that old city, and leave Dust empty at last. I took its name, and this much you know."

Mouana remembered. Dust's story had been what changed her mind about leaving—in her grief, she had seen her as a model of strength. To accept her brother's death and let go of the past, she had volunteered to die, and come through hardened, like the general had done. But now Dust held up a finger, and challenged the memory.

"Of course," she said, her voice dropping to a whisper like the desert wind, "I never told you the whole story. Just as you have done since your death, Mouana, I did something they did not expect me to do when they put me in the cave. I did not kill my brother."

"Then how did you survive?" asked Mouana, as she general's eyes bored into her vision.

"I told him we would escape the world together. That rather than staying in the cave, we would travel on foot to the Petrichor Gate, hunting along the way. Together we unsealed the entrance and left, with all the food we could carry." Dust looked down at the deck of the boat, and let out a scornful, rattling sigh.

"Of course, we had no hope of hunting without weapons, but my poor brother didn't realise that until too late. He was not a bright boy. Nor was he strong. On the second night while he slept, I blinded him with a stone and bound him with cord. We walked for days on end like that, my brother following behind me, taking sips of water as I allowed it, but no food. When he collapsed, I carried him on my shoulders, and his body kept the worst of the sun from me."

When Dust met Mouana's eye again, there was a fervour in her gaze, an elation.

"When the food ran out," she said, "I began to eat my brother. I do not know how long he sustained me on that walk, or where along the way he died, but when I saw the Gate shimmering in the distance, I dropped what was left of him and ran.

"I was crawling, by the time I reached its pillars. There was no shelter there, and the sun roasted me until I lost my wits, but I knew nothing living could pass a transit horizon unshielded, and so I waited. When vision began to fade, I dragged myself through with my hands, and I felt my heart stop as I crossed the horizon itself.

"I woke, much later, in the hospital of a Petrichor border krepost. And you know the rest of my story, save for one more thing. Much later, when I took command of the Blades and went to raze Dust to the ground, I did it not out of hatred or vengeance. I did it out of love."

Then Dust smiled, and the sight of it made Mouana gasp, but the general was too lost in rapture to notice. Her boat was right off the stern now, and she stared up, not at Mouana but through her, at the memory of flame. Then her eyes focused, and seemed to pin her to the spot.

"I owed everything to that city," hissed Dust, fierce as a serpent. "It had given me everything. It had made me who I was. A debt was owed. So I gave colour and feeling back to its people, after so long living in a world that starved their senses. The flames that night were the brightest, the most beautiful things that world had seen in centuries. And as the city burned, I knew it loved me back."

There was a long pause, and then Dust held out her hand across the water, reaching for her own.

"You understand now, Mouana, what I see in you. When you captured the Teuthis device, you weren't so docile as to bring it back to me like a dog. You ran with it, to your own ends, as I did with my brother—and you've used it to keep going, just as I did with that fool boy. You've seen off my army this far, and even now you may see it off for another few days. But you can't run forever, and this story can only end in defeat for you.

"Give me the device now, and we will use it to build a new world. With the power in that terrible brain, we can raise an army the worlds have not seen since the old wars. And you, Mouana, my pride, will command it for me. Teuthis is simply the mind of animal. With you piloting it, it will be something fearsome—a union of life and death, a creature of pure will."

Dust shook her arm, and her voice rang with passion. "Do this with me, Mouana, and let us become history together."

Mouana extended her hand towards Dust's, staring into the depths of those yellow eyes. The general was mad beyond measure, but there was no way to look at the situation, no way to make sense of it, other than to accept. She could not refuse. She was just opening her mouth to say 'yes,' when she thought of Wrack.

For all that Dust knew, and all she had planned, there was one card still hidden from her. She had called Teuthis the mind of an animal, and hinted at the power it might take on under human governance. She had no idea that awful union had already been made by her friend, or of the suffering it had put him through. Dust had no idea about Wrack.

Wrack who, without her knowing, had become the brother she had missed, and loved, and hated for so many years. And who she was about to surrender to a woman who had blinded and eaten her own. The Bruiser's accusation rang in her head, and she stood with her mouth open, gaping in disgust that she had even considered the offer.

No, thought Mouana. No matter how slim their chances, and no matter the consequences of refusing Dust, there was no way she was going to abandon Wrack now. She would carry her brother, and feed him, until they had no strength left to walk.

The Bruiser's words echoed in her head again, as she primed the cannon built into her arm. *This is for you, mate,* she thought.

"Fuck off," said Mouana, and shot Dust into the river.

The general disappeared into the water with barely a splash, and her boat drifted back into the mist like a fading nightmare. The shot startled birds from the forest canopy, and their cries brought life back into the world. Back came the hum of cicadas, the churning of the water, the hoots of waking apes; a swell of sound, as if the world had been holding its breath.

Moments later, Fingal came rushing onto the deck with a rifle, calling for backup as he scanned the mist. Mouana put her hand on his shoulder, and motioned for him to lower the weapon.

"Don't worry," she said, and the man looked puzzled. She was about to tell him it had been nothing, that she had simply been testing her gun, but immediately thought better of it. There was no point in secrets anymore. She had no doubt Dust had survived the shot, and once she caught up with them, there would be no second chances. If they were going to make it, they were going to do it together—she and Wrack and everyone, like it had been on *Tavuto*. And if that wasn't enough to get them to High Sarawak, then she would be proud to fail in the attempt.

"Gather the crew," said Mouana. "There's some things I need to tell them."

CHAPTER
THIRTY
THREE

WRACK WAS DREAMING the river when the voice began speaking to him. He was a turtle, bitten in two and tumbling along the bottom in a cloud of pink, and fishes were nibbling at him.

"I need your help with the directions again, mate. We're about to run out of map."

It sounded like that man who was always in his father's study. Fingal, was it?

"You're probably best off asking my Dad," said Wrack, and went on being the turtle.

"Your father's gone, Schneider. You're on the boat, in Grand Amazon. You remember?"

"I'm dead, aren't I?" said Wrack, the vision collapsing, and Fingal nodded. He was smoking his pipe, the bowl's glow illuminating his bite-pocked face in the dimness of the hold. Wrack was disappointed, but not surprised anymore. The remembrance that he was dead was fairly frequent now, coming many times in a day. Still, though, it was so easy to forget, when he let his mind wander to the water and the trees.

Even here below the waterline where his mind was stored, it was sweltering. Fingal was in a dreadful shape, his body dried and wiry like spoiled jerky. Wrack was worse. Almost all the ship's beasts had fallen apart by now; his crab form nested in the centre of those that could still move, shrouded in a pungent knot of fins, slime and sloughing scales.

To the left of them was the casket containing his mind. The dead were queued by a tap in its side, waiting wearily to draw cups of preservative from his own reservoir.

"They allowed to do that?" said Wrack, feeling a little invaded. Fingal nodded, then shrugged in apology as he puffed at the pipe.

"'Fraid so mate. We won't let you run out, but we need a bit of what's spare now we've used the whiskey from Rummage."

"Fair enough. How long has it been since Rummage, anyway?"

"Six days, mate," said Fingal, faint concern etched on his face. Wrack suspected he had already asked this question today. Nonetheless, he was amazed. With his mind in such a fluid state, the time had vanished like blood in the current. For the first two days, he had been barely cogent; thinking he had been back on *Tavuto*, he had grown terrified of the crew, and had cowered in the bilges of the ship, wondering where his friend was.

Then he had remembered his 'friend' had tortured a man to death, massacred a boatful of refugees, and attempted to sell half *Tavuto*'s survivors to a pub, and had been less keen to seek her out. As his mind had pieced itself together, he had wandered the boat, intermittently letting himself seep into other places for relief. He remembered there being a gunfight on one of the nights—no, two actually—but he had stayed well out of it. It had become more and more tempting just to let himself dream than to watch the struggles of the ship.

He wasn't sure when the dreaming—that weird inhabitation of Grand Amazon's dead things—had become possible, but he remembered the first time he experienced it. He had been watching a living sailor gut a fish he had caught and, for a bit of a laugh, had slipped into the fish's mind, had made it thrash and gurn on the sailor's lap.

And the further they went into the wilderness, the nearer they drew to that invisible glow in the deep jungle, the easier it became. He could just... lose himself, into the head of anything dead that drifted by. It had mystified him at first—the part of him that remained resolutely a librarian was baffled, as previously he'd only been able to see and operate through things created by the Lipos-Tholon factories or on *Tavuto*, by the application of miasma. Then the explanation had dawned on him—there must be miasma in the air out here. Not much, but enough for him to make connections, and connections that became stronger the further they went into the forest.

Even now, as he considered it, he was a salamander, being chewed by a centipede somewhere under a rotten log. The centipede coughed patiently, and sounded like Fingal.

"Sorry," said Wrack, coming back to the hold, and there was an awkward pause. "Why are you here again?" he asked sheepishly, as he had momentarily forgotten. Fingal sighed, and tapped his pipe against the barrel he sat on.

"Directions, Wrack. We're nearly out of map, and only you know where to go from here. I've left you alone for the last few days, figured you needed to rest, more than anything else. We'd pushed you a bit too hard. But now I need you."

Wrack felt a surge of bitterness, as he remembered the trireme fight, and the last time Fingal had 'needed' him.

"When you say 'I,' I presume you mean you're running an errand for Mouana since she won't speak to me, right?"

Fingal looked awkward, and his eye flicked to the far end of the hold.

"He means what he said, Wrack," said Mouana, stooped low under the beams of the hold. "He's the captain now, not me. And he needs you. But I'd like to talk with you, too, if you'll accept it."

"I'll leave you folks to it," said Fingal, getting up in a hurry. "I've still got those... repairs to finish up on the port turrets. Come on, you rotten lot," he added, gesturing at the sailors queuing for preservative, and they shuffled from the hold with an air of disappointment.

"Are you alright?" asked Mouana quietly, when they had left.

"Yeah, amazing," muttered Wrack, and she winced.

"I mean, are you alright to talk? You've had a rough time, and I didn't want to bother you until you were ready."

"I'm talking, aren't I? Anyway, I didn't think you were in the habit of caring."

"A lot's changed," said Mouana, looking down at her hands.

"Yeah, I heard. I'm not surprised they binned you as captain, but I have to say I'm shocked you didn't gun them all down for trying."

Mouana's face fell as he spoke, and her mouth contorted as if testing the shape of words.

"I stepped down, after Rummage."

"What? I suppose the Bruiser ratted you out, did he?" said Wrack with an insincere laugh.

"He tried," said Mouana, in a voice next to a whisper. "I destroyed him before he could speak. And that's why I stepped down."

"Oh," said Wrack. That was a hard one to take in, and he wasn't sure how to react. "You said you needed something from me again?"

"No, I told you already. It's you I need, Wrack, not what you can do."

Wrack dipped his eyestalks in consternation. "Maybe it's because they're draining my preservative, but I really don't have any idea what you're talking about."

"Listen... can you... can you read minds, Wrack?"

"This isn't making things less confusing, you know. But... yes, I suppose. I can tell you what it's like to be any number of dead bees right now, as it happens."

"I mean, could you read my mind?"

"What, go in your head?" said Wrack, incredulous. "I wouldn't want to, frankly!"

"Please," begged Mouana. "I'm not a great talker. In fact, I'm dreadful. But I need you to understand. I spoke with Dust, Wrack. I realised... look, please. Will you go in my head? This is the best way I can find to say sorry."

"Alright," said Wrack. "Sit down."

Mouana sank to the filthy deck, steel legs folded, and closed her eye. There was a long, sombre pause, after which Wrack made a noise through his speakers like he was straining to have a shit.

Mouana looked perplexed, and opened her eye again. "I don't think it worked."

"That's because I didn't do anything. I just wanted to irritate you while I had the upper hand. I'm going to do it now."

Wrack let himself fall sideways into Mouana's head, and the hold vanished. Before vision returned, a rush of feelings smashed into the back of his eyes; shame, rage, and far, far more fear than he would ever have expected. Then an image began to resolve itself. Wrack was in a tent, its sides flapping in the wind, trying to write a letter. He ground his teeth as the nib trembled on the empty page. He strained for words, but they wouldn't come past the shrieking of the 'drick...

"OH, DEAR, MOUANA," said Wrack, a long time later, touching a claw to her knee. "I'm so sorry. She... she really messed you up. I'm very glad you shot her."

"So am I," said Mouana, looking hollow, and held Wrack's claw between two of her huge fingers. "But it doesn't make it right, any of what I've done."

"Maybe not, but I can hardly blame you for having lost your mind, given I spent a lot of this morning being a dead catfish. I wish we'd spoken earlier. I just thought you were really into... you know, war."

"Yeah, well you can talk. You were a fucking battleship."

They shared a weak laugh, and Wrack spoke again.

"I won't lie; I'm still not comfortable with some of the stuff you've done. It could take a long time to get comfortable with. But we've both got a lot more past than we've got future left, and certainly there's no time to unravel it all. Shall we just let all this be, and help Fingal get this over with? I daresay Dust is the sort of person who has a habit of coming back from being shot, after all."

"I'd like that, yes," said Mouana, nodding solemnly. Wrack had never heard her speak like this; not since those early days when they had shivered together on the slave ship's deck. It was a world away from the grimacing warlord who had led them into Rummage, and a lot more like the woman he had just shared a head with.

"My legs are rotten as shit," he announced. "Could you carry me up on deck, and we'll see if I can work out where to go next?" Mouana fished him out from the mound of coiled sealife onto her slab of a shoulder, where he clung on with a claw.

"And bring my book," he added.

WHEN THEY CLIMBED out of the dark a great shout crashed over them, bright and fierce as the midday sun. The whole ship had clearly been waiting up here in silence, to see if they would emerge together. Now they had appeared, the crew exploded into a mass of roaring faces and raised fists. It scared Wrack at first, seeing all those dead faces split and screaming, but when he saw the joy in their eyes, he raised his claw back at them. Another cheer rolled across the deck, and even Eunice broke into a grin.

Wrack's speakers emitted a limp, tinny "Hooray" that was immediately drowned in the noise. It didn't matter—the sight of him and Mouana together was enough to keep the sailors waving their fists. For those who had been with them since *Tavuto*, riddled as they now were with bullet holes, burns and bites, it clearly meant the world. Whatever her sins, and whatever his madness, the two of them working together had saved them all from that place, and Wrack could see from their faces that they believed they would do it again.

They clearly needed the boost. There couldn't have been more than a hundred and fifty left, and many of them were hideously damaged. Even the couple of dozen living that remained were emaciated, and many of the dead were only held together with bandage, tar and staples. Their skin was peeling off in the heat, and insects swirled over the deck in a throbbing black cloud—only the weeks of preservative rub kept them from being eaten alive.

Wrack felt for them—even with the reinforcements the miasma had worked on the crab's body, and the mechanical enhancements Fingal's technicians had made, he was rotten through. Without Mouana carrying him, he would have been dragging himself across the deck on a trail of slime.

They wouldn't have to last much longer. He could feel High Sarawak, like a second sun that shed no light, boiling in perpetual dawn on the horizon. It drew him like their flesh drew the flies, something at once alien and achingly familiar. As he focused on that strange, silent pulse, it reminded him— he was meant to be navigating.

"Where are we, then?" he said, in a businesslike fashion, as Fingal waved the cheering crew back to their work.

"Upper Extrañeza, crab-man," said Kaba, who had appeared by their side as they moved to the bow of the craft. She had lost a forearm since Wrack had last seen her, presumably as they had duelled with Dust's outriders. "Up past the next bend's a settlement marked as 'Big Mistake' on the charts from Rummage, and then that's your lot. The ink stops there. There's a couple of shit drawings of monsters, but that's it."

"We passed Gustav's Rest yet?" said Wrack, with a burst of excitement. On his third and final expedition to Grand Amazon, when he was an old man and the main channel of the Sinfondo had been heavily settled, Waldemar had finally made a trip up the Esqueleto, and settled on the banks of one of its tributaries with his family. He had never written again, and history had forgotten him.

"Yeah, actually—it said that in brackets next to Big Mistake, now you mention it."

When they turned the bend, Wrack's excitement faded. The forest opened up into a narrow floodplain, where a few feeble patches of mud sprouted crops in shoddy, yellowing rows. On the bank, perched on stilts black with rot, stood a cluster of tumbledown houses, paint flaking with age. Collapsed dwellings sprawled to either side of the meagre hamlet, while ruins poked through the tall grass of the plain. At first the place seemed deserted, but as they chugged by, pale faces showed at the windows and ragged figures appeared on the sagging excuse for a dock. The inhabitants, who looked barely more healthy than the boat's crew, stood and watched them pass with hostile frowns.

Wrack could see why the town had been renamed. Clearly, the frontier metropolis Waldemar had dreamed of had never quite worked out. Still, now their voyage had surpassed the explorer's last reach into the frontier, he felt the moment needed commemorating.

"Mouana, throw them the book," said Wrack.

"Steady on, Wrack," said Fingal, sucking on his pipe. "That's all we've got, beside you and the map."

"Believe me, I know it by heart," he answered. "And anyway, the book runs out here too, just like the map. They're probably better off with it than we are. Go on, toss it on the dock, for Waldemar's sake."

Mouana pitched the book out over the river, and it landed on the settlement's dock with a dry *thud*. The villagers peered at it with a mixture of disgruntlement and fear, then went back to watching the boat.

"Well, there we are," said Wrack, "The end of civilisation. For the record, I think we need to take the next left."

And so they did, and sailed off the edge of the map.

*   *   *

THE DAYS THAT followed passed fitfully. Wrack spent some of the time playing cards with Mouana, as they shared what they could remember of their lives. Mouana usually won, but Wrack had his revenge by singing songs he half-remembered, rendered tuneless and mangled by the device that processed his speech. She was better company now she wasn't leading a crusade.

The rest of the time, he spent drifting between the dead things as they tumbled past them in the river, and trying to shake off the sensation of tentacles and terrible hunger. Sometimes he would be woken by Fingal or Kaba, to settle one of their arguments about the best course to take, but largely he was left to himself.

In the time he spent awake and on deck, he saw marvels, the likes of which Waldemar would have given his specimen collection just to glimpse.

A wormer's paddleboat passing in the night, refusing all contact, sigils of glowing blood daubed upon its hull. A figure crouched on its upper deck, silently nursing a harpoon.

A measureless lake, caked in grumous yellow skin, where pulsing larvae fired imagoes into the sky. The air thrummed with the hunger of the newborn, then with the clatter of rifles as the insects swooped.

The shell of a long-dead starship, strobed by lightning, as black-toothed cannibals shrank from their searchlights. Shouts and sirens in the dark.

Tracts of flooded forest, where osteoglossid titans swam. The crack of alien dentition on home-kind nuts; flickering shoals, and glowing worms beneath regis lilies.

Still waters, where church-gilled catfish cruised under duckweed, stately and ancient. The baking sun on silent water, songs chanted in a dozen tongues.

Shallows, and the perilous scrape of sand on steel; shouting and panic, as crates were hoyed to lighten the load. A gunfight, and Mouana's staying hand as she warned him not to intervene, lest Dust learn their secret. Bullets thudding into wood, and the gush of water.

Monsters on the banks; a thing that chased them through the shallows on its haunches, and an awful fight. Cries of loss when it was done, as the beast's mate followed them for miles behind the trees.

Pink shapes rolling; riverine orca, communing in clicks as they stalked lord-worms in the afternoon rain.

Species, taxa, systems that had never been documented, or whose origins had been forgot. Great leathery factory slugs, flesh-roots pulsing, as they struggled on the banks of nameless creeks. Metal ants, and smoke-belching spouts of cartilage.

True strangeness, where green lost its meaning in a forest of new colours. Places where the vines glowed black, and groves that ate light. Places where the water sang.

Determination, and bullets, saw them through. They were always *just* more aggressive than what they encountered, always made it through with a couple more dents in the hull, a few more bodies dragged into the water. Ahead of them, growing stronger with each mile, the ancient city called to Wrack. And always, a horizon behind them, their pursuit rumbled on in a distant wall of smoke and light.

AT LAST THEY reached a place where they could go no further. It was just past dusk, and Mouana was down in the hold, using a bit of pipe and some bones to show Wrack how a railgun worked. It was engaging at first, but she wasn't much of a teacher, and had soon veered away from the interesting stuff into a seemingly interminable discussion of what could go wrong with poorly-maintained coolant systems.

Now that Wrack's legs couldn't support his carapace, he had been taped to Mouana's shoulder, so he didn't have much choice but to watch whatever she was doing. Nevertheless, he made plenty of encouraging noises, and only occasionally gave in to the temptation to squawk "Pieces of eight! Pieces of eight!" in her ear. She hadn't laughed yet, but he was sure that was because she still hadn't gotten the joke.

The discussion of coolant methods was threatening to creep into its second hour when—to Wrack's relief—Mouana was interrupted by a strange horn blowing, followed by a commotion on the deck above. Her head jerked up from her diagram as the sound came again, and she hurried up on deck to see what was going on.

As they joined the crew in staring at what awaited them on the river, Wrack found words in his head, from an old treatise on mapping the Lemniscatus. *Travel far enough into nowhere, leave the borders of your own city far enough behind, and eventually you will come upon somebody else's.*

Across the river, as tall as the forest that crowded the banks around it, was a great stockade. At its centre was a gate with doors of blastwood timber, clad in the shells and hides of a dozen species, and stippled with patches of glowing moss. Painted skulls, yards long and gnarled with tusks, hung from chains across the barrier. A line of torches blazed on the parapet above it, and figures gathered before them in silhouette. The horn blew again, low and blatting, and *Gunakadeit*'s own foghorn sounded in answer as they approached.

"High Sarawak!" said an awed voice from somewhere on deck. "We're here," said another, and soon a murmur had spread across the deck. Wrack was not convinced; there was no denying they were close now, but he was sure he would be able to *feel* if High Sarawak lay just behind those gates.

Besides, he figured that whoever had crafted the necrods would be using more than logs and animal shells to guard their treasures.

When they came to within a hundred yards of the stockade, a volley of arrows hissed into the water directly ahead of them, and Fingal called for the crew to cut the engines and kill their lights. Kaba hauled herself painfully up the boat's central mast and called up to the ramparts in her mother tongue, but there was only silence in return. She tried again, in another language, and then haltingly in a third, clearly running out of options. She repeated herself, and at last a voice came back, low and rasping.

The exchange proceeded slowly, with long gaps in between responses, but eventually a word began to emerge from repetition—a word Wrack knew. "Dead?" questioned the unseen sentry. "Dead!" replied Kaba, whispering to Fingal to get the boat's searchlight turned on the mast. "Dead," she repeated, her good arm outstretched in the lamp's beam, spiralled in a raiment of moths. "Dead."

The horn blew again, and others sounded in answer from far behind the wall. Then, with a deep *crack*, the gates began to open.

WRACK WAS SURE he had fallen into another dream, the strangest yet, as the boat nosed through the gap into the still water beyond. The gates concealed a city like none he had ever read about— it sprawled across the surface of a shallow lake, stretching a mile at least within the long palisade. Its channels and streets were marked out with wooden pilings, and light twinkled everywhere—both the dry flicker of fires and the steady glow of bioluminescence. Buildings rose from the clear water on carved pillars, three storeys high in places, with lights strung between them in webs of vine. Tiered ponds thronged with floating vegetables, and squat trees bobbed on forested barges.

And everywhere swarmed... Wrack imagined he was Waldemar, and searched for a word that might seem believable to city readers. But there was no route around the obvious. They were lizard-people. Of course, they bore little in common with true lizards—their tails bifurcated halfway up their broad backs, and he could find as much of a mole shrimp or a bat in their anatomy as anything reptilian. But their lipless mouths and slit-pupilled eyes evoked pungent memories of the Lipos-Tholos reptile house, and that's what Wrack was stuck with.

They moved as gracefully in the water as out, membranes spreading as they surged along beside the boat, then folding away as they hopped out onto jetties and pilings. Hundreds were flocking to stare in fascination at *Gunakadeit* as it eased into the city, gesturing with three-fingered claws at the exhausted bodies on its deck. The crew stared back, some offering tentative waves, others flinching at every sudden movement from their watchers.

There was a sudden splash as a dozen or so of the lizard-people leapt into the water from a low hump, and a deep growl resonated through the shallows. The sound drew a low moan from the dead, caught between resignation and dread. Then the hump shook, and an eye opened on its side. It rose from the channel on a thick ochre neck, water sluicing from between tree-trunk-thick tusks as the vast head turned to regard them.

The boat rocked on a swell, and Wrack glanced over to see a second giant rising on their starboard side. It stood twenty feet clear of the water at the shoulder, and peered down on them from higher still, a spiked crest spreading above the tombstone battlements of its jaws. The monster gave a curious rumble and lights smouldered along its body, from its red-rimmed throat wattles to the tails swooping from its hindquarters. The light pulsed in jagged patterns along the behemoth; glyphs and cartouches that swam with bacterial calligraphy.

The beasts stood on either side of the boat, lowering their heads to inspect the newcomers; as their illustrated flanks shimmered, chanting began among the lizard people. Whether this was a ceremony of joy, the prelude to a swift ending, or both, Wrack had no idea. If he was honest with himself, he was too enchanted to care.

"Please tell me," asked Mouana, as the monster's head turned sideways and its tiny eye regarded them from its cliff of bone, "that you read all about this place, and were just saving it as a little surprise for us."

"I wish I could tell you that," said Wrack, as foetid lakewater fell on them from the titans' jaws. "I really could. But this is all excitingly new to me."

Of course, that wasn't strictly true; truthfully, there *were* stories about lizard people from Grand Amazon. There always had been. Waldemar himself had come across them in travellers' tales ancient even in his time, snippets from before the failure of the Gate. He had scoffed at them in footnotes, reading them with the same scorn he'd felt for tales of *rhinoceros* from long-lost Komkhathi. But that had been in his early writing. Now Wrack thought about it, his later work steered clear of such matters entirely. Either way, he figured, now wasn't the best time to get stuck into a discussion of narrative authority in the *Rückgewinnun*, and so he stayed quiet.

"What in the six skies are they chanting, Kaba?" called Fingal, hand curling around a shotgun as one of the lake giants nudged him with its snout.

"Not a lot I understand, boss. Only words I've got to share with 'em is scraps of old wormers' glot, and they're using scant little of that. 'Open again' is all I'm getting, though that's only a best guess."

"Well if that's all you've got, then shout it back," barked the rebel boss, patting the monster on its tusk with the enthusiasm of a cornered caniphobe. "Open again, Kaba, that's the ticket."

Kaba called the words back at the glistening throng, and the chanting intensified. She shouted the words, and they rasped back from all around, rising from throats not built to carry them. The lake beasts let out a strange sigh in harmony, then drew back their heads and let the boat chug on. Wrack was elated at their passage, if only because it let him see more of the place. Even as the monsters sank back into the warmth of their guard-hollows, he gazed at them with wonder. But there was so much more to see.

As they passed into the witching glow of the lake-city's heart, they passed ramshackle towers of woven wine, vertical pastures that rattled and thrummed as insects the size of hounds careened against their walls. Past them were floating butchery yards, where a bulkier breed of citizen worked; they hauled the bugs from the corrals onto tables before setting on them with cleavers, splitting off the meaty legs and throwing the shells into simmering stock pots.

In a viscous pool behind them, another giant lurked. This one was almost all mouth. Its huge scoop jaw lay half-submerged, churning in the mire as labourers shovelled heaps of detritus into its pit. At its rear, lizard-people daubed in nacreous script waited with broad pans, collecting its luminous excreta.

Further in they passed a series of corrals, circles of white gravel where fat, feather-gilled tadpoles wallowed. Most were the size of a person's torso, but each pen held one or two of truly enormous size, their mouths already budding with cartilage tusks. All were tended together by wading lizard-people, who sang softly as they scattered the water with smashed fruit and chunks of fish. By the time Wrack realised he was looking at the city's nursery, the larval pools had almost receded from view. He made a resolution to himself that he would come back and see this again, before the crushing realisation set in—this was a one-way journey. He had lived his life, and was crawling towards the end of its unintended epilogue.

Worse yet, he thought, it was unlikely there would be anything left to see here, even if he could manage to return. Dust was coming with guns and rage and roaring diesel, and would not stop to negotiate at the gate. All of this—the orchards and the tadpole baths and the beasts with their word-pocked flanks—would be gone soon, casualties of someone else's injustice. It stirred him to shame, quickly sublimated into black anger. High Sarawak tugged on his crackling nerves, and his mind raced with thoughts of surging brine. He could feel the world greying out, when a soft voice brought him back.

"Hey," said Mouana. "I guess it's time to get off the boat; looks like we've reached the end of the line."

Wrack's mind snapped back all at once, to a riot of colour and sound. The boat had come to rest in a circular pool, surrounded by cut stone and painted columns. Ahead of it, broad stairs led up a causeway to an island at the lake's centre, and they thronged with lizard-people. "Open again!" they cried in Kaba's old trader tongue, "Open again!" as they lowered gangplanks onto the boat's gunwales.

All at once the boat was flooded with the lizard-people; they scurried up the planks on their knuckle-claws, and moved about the deck taking reverent sniffs of its charnel filth. Wrack feared the blades were about to come out—but instead came garlands; ropes of glowing blossom were draped on the shoulders of the dead as three-fingered claws took their hands. Those who could no longer stand were scooped from the deck, and carried on the plated backs of their hosts.

"Stay together," cried Fingal as a pale creature scrawled in light led him from the bow, but the words were next to useless—they were caught up in a rapturous tide. Mouana allowed herself to be led by a trio with lilac-striped jaws, and they took their first steps on dry land since Rummage.

As they moved up the causeway steps, however, Wrack noticed that not everyone in their party was being offered the same reverence. The remainder of their living crew were huddled together in a knot as they hurried along, and nobody had taken their hands. Their hosts circled them warily, snapping and hissing at their limbs. Mouana had clearly spotted it too.

"Oi," she growled, yanking her hand free, and stomping over to the living crew's tormentors. "Leave off—they're with us." The lizard-people looked to each other in what seemed like disgruntlement, then glanced back at her with cocked heads— they kept their distance from the living after that, but Wrack had the sense that the incident had confused them mightily.

"What in grief was that about?" muttered Mouana, as they found their place in the column again.

"I'm not sure," said Wrack, "but I think a hypothesis is presenting itself. Look ahead."

"Oh, *fuck*," said Mouana.

The stairs ended in a great dais, carved with channels of light, and with a swirling green fire at its heart. Behind the fire waited a crowd of ancient-looking lizard-people, and behind them, rising into the night's gloom, stood a pair of vast, glowing skeletons.

The figures, unmistakably human, towered in blue light, painted on a pair of fifty-foot-high obelisks. Their skulls were tilted up towards their raised arms, as if calling something down from a high place. And above them, dwindling into dimness up the length of the great rocks, were painted countless stars.

"Yeah, does rather suggest we're on the right track, doesn't it?" said Wrack, marvelling at the giants in the firelight.

Up ahead, Fingal and Kaba were deep in conference with the city's elders. From what he could hear from Fingal, they were trying to leverage whatever strange goodwill they possessed for passage onwards to High Sarawak, a deal which Kaba was struggling to convey in detail. Wrack could only guess at the elders' body language, but there seemed to be an obvious and growing sense of affront at the lack of ceremony. Somehow, he doubted Kaba had explained the reason for the urgency of the discussion.

Then, as the negotiation progressed, it took on a more sinister air. Again and again, the elders would issue sharp barks of refusal, and thrust out their claws at the anxious bunch of living sailors. Wrack understood then, looking at the fear stretching across their faces, what the sticking point of the deal must be.

The gates opening when Kaba said they were dead, the skeletons on the stones, the cries of 'open again': it all made horrible sense. Whoever these people were, and however they fitted into this world's mangled history, they had clearly once traded with High Sarawak, and had been waiting centuries for its gates to reopen, and for trade to resume. How surprised they must have been—suspicious, even—for the dead to come from the opposite direction, and to come hand-in-hand with the living.

As the impasse continued, their hosts grew restless, and the elders began whispering to one another, glancing sidelong at Fingal. Fingal in turn was growing increasingly exasperated as he failed to understand what Wrack had just worked out—that they weren't going anywhere so long as the living stayed that way. If things carried on this way, it was only a matter of time before they were cut down on the spot as imposters, or Dust arrived and made the whole issue moot.

"Mouana?" asked Wrack, speaking as softly as he could.

"Yeah?"

"You know when you shot all those people at Mwydyn-Dinas? How you did something awful because it was the only way we were going to stay ahead of Dust?"

"Yes," said Mouana, after a very uncomfortable pause.

"Well, obviously I understand why you did it, because I've been in your head. But now... now I *really* understand. And I don't hold it against you one bit."

"Wrack, what the *fuck* are you talking about?"

"Look, there's no time to explain. I just wanted you to know that before this happens. Can you walk us to Fingal?"

"Alright, Wrack," sighed his friend, and stomped forward to the edge of the negotiation circle. Fingal looked round as she loomed, and frowned. "Wrack wants a word," she said, laconically.

"Not now, man," hissed Fingal, glaring at Wrack. "I'm in the middle of a bloody negotiation he—"

"We've got to kill them," said Wrack, cutting him off. "The living. Don't make me explain, but we have to kill them. There's no way we're getting past with them in one piece. They've got to die, and the longer we refuse, the more likely it is they're going to turn on us. We need to kill them, now."

Fingal was slow, but he wasn't stupid. Recognition flashed across his face as Wrack spoke, and he took one look at the living crew before putting a hand on Kaba's shoulder and cutting her off in mid-flow.

"Kaba, Wrack's right. New plan. Tell them we're going to slaughter the living."

Kaba's broken jaw fell in horror, but Fingal stayed stern. "Tell them, right now."

Kaba opened her mouth, and was about to speak when Mouana piped up, turning every head in her direction.

"Tell them," she roared, taking a mighty stride into the circle, "that I am the War Princess of High Sarawak, and that I have had enough of their *shitty manners*." She shoved one of the elders in the chest with a fingertip, rocking him back on his haunches.

The crowd exploded onto their feet and began hissing together, sounding like a sudden downpour. Mouana was undeterred. Scowling, the green light of the fire flickering on her face, she stalked around the circle and jabbed her finger at each of the elders in turn.

"I am heir to the skeleton throne," she boomed above the hissing of the crowd, "and I have come to claim it. How *dare* you stand in my way?" The elders scurried back at the force of her voice, and she threw her palm out to gesture at the living.

"These *quick ones* are my slaves, and among them is the Queen of Lipos-Tholos," she thundered, adding, "Pearl, get over here," in a hurried mutter. Pearl shuffled forward, looking thoroughly wretched, and stood with her head bowed by Mouana's side.

"I have conquered her city and *now*," she cried, slapping the woman to the ground with a monstrous backhander, "*now*, I am dragging her back to pay for her sins. Would you *dare* take that from me?"

Her words echoed into silence, broken only by the chirping of frogs far out on the lake. All around them in the dark, blades glinted, and a thousand bodies crouched in readiness for the tension to break.

"Alright, then, Wrack," she whispered, "work with me." Then, she began chanting. At first, he thought she was just bellowing nonsense, but as he listened closer, the words became obvious, disguised as they were by the weird rhythm of her ersatz incantation.

"*NEED-YOU-TO-DRAW-ON-WHAT-EV-ER-YOU-CAN-MAAAATE-MAKE-SOME-DEAD-THINGS-MOOOOOVE-THE-BIG-GER-THE-BET-TER!*"

She repeated the final words over and over, raising her arm to the sky in mirror image of the skeletons on the obelisks, and let her voice climb to a prolonged shriek. Wrack took his cue, and let his mind loose in the waters of the lake.

The small things came first; insects singed in the flames that began skittering on the stones, dead frogs that lolloped out of the water and began lurching up the stairs. He ripped through the minds of fish carcasses, had them thrash in the shallows beyond the firelight. Then his thoughts went deeper, probing the stony spaces beneath the island, and he found larger vessels to inhabit. Much larger vessels.

It began as a rumbling in the stone beneath them, deep and visceral, as if the world was shifting in its sleep. Then cracks emerged in the masonry, and a low howl echoed in the hollows beneath. In the wide plaza that encircled the dais, great humps of stone rose into the air, flagstones falling to reveal withered flesh.

First one, then two sets of vast jaws burst from the rubble, yellowed tusks parting to release natal screams in dread harmony. Wrack fought to hold his vision as he hauled the beasts from their graves, let his shriek of exertion billow from their throats as they crawled, immense and dessicated, into the night. Blackness hammered at the edge of his perception, but he held the weight. He would not buckle.

The grave-beasts lumbered towards the fire, and the etchings on their mummified flanks flickered into new light as they swung their heads. With his last shred of energy Wrack walked the monsters to either side of the obelisks and, as his thoughts collapsed into manic slurry, had them bow to Mouana.

The last thing he heard as darkness took him was the elders, crying out together in what could only be called joy.

IT WASN'T MUCH of a siege, but it would do.

The river—narrower, here—was packed bank to bank with her forces; the barges had to jostle past each other to move to the front, and it was easier to simply move infantry across the mass of decks than try to move the transports around.

Her flotilla had been compacted into a huge mass that filled the river for miles behind her. Even looting fuel and watercraft from every settlement they had passed, they had been forced to leave almost a third of the craft behind along the way. More still had grounded on sandbanks, or smashed on rocks or tree trunks.

Those that remained heaved with soldiers, and with sickness. Food had run scarce along the way, and medical supplies had been the first thing she had ordered left behind to lighten the load. The men and women on the barges, many already wounded from Lipos-Tholos, were growing thin, and swarmed with bites, infestations and fevers from the relentless insects. Some lost their minds each day and were executed, but tens of thousands still remained.

It did not matter how many she had lost in keeping pace with their quarry—once she seized the Teuthis device, she would be able to take it all back ten times over. Even now, every soldier that fell took the miasma, and joined the growing mass of dead in the column, the kernel of the legion she would build.

Still, the fight against attrition had enraged her. When Mouana had betrayed her, had scorned her generosity, she had been filled with a hatred like none she had ever known. For the first time, she had offered to share some of what she was with someone; had left something of herself vulnerable. Mouana had spat on her heart.

Ever since she had returned to the flotilla, she had been consumed by a fury that had no outlet in the glacial management of the army's progress. She had sent ahead what few speedy craft she had to harry her prey, out of sheer frustration more than hope of success. But the bulk of her force had been maddeningly slow. She had compensated by slaughtering and burning everything they had come across, setting vast fires that had left the river's bank blackened stubble, had raised a smoke cloud of continental size.

It had been tedious. Now, at least, it was time for a proper fight.

Far back in the column, the artillery barges fired another volley, and fire bloomed across the river gate. Impressive though the primitives' barrier was, it was nothing to an army built to smash energy shields. There was a ponderous creak in the dark, and something huge gave way. Then, almost gracefully, the entirety of the left gate collapsed forward into the water. Behind its wreckage, lit by the flames of the burning timbers, weapons gleamed.

Dust couldn't resist it. Protocol demanded she bombard the enemy for hours yet, reducing the whole place to mud before moving in infantry. At the very least, it made sense to break up the gate debris before launching an assault. But both protocol and sense had been left behind in the fires of Lipos-Tholos. What was left was *art*. She didn't care if she lost another few hundred now, when so much more lay just beyond her grasp. It would be so much more *beautiful* to assault the breach immediately.

Pumping boosters into her system, she climbed to the podium of her command craft and thrust her sabre out towards the collapsed gate. The sound of the firelight on the blade filled her to the fingertips, rough and hollow as warm milk poured onto embers. She could almost taste the dread of her army as the blade gleamed, as she held the order to charge for a full, agonising minute. Then she let the blade fall, and the engines of the assault barges sang.

The first screams from the gap curled round her with the smell of tea fumes, spiced with the cries of the defenders. They didn't sound human, and it lent a rich undertone to the sound of the fight, a blend she had never smelled before. Dust almost shivered in pleasure as a new sound rolled over the rest; the deep, undulating cry of something *big*. As if on cue, a monstrous form burst into the firelight; a sinuous neck and snaggled jaws that swept her troops from the logjam like children's toys.

Perfect, thought Dust, turning back to her army. She scanned the jostling boats, and found the torchlit bulk of the Atlassian's stable-barge. The expense of contracting the *Afferitter* brigade to travel through the Gate with her had been vast, but she had kept them on even when she had dismissed the other subcontractors. Because, despite the sheer logistical hell of ferrying a full pithecus unit with her, the smallest chance of an opportunity like this had made it worth it.

"Send in the apes," called Dust, and trumpets sounded.

As the Atlassian barge steamed towards the carnage at the gate, she took a deep breath, and closed her eyes. Perhaps Mouana's betrayal had been necessary. Without it, all of this would have been so easy. She would still have her prize, and it would be all the sweeter with the defeat of her former pupil.

The apes howled in the breach, the first hints of the feast to come, and Dust ran her tongue over lips that had been dry a hundred years.

CHAPTER THIRTY FOUR

THE SEABIRDS SQUAWKED, indignant, as he rolled limply on the grey swell. "Wrack! Wrack!" they cried.

He thrashed weakly at them with a hook-suckered arm, but it was losing strength and could barely breach the surface.

"Wrack, we're here!"

Where was here? His eye creaked in its mount, struggling to focus in the air. A bile-green slick lay on the water, his blood spreading out across the waves. Harpoons quivered in his flesh, trailing taut wires. At their terminus, black shapes moved towards him across the water. Pathetic, fragile. But they had conquered him. Behind them, grey and continental, a great ship waited on the horizon. The waves slapped over his eye and dissolved the vision.

"Wrack."

Agony, and confinement, and metal. Confusion, as drugs pushed their way through him. Monkey voices, endlessly chattering. A hundred thousand eyes, but none of them his.

"We're here. High Sarawak."

A swampy creek, overhung by trees that burst from ruins on the banks. Bats dipping low over the water to snatch fish. A night loud with life, but louder with death. He looked through the eyes of dead things—a hundred thousand eyes, none of them his—and saw a procession of reed boats, poled by corpses. In the last lay a huge cylinder, and a towering creature of metal and wrecked meat.

"Wrack, mate, we've nearly done it!" said the creature.

"Who's Wrack?" he said, drowsily, not sure where his voice was coming from. He couldn't remember who that was. Had that been the boat? Or the crab? Or had it been the thing before, dying on the surface of a bottomless sea?

"You are," said the metal one, talking to the cylinder.

"Right," he said, for lack of any better information. "Where am I?"

His voice was coming from a dead crab, nailed to the huge woman's shoulder. That didn't make any sense, but it was happening.

"High Sarawak, remember? We're here, brother. We have to leave the boats now."

She pointed ahead, to a glade where the creek petered out to little more than a trickle, and a huge steel platform waited on the bank. Behind the enclosing trees, he glimpsed crumbling ruins. They felt powerful, familiar. But he was exhausted, and all he wanted to do was rest.

"Good for you," he said. He was about to go back to sleep when the word caught in his mind. She had called him *brother*.

"Bear with me," said Wrack. "I lost the plot for a minute there. But I'm with you."

"HEAVE!" CRIED MOUANA, hauling on the rope with all the strength left in her body. Eunice pulled with her, and behind her the whole crew threw in their weight. Wrack's casket came up the bank inch by torturous inch, carving a deep trough in the mud. Her feet slipped on the bank, but caught on roots; she shoved against them with everything she had.

The lake city's elders had granted them passage, and boats that would handle the shallow water nearer the ruins, but would not send anyone with them onto what they saw as holy ground. Her performance with Wrack had left them awed, but wary; certainly, it would have seemed odd for her to have asked for help at that point. She was lucky to have been given the boats.

But now the river had run out, and the only way forward was overland. They had no choice left but to drag Wrack with them.

After an agonising climb, the casket finally tilted forward to sit on the top of the bank, and they paused to look back over the glade. They stood on a broad steel platform, sunk into the red soil and overlooking what might once have been a city, its streets collapsed beneath the shroud of ancient greenery. It looked as if there had been a rail terminus here once: a rusted engine lay in pieces, swathed in vines, and segments of track peeked through the loam.

The rail stretched into the distance, forming a long channel through the forest where no trees grew. Foraging animals snuffled over the leaf litter, indistinct in the gloom. At the far end of that avenue lay what could only be High Sarawak. There was little to separate it from the green darkness of the forest—just a single point of light, cold and faint as a distant star.

Mouana paused for a moment and leaned on the casket. The humid air thrummed with an insectile dirge, an eerie sound that swelled like a broken accordion from the eaves of the forest. She let the moment last, but there was no time to dawdle any further. Fingal was calling for them to take up ropes again, and she braced herself to heave, but Wrack interrupted.

"I think I can make it easier for you. Hold on."

The ground quivered as he spoke, and dead leaves rustled beneath the casket. Worms and worm-eaten animals rose in a hump, taking his weight: generations of dead things, soaked through with miasma and convulsing as Wrack swam through them. They rippled, and Wrack was pushed along, gliding on the ghosts of the soil as his friends walked beside him.

In time, Kaba began to sing a boat-loader's song; the one she had sung once before, when they had been adrift in a boat on Ocean's depths. The whole crew joined in, one by one, and the song soared above the moaning of the forest.

MUCH OF WRACK was lost to the soil, in the arcs of the worms as they bore him on their backs, the crackle of old carcasses. But what remained of him was lost in thought.

As memory came back to him, he remembered what he had done at the lake city. At first he had been relieved that Mouana's ploy had averted the death of the living sailors, that she had risked her own destruction to protect her crew. But had they swapped one atrocity for another? They had ploughed through a peaceful culture, tricked its leaders into obedience, and played with what, for all they knew, had been their deepest beliefs. And worse yet, they had drawn an army led by a monster to their doors. By now, the place would be in ruins.

And all for what? Wrack didn't even know what they were fighting for any more. Did they still hope to extinguish the technology that had enslaved the dead for Lipos-Tholos? Or were they just trying to stay ahead of Dust? How long would it be before someone admitted they had no real plan?

Fingal's voice broke his train of thought with something like an answer.

"See that ahead, lad? The dawn's coming now, and that's the end in sight."

Wrack looked. High Sarawak was revealed: a tight black filament, rising up past the clouds, that didn't so much as waver in the breeze. A squat tower rose from the jungle at its base. Still, other than the power that throbbed in his head, there was no sign of life to the place. Just that single white light.

High Sarawak. The vertical city. The bone-state. The place

where the dead walked as revered machines. The city that had dug too far into old tech and destroyed itself. Myth and rumour, condensed now by their insane journey into a tiny, cold twinkle and a crumbling hulk.

The power throbbed in him, kept him moving despite his every wish to sink. The tentacles waved in the deep water, beckoning him down to rest. It would be so easy just to lose himself, to cease caring. But even if she had no idea what she still hoped for, Mouana wanted him beside her. He had to anchor himself.

"Fingal," he said, from the crab on Mouana's shoulder. "Would you walk beside me, and talk to me about home?"

"Sure, lad," said Fingal. He began to talk.

He spoke about sports teams, and bakeries, and pubs and traffic restrictions, the minutiae of city life, and Wrack felt himself buoyed by memory. It was comforting beyond measure at first, but then began to hurt, as the stark gulf between the stories and their current reality became clear. They were memories of a destroyed city, and a destroyed life. The boy who had once played on those streets had torn them apart, had slaughtered men and raised monsters from alien tombs. Despite Mouana's desperate wish to believe otherwise, Schneider Wrack was long gone.

Nevertheless, the pain seemed to strengthen him, as if it catalysed the power he drew from the monolith ahead, and he quickened his pace. The sooner this was over, the better.

THE SUN ROSE somewhere behind the clouds, and the jungle's murmuring rose to a clamour. Kaba's song faded from their throats, leaving only the bass rumble of the casket as they pulled it along the restless ground, and Mouana looked ahead at their destination.

Stark against the sky, the line that sprung from the old city's crown was revealed without doubt for what it was—a skylift. She'd seen the ruins of the one on distant Shinar, as they had fought for the city at its base. Her own home, Mīhini, bore the scars of no less than three. But nowhere had she heard of one that remained intact. Looking at it, her engineer's heart soared, and she followed the line up through the clouds, aching to know what was tethered at its other end.

As they approached the skylift, the avenue broadened into a semicircular clearing against its vast foundation. The edifice must have been at least a mile across, yet only a hundred yards or so, here at the end of the rails, were clear of forest. Its side was sheer and featureless, save for the towering archway and its sealed gate, and that lone white light. Mouana hoped against hope that gate would open at their approach, but nothing moved.

Fingal called a halt, and they set Wrack down before it. Mouana stared up at the dull metal cliff, and Fingal came to stand beside her. There was nowhere left for them to go. Free of the jungle's cloying grip, and not yet warmed by the sun, the ground here was chill, and faint mist drifted across the gate's face. As a morning breeze kicked up, it sang against the cable in the sky, soft and low.

"How does this end?" asked Mouana.

"Same way it was always going to end," said Fingal, fetching his pipe from the pocket of his tattered waistcoat and lighting it. "We do our best to get inside that thing, and destroy any rods we find, or anything to do with them."

"And then?" said Mouana, before he could.

"And then, Dust comes," finished Fingal, and gave a meaningful look back at Wrack's casket.

"You can't," she hissed, covering the microphone on Wrack's crab and praying he couldn't hear them anyway.

"We must," whispered Fingal. "She's got an army with her, Mouana. There's no way any of us are getting away from here. What would you have us do? Run away into the jungle and live in harmony among the apes? Take him with us through the trees?" He shook his head, and drew on the pipe. "No. It has to end here. I can understand if that's hard for you, so I'll be the one to do it, when the time comes. Before we left the boat, I fitted a mine to the end of his casket, pointing inwards. All it'll take is a three-number code, one-two-three, and it'll all be over. He won't know it's happened."

"You can't," repeated Mouana. "We've brought him all this way. He's my friend."

"We needed him to get here, but he's done his job. This is the end, Mouana. We only ever set out to get this far, and when Dust comes—whether or not we've achieved our ends—it's over. You made me captain, Mouana, and you know I'm right anyway."

She tried to answer him, but the words wouldn't come, so she just looked forlornly at the gate.

"I know it hurts, but there's no time to come to terms with it," Fingal continued. "She can't be far behind, and there's work to do yet, especially for you. Out of all of us, you've got the best chance of finding a way past that door. So put your mind to the problem and I'll talk to the boy, make sure he stays calm. Don't worry, I'll be kind to him."

"Promise you won't hurt him."

"I promise I won't do anything until I have to, Mouana. Now go and see to that door."

Mouana trudged to the gate housing, and tried not to think about what was going to happen when Dust arrived. The wind sang around the cable, and she remembered how it had sang that night in the tent, blending with the howls of the injured 'drick. Then, she had thought herself the only one hard enough to put the thing out of its misery. Now, she wanted nothing less.

At least she had a problem to solve. Frowning up at the immense doors, she wondered what she wouldn't give for a decent artillery piece. But she wasn't out of options yet—what had appeared to be a featureless surface from a distance was stippled with panels and protrusions, and she would just have to start prying some of them open. She had gotten plenty of obscure tech working in her life, and saw no reason to stop now she was dead. Mouana sighed with her useless lungs, and got to work.

* * *

YOU NEVER TOLD me, you know.

"What's that, lad?" said Fingal, turning to face the casket as he puffed on his pipe. If he was surprised to hear Wrack's voice in his head, he didn't show it. And if he had realised Wrack had heard everything he had said to Mouana, he didn't show his fear.

How my father died. We never found the time to talk about it.

"I'm sorry, Wrack... in all the chaos as we left the city, it slipped my mind. We should have talked. I—"

How did he die, Fingal?

"He... he... it was all a mess, Wrack, when we rose up against the Chancellor. He caught a ricochet in 'Mander's Passage, holding it against the militia on day one. It... it was quick for him."

Oh, said Wrack, leaving plenty of time for the pause to ice over.

"You were, ah, you were a good lad, what you did for him."

What do you mean, what I did for him?

"Your sacrifice. When you agreed, you know, you agreed to be found with those pamphlets, to take the heat off him so he could keep on operating. I've not said it to you before, lad, but you did more for the Pipers than you knew, with that. The militia was on the edge of turning your old man over, when you stepped in for him."

That's very interesting, said Wrack, because it was. He had never agreed to be arrested. Remembering his human life now was like fishing broken glass from thick mud, but he was certain of that much. When they had arrested him it had come as a total surprise. He had been caught with his father's pamphlets, and that had been that. An unhappy accident. He had taken the sentence and not said a word all the way to the execution chamber, as he hadn't wanted them to punish his father for his failure. At no point, though, had he been in on any plan. Fingal's talk of an agreement was... fascinating. Keeping his tone casual, he continued.

I'm not sure I understand, Fingal. Do you mean to say that he planned for me to be found with the pamphlets?

"Well of course—you remember, mate, don't you?" said Fingal, a note of agitation in his voice. He had moved along the side of the casket now, sauntering all too unsubtly towards the mine. When he spoke again, his words were hurried. "That was always the plan. You were a hero for agreeing to it, lad. And you never said a word during the trial, neither. City thought... thought you'd been the one distributing the things, and never thought to raid your dad's place after you were gone. If you, ah, hadn't offered yourself up, that might have been the end of the Pipers."

Wrack had never agreed to anything. He had not sacrificed himself.

I don't think you're giving me the truth, said Wrack, and Fingal scrambled to his side. **So I am going to take it from you.**

The dead rebel shrieked as Wrack plunged into his head. He had eased gently into Mouana's mind, but he tore through Fingal's like a rusty saw through bone.

Fingal in his father's study, sneering at a boy playing with toy ships; wondering when the old man was going to hand the reins over to his useless son.

Fingal in the library at night, stuffing the shelves with pamphlets.

Fingal in an alleyway, whispering to a man in a uniform.

Fingal in the pub, his hand on his father's shoulder as he wept for his lost son.

Fingal in 'Mander's Passage, with a gun to the back of his father's head.

Fingal's hands, scrabbling to reach the mine embedded in his side before he discovered the truth.

That's really is all very interesting, said Wrack.

MOUANA WAS ON her hands and knees, peering in amongst the mouldering remains of the door's workings, when the blast hit her. She had managed to prise the cladding off what seemed to be a scanning mechanism, and was brushing cobwebs from its interior.

Inside were racks of glass tubes, and in them were scraps of flesh. She had no idea what they did, but she thought she recognised the look of them. Whatever they were made of came from the same anatomy as Teuthis, the mind Wrack was trapped in. No wonder Wrack had been able to feel this place; it contained what appeared to be *pieces of him*.

Wrack was the key to this door; she was sure of it. She was just getting to her feet, opening her mouth to shout Fingal's name, when the meat-scraps began writhing in their tubes. Then her head filled with thunder.

The detonation knocked her from her feet, screaming as if every ugly moment she had ever lived were racing through her head in the same instant. She blacked out, came back, and blacked out again, her back arched in agony. When she was finally able to move she looked back, expecting to see Wrack's casket blown open. But something very different had happened.

Fingal was being dragged into the ground by skeletons. They were erupting from the earth in a spray of soil around him, clawing at his body, gnashing at his flesh with age-greyed teeth. Their bones were picked clean, but strung with strange black filaments—the strange physical changes inflicted by miasma, laid bare by the complete disintegration of soft tissue.

Fingal screamed, but was cut off as he disappeared into the maelstrom of ancient bone. By the time the crew had picked themselves off the ground, there was nothing of him to be seen beneath the thrashing cadavers. Then the blast came again, knocking her flat on her back, and she knew it for what it was: Wrack's black pulse, but stronger and more feral than she had ever felt it before. As it washed over the clearing the ground quaked, and a fresh thicket of skeletal arms sprung from the soil. Even prepared for it, it was all she could do to stay on her feet.

"Wrack!" screamed Mouana, staggering towards the frenzy,

but it was too late. When the skeletal throng withdrew, nothing remained of Fingal but his pipe, smouldering on the broken ground. Hunched and chittering, the skeletons loped towards Wrack and clustered around the base of the casket, their mouths gaping in rage. More and more were joining them, climbing from the ground and scampering towards the growing pile with inhuman gaits.

GET BACK, shrieked the forest of skulls, half in her head, and half in the whicker of bone on bone. **GET BACK AND LEAVE ME.**

"What did he do?" pleaded Mouana, keeping her distance.

BETRAYED ME. USED ME. TRIED TO DESTROY ME.

"How?" she begged. "What do you mean?" It had all happened so quickly.

SEE, commanded the bone-mass, and light exploded in Mouana's skull.

The visions came with sickening speed, a zoetropic fever dream that hammered at her sense of self. Studies and tin ships and books and pamphlets, pipe smoke and rain and anger and courtrooms, cobbles and grief and guns. When they withdrew she was reeling, but the light came again, a star bursting in the centre of her mind.

Then darkness, and cold. A clinging chill that seeped into every pore. Deep water, that stretched forever beneath her feet, and silence. After what could have been hours, she became aware of something in front of her. A deep red glow, on the very edge of blackness, cast the edge of something vast into silhouette. A leviathan shape, hanging motionless in the abyss.

PREYMEAT, said the darkness.

"This isn't you, Wrack," said Mouana, ice-water flooding her lungs as she spoke. "Please, friend, come back."

COME BACK FOR WHAT, MORSEL? SO YOU CAN USE ME? SO YOU CAN *LIE* TO ME?

"Maybe that's who I was once, Wrack. But not any more. You've been in my head. You've seen the worst of me, and the best. And you've seen how I feel about you. I don't just want you back, I *need* you. Because you're my brother now, and I can't bear to see you hurt like this."

I AM NOT A TOOL, said the shape, mind-voice blasting like the heat from a furnace.

"No, mate; no, you're not. But you're acting like one. And while we're at it, you're not a bloody squid either. You're my friend, Schneider Wrack, and you're being a *fucking silly boy*."

I... I AM NOT A TOOL, said the dark again, but with the hint of a question in its tone.

"No. That's exactly what I'm trying to save you from becoming, so come back."

Somewhere in the distance, a trumpet blew, and Mouana clenched with horror. The sound was coming from outside the vision.

"Wrack..." said Mouana, voice flattened with dread. "She's here."

The trumpet sounded again, and the vision collapsed.

"Good morning," whispered Dust, from the edge of the clearing. Behind her, filling the railway avenue from edge to edge, was an army of the dead. There were thousands of them, ranks upon ranks, their grey faces haggard and hopeless as they stretched back into the morning mist. In the distant fog, huge shapes loomed; beasts or machines or worse. It was an army fit to level cities.

Mouana looked to Wrack's casket. The mass of skeletons had collapsed, little more than a heap of twitching bone on the ground around it. From the casket itself came a weak, muffled sloshing, but nothing more. And around it, shaken still from Wrack's blast, the shivering remnants of her crew looked across the clearing at their doom.

"I see you managed to get my prize working, Mouana," said Dust, still motionless. "I'm impressed. And intrigued, frankly. But you should know I came prepared for this. Look what I have brought."

Dust gestured behind her, as a strange mass struggled forward from her ranks. It staggered on beetle legs, moving painfully with the dull clank of ceramic plates. Its upper surface was smooth armour, open in the centre to reveal a throbbing mass of wire-studded flesh. Blue lightning arced and crackled across the exposed meat, while liquid gases dripped from its underside, splashing onto the sodden turf in sheets of ice.

"There are always countermeasures, Mouana. The number of old machines you've played with, you should know that, just as I do. Powerful though the prize is, it remains—alas—the mind of an animal. And all animals can be leashed."

Dust's eyes bored into Mouana, and she knew the general was right. While Wrack was lost in the throes of whatever madness Fingal had set off, he was an animal, and there was nothing he or any number of skeletons could do for them. It was just them, a hundred or so exhausted bodies, against an army. Against Dust. It was over.

"Time to give up, commander," said the general, almost kindly, and Mouana hung her head. Her thoughts raced. The mine on Wrack's casing was just a few yards away; Dust was fast, but there was every chance Mouana could reach it, and put him out of his misery, before the general was halfway across the clearing. Then it would at least be over for him, if not for them.

Tassie's shriek echoed in her mind as she took a step towards the casket. Then, as she repeated Dust's words to herself, she stopped. Why should she let anyone else, let alone *Dust*, tell her when it was time to give up?

For all her preparation, and all her prowess, Dust had no idea of what had happened on *Tavuto*. As far as she was concerned, the thing in that casket was the senile remnant of an old monster; an animal indeed, with nothing human to it. Mouana knew better, and she refused to think so little of Wrack. Whatever relic Dust had dredged up from history, she was willing to bet it was geared to constrain the mind of something so simple as an alien gigapredator. Faced with a sarcastic librarian, it had another thing coming.

"Right you are," called Mouana to Dust, raising a hand in casual surrender. "Just give me a moment to say goodbye." She turned to the crew. They looked utterly bewildered, but were looking to her with cautious hope, as if she could stand between them and annihilation.

"Form up around Wrack," said Mouana, as she met each of their eyes. "There may never be time to explain what just happened, but I need you to trust me." Every head nodded. "Eunice, I want you out in front. Kaba, you lead the dead. And Pearl?" The woman nodded, clutching her rifle along with the living crew. "You take the living, and run. I know it's not much of a plan, but there's no point you staying here."

"Not a chance," said Pearl. "We're dead anyway out there, and we'd rather be dead with you." The other sailors nodded, and Mouana gave them a tight smile.

"Okay, then," she said softly, "I suppose I'd better indulge the general." She turned to Wrack's crab—limp, now, like an appalling parody of a child's doll—and grinned at it. "I don't know if you can still hear me, mate, but watch this if you can. It's going to be a hell of a show."

Mouana walked out in front of her bedraggled crew, staring right into Dust's eyes, and doing everything she could to pretend fear didn't exist. She spread her arms wide.

"Alright, then," said Mouana. "You win. But let me ask you something."

"Go on," said Dust, as near as Mouana had ever heard to showing irritation.

"Do you really just want to march that lot over here and overwhelm us? Because let's be honest, you'll manage it in a heartbeat. Or whatever it is that happens inside your chest. I think you can do better." Mouana spat on the floor, then thumped a massive hand against her breast.

"Come on," she roared. "I'm the woman who fucked you over, after all those years of training. I ruined your clever plan, stole your prize, and made you take your whole army through a thousand miles of fucking mud and mosquitoes to get it back. I've made you look like a clown, general—and if I was you, I'd want to settle this in person. So come on, why don't you come over here and make a scene for the history books?"

"You're assuming that wasn't already my intention," said Dust, nodding once and starting to walk slowly across the field. Her troops began to advance morosely in her wake, their shambling footsteps making the ground tremble, but she held out an arm to stop them. "No one is to take a step forward until I have the prize," she commanded, unsheathing her blade. "I need no army for this."

The rest of the distance she walked alone, her gaze never breaking from Mouana's. When she got to within twenty yards, Mouana spoke again.

"Right. Rush her, lads."

And so they did. Eunice stormed past her like a freight engine, growling as she came, but Dust dodged her without so much as looking aside. Her armour sang with the impact of rifle fire, but nothing even registered. She did not speed up, she did not change her expression—she just strolled towards Mouana with blank rapture on her face, drinking the moment. Mouana fired a harpoon as she came within ten feet, but the general ducked it with the slightest twist of her waist.

Then she was upon her, and Mouana was blocking swipes of her blade, monstrous blows that came almost too fast for her eye to track. Shards of metal flew from her armour and only Eunice, flying in from behind with a wild left hook and forcing the general to dodge, saved her from the stroke that would have taken off her head.

Then the rest of the crew joined the fray. They came on, howling, with no regard for their own bodies, and swarmed the general. Dust danced through them, hewing the dead as if she were thrashing through mist, but there was no way she could dodge them all.

One arm seized her, then two, and then twenty—they kept piling on, weighing down her limbs as fast as she could cut through them. She slowed despite her unnatural strength, and for a moment, it almost felt like they might take her down. But only for a moment.

"Enough," said Dust, gesturing with her hand. Lights flashed on her armour, and something invisible rushed into the soil. The ground seemed to compress, to sink for a moment, then burst upwards and outwards, flinging Mouana high into the air. She crashed to the ground, bodies tumbling around her, and felt a wet crack as her body broke inside the armour.

Still she tried to struggle up, but before she could even raise her head from the floor, Dust was on her, springing up nimble as a cat and kneeling on her body. The general clicked her long fingers, and a sphere of light appeared around them.

"This will only last a minute, but that will be all I need to cut you free. After that I shall finish off the rest, and you and I shall be free to spend all the time in the world together."

Dust's blade hummed; it glowed white from hilt to tip, and she rammed it into Mouana's torso. The sword slid through the warbody as if it were gel, and settled deep in Mouana's chest. It sizzled, and filthy steam gushed from the collar of the armour. Even as Mouana felt herself cooking from the inside, she smiled. This was exactly the moment she had been hoping for.

"Hey, Wrack," said Mouana, voice hoarse as her core began to boil. "I've got a joke. You'll love this one."

Dust's eyes narrowed and her head jerked back, in what Mouana suspected was the first genuine surprise in her life.

"What does it take to make a squid laugh?" wheezed Mouana, and waited a long moment before winking at Dust.

"Ten tickles!" she shouted, steam leaking from her mouth, gaping at Dust with a foolish grin.

Something changed, then, in the world. There was something there that had not been there before. Something Mouana would never have been able to detect without having spent so long feeling its opposite. It was barely there at first, but it built and built, until the air trembled with it, and then broke like white water from a breached dam.

It was almost identical to the black pulse she had known since *Tavuto*, but in every way inverted—a searing wave of warmth and strangeness and mirth. It blasted across the field, and Dust spasmed as it passed through her. A high-pitched whining rose from her lines and she turned in horror, blade still caught in Mouana's chest, just in time to see her countermeasure device explode in a geyser of cerulean gore.

It had been overloaded. It could not cope with, had not been created to withstand, what was happening then in Wrack's casket. Dust goggled at it in disbelief, stunned to stillness, as gobbets of it steamed on the ground.

As she turned back, Mouana greeted her with a gargantuan, piston-driven punch to the face.

Dust was flung ten feet by the impact, landing in a rumpled heap, and the shield around them flickered and vanished. Slowly, achingly, with a black stew pouring from the hole in her body, Mouana rose to her feet and stood over the general.

At the edge of the clearing, her army were looking at each other with expressions of complete bafflement, flickering with questions that quickly congealed into dark purpose. They began to shamble across the field, not in the regimented march of soldiers, but with the hungry, disorganised lope of a mob.

Dust looked up at Mouana, eyes wide in profound confusion, and shook her head. Then a rattle of claws came from Mouana's shoulder, and Wrack spoke.

"It has to be said, Mouana, that... that was a terrible joke. I don't think she thought that was funny at all."

The ground quivered, and bone fingertips began to push through the loam like spring shoots. Hands emerged, then forearms, damp soil falling in clots from the bones. The arms curled around Dust's limbs and clamped down with horrible strength, keeping her fast to the earth. They clasped at her armour and tugged at her cloak.

Then a lone arm emerged from the earth, curled in front of

the general's face, and gave her a sturdy thumbs up. Mouana was in no doubt; Wrack was back with her.

DUST EXPECTED RAGE to come. She had been tricked by her betrayer, humiliated in front of her legion. Her prize, which she had schemed so many years to acquire, had been snatched from under her nose and used to beat her down. As the old bones creaked around her limbs, and the moans of her army grew louder in the dawn, she clenched her fists, waiting for the fury.

But there was something else there; something she wasn't sure she had ever felt. It shimmered over her bones, plucking her ancient muscles like harp strings and bathing her mind with warmth. Her interfaces nudged at the edge of her vision, urged her to activate the black mechanisms at her core. Even now, with their help, she could probably break free and fight.

But rage was such a stale old taste; it had blasted through her so often her nerves were dull to it. Even triumph felt flatter, more sour than it once had. This new feeling, by contrast, was intoxicating. To know defeat—to know the end was coming, at the hands of the army she had spent an age building—this was fresh, like sunlight on mountain snow. It meant no more fighting, no more planning, no more nights spent grinding her teeth in anxiety over how to fill the ever-deepening hole.

It was relief.

Dust let her fists unwind, and reached for the bone fingers that held her. Slowly, awkwardly, she clasped hands with the dead. It was, she realised, the first time anybody had ever held her hand. Even if this was the last thing she ever experienced, she thought, it was worth the trade.

But there was, of course, one last thing to experience. As the first of her soldiers loomed above her, Dust reached into the recesses of her endocrine rig and wrung it for every drop of synaesthetic boost it could give her. It would be an unsurvivable dose, but that didn't matter anymore. Her death would be music, and light.

The first blades fell, like waves breaking on endless white sand, and Dust smiled in welcome.

WHEN DUST WENT, she went silently, but Mouana had long since stopped watching. She was gone, and that was good enough—there was no need to stay for the gory details.

And besides, there was a more pressing concern. When she turned to walk back to the casket, she found her crew all staring the other way.

Silently, and slow as dawn, the gates of High Sarawak were opening.

AFTERWORD

IT'S ALWAYS AN honour to be asked to write the afterword to a book that exists partially because you tweeted something on your birthday once and a friend responded with a joke that then escalated over several months into the creation of a dark fantasy world that attracted the attention of a publisher. So I'm sure you can imagine how it feels to be charged with putting some words at the end of this book by Nate Crowley. Or perhaps you cannot. Either is fine, I think, because as you may have noticed Nate's writing strives to stretch the imagination. It pulls it taunt like old rubber on a hot day and twangs at it furiously so the vibrations permeate unevenly through your mind.

Nate's own imagination doesn't stretch so much as grow and blossom like a really messed-up tree. The seeds are always small and innocent-looking enough. A list of imaginary computer games, for example. An animated reality show about fighting. Some erotic furniture... okay, *innocent-looking* was the wrong term, but the point is they grow, far faster and more elaborately than you'd think possible, branches sprouting out like furious tentacles until daylight struggles to penetrate, creating countless nooks and no shortage of crannies—all populated with delightful and unexpected creatures. And still the tree squirms upwards, implausibly high and wide and gnarled as Nate's world-building takes root and characters fight and love and die and psychically inhabit a crab. And on top of the glorious canopy flower the stunning blossom's of Nate's wit, catching the eye and wrinkling the nose, blooms exotic and sometimes predatory.

As you may know, I inadvertently planted one of these trees myself. On my birthday, to be specific. I complained on twitter (jokingly... I promise) that not enough people had wished me happy birthday. Nate decided to wish me happy birthday. Repeatedly. Through Twitter. Every day for 76 days. It was quite an experience. He didn't know it was going to grow for 76 days when he started watering the seed. It was just a running joke. Tweeting a little poem one day, a cheerfully surreal birthday song the next. But the more he nurtured the idea, the faster it grew. Twitter as a medium for micro-fiction turned out to be an astonishingly fertile terrain. Themes and motifs emerged and a running joke gave way to a narrative. The scale and ferocity of the birthday celebrations grew, and grew, and days turned into weeks, never letting 24 hours pass without "happy birthday" in some form appearing. In that time the character in his story that had my name developed into a vicious yet fragile tyrant, destroying worlds and dispensing death with celebratory casualness in an increasingly complex fictional cosmos. Jelly, Skype, mutants and various types of animal blood were just some of the branches that knotted their way together through my social media. Imagery that would cause JG Ballard to wake in a cold sweat tripped merrily across my notifications tab. Clowns took on a whole new meaning for me. I learnt a lot of new words.

I should point out that I've known Nate for a few years and consider him a dear friend. It's important to note this, because otherwise the whole venture could have looked like unusually elaborate cyber-bullying. But it was honestly a delight to be part of such a ridiculous thing. And as it spiralled out of control we enjoyed picking apart the joyous silliness of it all over beers and spirits and an excellent stew. Because it's necessary to remember that, as well as being a writer who conjures metaphors that could derail a freight train and treats adjectives as a form of artillery, Nate is one of the loveliest men you could hope to meet. He's the only man I know who can speak with complete authority on both distressed securities investment strategy and the varying musculoskeletal characteristics of extinct megafauna whilst at the same time exuding charm and genuine warmth for anyone caught up in his path. He has a rare faculty for being hugely impressive yet hopelessly likeable at the same time. Which is why I managed to quite enjoy my extended birthday. Even when my phone nearly broke from the sheer volume of people tweeting "happy birthday." And when I had to check Wikipedia to understand which celebrities were joining in. And when people started creating fan art.

Because, you see, this venture wasn't purely for my benefit or punishment. It developed quite a fan-base. In the end, it culminated in a real-life party in the basement of a London bar, with clowns chanting my name and people dressed as leopards offering me chalices of fake blood. That was a deeply surreal evening for me, and I promise you can't imagine quite that was like. It's quite a demanding thing, cosplaying someone else's fictionalised version of yourself as a hundred strangers in costume recreate a Twitter-based hellscape around you. But a fantastic party was the only reasonable conclusion to it all and we remain indebted to Nate's partner and others for making that night happen. Two years on, I have a lot of friends who I made as a result of that ridiculousness and the enduring memories are of baffled glee and unexpected warmth as people came together to celebrate a bunch of tweets which got out of control.

Quite a towering achievement from one small seed. And so after *Buzzfeed* features and live performances and award nominations Nate was offered a book deal. A new seed. An opportunity to exercise his great love of ocean horrors and try his hand at a rollicking undead cyber-fantasy thriller. An opportunity to take some of the superscaled world-building and crypto-zoological buccaneering of The Birthday into a more sustained and considered piece of story-telling. And the end result is this assemblage of pulped tree bits that you've been holding in your hands or propping up on a surface. Every page is a testament to Nate's brilliant mind, except the few which I have taken up here to indulge in a little affectionate gratitude. I hope you're as grateful as I am to have spent some time strolling through the arboretum of Nate's imagination.

Daniel Barker
April 2017

ACKNOWLEDGEMENTS

THIS BOOK STARTED life as two novellas, each with their own sets of acknowledgements, and so the below is a sort of gratitude mash-up to everyone who helped me get in a position to make the whole project happen. Here goes:

Daniel, who is one of the kindest souls I know, to the extent where he let me launch a career in fiction by depicting him as an inhuman galactic tyrant. Mate, I owe you big time. Ashleigh, who makes my life a proper pleasure to live, always has patience to spare for me, and convinced me to put in the lizardmen. Mum, who always believed I could write, even if *TSHAC* didn't end up being quite her cup of tea. Dad, who continues to inspire me even though he isn't around any more. Words are hard. Josh, Chris and Anna for being superb test readers, and Dave at Abaddon for being a far nicer man to work with than he has any duty to be. Mark, for being a complete SF ideas machine, and letting me nick a concept or two. Lydia, for kicking off the unlikely process of publishing me in the first place. Jamie for agreeing to take on the fell burden of representing me. Dave M for being a hell of a support, as ever. Ewa, for helping me feel less daunted by publishing in general. Nikki and Dean for plugging my work way more than I deserved. Joy for her tremendous penwork. Guy, Cat, and all my other mates who keep me from losing the plot. A huge cohort of people off twitter, who were not only kind enough to read my work, but in many cases contributed to it with their expertise (particular thanks to Emma for helping me make up a word). Finally, the absolute bucketload of authors, living and dead, who I've borrowed from both consciously and unconsciously in my work.

Thanks to you for reading, and see you all in High Sarawak!

Nate Crowley
April 2017

ABOUT NATE CROWLEY

Nate Crowley lives in Walsall, near the big IKEA, with his partner Ashleigh and a cat he insists on calling Turkey Boy. His writing career began on twitter where, as @frogcroaklcy, he authored Daniel Barker's Birthday, a dystopian space opera in 700 installments. Nate is currently writing *The 100 Best Video Games (That Never Existed)*, a fictional history of gaming, with art from games studio Rebellion Developments, as well as working on a new novel. He is also writing a text adventure game about a haunted sales training manual called *Big Mike Lunchtime's Business Training '95*, and the second series of animated show *Realms of Fightinge*. Nate loves contemplating unusual animals, cooking stews, playing complicated games and being in wild places. He is represented by Jamie Cowen at the Ampersand agency.